CAGED

CLARISSA WILD

PROLOGUE

CAGE

My thumb brushes over the reflecting image of a girl with hair so white it could blind a man like me. Licking my lips, I stare at her delicate shape in the white dress, her soft posture as she leans into the green trees around her, and the way she wistfully stares at the blue sphere above her head. One moment is all it takes to capture her beauty. And I know I'll have a lifetime to discover it.

I smile, cocking my head. "Her."

That's all it takes. That one word ... and she becomes mine.

I can't stop staring at her eyes. Those soul-crushing blue eyes seem so pure. So vulnerable. Unlike me.

But when the image is snatched out of my hands, my

smile immediately dissipates. I turn my head and watch him take the pictures down from the glass, one by one, until nothing's left but a gray stone mass behind it. No life. No green. No blue. No nothing.

I sigh out loud.

A hand touches my shoulder, squeezing. "Don't worry … You'll see more than just a picture soon."

The hand disappears, and I'm left alone again in my cold, dark space.

But one thing has changed.

Me.

ONE

Ella

The scent of freshly baked bread enters my nose and fills me with joy. I point at the loaf I want and smile.

"That one?" the baker asks.

I nod, and he grabs it from the shelf and wraps it in paper then puts it on the counter. I already have the money ready to pay, so I place it next to the loaf. He swipes it off and stuffs it into the cash register.

"Thank you very much," he says. "Enjoy!"

I smile again while picking up the loaf and tucking it into my bag. Waving, I leave the store and face the sunlight again. I love how the warmth radiates over my skin, how it makes me want to close my eyes and take a deep breath.

Summer is the time I come alive.

On my way back home, I take a detour through the park and pick up all the flowers I like. Red, pink, yellow—as many of the crazy colors as I can gather. Their aromas waft through the air with every summery breeze, and I love to just take it all in. Like a moment frozen in time, where everything is exactly the way it should be.

Untouched.

Perfect.

Unlike me.

***

Twelve Years Ago

I pick up two rocks and stuff one into Suzie's hand. "You go first."

"No. Why do I have to go first? You know I'm not good at this," she whines, putting out a pouty lip. "Why can't we just do it my way?"

"Because we already did that yesterday. Now, we do it *my* way," I say, frowning. "Now c'mon. Throw it."

She sighs, so I rub her back. "You can do this. Just throw it like this." I bend my arm and chuck the stone at the pond, and it skips across the water like a bug until it sinks.

"Wow, that's far!" Suzie yells, her face full of amazement. "But wait ... I was supposed to go first, right?"

I shrug. "We weren't playing for real yet. But now we are. C'mon. Throw the stone."

Her face lifts with a smile. "Okay, I'll try."

I nod a few times, which only makes her smile bigger. I cheer her on. "Go!"

She aims and then throws as hard as she can, but the stone immediately sinks to the bottom just a few feet from where we stand.

"Aw ..." she mumbles with chagrin.

I clap my hands. "My turn."

I snatch another stone from the ground and do it just as I did before, and it pitter-patters across the water farther than Suzie's stone did.

She puts her hands on her side. "Fine, you won."

"Yay!" I jump up and down. "I get to be the princess now."

"But we do it *my* way tomorrow," she says, grimacing. "Rock, paper, scissors."

"But that's just boring," I reply.

"No, it's not!" she quips. "I do it all the time with Bobby. He says it's much better too."

"I don't care about Bobby. Bobby's a boy; I'm your sister. Big difference."

"So?"

"So I get to say what's much better. And this is much better." I pick up another rock and hold it out to her. "If you want to get better, I can teach you."

"Really?" she asks, taking it and tucking it into her pocket.

"Yeah, of course. That's what sisters are for, right?" I grin, and she hugs me. "All right. Now, let's play," I say, wrenching away from her arms.

As I run for the tree, Suzie chases after me, and I glance over my shoulder and giggle. "You won't catch me!"

7

"Yes, I will!"

"No!" I pat the tree just before she does. "I win!"

"Fine," she snaps as I climb up the shoddy ladder to the makeshift treehouse. It's just a bunch of wooden planks stuffed between the trunk and some curtains hanging from the branches, but it's my house now.

"Here!" I say as I pick up the clothes I brought here from home and throw them down to her. "Put this on!"

"Why?"

"Because you're the prince, of course," I say with a cocky face. "Why else?"

She rolls her eyes but does it anyway while I put on the pink dress I brought. Mom doesn't exactly know I took them from the dress-up box, but she won't notice. I'll bring them home without a scratch, and if they have smudges, I'll wash them out myself. I'm a big girl.

I pat down my dress and twirl. It looks so pretty.

"Ready yet?" I yell down as I wait for my prince to come rescue me.

Except when I peer over the edge of the treehouse, no one's there.

Suzie's gone.

"Suzie?" I yell.

It's quiet. Too quiet. I wonder where she went.

I step to the other side of the treehouse and look down there. She's standing near the road just a few steps away from the trees … and she's talking with a man.

A man I've never seen before.

A tall … no, a big guy with a beard and scary looking scars. His face is dark as he speaks to my sister.

I wonder what they're saying. I think it's something I

should hear too.

I try to listen to their conversation from where I'm at up high, but I can barely hear anything. Except for a couple of words …

"Will you be my friend?" the stranger asks.

"Sure," Suzie says.

She keeps talking to him even though Mommy told us not to talk to strangers. Did she forget? Or doesn't she care? Either way, I'm worried, so I start climbing down the ladder.

"Ella?" It's Suzie, and she sounds like she's in trouble.

"Who is that?" I yell, but she doesn't respond, and I can't see her anymore as the trees block my view.

But I can clearly hear her scream.

I immediately jump down the last few steps and run to her. The man has grabbed her hand and is dragging her to a car.

"Ella!" she screams as he pushes her inside and closes the door.

"No!" I scream, my lungs barely able to handle the force of my voice.

The man gets into the car, and before I can get to her, he drives off.

Within a second, I've grabbed my bike and jumped on it to race after them. I don't care that I'm wearing a pink dress or that I'm crying my eyes out. I have to get to her. I promised Mom I'd look after her. I promised Mom I'd take her back home. I have to.

I have to bring Suzie home.

The car's right in front of me, but I can't seem to catch up, no matter how hard I push the pedals of my bike. I'm out of breath, out of energy, but I won't give up. However, the longer it takes, the more I'm left behind.

I can't keep up.

The car disappears, but I keep going. Keep biking. I'll go on forever if I have to. Because I have to get her back. I'll get Suzie back. No matter the cost.

It's almost sundown, and I'm supposed to be home by now, but I can't go back. Not without my sister. My mom would kill me. I promised. I promised.

Tears run down my cheeks as I follow the only road the car could've gone.

And then out of nowhere, it appears.

My heart skips a beat, and a hopeful burst of energy makes me bike harder to get to the car. Parked on the side of the road, it's near the forest my mom told me not to go near because it was way too big and we could get lost.

But getting my sister back is more important than rules.

So I dump the bike between the fallen leaves on the ground and make a run for it. Through the woods, I follow the trail. Tracks in the earth and leaves show me where they went. It can't be far.

The salty tears on my face have dried up, and determination has taken their place. I keep going and going without knowing where I am, but as long as I find Suzie, I'll be okay. We'll be okay.

Thick branches push me back, but I don't stop wading through the darkness of the forest. I don't stop for anything. Not for the pain I feel in my legs. Not for the monsters that could lurk in the dark.

Except for a cliff … right in front of my feet.

I barely manage to stop in time before I fall.

That's when I see it.

A body lying down there on the cold, muddy ground. Hair tangled with twigs, face bloodied and twisted.

It's Suzie.

I scream, but the sound disappears into a sea of trees echoing my voice.

"I'm sorry."

A voice makes me turn my head toward the direction its coming from, just behind a tree not far from Suzie.

"I only wanted someone to talk to," he adds.

It's him. The man who took Suzie.

He quickly turns and runs, disappearing into the forest.

Without thinking, I slide down the slope of the cliff, careful not to fall as I rush to her. I wrap my arms around her and shake her, but she doesn't respond.

"Suzie?" I call out her name maybe three, four … fifteen times.

Nothing I say or do reaches her.

No matter how many times I push her, how many tears roll down my cheeks, how many times I scream—nothing will bring her back.

The more I cry, the less my voice is heard. And even though I try, the sound of my voice keeps fading until nothing's left.

Nothing.

Suzie's gone and so has my voice.

She screamed my name, and I didn't get to her in time. She lost her voice because I refused to use mine. And now it's all gone.

She's *gone*.

But I promised Mommy … I *promised*.

And now I'll never bring her back home.

TWO

Ella

Present

When I've gathered enough flowers, I stroll through the streets until I get to the cemetery. I open the iron-clad fence, its loud squeak a stark difference from the silence up ahead. As I walk along the pebble path, I notice I'm not alone, but that's okay. Everyone here has lost someone dear to them, and not a single soul would dare to say they don't miss them.

I do too.

I place my hand on top of the cold stone in front of the grave and say a prayer. Sometimes, I even talk to her in my head.

I brought you these flowers.

I place them on the grave.

I know you always loved to steal them from the park, so I thought I'd pick them for you instead of buying a bouquet. Are you okay here? Do they treat you well in the afterlife? I hope you don't miss me too much. I promise I won't be long. But I won't come until it's my time. I know you'd want me to enjoy the life I have here. It's just hard, you know? Of course, you know ... you lived it.

I sigh and bite my lip.

Twelve long years. And still, nothing has changed.

The world still revolves around the sun. People live their lives, oblivious to the pain of others. And me? I'm still stuck in that same memory ... still unable to move on.

I turn around and make my way out of the cemetery, determined not to stick around for too long or else I might even spend the day. I have to get this out of my head. Have to find my happy place again.

Turning the corner, I start across the bridge over the river and stop in the middle. I grab my loaf of bread and pull off a few pieces, chucking them into the water. The ducks and seagulls quickly gather to gobble them down, fighting over every last bit as if it's the only food they've gotten in a week. Except they're as fat as can be, so that can't be it. They're so used to people that they practically follow me around just to get more of that bread, and it makes me giggle. Especially when one of the ducks nibbles on my dress.

I try to shoo it away but have no luck. When I twist and spin on my heels, I notice a car with tinted windows on the road at the end of the bridge. A man in the driver's seat has rolled his window down and is staring at me.

A chill runs down my spine.

I don't know why, but when he drives off seconds later, I feel like I can finally breathe again.

To this day, every single incident scares me. Makes me want to scream with the voice I've lost long ago.

I'll do anything to stop the terror, so I start walking. Even with all the ducks chasing me, I keep going. One of the ducks latches onto my dress again. I pull it back and throw another piece of bread behind me. They're so busy and distracted that I can make a run for it.

I'm completely out of breath when I get home. I can't believe I got so worked up again over just a car. It was fun feeding the animals, though.

I take off my coat and put the loaf away then I put a cup of water in the microwave and heat it up. After I make a cup of hot tea, I sit down on the couch and pick up my Kindle. I love reading … and I love tea. It's odd because most people I know don't drink tea, but I love it. Then again, I'm not like most people.

I like silence. I like the serenity it brings. Silence is when the world is still spinning, and everything is okay. Silence is what I'm used to. It's all I've known since …

I choke up just thinking about it.

I gaze at the clock and at the pictures on my bookcase. They're so unique and detailed. I can't stop looking at them from time to time. I made them myself. Dad always says it's okay to be proud of yourself even if it's a small thing.

I smile to myself, thinking of how happy he was when I picked up this hobby, as he calls it.

To me, it's my job. I sell these pictures to newspapers and magazines—whoever is willing to pay for them. They're my bread and butter. I can live off it, so it's more than just a hobby. Even though it doesn't make me rich, it's something I can do. Something that doesn't require me to talk to people. Something that makes me feel less out of this world.

Sipping my tea, I enjoy the day until it's time to cook. However, just as I'm about to get up, I hear the lock in my front door rattle. Seconds later, Bobby, or Bo as he likes to call himself nowadays, bursts in with a paper bag filled with groceries.

"Hi, Ella!" He's always so vibrant; it amazes me.

I wave.

"Feeling good today?"

I nod.

"Sorry about the sudden entry. I just thought I'd surprise you by cooking for you. That okay?"

Bo's sweet; I have to give him that even though he just barged into my home.

He does that from time to time—to check up on me, I suppose.

Ever since my sister's gone, he's been keeping an eye on me. It's like he feels responsible for me, in a way, which is cute.

"I've got some fresh veggies here that we can cut up," he says, placing the paper bag on the counter.

He didn't have to buy all that, but I can't say no to a hearty meal either, especially when he cooks it. His dishes taste much better than mine do.

"Mac and cheese but with veggies?" he asks, turning around to wink at me.

I nod, smiling.

"I knew you'd be a sucker for it." He points at me and

laughs. "One mac and cheese coming right up."

He's too sweet for his own good. Always taking care of everyone. I don't remember him being any different, at least not toward me.

Other people sometimes say he's a weirdo because he's so shy and doesn't have many friends. But I don't mind. I'm the same, so I guess that makes us friends by default.

I smile to myself, watching him toil about in my kitchen. He's such a kind soul, despite being so closed off to the outside world. He hides his pain and sorrow underneath thick layers of fake happiness. Anyone can see that. But I won't judge him for it. After all, I have baggage of my own to deal with.

When the food is done, we gobble it down together while watching television. Then we wash the dishes and play a board game. He doesn't talk much, but I like it that way. We both like the silence.

I just enjoy the time I have with him without feeling judged. When we're hanging out, we focus on the good things in life. And it makes me happy ... if only for a moment.

A few hours later, the day has already passed, and Bo has gone back home.

In bed, I lie awake and stare at the ceiling, wondering if my simple life will ever be anything other than boring. If I could ever handle anything else again.

Because as I turn in my bed and curl up into that comfy position, I still feel my heart banging out of my chest. The crippling fear that has chased me for so long still holds me in a vise grip every single day of my life.

And there's no way to escape.

No other way … but sleep.

***

I wake up to something covering my face. A sickly sweet smell enters my nostrils as I breathe, but it makes me want to vomit. My eyes burst open.

A man is standing mere inches away from me.

His hand covers my face. A damp cloth between us.

My eyes dart around the room, looking for an object I can use to smash his face in, but he's holding me down with his other hand. I'm paralyzed from both my fear and his control. And the more I struggle, the harder it becomes to breathe.

To move.

To see.

I'm weak—so weak and tired—but I don't want to close my eyes.

What is he doing to me? Who is he? Why is he here? How did he get in?

I want to open my mouth and scream, but when I do, nothing comes out.

His voice is all I hear … whispering to me like a snake right before I fade away.

"Shhh, it'll all be over soon."

***

When I come to again, the first thing I feel is a roaring headache. My lungs burn when I breathe through my mouth. A metallic taste lies on my tongue, and I swallow to make it go away, but it lingers. Everything hurts. My head. My mouth. As if I've been hit a couple of times, but I can't remember a thing.

And when I open my eyes, I'm still so dizzy; I can barely make out a thing.

It's dark as night. Not a single light surrounds me except the one at the far end of the room.

The room ... with no windows.

No plants.

No sunlight.

Nothing.

All I can see is a gray concrete wall surrounding me.

I try to get up, but my feet don't feel like they belong to me, and I struggle to get anywhere. But I don't give up. I keep crawling across the floor, hoping to make it to the light, just so I can see where I am.

But I can't.

Not because my muscles gave up.

But because I physically, literally can't.

Between me and the light ... is glass.

I turn around, trying to find a way around it, but there's no crack. Not a single one in all the glass surrounding me. Not even at the top as I try to stand on my toes. Nothing ... but glass.

A cage.

My heart stops beating.

The panic rises again, bubbling to the surface.

I open my mouth and scream, but no sound comes out except for a faint sigh.

Just like always. My voice was taken from me a long time ago. And I know no matter how hard I try that no one will hear me.

Where am I? Who was that man? Where did he bring me and why?

With my back against the glass panes, I sink to the floor.

I can still barely make out my environment or feel my own skin. I'm numb from the drug he gave me and numb from the shock.

But I still don't cry. I close my mouth and stop breathing. I stop moving. Like a rock, I stay put and pretend I'm not there.

Why?

Because something across the room, not far from me, still captures my attention.

Something lurking in the dark behind the glass.

I'm not alone.

THREE

CAGE

There she is. In the living flesh.

The girl from the picture.

Mine.

I stare at her from across the room, not moving an inch. She seems locked in place. Her lips trembling. Her fingers clutching her thin clothes. She seems terrified.

She should be.

It's dangerous here.

She shares my fate now.

But I don't want to scare her any more than she already is. So I stay put and watch her from my bed. I don't want her to do anything to hurt herself. She's too precious. Too important.

Too pretty.

Her long, pearly white hair is completely in tangles from her ordeal, but it doesn't make her any less appetizing. Especially with those doe-eyed looks she keeps giving me.

She smells nice too. I can't stop sniffing the air around me; that's how in love I am with her scent. I can't stop looking at her. Can't stop wanting to inch closer. It takes every ounce of self-control not to. My body is greedy … yearning to finally meet this girl sitting only inches away from me. But I know I have to be patient.

Patience … that's what he always says.

So I sit and stare … all through her waking up … and even after she's already seen me.

Our eyes lock.

I'm not going to pull my eyes from hers.

I want her to see me.

I want her to know I'm here.

And that neither of us is going anywhere.

***

Ella

The room is so dark I can barely make out a thing. But there's one thing I can clearly see.

A man in the corner sitting on a bed.

I swallow away the lump in my throat and try not to move.

I don't know who he is or what he wants, but I know it

can't be good.

Is he the one who took me? Or a fellow captive? Or something worse?

So far, he hasn't said a word or moved a muscle, and I'm beginning to wonder if he's sleeping … if he's even alive. But it can't be because he's looking straight at me.

And for some reason, it feels impossible to take my eyes off his.

After a few seconds, I manage to tear them away and I quickly scramble to the bed. Then I gaze around the room, looking for an exit. My cage is made entirely of glass. To my left is a black door leading into my cell, which I assume is locked. To my right is a small, square box inside the glass wall. I wonder what it's used for.

Outside this glass prison, I see another black door, which I assume leads to a room from which my captor can walk in and out of the prison. A sort of in-between room.

A tiny rug on the floor in the middle of the cell provides little softness. Above me is a vent, which blows air into the cell. There's another one up ahead. In the far-left corner is what looks like a toilet, and in the right corner of my cell, right next to my bed, is a small water tap.

I wonder what else this place is hiding.

However, the moment I think about getting up and exploring my cell, I'm immediately reminded of the dark figure across from me, breathing in and out loudly.

His arms fall off his thighs, and his hands clutch the bed. They're huge.

Every muscle in his body flexes as he slowly gets up from the bed and saunters my way, his footsteps heavy … like that of a giant.

My heart is beating in my throat as I slowly back into a corner as far away from him as I can. Something inside me tells me I should be more scared of him than my environment.

The closer he gets, the more menacing he appears. The small light hanging from the wall at the far end of the room only barely lights his presence, but it's enough to see him. His posture is like that of a bear … broad as if he's about to break through the glass. But he doesn't. Instead, he approaches me with hawk-like eyes, coming to a stop right in front of the glass. He's so big; his head almost touches the ceiling while mine doesn't even come close.

I swallow again at the sight of his size.

And I'm not just talking height.

Muscles everywhere, nothing covering him but simple camouflage shorts. I can't imagine the size of what's inside although I can make out quite a bulge. I can't even focus; that's how flabbergasted I am by the man who looks more like a beast than a human.

He looks unkempt.

Savage.

The scruffy beard and moustache can't hide the scars underneath. They're all over his body and face, and there's one right under his eye and across his thick, bushy brow.

My lips part, but nothing comes out.

As usual.

The moment I need my voice the most, it fails me.

He paces back and forth in front of the glass as if he's deciding what to do to me. Observing me.

His nostrils flare.

He takes a sniff.

A hint of a smile tips his lips up briefly.

Goose bumps scatter across my skin.

Who is this man? And what does he want with me?

He cocks his head and his eyes narrow … and then he turns around and walks back to his bed again, sits down, and pretends he's not there.

I wonder why.

I slowly get up from my corner, trying not to aggravate him. It feels like I'm stuck in a cage with a tiger mere feet away from me, ready to pounce. Any movement could kill me, so I go slow.

However, I'm too curious to stay put. Too desperate to get out that I just have to feel my way around every nook and cranny. Every inch of glass, I have to feel it. From bottom to top, my fingers leave nothing unscathed. But there isn't a single crack to be found.

"There's no way out."

The voice is deep … so deep it feels like a growl from an animal even though I know it isn't.

It's *him*.

The man across the room.

I can tell because the sound came from his direction, and I haven't seen or heard anyone come in.

But that voice … it instantly draws my attention.

I glance over my shoulder at the dangerous figure on the bed, wondering why he's telling me this. If this is his way of testing me.

But nothing indicates he wants to continue. No other words come from his mouth. There's only that slight smile on his face.

Suddenly, a loud screeching noise startles me. I turn my

back against the wall, searching for the source. A door in a far corner of the room opens right next to the lamp, and a middle-aged man steps inside. When he spots me, he rubs his head, specifically the spot where he's going partially bald.

He clears his throat and walks up to the glass cage.

***

I freeze and make myself as small as I can, pushing myself against the glass as far away from him as possible.

With a creepy smile on his face, he stalks around the cage, and I get the feeling he's trying to gauge my reaction. I guess he must be wondering why I haven't screamed yet. I'm wondering that myself too.

The man's eyes betray his fascination with my reaction. Amusing, maybe, judging from his vicious smile. But to me, the strangest thing isn't him pacing around outside the glass cage. It's the man in the cage right next to me.

Because he doesn't respond to this man outside watching us.

I look at him then back at the man lurking around, and I can't help but notice he doesn't even seem to care.

What is going on?

Frowning, I try to get his attention, but the man in the cage doesn't seem to be interested in me anymore. All he does is stare at the other man outside and wander around.

Who are they?

Suddenly, the man is right beside me with only the thick glass separating us, and I'm spooked.

For an instant, I forgot to keep an eye on him while I was staring at my cage companion, and now this scary man is inspecting me from up close.

"No need to be afraid …" he hums.

His voice is soft but slimy. Totally not like the other guy's gruffness.

He cocks his head. "Are you okay? How are you feeling?"

I narrow my eyes and cringe from the way he seems so interested in me, despite being the man who's outside the cage, not in.

He must be the one who took me from my home.

The one who keeps us here.

I just stare.

His eyes narrow too, and he focuses on my forehead. "You're bleeding. Must've been from the trip. You put up quite the fight. I even had to restrain you while driving." He smiles again. "We'll get that wound taken care of."

The word 'we' makes me shiver. But why can't I remember anything about the whole ordeal? Must've been the drugs in the cloth he held against my mouth. Or maybe he gave me something else too so I'd finally calm down.

"Tell me your name," he says.

My lips part, ready to answer, but my voice is as hollow as his heart.

The only thing that follows is silence.

"Not the talkative type, are you?" he muses after a while. "Doesn't matter."

He wanders around the cages again, seemingly checking every nook and cranny. I wonder if he's testing whether his contraptions will hold up.

"So … since you won't talk, I'll start. You can call me Graham. Nice to meet you, Ella."

Just the mere mention of my name makes my eyes widen.

How does he know?

I glare at him, absorbing his facial expressions and posture, but no matter how hard I look, he doesn't seem remotely familiar. I don't know him, so then how does he know me?

"I take it you've already made yourself at home?" he asks, giving me that creepy smile again.

I don't answer, but I don't look away either. I want him to see me. I want him to look at me and me alone. I want him to feel the pain that I feel. Maybe one day I'll make him feel.

"Good." He nods a few times even though he's conversing entirely with himself. I wonder what the purpose of his visit is. If he's checking to see how I've settled in. If he's figuring out a way to make me talk. Or if he's just trying to make me feel uneasy. Whatever it is, it's working all right.

I'm waiting for his next words, but then he suddenly turns and starts walking.

I can't let him leave.

I have to know why I'm here.

So I bang on the glass as hard as I can ... as fast as I can.

The sudden noise makes my neighbor home in on me like a drone. The look on his face switches between shock and worry, causing me to instantly regret what I just did. What if the man who just froze in his tracks flips out?

Pulls me from my prison?

Hurts me?

Murders me?

Shivers run up and down my spine as I slowly lower my

hand, hoping he didn't hear.

But of course, he did.

Because he's turning around and walking back to me. He wears pure determination in his eyes. The kind that could make you scream. But I can't. No matter how much I wish I could.

Right in front of the glass, he stops.

We stare at each other for what feels like minutes before I finally gather the courage to do something about my questions. The desire to know is greater than the desire to stay safe. I'm already in danger just by being here. And answers to my questions may just be my way out.

So I slowly raise my hand and point at myself.

He purses his lips. "You want to know why you were chosen?"

I nod.

A wicked smile spreads on his face. "You'll find out soon."

Before I can make him tell me more, he's turned around and walked off.

FOUR

Ella

The first night, I don't sleep at all.

It's horrid. Being here. As if the world has suddenly disappeared to be replaced with a black void. The only thing I have is my memories, and I often just shut myself off and go there just to feel secure.

But I'm not.

I'm far from okay.

I'm in a glass prison with an unknown stranger, being held like some caged animal.

For what reason?

Will I ever get out?

Graham ... how can such a cruel man have such a sweet

name?

In the morning and evening, he stops by with clean clothes and food. The food wrapped in aluminum, he places it in the box then pushes it my way so I can take it out. The box only opens from one side, obviously. He took precautions so he wouldn't get attacked. Smart. Because I would've definitely taken the opportunity.

The food doesn't come with utensils, so I'm left to eat with my hands. Rice and chicken were on the menu tonight, but it's not enough. I'm still hungry, but I won't ask for more. I'll be damned if I beg that man. I'd rather starve.

The small toilet in the corner is visible to anyone, so I usually wait until the man next to me is asleep before I go. But it's hard holding it all day. I can't imagine keeping this up for months. I'll probably have no other choice, though.

Now, I'm lying on the bed with a rumbling stomach, and a stranger is staring straight back at me.

Ever since I've gotten here, the stranger on the other side of the room hasn't taken his eyes off me. Not unless Graham is in the room, which makes me wonder if he's scared of repercussions. But the moment Graham's gone, he returns to watching over me with a certain vigilance that's as much endearing as it is scary.

He seems so calm, unlike me.

Collected? Maybe.

But I can tell from the way he's looking at me that he's not.

It's just his body that's still, but his eyes … they're burning with a fire that's not easily quenched.

But why?

Why is this man watching me the way he is?

And how long has he been here?

He's obviously not trying to escape, which begs the question if he's ever tried. With that kind of physique, you'd be crazy not to. If he has, then there's no hope of me ever getting out. If he can't break through, then neither can I.

So am I doomed to stay here forever? Or until Graham decides he's going to pity me?

I sigh. There's got to be more to this. Some sort of sad story I can use to my advantage to get him to let me go.

But this man right next to me … I feel like he's part of it all. Like there's a reason I'm here. Why *he's* here, right next to me.

I wonder if we're part of some kind of big plan Graham has in store for us.

I shiver at the thought.

To distract myself, I gaze around the room again as I've already done so many times before. It makes me feel sick to my stomach. But I'm not about to give up the much-needed food.

Instead, my eyes find their way back to the only thing that relaxes me whenever I look at it.

Him.

That man … I don't know what it is, but something about the way he watches over me makes me feel less alone. Less like I'm about to collapse and cry.

But it's damn scary too.

It's the middle of the night. I only know because a clock hangs on the far end of the wall near the lamp that's still on.

I can't close my eyes, though. His eyes are on me like a hawk.

We should be sleeping, but instead, we're staring at each

other.

Like I could ever sleep when a mountain-sized muscle man is eyeing me from the corner.

Suddenly, his lips quirk up into a smile, catching me off guard.

"Sleep." There's that rough voice again, the one that sizzles with power with every spoken letter.

I don't know why I feel like his commands make me wanna do exactly what he says.

Like he's saying, "It's safe; I'll be here, watching over you." But that wouldn't make any sense because I don't know him.

Then again, he is a prisoner in this place … just like I am.

We're both in this together, so I guess I should trust him.

Still, I'd sleep a lot better knowing his demanding stare wasn't penetrating my back.

I shake my head and point at him.

He frowns and tilts his head up. "Why not?"

I point at him again.

He leans up on his elbows, his abs bulging like mad. I'd be lying if I said I didn't completely zoom in on them. He's quite handsome—like one of those models from a magazine—but much bigger, and he looks so strong.

However, his well-trained body is a distraction I don't need right now.

I need sleep, desperately. I don't intend to collapse; I have to avoid it at all cost. Especially when Graham's near … when he could come in at any moment.

Still, this man on the other end of the glass is staring at

me, and it makes me wanna shout.

Stop looking at me like that!

But of course, nothing comes out.

It's been like that for twelve long years.

I still can't get used to it, but my body won't listen to my brain.

For some reason, whenever I think about talking or screaming, it jams shut and my vocal cords clamp up. I don't have a choice. My voice isn't mine to control anymore.

The man smiles at me again, and then he turns around on his bed and faces the wall.

I stare in disbelief. He actually turned away from me and stopped looking.

Did he do that because I pointed at him? Because I made him aware of what he was doing?

Or is just because he's tired now?

Whatever the case, I have to grasp this opportunity to get some sleep too, despite being nervous about whatever may happen when I do go to sleep.

I can't hold it off any longer.

I'm too tired.

But my mind keeps going in circles, wondering where I am. If I'll ever get out.

If ... anything.

***

Twelve years ago

I stand in front of the hole in the ground and stare at

the wooden casket deep inside. My hand rises and releases a few rose petals. Slowly, they drift to the bottom, just like my heart. I'm leaving it here with her for safekeeping.

Mom said I should say something, but I don't know what.

Goodbye doesn't sound right.

I don't want to say goodbye.

She should be here, with us, but nothing I do will ever bring her back.

Suzie's gone … and it's my fault.

The detectives said she broke her neck when she fell off the cliff, but she died because that stranger took her.

I could've stopped him from taking her. I could've gone after her faster on my bike. I could've done so many things. But I didn't, and now she's dead.

I sigh as the tears roll down my cheeks. Glancing over my shoulder, I can't help but look for Mom who's weeping against my dad's chest, clutching him tight. When our eyes connect, the sadness in hers breaks my heart in two.

Every word I could say would only make it more difficult.

When we sat at the table and I tried to discuss what happened, Mom said, "Don't discuss it. Please. I don't want to hear it."

When I was at the funeral home with Dad, he said, "Nothing will bring her back."

I said I was sorry. I said it again and again until my throat hurt and my voice became hoarse.

But Dad is right. Nothing I say will ever bring her back.

Nothing I say will ever make them happy again.

Nothing changes what's been done.

So why talk at all?

As I stare at my sister's grave, guilt washes over me. Even though I haven't done anything … that's exactly what I did.

Nothing.

Because if I had done something, she might've still been here.

If I'd biked harder, yelled louder, or let her win so she would've been the one up on the tree, she might've still been here. I would've done anything to trade places with her.

But it's too late for that. Too late for saying I'm sorry. Too late for anything.

She's gone …

And my voice disappeared with her.

***

Present

A loud banging on the glass wakes me. I sit upright in my bed, completely freaked out. It's Graham with another plastic plate of food.

Waking up out of nowhere in a place like this still makes my heart drop. Every time I open my eyes, I see dull grayness … and a glass prison surrounding it. No sunlight. No fresh air. No green trees and flowers. Nothing. It's like waking up in a nightmare.

I don't know how much time has passed, but since he's back with food, I guess it's already morning. I barely feel rested, though.

I get up and walk closer. Graham puts the plastic plate into the box and slides it inside.

"Eat," he says. "You're gonna need it."

My lips part.

For what?

I sign.

I actually sign the words.

Graham seems confused as he watches my fingers move, and then he bursts into laughter. "Right. You think I can understand that?"

Of course, he can't.

He's not a signer. He's a talker.

I used to be like that too. But when I stopped talking, my parents had to think of something to get me to communicate with the outside world again. I only talked to them but no one else. I'd go completely silent in the presence of others but flourish in their vicinity. I couldn't tell them what was wrong because I didn't understand it. The doctors didn't know what to do with me either. An unusual case of Selective Mutism, they said. No cure.

That's why my parents brought me to a special school where they taught me how to sign, so I could at least communicate with the rest of the world again. I had deaf and mute classmates, which made me feel much more at home there anyway. By the time I was out of school, signing felt like second nature.

It's all I've ever known. But now, I feel lost in oblivion, a place where no one can understand me. My words mean nothing if they don't come from sound.

I sigh.

Graham stuffs toilet paper into the box and says, "Use

this if you have to go."

Thanks, I sign.

He smiles. "You're welcome. If that's what you said."

Yes, but I guess he doesn't need to know sign language to understand the basics of language.

Then again, I didn't thank him to be kind. I thanked him sarcastically. At least, in my head.

"I might be keeping you in here, but that doesn't mean I'm a monster. I'll take good care of you."

Good care? Right.

I point at the guy in the cage next to me.

What about him?

Graham briefly glances at him before turning his head back to me. "Don't worry about him."

I don't understand any of this.

"Now eat. Sleep."

When he turns around, I knock on the glass again.

I mouth the word, "Please," and use my hands to mimic opening a book.

A tentative smile forms on his lips. "You want ... a book?"

I nod. Anything. I don't want to ask for big things. I don't need a TV. I don't need games or any of the flashy things. Something small is enough. It's all I can ask for without him getting pissed. And a book is all I need to escape, if only just for a little while.

"Well, since you asked so nicely," he says, and then he turns around and walks off again.

I wonder if he'll come back.

I quickly grab the plate of food and gobble down the tortillas. It's something. Any food is welcome at this point. I

37

fill my belly with water that I filled a plastic cup with using the small faucet and then put it all back into the box again.

After a few minutes, Graham is back again, his hands behind his back. When he's near my prison, he holds up a book I don't recognize. *Captive and Free.* And the smile on his face seems to indicate he genuinely thinks this is a good surprise.

"For you." He winks and places it in the box. I reach inside.

He doesn't pull back. Instead, he grabs my wrist.

I try to jerk myself free, but he's much stronger than I am.

"Make no mistake, girl. This isn't a gift. This is a transaction."

My brows drop, not liking where this is going.

He looks me dead in the eyes. "Things work a little bit differently here. If you behave, you get good things. If you don't behave, I'll take the good things away again," he growls. "Got it?"

I nod.

"Good." He releases my wrist, and I immediately pull back, not giving a shit about grabbing the book.

I sit down on my bed, too scared to even come close to him right now.

He cocks his head and grins. "You're a good girl. Exactly what I was hoping for. He picked well."

Picked well? Who did? What's he talking about?

When he turns around, I'm almost tempted to bang on the glass again, but at this point, I'm not sure I could deal with more of these surprise touches. Because his hand around my wrist felt like a snake wrapping itself around my arm so it could bite into my veins.

I'm still shivering from the encounter.

And I can still feel his grip.

See his stain on my arm.

I wipe it off, again and again, but it won't work.

Defeated, I stare at my cell and the book luring me in from the box where it lies. It only takes me thirty minutes to give up. Thirty minutes for the promise of a world beyond this one to seduce me.

So I get up from my bed and pull the book from the box, caving in to my only desire.

To escape.

FIVE

CAGE

She paces around her cell with an angry gaze. Her nostrils flare every time she glances at me. I wonder what she's thinking. She hasn't spoken to me yet. Can she even talk?

She seems absorbed in her thoughts, and I don't want to disturb her, but I don't have much else to do in this place. She's got her book even though she's only read a few pages. But me? I've only got myself ... and the bars in the corner that I use for exercise.

That's all I can ever do. Exercise. Focus on the next time I'm going to need that added strength. I always have to figure out a way to get stronger. That's why I get more food than her because he wants me to be strong and powerful.

But it's not fair. I think she should get as much as I do,

or at least more than she gets now.

She must be hungry half the time, looking at how small her portions are. I wish I could give her some of mine.

I blow out a breath and try not to think about it. It's no use because I'm here, and she's there. That's it.

However, I can't stop watching her fume in her cell. She keeps looking at the toilet and then glances at me.

Suddenly, it hits me. She hasn't used it in some time. Does she need to go?

Maybe. Is that why she's looking at me? Because she doesn't want me to see her?

I frown and cock my head at her. "Go," I say. I never use more words than needed. I don't like to talk.

I turn around on my bed and look at the wall. It's covered in cracks, like me.

My ears pick up the sounds of her sitting down and relieving herself, and I smile.

I'm glad she can finally let go. It must be hard for her even though I don't understand it myself. I never had this feeling. Never needed to hide. Never needed to do anything but be myself in here. If this is who I am. I don't know … It's all I've ever known, so that's just what I am I guess.

When I hear the metallic sound of the toilet and a flushing noise, I turn around again. She's swiftly up on her feet again, pretending as if nothing happened. As if she's embarrassed even though she has nothing to be ashamed of.

Not with me. I don't feel shame. Or guilt. Or regret.

Hell, I'm surprised if I even feel anything.

But when I look at her … I know there's something. Something I've never felt before. Something that makes me want to get close and touch her. I want to see her smile. I want to see her ... naked.

I wonder what she looks like.

She clears her throat, making me look up. She's standing underneath the vent, holding out her hands and waiting for something, but what? Nothing happens, so she starts looking around her cell, for what I have no clue. After ten minutes, she gives up and grabs the cup from the bed and fills it with water ... Which she then chucks all over her face.

What is she doing?

Frowning, I watch her pour water into the cup and throw it all over herself. Her arms, her legs, her face. Even her feet. Then she washes her hair and squeezes it out. It looks so different when it's not flowing over her shoulders. But still, she's beautiful. Even when she's soaked.

She squeezes out her dress and puts her shoes in the corner. Then she grabs the book she got and rips out one of the empty pages in the back. She goes on her knees and starts fiddling with the paper close to the floor, trying to shove it underneath the glass.

"Won't work," I say.

She stops for a moment, not even caring to look at me, and then continues.

She doesn't stop trying to push it underneath until she's gone through every inch of glass. When she gets back to where she started, she sighs and throws the paper onto the bed. Pulling herself up, she grabs a loose plastic stool and throws it at the glass.

I don't make a noise, but fuck, I'm surprised she'd do that.

She's so frail and small; I never expected an outburst like

that.

Then again, I can imagine how it must feel, being confined to a small space after having been free your entire life.

She keeps going, throwing stuff at the glass again and again. One after the other, everything she can lift, she tries. But nothing works.

"Stop," I say, to try to calm her down, but it obviously doesn't work because she immediately glares at me as if I've hurt her.

Still, she eventually puts down the stuff she was trying to use to break the cage. There's not even a mark on the glass.

She sits down on the concrete floor in a really weird position. Her legs are crossed, and her hands are resting on her knees, and she's making an o-shape with her mouth that reminds me of the face I make when I rub myself.

I wonder if she's doing that now, but that's not possible since her hands aren't anywhere near that place.

Still, it looks odd. What is she doing?

She breathes in so loud I can hear it, and I do like the sound.

Ten minutes of doing that, and she lies down on the floor, facing the ceiling. Her hands and legs lie flat on the ground. Her face is pale, and there's no smile to be found. Her eyes squint and turn watery, after which droplets begin to roll down her cheeks.

Watching that … it stirs something inside me.

I don't know what. I've never felt it before.

Never knew this feeling, this overpowering urge to go to her.

It's nothing I've ever experienced.

Something that scares me.

I never get scared.

I take a deep breath, watching the drops cascade down onto the concrete and leaving dark marks all around her. My smile dissipates as I feel the happiness drain from her.

I don't want her to feel this way.

No one should.

So I get off the bed and tread toward her. Normally, she'd immediately look at me, probably wanting to know what I'm going to do. Not now, though. No, she's still staring at the ceiling in a way that makes me think she's given up.

Like her fighter spirit is leaving her slowly but surely.

I can't let that happen.

She can't give up.

I place my hand on the glass and wait until she looks at me. But the longer I wait, the more I start to worry. So I place another one against the glass, still staring at her.

She might give up, but I won't.

I won't ever give up on her or myself.

I rest my forehead against the glass and look down at the body of the girl who came here after me, not knowing what would happen. I know what will happen. He told me a long time ago why she would be here.

I swallow as my gut feels constricted and my chest tight.

This girl ... she doesn't even know why she's here. Am I even allowed to tell her? Should I?

It'll probably only make it worse.

So even though it kills me to see her like this, I don't.

She's just lying there, motionless ... glaring at the specks on the concrete ceiling with eyes that are emptier than this room.

And I realize, then and there, I can't do a single thing about her situation.

All I can do is wait while gazing at her, hoping she might one day look back at me with the same gaze.

Because I will keep on looking. As hard as I can. As long as I can.

I won't give up.

Even if she does.

I won't give her up.

And from the way she briefly glances at me with reddened eyes, I can tell she knows.

**

Ella

I can't stop crying.

I don't know why. It just keeps coming and coming like an endless stream of sorrow.

It's as if the realization of my situation has finally settled in.

As if I've finally come to terms with the fact I'm stuck here and might not get out.

And that hopelessness … it feels like death.

I wipe away some of the tears, but it's no use. My whole body is shaking as I lie on the floor, wondering why I should go on. It's been days … how much more can I live through? In the darkness, nothing can console me.

Except him …

The man standing behind the glass, holding up his hands as if he's trying to reach me.

He sought me out on his own, and I don't quite know how to respond.

It doesn't matter how long I ignore him or how long I keep crying. He refuses to let me be.

Instead, his gaze only becomes stronger, boring into mine like he wants to dig into my soul.

And for some reason, I want to look back.

Once.

Only once, but it's enough.

The gentle giant I see in front of me is trying to make me feel better … and for that single moment, it's enough.

It's what I need to smile.

If only for one single moment.

It's enough to make me feel like I'm not alone.

And for that, I'm grateful.

SIX

Ella

I only just finished my breakfast and washed my face when noises behind me make me look around. Mr. Unknown is sliding some metal bars out of the ceiling.

What the hell is that for?

I didn't even know they were there to begin with. Does my cage have them too?

I look up, but there's nothing there. Odd.

But what's even odder is that when I look at him again, he's taking off his tank top.

And oh God … the muscles that appear from underneath still make me gulp.

He throws it on the floor and starts jumping up and down in his cage, waving his hands and legs while he's at it.

Jumping jacks? Really?

He keeps going until his body glistens and his breathing becomes hard and loud. Then he switches to the bars hanging from the ceiling, lifting himself up. He can do complete body pull-ups as if it's a cake walk. And for some reason, I can't stop staring.

That is, until he glances my way, and our eyes lock.

Embarrassed, I immediately grab my book and pretend to read. I know he knows I wasn't. And I know he saw me looking.

From the corner of my eye, I see him grin briefly before returning to his pull-ups.

Only this time, he's doing it with one hand.

Jesus Christ. He's like a beast. An animal in human form.

His abs twitch with every pull-up, sweat dripping down his body, and his face is all scrunched up. I can honestly say it's one of the most beastly things I've ever seen. Sexy, even. And somehow, I can't stop staring.

Even when I'm pretending to read.

And when he looks at me again, my whole face turns red.

Shit.

I quickly change my position, hoping he didn't notice, but of course, he did.

I can see his smug smile from where I'm sitting.

He enjoys putting on a show for me; I can tell. I wonder why he's going through all this trouble, though. It can't be all because of me.

After a while, he drops down from the bars, a resounding boom sounding from his feet as they crash into the concrete. Immediately, he drops down to the floor and starts doing push-ups. Hundreds. Maybe more. I'm not keeping count. But the most amazing part is that he's doing more than half with just one hand, alternating both like he's attempting to train to the max. As if he's preparing for something. But for what?

When he catches me staring again, I quickly turn away and shake my head.

I've got to stop letting this man who's obviously not in my reach distract me. Literally. A thick, impenetrable glass wall separates us, and nothing he does is going to change that.

I've already tried throwing everything at the glass, but to no avail.

He's probably done the same thing loads of times. If it didn't work for him, I don't know why I thought it'd work for me.

Oh, well … guess we have nothing to do here to waste time except read books and work out like we're in the Army. I can't blame him.

I just hope the waiting ends someday, and that Graham will just tell us why we're here because I can't handle being here forever without knowing why.

I just need to know why. So I make a promise to myself right now that the next time I see him, I'm going to make him tell me.

The sweaty, pumped-up man next to me gets up from the floor and stands still in the middle of the room. When I look up, I notice he's staring at me. And no matter how hard I stare back, he won't stop. It's the same as last time … only worse …

More … raw … and hungry.

And why do I get the feeling he's undressing me with his eyes?

I swallow hard and return to my book, determined not to let his ample physique distract me from my objective … which is getting out of here.

With or without the unknown man.

***

Just as I'm about to fall asleep on my belly, my eyes spring open, and I look up. All visible lights have gone out. I push myself further under my blanket until only my eyes peek just above the pillow. I shiver, wondering what's going on. I feel like anything could happen. The lights have never gone off.

What does it mean?

Is Graham gone?

Was there a power outage?

Or did he do this on purpose?

Noises from below us make me place my hand on the ground to feel the vibrations. Nothing penetrates the thick concrete, though. But now I know there's not just earth underneath us. We must be up a floor or more—how many I don't know—but I'm sure it's not a basement.

The realization gives me a jolt of energy, an indescribable feeling of power. Why? Because I just discovered something Graham probably doesn't want me to know. And it feels fantastic.

Even if it's just a tiny bit of information, it's enough to fuel the desire in me to discover more about this place. To learn the ins and outs. Because that is the only way to plan an escape.

Suddenly, the door on the other end of the room creaks and opens wide. I can barely tell what's going on because it's so dark, but I can definitely make out a figure … and a moving chair on wheels. And inside is another person.

Groans are audible.

I hold my breath as the wheelchair approaches, and I pretend to be asleep even though I'm still lurking underneath the blanket. As it's rolled past me, I can clearly distinguish the shape inside … It's a girl, judging from the long hair and voluptuous chest.

But before I have another chance to look, she's rolled past my window and into the room behind the dark doors. Not long after, another door creaks open. It's in the far corner of the room in the cell on the other side of the handsome stranger next to me.

He's fast asleep, snoring on his bed, while I'm lying here with a pounding heart, wondering what's going on.

The wheelchair is pushed into the cell, and the girl is taken out. Then the figure leaves with the wheelchair. I assume it's Graham. It must be.

He rummages in his pocket, and I hear a clicking noise. The light turns back on. Then he exits the room with the wheelchair, leaving us all alone again.

I wait a few minutes to make sure he's not coming back before I slowly slip out of my bed and walk up to the glass. Peering through, I can clearly see the woman lying on the bed in the far corner beyond the mysterious man's cage.

Another captive.

Why is she suddenly here?

Did she come here after me or before me?

And what did he do to her to make her pass out?

Because she's clearly not awake, judging from the way her face is smashed against the pillow. I wonder if he did the same to her as he did to me when he took me. Just thinking about the awful smell that was inside the cloth pushed against my mouth makes me sick.

But I don't give into the sensations of wanting to hurl. Instead, I gently tap the glass, hoping to wake her up.

She groans and turns, and my heart does a flip-flop. However, she immediately drops back down onto the bed again, and I hear nothing.

Shit.

She must be completely wiped out.

But then another groan slips from her mouth.

Is she trying to wake up? Maybe she's fighting the drugs.

I have to help her.

Without thinking, I start banging on the glass, hard.

So hard even my next-door neighbor wakes up. He groans loudly like a bear as he leans up and looks at me with furrowed brows. "Sleep," he growls.

He's never spoken more than two syllables to me, but I can tell he's mad because I woke him up. He shouldn't be. I need his help. So I point at the window behind him, desperately trying to get him to look.

When he finally does follow my finger, he just shrugs and turns around again.

My jaw drops.

What the …?

I knock on the glass again. He looks annoyed. "What?"

I point at the woman again and make an angry face.

"She's sleeping."

She's not. She's struggling. She needs help. Wake her up.

Of course, whenever I try to sign, he understands zero of what I'm trying to say.

Why is he completely not interested in the woman right beside him? She's the first new thing that's happened to us since I came here, and he seems totally oblivious to her presence. As if he doesn't care. Or as if he doesn't feel that it's special.

But it is. It's a person. Someone to talk to. Someone who could help me figure out what this place is, and what Graham wants with us. Someone who could help us get out.

But I'm tired of waiting until the stranger beside me does something, so instead, I bang on the glass harder. As hard as I can. I don't care if it keeps him awake. This is too important. I need to know who this woman is. Why she's here. If she knows more, anything, I just have to know.

I can't sleep knowing she's here. Not without having at least tried to wake her up and get her to talk to me.

But my wrists feel like they're about to fall off, that's how painful it is. And Mr. Unknown jumps up from the bed and pounds the glass near me once, his strike so hard that it makes me jump back.

"No …" he growls.

No? What the hell?

Why wouldn't he want her to wake up? Is he insane?

I frown and make a face. Then I continue to knock anyway. I don't care if he likes it or not, I'm not stopping until she's awake.

However, the vents above me suddenly open wide, and a gas filters inside.

53

I cough, backing away from the glass, and try to escape the gas by rushing to a corner. I cover my mouth and nose with the bed sheets, but as more gas flows inside, it's becoming harder to breathe.

Shit.

He's drugging me again.

Mystery man beside me starts punching the glass out of nowhere. And not in an angry way, but as if he's trying to actually break the glass to get to me.

"NO!" he yells loudly.

My vision is getting blurry as I sit down in the corner of my cell, covering my face with whatever I can find. But it isn't enough.

I struggle to breathe.

A few seconds later, the lights go out.

***

CAGE

"No!" I yell as he comes inside her cage and drags her into a wheelchair.

"Silence," he barks at me.

I frown as he rolls her out of her prison. "Give her back."

"Don't you worry about her …" he says as he takes her out of the room and out of sight.

What is he going to do to her?

I don't want her to get hurt, but I'm so damn scared he

might do something to her. Especially after she made so much noise. He must've been angry with her. I just hope he won't take his rage out on her.

The girl in the cage next to me groans, and her eyelids struggle to open. "Where …?"

"Cage," I say.

She blinks a couple of times and then sighs. "Fuck …"

She sits up on the bed with her head still hanging low, and she scrunches up her face. "God, I feel fucked up."

"It's the drugs," I say.

She nods and tries to get up. Her body is still weak, so she collapses on the floor. "Fuck!"

She swears a lot more than …

Just thinking about the girl makes me clutch my bed and make a fist with my hand. I wish I could get her back, but I can't.

"Food?" she asks.

"In the box," I reply.

She immediately gets up to grasp it before quickly sitting down on her bed. I can tell she doesn't want to stay on her feet too long because she keeps pulling them back up on the bed.

She tears off the wrapper and munches on a sandwich, practically stuffing her face with it. "God, I can't believe I could ever love a peanut butter and jelly sandwich this much."

Only when she turns my way can I finally see what happened to her feet. They're completely red and covered in sores.

"What happened?" I ask, getting closer to her side of the glass.

After swallowing the last bit of her meal, she takes in a deep breath. "Pain, that's what happened."

"How?"

She sighs. "I had to dance. Day and night. They wouldn't let me stop."

Dancing, a whole day long? I don't even do my workouts for an entire day; I'd be too worn out. Yet she's been up on her feet the entire time. No wonder she's hesitant about using them.

Water fills her eyes, and she wipes them away with her thumb.

"I'm sorry," I say.

"Don't be," she says. "It's not your fault I'm in here."

I swallow and look away, wondering what I can do to help. But that's just the thing. I can't do anything. I can only sit and wait out our time.

So I walk back to my bed and sit down to stare at the door he disappeared through with the girl.

A few minutes pass, and suddenly, a voice reminds me I'm not alone. "What are you doing?"

"Looking at the door," I reply.

"What for?"

"Waiting for her."

"Who?" The pitch of her voice changed, and I know exactly why.

She doesn't know yet that we're not alone anymore. "The new girl."

SEVEN

Ella

When I come to, my head feels like it's exploding. I feel so drowsy, and when I try to open my eyes, everything is blurry. I shake my head to try to make it go away, but it doesn't work.

Crap.

"Stay still …"

That voice brings chills to my body.

It's Graham, but I can barely make out his figure hovering over me.

"This'll only take a few seconds." He's so close to me right now, yet I have no idea what he's doing.

It's freaking me out to the point that I want to flail just to get him off me.

Except when I try to move my hands, they won't budge. I'm stuck ... literally. He bound me to the wheelchair with restraints. My legs too. I can't move.

Oh, God.

"I said stay still," he growls, putting his filthy hands on my wrists. "You'll hurt yourself if you don't."

I don't listen. I have to get out. I have to free myself. I don't know what he's doing to me, but I can't let it go on. So I fight with every bit of strength I can muster.

"Stupid girl," he growls.

The binds around my wrists and feet tighten again to the point they're painful.

My lips part, but no sound comes out. I can't form the words in my mouth even though I try so hard to speak. To scream.

"I told you to stop moving so much," he says. "Are we going to behave or not?"

My vision is getting better already, and I can clearly make out his hand as it comes closer. He's holding a needle.

"If you're going to resist again, I'm going to have to put you under. Do you want me to do that? Hmm?"

I shake my head.

"No?" The needle comes dangerously close to my skin.

I beg with just my eyes, desperately wanting to escape.

When I look at him, I can see the fire dancing in his eyes. The excitement at seeing my pleading face. And the wretched smile that appears a few seconds after.

"Good. Now hold still and be a good girl."

He places the syringe down on a desk, and I calm down a little. While he's not touching me, I quickly scan the room. It looks like a small office. There's a desk, a cabinet, a bookcase, and even a computer. Is this where he spends most of his time?

Graham grabs a bottle of liquid from the desk, so I raise my brows and stare at it.

"Alcohol." He pours it on a cotton pad and says, "This'll sting a little."

He dabs it against my hand, right where a wound is from banging on the glass. It burns so much, I hate the feeling, but I'm also wondering why he's doing this.

I watch him like a hawk as he picks up a Band-Aid and sticks it around my hand, right on top of the wound.

"There," he says, holding my hand in an eerily soft way as he checks it for more scratches.

"That wasn't so hard, was it?" he says.

He makes it sound as if he's doing me a favor.

As if I owe him something when, in fact, he was the one who took something from me.

My freedom.

"Now ..." He pulls the wheelchair so close to him I wanna sink back. He picks up something from his desk. Photographs. "I want you to look."

He holds them out in front of me, one by one.

All the pictures are of girls.

"See them?"

I nod.

He places them back on the desk and scoots even closer to me. So close, his disgusting breath seeps into my nose, making me cough.

"Remember those faces, Ella," he says. "All four of them."

Who are they?

"Wanna know why you have to remember them?" He narrows his eyes, clutching my arms. I feel sick from his touch. "They're the girls who came before you ..."

I swallow as he says the words, the realization of what it means hitting me like a brick to the face.

"Let's just say they didn't go back to their families."

I want to puke.

I can already feel the bile rising.

Shit.

"And you ..." He points his finger at me and chuckles. "You're pushing it too."

This isn't just a warning. It's a threat. I might disappear.

I stare at the pictures of the girls, wondering where he buried them. But he grabs my chin and forces me to look at him.

"Do you want to end up like them?" he asks.

I vehemently shake my head.

"You'll stop banging the glass until you bleed. You will do exactly what I ask you to. No objections. Got it?"

I nod harder than I ever have in my life.

No matter how much I hate this man for ruining my life, I don't want to die.

He cleans up the stuff he used and returns the items to the drawers. While he's busy, I secretly look around again, and my eye catches a bunch of papers lying on the corner of the desk. The top one has my name and photograph on it.

"Oh ... you saw that?"

I pretend I wasn't looking at it, but of course, it's too late now.

Shit, I'm caught.

"Yes ..." he says, deviously smiling at me. "I did my

research. You were perfect."

Perfect for what?

Suddenly, he walks away, leaving me alone in this small office that feels more like a closet than anything else.

Panic rises to the surface, and I feel the urge to break free from my bonds, but no matter how hard I try, it's no use. Despite having regained a bit of energy that I lost to the gas, it's not nearly enough to work out of these leather straps. And I can't reach them with my teeth either.

Dammit!

The stomping behind me stops me immediately. He came back with a smile on his face … and a dress in his hands.

"Like it?" he asks.

It's a navy blue, floral dress that looks like it belonged to a girl similar to my size.

"I think it'll fit." Graham places it on my lap with something else. Lipstick.

I want to shove it off and erase their mark from my body because I don't know how he got these.

What if these belonged to one of his victims?

It makes me want to scream.

"Tomorrow's a big day," he says, his underlying tone twisting my stomach.

Tomorrow. What's happening tomorrow? Something I'd need a dress for. A dance? Or is he taking me outside?

The questions are killing me, but then he grabs the wheelchair and spins it around.

I can't make eye contact with him, despite wanting to so desperately. I need to know what he meant by 'tomorrow.' What will happen? Why did he give me the dress and lipstick?

Right before we exit the room, he grabs a piece of cloth and stops to tie it around my head. Not being able to see makes me nervous. I want to know where we're going and if I need to prepare for something, but not seeing anything makes that impossible.

He brings me somewhere ... comes to a stop ... and I hear a soft beep. We wait. A rattling of metal. He pushes me again and stops. Something closes. It must be an elevator. I know for sure when I feel the familiar sense of gravity intensifying for just a second. We're going up.

It doesn't take long to come to a stop again. He pushes me out again and keeps going. It feels like forever until he stops again, and a clicking noise is audible, followed by a creak. The wheelchair lifts and is pushed over something. A loud bang behind me makes me jolt in my seat.

"That's just a door," he says, chuckling as if he finds it amusing that I'm scared shitless.

I'm pushed again through another door and then into another one. After which he pulls the cloth away from my face.

And I'm back in that familiar glass cell again.

The only place I didn't ever want to return to.

But when I turn around and look at Graham once more, I know any place—even this place, this glass prison—is better than being anywhere close to him.

"Tomorrow you'll put on that dress and lipstick. Understand?" he asks.

I nod, hoping he'll get me out of the restraints.

Maybe I might even be able to catch him off guard and overpower him. Attack him. Throw the wheelchair at him.

Anything.

But then he pulls out a cloth and a bottle from his pocket, dabs the cloth with the liquid, and holds it over my mouth. The same disgusting odor enters my nostrils ... and it reminds me of the night he took me.

I struggle. I fight it, I really do. But it's no use. Within seconds, I feel drowsy again, and my limbs don't respond to my intentions to move. My vision is hazy, and I fade in and out of consciousness.

I can feel his hands on my wrists and legs, freeing me from the restraints. He lifts my body, holding it close to him as he carries me to the bed and lays me down.

I feel like a puppet on strings.

From the corner of my eye, I can see him walk off with the wheelchair through the door he brought me in. Too late do I regain any bit of control over my body. Too late ... because the door's already shut tightly before I can make my way to it.

I shove the dress and lipstick off me with what little energy I have then I try to clean up. I can't even sit up straight without seeing the world revolve around me.

"You'll feel better in a minute," Graham says as he walks past my glass chamber.

I want to say, "Fuck you," but as always, my mouth fails me.

I just sit there in silence, waiting for the drugs to leave my system.

Another door closes, and I know by now Graham must be gone. I'm back inside the lonely cell again, but it's not like before. Something's changed.

There are three people now.

EIGHT

Ella

The memory of the girl lying on the bed pulls me out of my haze. I need to talk to her. The mere thought of going to her pushes my body to drive out the drugs quickly.

Focus, Ella. Focus!

My eyes adjust to the spinning motions around me as I get up from the bed and wobble to the glass.

"Don't," the man in the cell next to me says. "You'll get hurt."

I ignore his pleas and walk until my head hits the glass. Touching it, I slowly slide down until my butt hits the floor. My vision is already improving, and I can clearly see her bed from here.

"Is she awake?" It's a girl's voice.

"Yeah," he says.

"Hey ... are you that girl he mentioned?" It's her. The girl in the other prison.

I nod even though I can still barely make out her figure.

"The drugs wear off quickly. Don't worry," she says. "Just breathe deeply."

She sounds so calm. How could anyone be this calm if they were just taken and put into a small box like some kind of pet?

"It's okay. I've been through the same thing ... lots of times, actually," she says.

But that means she's been here ... before me? I stare at her with my mouth open.

"I'm Syrena. You?"

That's a beautiful name, I sign.

Her face is already becoming a bit clearer, and I can definitely make out her dark complexion and the curls in her hair.

"She doesn't talk," grumpy guy next door says while leaning against the glass.

I look up at him standing just a few feet away, and he crosses his arms and looks away as if he's upset at something. If only I knew what.

"Oh ... you're mute?" she asks.

I nod. Well, selectively anyway. But it doesn't matter because it still doesn't mean I speak. At least not here, in an unknown place with people I don't know.

The only ones who've heard my voice since my sister died are my parents because they're the only ones I trust.

I'm not expecting my voice to return to me anytime soon.

"No problem," she says. "I can just ask questions. So the guy next to you, his name is Cage."

Cage. How fitting.

When she calls out his name, he gazes at me instead of her. And the way he looks at me is just so … overpowering, somehow. Like he wants to possess me. Own me.

Syrena coughs. "Actually, that's just what Graham calls him. Cage. And then he points at this glass box we're in, saying Cage every damn day." She shrugs. "As in 'Get in the Cage.' He's never called him anything other than that."

Wait … that means his name is literally this place? Cage? His name is also his space? It doesn't make sense.

"I know, it's weird." She still seems so unfazed. "Everything is, here. Graham took me a few weeks ago," she says. "He's been keeping me locked up ever since."

But you weren't here before, I sign.

She continues to scrunch her face, but nothing I do helps her understand what I want to say. There must be some way I can tell her what I'm thinking. And then it hits me. Graham gave me lipstick.

I immediately reach for the dress and snatch the lipstick off the bed. And for the first time in ages, I write something down … Right on the glass.

Where were you?

The letters are thick, greasy, and bright red. The text is so vivid. She must be able to read that.

"Uh …" Syrena mumbles.

I look up at Cage who raises his brow at me. He points at his eyes and then cocks his head at Syrena. I follow his lead … and when I finally take a good look at her, I notice her eyes don't focus on me. And they're just as white as my hair.

She's blind.

Shit.

How in the world am I going to communicate with her?

"She wrote on the glass," Cage says to her.

"Oh ..." Syrena says. "I can't read." She laughs and points at her eyes. "Blind, you know?"

Well, that's ...

"Unfortunate when I'm stuck in a cage with a guy who can't read and a girl who can't talk." She laughs again. "Just my luck."

She's right. It's almost ... too much of a coincidence. Maybe Graham intentionally put us here together.

"Well, anyway, it doesn't matter. I might be blind, but I'm not stupid. What's in your cell? Look around you? Anything you can make noise with?"

I do what she says and look around, but there's nothing apart from a plastic cup and a book that I can pick up. That's when I realize what I need is right here in the palm of my hand.

I put the lid on the lipstick and tap it on the glass.

A bright smile appears on her face. "See? That was you, wasn't it?"

I nod, but obviously, she can't see that, so I tap again.

"Okay, two taps for no, one tap for yes."

I tap once.

"Good." She clears her throat. "Now, when I ask you a number, you can tap the numbers too, right? One to ten."

I tap again.

"Great ... See? It works."

"Amazing," Cage adds with a grumbling voice, rolling

his eyes.

"Stop being such an ass, Cage," Syrena says. "You're just upset that two girls are busier talking with each other than fawning over you."

I sniff a little, laughing through my nose, which she apparently hears because I can definitely see her grin.

Cage rolls his eyes and sighs after which he directs his attention to me. "Go on …"

He points at Syrena, and I'm wondering if he means he actually wants me to communicate with her. Or maybe he just doesn't want to deal with being locked in with two girls. Who knows.

"All right," Syrena says, groaning. "So tap one time for the letter A, tap two times for B, three for C, etcetera. You get it? You can make a word. Now tell me your name."

I tap five times. Then twelve times and then twelve times again. Then once.

"Is it Ella?"

I tap once, and she smiles.

"I like it."

I smile too, but then Cage opens his mouth and says with a gruff voice, "Ella."

A shiver runs through my body.

He didn't just *say* my name.

He claimed it.

Owned it.

Licked it.

Fuck.

I don't normally swear, but that's how it felt. Especially with him looking at me like that.

"God, my feet hurt," Syrena mumbles, pulling me from

my thoughts.

My lips part and I give Cage some looks, wanting him to ask for me.

"Tell her," Cage growls.

"What? How it happened?"

"Yeah."

"Well ..." She sighs. "Graham takes me out of the cage for days on end. He makes me dance ... in front of a whole audience of slimy businessmen. They're all there to make fun of me. To hurt me. To ... use me."

It's quiet for a few seconds, and I can imagine why.

A 'rough time' doesn't even begin to describe what she's been through. What we're all going through. But it sounds like she's had it the worst.

"They make me dance until my feet can't take it anymore, and sometimes they find it funny to poke me or burn me."

I swallow at the thought. I can almost feel my own feet burn just from her description.

"I don't know who they are; those ugly old men who are just there to enjoy whatever the fuck Graham gives them. I don't even know what Graham's doing and why. I just know that he uses us for cash. The men pay him to make me do things."

Do things? Payment?

We aren't just here for nothing it seems. I was right after all; so that means he intends to use me too.

"I think those men are just there to buy ... people. You know?" she says.

The thought alone makes me shiver.

"Because I wasn't the first girl here, and neither are

you."

She's right. Graham even told me so.

"I know for sure Graham's just showing me around like some expensive porcelain doll because I already heard some whispers around the huge room I was kept in … some of them were saying they were interested in buying me."

"Sorry," Cage says.

"Don't be. It's not your fault, right?" Syrena says.

Cage just shrugs and looks away. I know it must be horrible for him too, to know that's what's happening to her and not be able to do anything about it.

But the only question I have is why does Graham have Cage locked up in here? What is his purpose? Is he going to sell Cage too? And what about me?

"But anyway … I don't know why he took you, Ella, or what he plans to do with you. If he wanted to sell you, he would've already introduced you to the men. I mean, you're special. New. Innocent."

Innocent.

If only.

"You would know by now if Graham wanted to sell you … which is what I can't wrap my head around. Why would he keep you here? It must be something else. You have to be here for some other reason …"

Cage's brows furrow as he stares at me, his face rigid. Without looking away, his lips part, and I feel like he wants to complete Syrena's sentence.

But I'm not prepared for what he says.

"Me."

NINE

CAGE

Ella hasn't looked at me the same since I told the truth.

Something's changed. I can see it in her eyes.

She fears me now.

I hate the way she glares at me from her bed as if she's keeping an eye on me. As if I could snap at her at any moment and break the glass confining us.

If I could, I would've already done it if it meant being closer to her.

I want her ... I've wanted her ever since she came here. That longing has only grown the longer we're separated. Now it's at its peak. My muscles tense at the thought of touching her with my bare hands, feeling her skin against mine, tasting her on my tongue. My whole body roars with excitement when I think of her. And it's only gotten worse these past few days.

I gaze at her sweet, succulent-looking skin, those perky tits, and the sweetness that's between her legs. My cock tents in my pants. I can't wait to get my hands on her.

However, I know I have to force myself to focus right now because the door across the room just opened, and *he* steps out. The girls immediately get up, and Ella watches him closely as he walks toward the black door and opens it up, disappearing inside.

Minutes later, the door to my cell opens, and he comes inside.

I close my eyes and take in a long whiff. I can smell the scents from the room beyond, husky wood mixed with leather. Delicious.

"Ready?" he asks me.

I nod.

He holds out a bag containing gauze, tape, and a bottle of energy drink. I take the bottle out and immediately chug the liquid, throwing it away in my cell. Then I take off my shirt and toss that in the corner too.

For a split second, I spot Ella gazing at my chest in amazement before she looks away at Syrena again. Both of them seem on edge … and for the right reasons.

I wrap my hands with the gauze and tape and make sure they're tight and patted down.

"Now, make sure you give it your all. You know what's at stake here," he says.

I nod. "Yes."

He squeezes my shoulder. "Don't let me down."

"I won't." I make a fist with both hands and mentally

prepare myself.

"Good." He pats me on the back. Then he pulls the rug away from the floor to reveal the circular pad, and I step on it.

Ella's jaw hangs open as she approaches us and taps the glass. Nothing comes from her mouth, but I can tell she's confused. Her eyes move back and forth between me and the black door, which is wide open. With a cocked head, she beckons me to go there.

She still doesn't see it ... still doesn't understand.

"He won't run," Syrena says.

Ella's hand retracts from the glass as she slowly steps away, her body quivering as she stares at me while shaking her head.

It finally begins to dawn on her.

I look down at the floor, refusing to see the defeat in her eyes. It doesn't matter what they're saying right now. All that matters is what's to come.

He leaves my cell and walks out again, but before he disappears completely, he says, "I'll see you down there."

One final nod at him and I wait on my designated spot. He closes the door behind him and leaves me alone with the two girls again. The faster this is over, the better.

"You wanna know why he didn't flee?" Syrena adds. "Graham is his father."

Ella's eyes widen, and the shock and desperation seep in like poison. I don't know why I expected anything else. Yet it kills me to see her look at me like that. As if I just murdered the Cage that resided in her mind and replaced it with a monster.

Betrayal.

I know that look all too well.

But before I can say what I want to say, the floor underneath me begins to shake, and I know it's time. The lever was pulled … and I slowly descend to the room below.

***

Ella

"What happened? Where'd he go?" Syrena clutches the glass as if she's trying to hear what's going on. "What's that noise?"

I rush to grab my lipstick and immediately begin tapping the letters on the glass as fast as I can.

Hatch.

When I've tapped the final letter, she opens her mouth. "Oh, God. Did Graham make him put on something? Gloves?"

I tap once for yes.

"I think I know what it is," she mutters. "Shit!" She seems in a rush as she yells at me. "Grab the rug."

I do what she says and pull it away … only to discover a thick, round glass insert. With my jaw dropped and my eyes wide open, I peer through the hole into the deep room below. A gigantic pit lies below with a stage in the middle defined by a ring of ropes. Surrounding them are rows and rows of seats. About fifty men sit behind the ring, all of them wearing expensive suits. Scantily clad women pour drinks for them and give them snacks, some even sitting on their laps.

I can barely breathe as I notice a buff figure walking into the ring. It's Cage.

I gaze at Syrena who seems clustered to the glass, waiting for me to tell her what it is.

"Well? It's him, isn't it?" she asks.

I pick up the lipstick and tap once.

"Fuck, I knew it. I've been hearing so much noise coming from beneath that rug that I knew there must be some sort of window. I knew that motherfucker was providing more entertainment for his customers." She sighs. "Jesus. I'm sure that's the exact place where they made me dance. A stage of some sort is in the middle and used for whatever they think is fun to see. The ultimate fun pit for rich men who want to throw away their money to see people do their bidding. It's sick." She looks away, swallowing as if she has trouble holding the bile down. "I wasn't the only one. There were more girls, boys. Anyone they could get their hands on. I heard some of them. They begged to be spared. Some of them I never heard from again."

I bite my lip, clutching myself as I listen to her story and then watch as another man walks into the ring to face Cage.

"I never imagined he'd put Cage there, though. Probably to fight, right?" she says.

I tap again for yes.

"Figured. But why'd he do all this for his father? Why would he let himself get beat up just for other people's amusement? He doesn't get cash. He's not even free. He's stuck in the same glass prisons we are. Why would he do it?"

I don't know. I don't understand any of this.

All I know is that Cage is about to fight this other man

… because they're definitely taunting each other.

In the corner of the large room, Graham enters and greets all the male guests, sitting down with them while smoking a cigar. It's as if he's using his own damn son to entertain his guests.

Sickening.

"Can you see Graham?"

I tap again.

"He must be trying to sell them on something, but what? He'd never sell his own son, right?"

At this point, I don't know anymore. The sick bastard seems willing to do anything to get his hands on more money.

I can't believe this is happening. One man, running an elaborate underground market … selling people.

Hiding us in the attic makes it very unlikely that anyone will find us here. It's the perfect way to avoid visits from the police. If they break in, he'll just pretend he's paying people for their service instead of locking them up in glass prisons for his personal use. And if they don't believe him, he can just pay them off.

Just thinking about it makes me wanna puke.

"Are they fighting?" Syrena asks.

I tap out the word *no*.

They're still circling each other, and the men on the benches seem riled up about it. One of them stands up and yells.

Suddenly, Cage and the unknown man clash.

I quickly tap once to let Syrena know the fight has started.

Their hits are vicious. Powerful. Like mountains

colliding.

It's rough and coarse and not at all fair. The man hits him in the nuts, but Cage responds with an uppercut to the chin and then another one right in the nose. They're equally fierce and brutal, but the look in the man's eyes is murderous.

It scares me to the point where I'm actually hoping Cage might win just because he feels like the lesser of two evils right now.

I don't know who that man is or why he's fighting Cage, but it doesn't look like an ordinary fight. They aren't just fighting to win.

They're fighting to the death.

It's as if I'm watching two animals clawing at each other, and the men in the audience seem to be enjoying it even more. The harder they slam into each other, the bigger the wretched smiles on their faces, and the more they cheer. It's wrong, so wrong, but when I look at Cage and the violent spark in his eyes, I know he's enjoying it too.

It's his footwork and the way he punches his opponent that gives it away.

This is not the first time he's done this.

I just wonder ... how many times has he killed someone?

This is cruelty, yet Cage doesn't seem to see it that way. It's almost as if he's truly come alive down there in the ring. He's no longer that shy caveman who barely communicates while locked in a cage. He's a ferocious animal living for the kill.

And right then and there, he smashes his opponent to the ground.

Beating him to a pulp.

He doesn't stop. Not until Graham whistles.

When he gets off the ground, blood is everywhere. I'm not sure which is his, but he's covered in it too. Cage doesn't even seem fazed by it. In fact, he almost looks proud.

My heart is beating in my throat as he breathes in and out so hard I can see his heavy chest muscles move. His eyes turn up toward the sky. Toward me.

I freeze the moment our eyes lock. The fire inside his seems unquenched. But I can't look away. It's as if he's demanding me to see him. To see what's become of him now that Graham put him down there. As if he wants me to see the real him.

Graham flicks his fingers and severs our connection again just like that.

Cage walks away from the body and jumps out of the ring. What's left is a testament to a bloody fight where only one man could be victorious.

I lean away and sit down on my ass to process what I've just seen.

"Is it done? Is he alive?"

I tap once with the lipstick, but my movement is so damn slow. I still can't believe what I just witnessed.

"Is he coming back up?"

Why does she want to know that?

He isn't a prisoner. At least, not like us. That man down there is his father. The same man who took us. They're family. There's no way he could be a prisoner in here. Right?

But then why was Cage practically living right beside us in that very glass cage I'm looking at right now? Does Graham keep him there like some kind of animal? Just to make money off fights?

Just thinking about it makes me wanna punch the floor, but I don't.

It's no use. If Cage, the most powerful one of us three, didn't flee ... never got out ... There's no hope for us.

The ground begins to rumble again, and I recognize the sound. That makeshift lift is coming back up. I crawl away from the glass pane in the floor and quickly cover it with the rug. Not soon after, I see Cage's head pop up from the ground. He stands rigid and proud, like a brave warrior returning from war, covered in blood.

"Welcome back ..." Syrena says, clearing her throat.

She's looking for an opening. She's much more courageous than I am.

If he's Graham's son, then whose to say Cage is on our side?

He immediately unwraps his hands, not granting either of us a look. The shower suddenly turns on. I suspect it's Graham's doing. He must have a remote switch.

However, my attention is immediately pulled toward Cage who takes off his training shorts like he's all alone and walks to the shower butt naked. He doesn't even give a shit that I'm right here, looking at him.

Maybe he's so used to Syrena not being able to see him that he forgot I could. Or maybe he *wants* me to see him. Because damn ... the way the water forms rivulets as it rolls down his naked body has me enchanted.

I shake my head and put it out of my mind.

But then the door at the end of the room opens, and Graham pops in. Just his head. "I'm proud of you," he says. "You did well."

Cage doesn't respond.

"You," Graham says, looking at me now, "put on the blue dress and the lipstick." He snaps his fingers.

I quickly get up and do what he says before I get in trouble. I don't know why he wants me to do this, though. I don't understand any of it.

Cage doesn't seem to react to the man being here either. He just stares at the water on the floor pooling at his feet while his hand rests on the glass prison. Blood mixes with water as it disappears into the drain, and I can't help but wonder ... Did he really fight that man because he wanted to? Or is there some other reason?

It doesn't take long for me to find out.

"Here's your reward."

Graham presses a button, and the shower stops running. While Cage grabs a towel to quickly dry off, Graham presses another button ... And the black door from the glass cage to the room beyond opens for him.

And it also opens for me.

TEN

CAGE

Like a wolf that's sniffed its prey, my nostrils flare with excitement at the sight of the open door. Finally, after all this time, she's mine.

I rush to the door like a rabid animal, wanting to claim her this very instant.

I can't wait any longer. I want her so badly; I feel like I'm about to explode with need, so I storm through the door, ready to take her.

I kick the door to my cage closed and march toward hers. I ignore everything else in the room and focus solely on getting to her. I peer around the corner through the opening. There she is.

My woman.

My Ella.

I rush to her, not giving a shit that Syrena is yelling at me, asking what's going on. I want her. No, I *need* her.

I want to bury myself deep inside her and hear her moans as I fill her with my seed. I want to feel her skin on top of mine; I want to lick her crevice and taste her sweetness on my tongue. I want it all.

But when I approach her, she cowers in a corner, diving away when I get close.

Her eyes are filled with fear as I stare at her for a moment, her body shivering.

But there's no need to be scared. I'll take more than good care of her.

I'll give her every lick she'll need, every kiss she asks for. I'll protect her from anything and anyone. Because she's mine now …

My woman.

My Ella.

I reach for her and grasp her arm. She resists, jerking free, so I take her other arm. Again, she pulls back and gives me this look as if she doesn't want me to touch her. But that's not true. I saw her looking. I saw those hungry eyes. I saw her practically begging for my cock when she licked her lips at the sight of it.

Just as her eyes slide down my body this very instant, taking in every inch of my length. She gulps, visibly impressed. A smirk spreads on my lips.

I know she likes what she sees.

She can't deny her own body's desires.

So I put my hands on her tiny waist, lift her up from the floor, and throw her over my shoulder.

Then I turn around and march right back into the room

I came from, kicking the door to her cage shut.

With her fists, she pounds on my back.

Feisty. I like that.

It makes it much more interesting when she's just as eager as I am. I'll make sure she's opened up to me before our time is over.

I put her down on the bed, and she immediately tries to crawl away. Towering over her, I grasp her ankles and flip her over. That blue dress looks pretty on her ... but it's in the way. So I lean over her and push it up with my hand until it's right above her waist. I can see she's struggling, her fingers desperately clinging to the fabric as if she's afraid of what's about to happen.

But the look in her eyes ... it's different from anything I've ever seen before. Like she doesn't know what's about to happen. Like it's never happened to her before.

Could she be ...?

I smile at the thought.

My seed will be the first to lay claim to her womb.

As I hover over her, she places her hands on my chest and face, pushing me away. I grasp them and pin them above her head. My face is so close to hers now ... I can smell her delicious scent. With my eyes closed, I take a whiff, and they almost roll to the back of my head. That's how good it smells.

But when I open my eyes again, hers are red, and water fills them again. With my thumb, I brush away the single drop rolling down her cheek. Then I tuck her beautiful white hair behind her ears, and I lean in to press a kiss to her lips.

It's agonizingly slow for me, but I know I need to be

gentle with her.

For all these years, her body went untouched, and it doesn't know how to respond to a man like me. Doesn't know how to yield.

But I'll show her. With my body, I'll teach her how to submit.

As I kiss her, she bites my lip, and the bitter, metallic taste of blood enters my mouth. I'm used to it, so I shrug it off and continue. I like a woman with a bit of fight in her.

I press another kiss to her chin and one on her neck, before returning to her mouth.

My kisses are soft but overpowering. My hands are still on her wrists, but I can tell she's resisting less and less. And after a while, I release her from my grip.

My cock bursts with arousal as I feel her heated body beneath mine. With every kiss, I crave her more and more to the point I can barely take it anymore.

So I rise and allow her to look at my ample length before grabbing her waist again and flipping her over. I pull her up on her knees, ready to mate.

But she sinks down on the bed and holds out her hand right in front of me. The look in her eyes is serious.

"STOP!"

That yell … it came from her mouth.

I can't believe it.

She actually spoke.

***

Ella

Scream. It was the only thing I could do, the only thing I could think of. And then suddenly it happened.

My voice returned.

I breathe in and out through my mouth, my body shaking from the shock. I can't believe I almost allowed that to happen.

He leans up away from me for a second, equally surprised by the sound that came from my mouth. I immediately take the opportunity and pull my legs out from underneath him and scramble off the bed, crawling away.

Clutching my dress close to my body, I huddle into a corner. I can't believe what just happened. The door opened and in came Cage to sweep me off my feet and carry me into this room. This ... sex room.

Because that is what it is.

A room with just a closet, a water faucet, and a bed.

Its sole purpose is to connect the glass prisons.

It should've dawned on me that this was the reason for the room in between. Why Graham kept me instead of trying to sell me. Why I'm here in the first place.

It's for him.

Cage.

I'm his prize for winning the fight.

How could anyone offer up a human being as a prize? And why would Cage accept? It's as if he doesn't even know any better. I can tell by the way he looks at me as he sits on the bed naked with a full-blown hard-on that he doesn't have a single clue what's going on.

I want to rage so badly, but the sounds have disappeared from my throat again. I still can't believe I actually made a noise around him. It only happened with my parents because I knew them. I trusted them.

But this? This is completely different.

I don't know Cage.

Yet ... I could speak.

I shudder. It couldn't possibly be because I trusted him. No. Absolutely not.

But then why do I feel this sorrow when I look at him? As if I should feel bad? The worried look on his face doesn't make it any better either.

I'm not the one who did this.

"Ella?"

The way he speaks my name—in such a guttural tone— brings goose bumps to my skin. It sounds so innocent as if he's sad and wants to make things right. Even though he's the one who ... who ...

I don't want to feel the way I did when he touched me. I don't want to have these goose bumps whenever I hear him talk. I don't want this heat that rushes through my body after he kissed me. I don't want any of it because it's wrong.

It's so damn wrong.

Yet when he looks at me like that—with those hungry yet thoughtful eyes, licking his lips like he's contemplating what to do next—it makes me weak.

I can't be weak. Not in here.

Suddenly, he gets up from the bed, and his erection becomes huge in my eyes. Or maybe it was always like that, but I've only now gotten the time to actually look at it. And holy shit, I can't believe that thing was about to go into me.

I swallow away the lump in my throat.

I admit I have seen a man before, on several occasions, but it was mostly on the internet. I know how it works. But this is different. I've never actually been with a man in that way.

All I ever did was make out with boys when I was younger, but I never allowed any of them to get close to me. Never. I couldn't take it. Not with my baggage. Not without a voice to speak up when things went awry.

I wasn't ready for them, so I didn't go all the way.

But now ... I have no choice. No voice. Nothing.

Nothing to keep him from taking me.

Because that's what Graham wants. I am Cage's prize, and now he gets to have me.

But what I don't understand is why Cage doesn't see anything wrong with this? Why would he not see I'm more than just that? Why would he let Graham do this to someone? And why would he participate?

But as Cage stands there, gawking at me with these lustful but confused eyes, I conclude he honestly doesn't know either.

When he takes a step toward me, I panic and reach for the door, but it's locked. So I cower against the wood, hoping he won't drag me back to the bed again.

Except he stops in his tracks the moment he sees me flee like a hunted animal. His brows furrow and confusion replaces the gentle look on his face. He goes down on his knees and sits there in the middle of the room right in front of me, just staring at me.

Waiting for me to ... come to him?

Why would I do that?

He holds out his hands as if he wants to make up.

Why do I get the feeling he thinks this is normal?

I don't come near. I just glare at his hands, hoping he isn't going to use them to grab me once again. I always told myself that when and if I ever gave myself to a boy, it'd be on my terms. When *I'm* ready.

But him ... I'm not ready for him.

Holy shit.

He's like a super human. A beast amongst men.

How could anyone ever be ready for him?

That's what scared me the most. That this man would want me to the point of actually claiming me. And that he'd be this pumped up, this excited about it. It's that look I've seen in his eyes ever since I came here. That gaze of pure need ... as if he's been thinking about this one moment forever. And now that he finally could, he went for it like an animal in heat. And I'm the meek lamb thrown into the lion's cage.

I suck in a breath as I come to this realization.

But then why do I get the feeling he's not only a caged animal? Because that look of despair I see in his eyes now is not the look of a hungry beast. It's that of a sympathetic human being. Someone who cares.

He slides closer, still completely naked. It's like he's not even aware of the fact that his dick is still huge and hard, and I can't stop focusing on it because it makes my jaw drop. Or maybe he doesn't care at all.

But why doesn't he care? It makes no sense at all. It's as if he doesn't even know the rules of our world ...

Still, he doesn't grasp me, so I guess he finally

understood what I was doing. But I can tell from the way he bites his lips and keeps his hands locked firmly on his muscular upper legs that he's struggling with it too. As if he wants me so badly he finds it impossible to resist the urge. Yet he is …

His hand reaches for me, and I flinch because I'm still scared.

He immediately retracts it.

Lowering his head, he gazes down at the soft carpet underneath his feet before standing up and turning around. In amazement, I watch him stroll to the closet and take out a shirt and pants from it.

I hear a clicking noise.

Cage walks towards his door. He pushes the door handle, which actually moves, and he goes back into his cell, leaving me alone in this room, completely shaken and mesmerized by what just happened.

He did something I never expected for someone so addicted to the smell of a woman, to the need to fuck.
He let me be.

ELEVEN

CAGE

As I sit on the bed and wait for the door to her cage to open, I think about what just happened.

Father told me I could have her once I won the fight. That she'd be mine, and that she'd be willing. My woman. My girl. My Ella.

But he never prepared me for this. This ... reluctance ... this ... shame that I feel deep inside me whenever I look into her scared eyes.

I never wanted to make her feel that way, and I don't understand. All I want to give her is warmth and tenderness and satisfy our needs. I don't want to make her feel bad; I want to make her feel good. Real good. But she won't let me.

I don't understand anything about this.

"What happened?" Syrena asks, crawling closer to my cell. "I can hear you. You're back."

"Nothing."

"But I swear I could hear her voice."

Grumbling, I pick up my cup and take a much-needed drink.

I never thought women could be this confusing. She looks at me, practically eye fucks my body, but when I come to take her, she won't let me.

It's what we both wanted, so why not?

I fought hard for her and earned him money, so now I get to pleasure her. That's what he said would happen, and I trusted him.

But then why won't she accept me? Am I not good enough? Am I wrong for her? Or did I not give her enough kisses? Not enough attention?

Next time I try, I'll make sure to rub her too. Maybe that'll warm her up to me. Even though her mouth felt like it was ready, maybe her sweet pussy wasn't.

That must be it.

I just have to put more effort into it. Maybe kiss her down there too and let my tongue do all the work. Then she'll open up to me; I just know it.

After finishing the last drop of water, I crush the plastic cup in my hand and clear my throat. Something just clicked, and I know it's her door. Within seconds, it opens, and I see her stepping back into her glass cage slowly, carefully sliding along the concrete floor as if she's scared something's waiting for her.

But there's not. He'd never do that to her. She's mine, and he'll be kind and gentle to what belongs to me.

At least, that's what he told me.

But he also told me she'd like me, and that was a lie.

So maybe not everything Father says is true.

***

Ella

I sit on the bed and try to calm my heart down, but it's still pounding out of my chest. Images of what just happened keep flashing in my head, making me wonder if I could've done anything differently to prevent what happened.

But that's bad. I didn't do anything wrong. I'm here, captured, taken from my home. None of this is my fault. Not the room, not the door opening, not Cage plucking me like a ripe fruit to devour.

Yet I can't help but feel sorry for him as he sits there across the glass pane window, staring angrily at the wall like he knows he did something wrong.

Like he's beating himself up over it.

And for some reason … I almost want to reach out to him.

Even though I can't. Not anymore.

The second I entered this room again, the door behind me locked.

Graham made sure no one can go in and out without him knowing.

Suddenly, the door in the back of the room opens, and

Graham storms in with a look on his face that predicts thunder.

"Why? Why didn't you take her?" he yells, glaring at Cage, who gets up from his bed and stares at him with parted lips. "How dare you defy my orders like that!"

"She doesn't—"

"I don't care what she wants!" Graham snaps, interrupting Cage.

"What happened?" Syrena asks. "Did Cage try to do something to you, Ella?"

"You, shut up!" Graham barks. "And you ..." Now he points at me. "Your only purpose here is to do exactly what I want. Did you forget the little deal we made, missy?" He approaches the glass, so I scramble up from the bed and back away into a corner as far away from him as I possibly can.

"We had an agreement, remember? You'd be a good girl, and in exchange, you'd be rewarded."

Rewarded.

Yeah, right.

It's almost sickening how much indignation he seems to feel, despite offering me up like some gift to the gods.

I'm a human, not an object for him to use whenever he sees fit.

And I am *not* a prize to be given away.

So I stare at him and stand my ground without fear, without yielding.

"You play by my rules," he spits, pointing at the glass. "And my rule is that when I let him out of his cage, you are his."

"What?" Syrena quips. "Cage can take Ella? As in fuck

her?"

"I told you to shut up!" Graham growls, and then he focuses on me again. "You ... you'll pay for this."

He rummages through his pocket and takes out a knife, pointing it at me. Threatening me with it.

I swallow the lump in my throat at the size of the thing.

"NO!" Cage growls, furiously staring at Graham in a way that I've never seen before. As if his gaze could split mountains in half.

"What? She won't have permanent scars ... It'll only be a small cut. Just enough for her to learn her lesson."

Cage rams the glass cage so hard it quivers and catches everybody's attention, even Graham's.

It's quiet for a few seconds before Cage's resounding, booming voice echoes through the chamber again. "No ..."

Graham's nostrils flare, and he takes a deep breath. Narrowing his eyes, he seems to look past me ... beyond the glass prison ... and I follow his gaze to find him glaring at Syrena.

"Fine. But I *am* going to teach her a lesson. Everything has a price."

Just with that one look ... he's sealed the deal.

He couldn't get me because he'd go against Cage's wishes, and he wants to keep Cage happy. Cage is his prized fighter, the one he cares about the most. The one that everything here revolves around ... So now he's going to take Syrena instead.

He marches to the black door that leads to the back bedroom, and I try to scream, but my voice has abandoned me once again.

I hear the door unlock and watch as it slams open and

Graham disappears through. Seconds later, the door to Syrena's prison opens, and she screams.

"Who is it? Graham?" she pleads, desperately searching for a way out with her hands, but a blind woman is no match for a man who can see.

When he grasps her wrist, she screams. "No!"

"You're coming with me," Graham growls, dragging her out of her cell and through the bedroom.

In horror, I watch as he pulls her all the way outside, beyond the glass, and to the door. I keep knocking on the glass, but he won't turn around. He won't even give me one look before slamming the door shut behind him.

The last thing I hear is Syrena's loud squeal as it penetrates my brittle heart and shatters it into tiny little pieces.

***

Tears run down my cheeks as I keep banging the windows, but it's no use.

She ... won't come back.

Syrena's been taken from us, and why? So Graham could fulfill his sadistic needs.

So he could hurt her instead of me because Cage wouldn't let him take me.

I want to know where he took her. What she's going through right now. I hate the thought of her being in more pain.

And it's all because of me.

I didn't do what Graham wanted, so now he punished her instead.

Probably to get me to listen—to do his bidding—and it's working. I'm no match for this emotional blackmail. I never wanted Syrena to get hurt. I never expected he'd go to this length to get to me.

God, if I could switch places with her, I would.

It's all my fault she's there now … wherever she is.

I turn around in my cell and knock the glass near Cage. He glances over his shoulder at me. The mere sight of his wistful gaze makes me so furious, I scream.

Out loud.

The sound that exits my mouth is as formidable as it is frightening.

And it feels good.

So good.

To finally let it all out.

To finally capture his complete and utter attention in a way I didn't think was possible.

And I will make him listen to me, no matter the cost.

"How dare you?" I yell.

His lips part again, but now he is the silent one as he stares at me in disbelief.

I'm just as much amazed at my own ferocity as he is, but I won't back down. Not now. Not anymore. I've reclaimed my lost voice. Found what always belonged to me. And I won't let anyone or anything take it from me ever again.

"You let him take her!" I scream, my voice hoarse and uncontrollable.

He still doesn't respond even though tears stream down my face. I feel so out of control of this world, this place, these people. So let down by fate. My voice was the only way I could regain a little bit of my self-worth. My soul.

"Why didn't you do something?" I ask, banging the glass with my fist. "Answer me!"

His eyes lower to the floor, and he frowns. "No choice. This is my life."

"What do you mean your life? You're a captive, just like we are. Why don't you fight back?"

"He's my father." He swallows it down as if it's a tough pill. "I was born here."

TWELVE

Ella

Shuddering, I lean back, pulling my hands away from the glass.

"Born here?" I repeat.

It makes no sense.

No sense at all.

Yet the sincerity in his eyes makes me feel as if I've just been hit by lightning.

No wonder he never sought to escape. Why he never tried to hurt Graham. Why he shrugged off being in the cell as if it wasn't that bad. Why he seemed so eager around me.

He literally … doesn't know any better.

He looks away as if he's ashamed of the fact even though it might not even be his fault.

"Do you mean … your father kept you here all this time?" I ask. "In this cage?"

He nods and then sits down on the floor, so I do the same.

I guess this is the time where we finally have a sit-down and actually talk. Like real grown-up people.

But still, it's quiet. Too quiet. Neither of us knows what to say.

I'm too occupied with all the possible scenarios that could currently happen to Syrena, and he's conflicted about telling me the truth.

"I'm … sorry," he suddenly says, licking his lips as he looks up at me. "About Syrena."

I frown, wiping away a tear, not knowing how to respond.

"I don't want …"

"I know," I say, smiling a little bit.

It's not entirely his fault. He could've stopped Graham, yes, but ultimately, I was the one who didn't do what Graham wanted. I rejected Cage, and by doing so, I set certain events into motion I couldn't have anticipated. And it sucks. I wish I would've known how much of a cruel man he truly was.

I wrap my arms around my legs close to my body, clutching myself for warmth and comfort.

"It's not your fault," Cage says.

"It is …" I mutter. I know he's talking about Syrena.

"It's *his*."

With a look of dismay, I gaze at him. "But he's your father."

"Syrena deserves better," he growls, making a fist with

his hand.

"She does," I agree. "But there's nothing we can do to change it."

He briefly glances at me again. "I could."

"But as you said, he's your father. You love him."

He doesn't respond anymore. Instead, he just stares at my body, up and down, again and again. I wonder what he's thinking. If he's still contemplating what happened back in that room behind the black door. Or if he's thinking about something else entirely, like feeling sorry for what happened. Or maybe he just doesn't know what to do with himself.

Hell, I don't even know what to do with me, and Graham isn't even my father. It only makes things more complicated.

More complicated than being able to talk to a stranger after so many years of silence? I don't know. I'm still flabbergasted I can use my voice in front of Cage.

I don't understand why I can suddenly talk to strangers again. Maybe it's because of my horrible situation. Being stuck in this prison makes one feel exceptionally appreciative of the little things. Like contact. And smiles. Like the one he's giving me now.

"I like your voice," he mutters.

It makes me smile too. And I blush.

Maybe I'm actually getting used to him.

But it's not right. I can't sit here and smile while Graham does unspeakable things to Syrena. I can't just sit around and do nothing. But when I look around my cell, I come face to face with just how impossible our situation is. And how powerless I really am.

I need a distraction from my thoughts. Anything to

occupy my mind so I don't think about what he's doing to Syrena.

"Tell me about yourself," I mutter.

He cocks his head and points at himself, so I nod.

"This cage …" He glances around and above him. "It's all I know."

"But why? Why does he keep you here?"

"Fighting. And … sex."

When he says that word, I find it hard not to zoom in on his lips. I have to stop myself from thinking about anything that involves him and sex … and me.

"Was I the first girl in here?"

He shakes his head.

So the girls in the pictures I saw in Graham's office were really here. He wasn't lying. They might've all been in this very cage, living this trapped life I'm living right now. Being offered up to … him.

I swallow away the lump in my throat, thinking about the way he came for me.

"Did you …?"

"No. They died."

"Before you could …?"

"Yes."

I nod a few times, looking away. It's hard, coming to terms with the fact that Graham might've killed them or that they might've killed themselves just to get away.

The way Cage talks about it seems so distant. As if he doesn't really know what happened. Or maybe he just wants to forget.

I can imagine it's tough seeing girls die or disappear when all you want is to have them close. It must've been very lonely for him.

"Were all the girls prizes?" I ask.

He nods, which makes me shiver.

"So your dad gives you girls instead of freedom?" I feel weird just saying it out loud.

"Freedom?"

"Yeah ... like a real home," I explain.

"This is home."

I frown. "But you're not free."

"I don't need freedom," he replies.

I grimace. "Everybody needs freedom."

He shrugs and looks away, annoyed.

"Don't you want to go ... you know ... outside?"

When he finally looks at me again, his narrowed gaze is full of confusion, eyes blazing with curiosity. "Outside?" He takes a deep breath. "Tell me more."

My lips part, but nothing comes out.

I don't know how to respond.

In shock, I ask, "You've never seen it?"

He shakes his head. "No."

THIRTEEN

CAGE

With her lipstick and pieces of toilet paper, she's been drawing the world to me.

Picture after picture, nothing is left untouched, and we sit here for hours, maybe even days, just talking to each other.

I'm overwhelmed with information, taking it in like a sponge. I can't stop listening and looking at everything she's showing me because I can feel the excitement whenever I think of the possibilities.

She asks me what my father has taught me, and she seems surprised. Apparently, he didn't teach many things. Only what was necessary ... Like what's food and what isn't, he's shown me a few colors and their names, taught me how to train my body and how to fight, how to talk… and how to fuck.

Her stories are never-ending. She talks about cities and people, what they look like, where they live. Houses and trees, gardens and flowers. All kinds of animals, big and small, mountains and rivers. Summer, winter, fall. I'd never even heard of them before she told me about them.

The world is so big … it's almost hard to believe.

My father was my teacher, but he never told me anything like this. He never taught me to read the words either. I almost envy her for being able to read and write them with her lipstick when I can't.

I wish I knew all this before. My father always told me there was only this room and the rooms beyond. The pit where I fight and all the rooms in this place are my home. I don't know anything else.

But she … she's seen the world.

She's lived it all.

I don't know why he didn't tell me, but it doesn't matter right now.

All that matters is that she's here … showing me life.

Real life.

Inside her eyes, her mouth, her whispers.

Her voice sounds like that of an angel calling out to me from heaven.

It's too beautiful. Too perfect.

And so is the world.

Where we live now is just a dark, damp hole far away from any of the life she spoke of.

I yearn to see what she's seen. To watch the fish swim

through the sea. To see the birds fly in the sky. To experience the people and their habits. To see where she lives.

I want to learn it all.

But I already know it's impossible.

Despite telling myself not to think about it, the realization that we're stuck here still creeps back into my head every time the conversation ends.

Because I know damn well I was born here … in a place where no one will ever know my name … a place that might as well disappear from the world, and no one would notice.

That place is my home. And she doesn't belong there.

I can't help but grind my teeth. I'm actually jealous of her even though I don't want to be.

Because it makes me feel out of place … and it's not fair to her.

My father put her in here with me. He took her from that place. That place where the sky is blue and the ground is green. That place she calls home. He had no right.

Yet I can't stop wanting to know more. More. *More.* It's never enough. I need to know everything there is to know, and I need to know about her. Who she is. What she likes and dislikes. What she wants.

If she could ever want me the way I want her.

And if I could ever give her what she truly needs.

Freedom.

I sigh.

"Talk … more about you," I say.

"Well … I have parents too. A mom and a dad, like you." She smiles.

I shake my head. "No mom."

"Right ..." She frowns, rubbing her lips. "Where is she?"

I shrug, not knowing the answer. Father never told me about her. All I remember is him. There was never anyone else but him.

"Oh ..." She takes a breath and sniffs. "I'm sorry."

I bite my lip. "Tell me more about you."

She looks up, a tentative smile briefly appearing on her lips before a delicious blush overshadows everything.

"I used to have a sister a long time ago ..." She looks down at the concrete floor briefly.

"Sister?"

She frowns, surprised at my question. "You were born, right? What if another girl was born from your mom and dad? That's a sister."

Interesting. I never realized it was possible to have more than one child. Father always told me that I was the only child who mattered to him, and that he never wanted anyone else but me. And that I was to make a child just as he did. Someone who would follow in my footsteps.

But I am curious ... what my sister would've been like if I had one.

"And a man?"

"That's a brother," she explains.

I wish I had a brother. Or a sister. Doesn't matter to me. I just want someone to talk to.

I imagine Ella talked with her sister all the time. I wonder why she isn't here, though. Why Father didn't take her too.

"Where's your sister?" I ask.

She takes a deep breath, making a face as if it's difficult.

"She's ... dead."

"Dead?"

"No longer here. Moved on. Like those other girls your father brought here before me."

Father told me those girls would never return, so does that mean her sister will never return either? That's sad. Sad for Ella. Sad for her mother and father. Sad for the world. But why? Why would she go?

"Why?" I ask.

"She was murdered."

I shake my head, not understanding.

She sighs out loud. "Do you know what life is?"

"Yes."

"Then you know it can end. Someone else can end it too."

Someone else? Snuff out life?

"It's what you do when you fight," she adds.

"Oh ..." I growl.

Those bloody fights with my opponents always end with them not moving. If that is what it means to be dead, I hope I never end up like that. Then again, if it could happen to anyone, it could happen to ... Ella.

"You *can't* die!" I bark, infuriated.

"Well, technically, I can." There's a pause. "Your father could kill me."

Rage boils up inside me at the thought of her being taken away from me. Especially by him.

"No." He wouldn't do that.

"You're the only one who can stop him," she says.

I feel so angry right now. I want to break things, fight an opponent, scream, anything. Just to get it out of me. But I don't. I don't want to scare her.

So I stay put and listen, despite feeling enraged.

"I get it; he's your father."

"Don't …" I growl.

Her brows furrow. "Fine."

She looks away, and so do I, and for a few seconds, it's quiet again.

But I could never stay mad. Not at her. She didn't do anything bad. Nothing about this is her fault. It's all Father's fault, which is why I'm so confused.

Thinking about it won't help, though. I'd rather focus on her because she's the one thing that keeps me happy. She makes me feel good about myself and my place in this world.

"More about you," I say.

With folded arms, she just glares at me as if she's mad at me too. I don't know what to do to make it go away, but I think girls like it when men are a little bit less commanding sometimes, so I opt with a question. "Please?"

This makes her face less grouchy and more relaxed again.

"All right …" She sighs. "I live on my own in a small neighborhood. I work as a freelance photographer."

"Photogaf—fotho…"

"Photographer," she repeats. "Someone who makes pictures." She holds up the toilet paper she drew on. "Like this."

"Oh …" No wonder she's so good at it, if she does it all the time. It's like me and my fighting skills. Only hers don't involve blood, I think. Unless she normally draws pictures with the blood of her enemies. I'd like to see that.

"I don't have any other family but my parents. My mom and dad always worried about me even when I moved out to live on my own." She twirls her hair with her index finger and points at her mouth with her other finger. "Talking. You know. It's difficult."

"But you speak …?"

"Now. Yes." She chuckles a little, and it's the sweetest sound to my ears. Like that one time Father whistled. He called it a song. Her voice and laughter are just like that. Sweet and fun.

"My voice … disappeared when my sister died. It just became so hard to speak that I stopped entirely. They call it selective muteness."

"Muteness …?" I repeat. Sounds difficult.

"I physically couldn't bear my sister being gone, so my voice died with her."

"Why?" I ask.

"Because …" She sighs. "She spoke to a stranger, and he killed her. In my mind, speaking meant death. And I blamed myself for her death."

"It's not your fault."

"I could've gone after her sooner. Could've stopped him. Could've done something …"

I nod, swallowing. I can understand what she means. I, more than anyone, know what it feels like to feel guilt for something you didn't do but could've prevented.

Her being here is one of them.

"My parents … also didn't take it well when my sister died. Their screams made me pull back. I shut myself in," she continues.

"But you're here …" I say, not really understanding

what she means with it.

I do know one thing, though … no one can change what happened. The past is the past.

But why her voice works now is a mystery to me.

"I don't know why I can talk. My voice normally never works anywhere but with my parents. People I trust," she says after a pause.

Does that mean she trusts me?

She gazes up at me with those pristine eyes again. I want to touch her so badly right now, but the glass is in the way, so I settle for placing a hand on the cage instead.

She reaches for my hand and lines her hand up against the glass on her side.

I can't stop looking at her. Can't stop falling into the depth of her eyes. I don't ever wanna crawl back out. If this is hell, I'd stay if it meant I got to spend more time with her.

But suddenly, the door in the corner of the room cracks open, and she pulls her hand away from the glass.

***

Father steps in with an angry look on his face. Like I look when I'm ready to fight.

The two plastic bowls in his hand are probably food. I eagerly await mine near the box, but Ella's not so happy.

She bangs the glass hard. Father doesn't even seem surprised. Just irritated.

He shoves the bowl into her box and continues to me without even acknowledging her.

She smacks her fist on the glass again, visibly restraining herself from screaming. I don't know why she doesn't say what she wants to say to him. Why not use your voice if you have one?

He gives me an annoyed look as he chucks the food into the box and pushes it my way. He keeps grinding his teeth, chewing on the inside of his cheek and eyeing me from the side as I bring my bowl back to my bed and gobble down the fried rice with eggs.

She refuses to eat even though I know she's hungry. I also know why she's doing it.

My father looks at her and then gazes at me as if he expects me to speak.

When my bowl is empty, I growl, "Syrena?"

Father narrows his eyes at me and then directs his attention to Ella, approaching her glass with slithering footsteps. He seems amused by the fact she's inside and he's not. As if he's reveling in the fact she can't reach him.

"You wanna know where she is?" he mumbles.

She nods vigorously.

His smile is bitter. "Yeah, I bet you do." Then he turns and walks off. "Eat your food."

Ella's resistance is admirable, the way she keeps pounding on the glass until she sinks to the floor.

I can hear her belly grumble from where I'm at, but she won't eat.

She just sits there and stares at the door through which he just disappeared.

I know she's hungry, but she still won't eat.

Not because she can't, but because it's her way to remain in control.

To stop the guilt from eating her instead.

FOURTEEN

Ella

A few days later, in the middle of the night, the door creaks open again, and Graham pushes in an all too familiar wheelchair. I gaze through the tiny slit of my blanket as he rolls Syrena inside. I can't stop looking at her, but he walks by so quickly I barely have a chance to properly assess her.

All I can see is her arms as they hang motionless over the edge ... and the needle marks and bruises that cover her skin.

I swallow as the black door opens, and he disappears. The few seconds that pass are agonizingly slow. Her cage door opens again, and she's rolled inside. I watch him as he places her on the bed and pulls the blankets up, pretending to care about her even when he doesn't.

I know he'd get rid of her the second she wasn't useful to him anymore.

But I guess it won't take long for him to sell her to the highest bidder.

I wonder if I'm awaiting the same fate after Cage has had his fill of me.

When Graham's gone again, I wait a few minutes to make sure he doesn't come back before I crawl out of bed and inch closer to the glass, tapping it a few times.

She seems completely out of it and doesn't respond, but I can clearly see the wounds on her body from this far away.

What did he do to her?

I can only imagine.

I shiver at the thought of being the one to put her through all that. It couldn't have been easy.

Once she wakes up and realizes she's back in here, she'll probably break down. I can't let her go through that alone. Not on my watch.

So I sit down in front of the glass and keep on waiting. Until morning or longer, if I have to.

Anything to prove I'm here for her now even though I let her down before.

It won't happen again.

***

My eyelids have trouble staying open, and I'm fighting sleep. However, when I finally see some movement, I feel instantly invigorated. I lean up from the floor when I hear her groan.

"Fuck ..." she mumbles.

I immediately get up and stare, knocking on the windows so Cage wakes up too.

"What?" he growls, rubbing his eyes.

I point at Syrena. When I open my mouth, my voice refuses to make itself heard. I don't know why, but something feels like it's in my throat, preventing me from talking. It must be because I'm not alone with Cage anymore.

I wait until she sits up in bed, clamping her stomach with her arms.

"Ah … I …" I mutter.

God, it's so hard. Why does it have to be so hard to speak?

I'm fighting as hard as I can. I won't give up. Not until she hears me. She deserves to hear these words.

"I'm …"

She turns her head at me in shock as I try to vocalize what I'm thinking.

"I'm s-s-s …" My voice is hoarse, but I persist. If I can do it with Cage, I can do it with Syrena. I trust her. "I'm … s-sorry."

I clutch my hand near my chest and place the other one on the glass, hoping she understands. I feel terrible for what happened to her.

"It's m-my … f-fault," I say slowly, trying to pronounce the words right.

She groans again, clearly in pain, and it only makes me feel worse. I wish I could come close and hug her, but I can't. I hate being stuck in here.

"I'm … s-sorry," I repeat, hoping she can hear it.

"Don't …" she says, her voice squeaky.

I know she must be so pissed at me, and I'll understand if she never wants to talk to me again. After all, it's because of me she's in this state.

"Don't apologize," she mutters, catching me completely off guard.

"Wha—"

"You can talk," she says, her lips still parted as she's still facing the glass, trying to find me with eyes that can no longer see.

"Selective muteness," Cage grumbles as he leans up from his bed, rubbing the back of his head. I'm surprised he remembered.

"Wow …" Syrena says, but then she cringes again, touching her stomach.

It's weird to everyone, I guess, not just me. I don't know why I'm suddenly capable of talking. But when Cage didn't stop Graham from taking Syrena away, I was so mad. It just felt as if I couldn't hold back something huge bottled up inside me for so long. And then my voice burst out of me like lava from a volcano.

However, talking isn't important right now. What's important is finding out what happened to Syrena.

"I …" I mutter. "What did they d-do to y-you?" I ask with great trouble. My voice isn't a hundred percent yet, but I'll take having one over nothing at all.

She hisses from the pain. "He gave me to another client. Said I was his gift. Only while he was here, though, because Graham didn't let him take me with him. He's still waiting until someone pays up for me, but in the meantime, he'll use me as entertainment for his guests. And this one was extra vicious. Like … ow …"

"He hurt you?" Cage asks, his voice low and gravelly.

"Graham? He ... used a Taser on me," she says.

I grimace at the thought of feeling a current of electricity run through my body.

"But that man ..." She shivers. "He was pure evil. I'm lucky to be alive. Lucky Graham didn't want him to ruin something he could still sell," she scoffs, making a fist with her hand. "Bastard."

"I'm s-sorry," I say again.

I know she doesn't want to hear it, but I don't know what else to say.

I can't make her pain go away. I can't stop Graham from doing this to her.

I could've prevented it from happening if I had only done what he wanted, though, and I didn't. And that will always be a part of me now.

"It's not your fault," she says, coughing then immediately making a face again from the pain.

"I should've ... done what h-he asked."

"And then what?" She raises a brow. "Have sex with Cage?"

I almost break out in a sweat, thinking about that very thing.

"No, I'd never ask that from you, and it wouldn't be fair to ever agree to something like that," she adds.

"But ..."

"No." She purses her lips. "It's *his* fault."

Cage grimaces as he realizes she's talking about him.

"N-no," I say. "He c-can't ... h-help himself."

"Really?" She folds her arms, but she doesn't last long from the pain and immediately leans back on her bed.

116

"He's a c-caged animal," I say.

I don't want him to feel bad, but … that's what it is.

We're all caged animals. Except, he's never known any better. It's who he is.

And I feel sorry for him.

"Doesn't matter. It's his dad. You can't trust him."

"He doesn't k-know any better," I say.

"If Graham opens his door, he wouldn't even try to escape," she scoffs. "He plays on the wrong side, Ella."

"I don't play on any side …" Cage barks.

"You don't k-know that … y-yet." I swallow.

"Well, I'm not going to wait and find out." She perches herself against her pillow and lies down again.

She's right, though.

We can't wait until Cage finally does something to thwart Graham, but I don't feel we should write him off. He's strong. He absorbs information. He loves everything I tell him. I know it's in him— the need to see more, and the desire for control over his own life.

And if he doesn't want to escape, who knows, maybe he'll become useful to us in another way … someday.

Suddenly, a beep is audible. Syrena and I both try to find the sound; she listens with her ears while I watch the door. But nothing happens.

Not there, anyway, because in our cages, the showers just turned on.

Water pours from the ceiling, and Cage pulls off his tank top and shorts, standing butt naked in the cell once again. It doesn't even faze me anymore. I'm just impressed that he casts away his shame so easily. I wish I knew how to do that.

I wish I could just shower without feeling watched.

But I can't.

I can't help but stare at him, hoping I might have the courage to step underneath like he does. Because when I touch the warm water with my hand, I want nothing more than for the water to engulf me and take away the grime of the cell surrounding me.

Syrena stays in bed, mumbling, "I can't get up. Fuck the shower. Fuck this whole place. Just fuck."

I can't help but snigger. I like how often she says fuck. It brings some much-needed reality back into this place.

Cage glances at me, beckoning me with just a head nudge toward the shower. I shake my head, and he nods at it again. I know I should shower when possible, but it just feels weird to undress in front of strangers. Especially in front of Cage.

He furrows his brows and sighs then turns around, facing away from me.

I don't think it's random, and he didn't look upset.

He's trying to make it easier for me.

I lick my lips and tentatively pull down my clothes, hoping he won't notice. But he doesn't turn around once. Not when I'm completely nude. Not when I step under the shower. Not when I look at his muscular back and ass … which is very firm, by the way.

What the hell, Ella? No.

I shake my head and allow myself to enjoy the warm water scattering on my skin. I close my eyes and transport myself back to my home, pretending I can smell the liquid soap I use. Pretending I can see the light coming from the windows, and feel the white stones on the wall. I pretend because it's the only way to survive.

When I open my eyes again, I can clearly see Cage glance at me over his shoulder. But he immediately looks away the moment I catch him staring.

A blush spreads on my face as I cover my body with my arms, wondering what he's thinking. If he feels the same buzzing feeling I do whenever I look at him. If he still yearns to touch me the way he did back when the door opened.

I wonder when it'll happen again.

Last time, it was right after he showered.

The water feels hotter than before, but maybe it's because I'm sweating. Why? Because it just dawned on me that this could be it.

This could be the exact moment Graham flips that switch.

He's done it before … and I'm sure he's going to do it again.

I quickly step out of the shower and dry off with a hand towel I received through the box yesterday. I put on my dress and stand in the corner, glaring at the door and walls. I wonder when he'll come inside and tell us it's time.

I wait and wait.

Soon the showers turn off, and Cage dries off too.

I'm still staring at the wall, waiting …

But nothing happens.

Except for when that one voice suddenly booms from the walls.

"Last. Chance."

It's him. It's Graham.

Click.

I turn my head and watch the black door unlock.

FIFTEEN

Ella

I hold my breath as both Cage and I gaze at the black doors. I know he heard it too. The click that sets the lion loose.

I glance at him then back at the door and at Syrena, wondering if she heard.

Before I know it, Cage has made a run for it.

He doesn't even take the time to put on shorts or a tank top.

I realize if I want to stop him I should block the door, but by the time my legs actually move, he's already stormed into my room.

It's too late now.

We're face to face again.

Something indescribable overwhelms me as I stand frozen in a corner, staring at his chiseled body, his v-line … and what's below that. His length bounces up and down the moment I glance at it.

I swallow away the lump in my throat when I look up and see him staring straight back at me. I know he saw me looking. I'm just shocked anyone could walk around like that and not give a shit. But he can. And he *wants* me to see him.

He strides toward me, and I open my mouth, but nothing comes out.

My voice fails me. It always does whenever I need it most.

Or maybe it's because I'm too shocked to force myself to speak.

He's quickly close enough for me to feel his warmth and see his dark eyes slide over my body. I stay put like a deer cornered by a wolf. He towers over me as he stands in front of me, his still half-wet body dripping water onto the floor … onto me. Droplets rolling down his sexy abs have my mind spinning in circles, my tongue almost dipping out to have a lick.

God, what's wrong with me?

I suck in a breath when he leans in. I can practically feel his breath on my skin. He grabs a few strands of my hair and takes a deep whiff as if he's trying to memorize my scent. A low, rumbling noise comes from deep down in his throat, and I don't know why, but that just made me tingle.

Shit.

I don't want to feel that way. Not around him. Anyone

but him.

His face is still dangerously close to my body, and my breath hitches in my throat when his lips part. My nipples tighten as he blows out a soft breath near my ear.

And then he places a gentle kiss just below it ... right on the side of my neck.

I almost melt into a puddle right then and there.

I can't. I shouldn't.

But his lips ... God, I've never felt anything like it. Something this consuming should be forbidden.

He plants another kiss, this time on my jaw, and my head actually leans back. I can't believe I'm letting him do this, but it's just too ... enticing.

For some reason, the need to push back completely disappeared the moment he put his lips on me. It was the same as last time ... only then he tried to ...

Suddenly, his mouth is on mine.

And just like that, he completely wipes out my conscience, making me forget where we are and why. All I can do is feel. Feel him kiss me. Feel his hands creep up my dress. Feel him cup my breasts and squeeze lightly.

I can feel his every ounce of self-control.

He wants to ravage me but be tender with me as well. And these polar opposites of him are driving me insane with lust. I've never felt this before, this need to be swept off my feet, to be taken by him and to lose control.

I don't *want* to lose control. Not in a place like this. Trapped. Caged. Locked in a prison. With a man like him.

But he makes me forget everything I am and ever was, reducing me to my most primal self; a woman filled with unanswered needs.

I can feel his cock against my leg, swelling with greed, and my body responds with equal desire to be close despite my brain telling me to stop him.

I can't. I just can't do anything but be overtaken by his desires ... and mine.

Suddenly, he grabs me by the waist and lifts me into his arms like I'm some kind of princess and carries me off into the room behind the black doors again.

I stammer as he puts me down on the bed ever so gently. "But I ..."

He silences me with his index finger, replacing it with his lips soon after. He pushes me forward with his mouth, overpowering me and forcing me to lean back on the bed. His hands capture my breasts again, finding my nipples and playing with them. I suck in a breath and let out a moan when he pinches them.

The sound winds him up, and a smile creeps onto his lips. His dick bounces again, this time against my thigh, and I feel something thump between my legs.

Still, it feels so wrong despite everything feeling good.

I don't know him. This place is my prison. And he is part of the reason I'm here.

Yet ... I can't say no.

I can't. Not anymore.

When I look into his eyes, all I see is his innocence in all this ... and his greed. His desire to claim me. His need to fill me with his seed.

A shiver runs up and down my body as I realize what's about to happen.

He's my first ... or will be if I keep up this meek act.

I can't falter in my resolve. I don't want to get pregnant.

Not in here.

So I place my hand on his chest and push him away.

The look on his face immediately changes from excitement to sadness as the guilt washes over him again. I know he feels bad. As if he's letting me down. He doesn't have to tell me because I can see it in his eyes. They're like an open book to me. Emotions spilling out like words, showing me that he's torn between taking care of me and needing me more than the oxygen we breathe.

I don't want this to end up like before. When Syrena was taken from her prison and hurt because of my decision. But I know something else that could fix this problem.

There are more than one ways to pleasure someone and give them what they want.

And I know just the thing to do.

With a flat hand, I push him away from me until he's off the bed, standing in front of me with that huge cock of his pointing right at me. I gulp at the sight of it so close to me, and wetness pools between my legs. But I can't give in that easily.

I slide to the edge of the bed and take a deep breath as I see him stare down at me, his eyes all broody and wild. My fingers wrap around his ample length, and I begin to jerk him off. Slowly, with calculated movements, I try not to entice him to pounce me again while giving him just enough to stay.

I tell myself I'm doing this because I want to prevent Graham from taking Syrena again. That I'm doing this to save myself from the guilt. But that's not the only reason.

A small part of me actually enjoys gazing up into his hungry eyes and watching his body twitch with arousal—his balls tightening, his abs flexing.

I love how the rivulets of water are still dripping down his body from his neck, and how his whole body tenses the moment I apply pressure.

A guttural sound escapes his throat, and my pussy thumps again, feeling the excitement bubble to the surface. I don't know why I'm feeling this way, and I know it's wrong, but I can't help it.

I just know that I have to do this, for all our sakes. At least, that's what I tell myself, but I can't stop thinking about the way he kissed me. The way he touched me. How he's tried to control himself, for my sake, even when it became impossible to manage.

I don't want him to be my enemy. I want him to be himself. I want him to be the ravenous animal he truly is.

So I increase the length of my strokes, apply more pressure to the tip, and pleasure him the best I can. Pre-cum drips out, and I wipe it along the shaft to make it smoother, and he seems to enjoy it, arching his back to get closer.

But then I do the weirdest thing.

I actually lean in and press a kiss onto his abs.

God, he tastes delicious.

I couldn't stop myself.

I lick up a drop of water and let my tongue slide down until I hit the base. His cock tenses, veins pulsing as my tongue rolls over it all the way to the tip.

Then I take him into my mouth.

I'm stupid.

Crazy.

But I want to do this.

I want to feel him come.

Even if it's wrong.

***

CAGE

When her tongue wraps around my cock, I almost shoot my load right then and there. The only thing stopping it from coming is a pure force of will.

I've never felt anything like this before. I've pleasured myself with my hands but never a mouth.

The sensations are overwhelming to the point of wanting to thrust into her mouth. But I must restrain myself. I don't want to scare her away again.

She's doing this on her own terms. She's taking control of her own needs and desires, and I like that.

I smirk, gazing down at her licking my shaft. It bobs up and down with excitement, wanting to feel the inside of her mouth and the wetness coating it.

God, I want it all.

I arch my back and let her explore me with her tongue while I enjoy the view. Too bad I didn't have the time to tear off her dress and look at her naked body. But no matter, we'll get to that soon enough.

First, I have to get this pent-up need to go, and the only way to do that is by coming. Hard.

She's working my cock diligently, as if she's eager to receive my seed, and it pleases me. I groan with delight as she takes me into her mouth and sucks hard.

She slides off the bed and kneels on the floor at just the

right height. Her tongue rolls around my dick and lathers it with wetness and pre-cum. When she looks up at me with those doe eyes, all I want to do is thrust hard.

But I have to keep calm. I have to stay focused.

I wanted to take her so badly, but now she's giving me something I've never felt before, and I can't say no. Even though I should, I don't want to stop her. I just want to feel her sucking me until I blow my load. Is that so wrong?

I know I'm supposed to take her pussy, but her mouth feels so good. Too good. I can't deny her sexually, so I stand there and let the arousal wash over me.

She sucks me down to my base, and I can't help but apply a little extra push. She coughs, and saliva runs down her chin. I lick my lips at the sight. When I pull out, I almost want to lean down to claim her mouth again, but she quickly takes me back inside again.

She repeats this until I can't hold back any longer and start thrusting.

Back and forth, quicker every time. And she lets me.

My hard-on is pulsing with need, and my sack tightens when I'm completely inside her throat. I grab the sides of her face to push in farther until I hear that familiar, throaty sound again, and then I pull back.

As she takes in some air, I rub myself before shoving back in again. Her tongue circles around my length as I thrust in and out, eager to receive.

I clasp my hands around her throat and pound hard.

It's wrong, so wrong.

But that desperate look in her eyes makes me do it.

I can't stop fucking her mouth.

Can't stop wanting to feel her throat tighten around my

cock.

Can't stop the desire to come all over her tongue.

So I do.

With a roar, I jet deep into her throat, coating her tongue and the inside of her mouth.

She moans, and it's the best sound I've ever heard after listening to her swallow it. Her tongue rolls around me as she struggles with the stream of cum, which keeps on coming. I only let go of her face once I'm sated, and my cock is flaccid again.

When I pull out, she gasps for air, coughing.

I lean down and press a long, soft kiss onto her forehead and smile to show her my appreciation.

She briefly smiles back, and it's all I need to feel the full brunt of my greed for her again.

I don't want this to end with just my pleasure.

I need to sate her too.

I can see it in her eyes. That wantonness that's been dormant for far too long. Her body is yearning for it, so I will give her what she deserves.

Tipping up her chin, I make her stand on her feet, and then I push her down to the bed again. With a flat hand against her belly, I make her lie down and prop myself between her legs.

She stammers again, "But—"

"Shh …" I murmur, placing a kiss on her thigh.

She sucks in a breath as my fingers reach up her dress until I expose her pussy once again.

Slowly, my mouth roams up to her crevice until I reach the top, where I place another tempting kiss. I take a whiff, her scent arousing me to the point of getting hard again.

I dive straight into her pussy, claiming it with my mouth.

She arches her back on the bed, her mouth wide open as I lick and suck as much as I can. I don't need experience to know what she likes. The only thing I need is to hear her moan and feel her squirm.

My hand snakes around her waist, and I push her body up to access her more easily. Pushing my tongue into her makes her go crazy as she bucks up to meet my lips.

I place gentle kisses and suck in between, creating a whirlwind of sensations she can't seem to cope with. She desperately clings to the blanket, scrunching it up with her fingers.

Her face shows she's struggling with the feelings inside her even though I know she wants this.

Her clit is engorged, and when I twirl my tongue around it, she moans again, making me grin. I alternate kisses with suckling, mixing it with my tongue.

I push two fingers inside her wetness, and the mere idea of touching her there makes me grow even harder. I thrust in and out of her, and she seems to like it, judging from the blush on her face.

I want her to be pleasured, but this is also my way of preparing her for what's to come, eventually. Because soon, it will be my length inside her instead of my fingers.

As I roll my fingers around inside her, I can feel the heat rising, and I even need to hold her down to the bed with my other hand.

Her muscles contract around my fingers, and she holds in a breath only to let it out seconds later. A soft moan escapes her mouth, and her whole body tenses up as she quivers underneath me. I grip her waist tight and lick up all her wetness, loving the taste.

This … the way she scrambles for air, the way her eyes roll into the back of her head, the way she is unequivocally mine … this is what I live for.

SIXTEEN

Ella

The black door has long closed but not the one to my heart.

With every smile and every innocent gaze as I tell him more about my world, he nudges it open bit by bit.

It makes me wonder if I'm starting to lose my mind.

It can't be normal to fall for someone in a place like this, let alone for the son of your captor.

But when I look at him and see the primal, animalistic man as he works out on the bars, all I feel is warmth. Comfort. The only bit of light in this cell.

And I think Syrena's noticed it too.

She keeps raising her brows at me, giggling to herself. I know she can tell. She only needed to hear the sounds I made in that room. That, and our complete and utter silence about the whole issue.

I can't even discuss what I did. Not to him. Not to her. Not to anyone, including myself.

It's too shameful ... even when I don't want it to be.

Because who'd offer themselves up like that?

No one. Except me, of course. And I keep telling myself I did it for Syrena even though that's not the entire truth. It's the only way I can stay sane in this place.

"So are we going to discuss this ... thing?" Syrena suddenly says.

I already cringe at the thought of her listening to the sounds I made in that room while Cage was licking me. Just thinking about it makes my heart do a backflip again.

"Thing?" Cage growls.

"Yeah. You two hooking up. That thing."

He just makes a face and returns to doing his push-ups, just as he always does when he doesn't want to discuss something. We've got more in common than I thought.

"I did it ... t-to s-stop Graham ..." I say to the best of my ability. "From t-taking you."

It's my way of talking things right. That, and I don't want her to have to go through all that pain again because of me. If I have to fuck Cage to prevent it, then so be it.

"For me?" She snorts. "Thanks, but you didn't have to."

"His will is law ..." Cage says, narrowing his eyes at her.

"So? Doesn't mean we have to listen." She leans back on her bed. "I don't care what he says or wants; I'd rather die than play by his rules. I'm not going to be some easy captive. No way."

I love her tenacity. How, in the face of death, she still

132

maintains her resistance. That's real power. No one can bend her, no matter how hard they try.

It's the kind of resolve I'm jealous of.

I wish I was that strong, but my weakness is seeing other people in trouble and being the cause of that trouble. I learned that a long time ago.

I stare at Cage as he keeps doing push-ups until beads of sweat roll down his body. His eyes constantly switch from the floor to me and back again as if he enjoys me watching. To me, it's entertaining. The only thing I can do in this place is communicate with people.

I feel like a caged pet.

Something to play with.

I'm specifically here for him, but even after knowing why, I still don't fully understand it.

Why was I selected over all the other possible girls? And since I'm sort of selectively mute and Syrena blind, does that mean Graham has a thing for disabled people? Or are we just easy targets?

So I open my mouth and let the words roll out, hoping Cage might have the answer. "Why me?"

He frowns and stops pushing himself up.

"Why did Graham take me?"

He answers with a guttural voice. "Because I wanted you."

His admission makes me shiver, and I can't help but glare in disbelief.

Even Syrena sits up straight in bed.

"You chose me?" I exclaim. His nod confirms my suspicions. "So it was you."

I don't know why I feel the way I do, but it's as if he just rammed a knife into my back, and I helped him shove it in farther. I should've known this. It all makes sense, yet I refused to even think about it because I didn't want him to break that magical version of him I'd created in my head.

Stupid. So stupid.

"No regret," he adds, licking his lips. "I liked you …"

"Why?" I ask. "How?"

"Pictures." He points at the drawings I made on the toilet paper that I tucked underneath my bed, and it makes me want to tear them all up.

"I wanted you …" he adds, the left side of his lip quirking up into a smile. "Pretty."

"I'm not a doll!" I feel like I'm boiling on the inside.

He grimaces, clearly upset as his head hangs low.

He should feel ashamed. It's his fault that I'm in here.

Out of all the girls he could've picked, he chose me. That is *not* a compliment even though he seems to think it is.

"I don't care if I'm pretty. You had no right."

"But …" He places his hand on the glass, hoping I might place mine on as well, but I walk as far away from him as I possibly can.

"You could've chosen anyone, but you picked me."

"I … like … you," he says softly even when his voice still sounds like that of a grizzly bear.

"If you liked me, you wouldn't have condemned me to a place like this! You don't do this to someone you like. You don't get to pick them and trap them like … like …"

Tears spring into my eyes. I can feel my throat clamping up again, so I clutch it and sit down on the bed.

Every time I look at him, all I see is that he's the sole reason I'm in here. And I hate myself for feeling so guilty for ever even letting him into my heart. For letting him take what he wanted. For me ...wanting him too.

He took my freedom away from me.

How could I ever look at him the same again?

***

The next day, Graham storms into the room. "Why the fuck didn't you two have sex?"

I almost tumble over my own feet; that's how fast I'm trying to get up from the bed so I can get as far away from the glass as possible. As far away from him as I can.

He paces along the cages, gazing at us with an infuriated look. "Hmm? Got an explanation for me?"

"Sex. In the room," Cage says.

"Yes," Graham barks. "You were supposed to fuck her hole, remember?"

I don't understand. Why is he so mad? Cage got what he wanted, right? Wasn't I just a reward to him for winning the fight?

"We fucked," Cage says.

"You let her suck your dick," Graham growls, banging the cage and scaring everyone. "I told you to ram your dick inside her; I didn't mean her fucking mouth."

There's only one way he can know that ... and that is by watching us. So there's a camera in the bedroom.

Shit.

How often does he watch? And how long?

Just thinking about it makes my skin crawl.

Cage doesn't respond. All he does is stare stoically.

"Calm down," Syrena says.

"Don't tell me what the fuck to do!" Graham spits at her, making her take a step back. Then he walks back to Cage. "And you ... do what I fucking told you to do."

Cage sighs.

"What was that?" Graham says, holding his ear up to the glass.

"Yes, sir," Cage mutters, clearly not impressed.

Graham nods. "You'd better remember your place."

He turns and walks straight to my cage. I don't want him anywhere near me, but that's just the thing ... I'm not in control. And that's what this is all about. Control. He wants it, yet Cage and I took it away from him by deciding to do it differently than he had in mind.

"You think you're so clever, don't you?" he says, cocking his head as he points at me through the glass. "You think you can avoid my rules forever?"

I shake my head, but when I part my lips, just a tiny squeak comes out.

He chuckles, but it quickly turns into fully fledged laughter. "Not anymore. If you won't do what I say, I'll have to make you." The creepy smile on his face makes a chill run down my spine.

Then he turns and storms out again, slamming the door shut.

I shiver again, wondering what his threat meant. What he's planning ... it can't be good.

I sit down on the bed again, feeling nauseous.

"Guys? You gotta step it up, man," Syrena says. "If y'all wanna avoid getting caught in his rage. All I'm saying is ... make him happy, and he might give you what you want too."

"Freedom," I say, looking at Cage as I say it even though I'm replying to Syrena. "N-no one can g-give me that ... except me."

***

I wake up in the middle of the night when a foul stench enters my lungs. When I open my eyes, my vision is blurry, but I can definitely make out the gas pouring into my room.

Shit.

He's turned on the valves again.

I don't want him to take me, so I immediately roll out of bed with my blanket and stand on my bed, stuffing the blanket into the vents letting all the smoke in. But it's too late. The smoke's already in the room, and I'm coughing and heaving. Worse, my legs are shaking, and I feel weak. Not soon after, I collapse onto the bed, unable to keep the blanket against the pipe. The smoke now freely flows into the room, pulling me with it into the darkness.

I don't know how much time has passed since Graham drugged me, but a roaring headache pulls me back into the here and now. I try to rub my temple, but I can't. My hands are stuck.

That's when I realize ... They're tied to something.

And I'm lying on it.

I try to open my eyes, but everything's still blurry.

That's when I hear his voice.

"Relax, Ella. You'll need to learn how to use that body of yours."

I look around me, and despite not seeing much, I clearly recognize the room. We're in the bedroom, but the bed is

137

gone, pushed into the wall behind it. I'm there, on the spot it's supposed to be, but I'm strapped to a contraption.

I jerk the shackles around my wrists, but they're tight and bolted into the wood below me. Even my feet are shackled, and there's nothing I can do but wait. As my vision slowly returns to me, I realize I'm on a device…

A sawhorse.

SEVENTEEN

Ella

I swallow away the lump in my throat as I feel the soft padding underneath my belly and the coarse wood pinching my legs. What is he planning to do with me?

"You've been bad, Ella," he says, whipping his fingers at me. "I'm guessing you found it difficult to let him in, so I made it a little easier for you."

Panic washes over me as I realize the use for this type of thing.

Especially when his hand slides across my body and down my dress, pulling it up toward my back to expose everything.

I want to scream, but when my lips part, the sound is

nothing but a vapid sigh.

He chuckles. "Patience, Ella. He'll come soon. Literally and figuratively."

He chuckles again at his own horrible joke. "But first, we need to prepare you. I've placed a nifty device under your pussy that will make sure you're ready for him when he comes."

I shake my head, cringing. I don't want him to do this. Not him. Anyone but him.

"Don't worry. I'm not going to watch, if that's what you're worried about. I don't care about sex or girls, for that matter." He smiles and pushes aside a strand of my hair with his filthy hands, making me want to bite, but his finger is already too far from my mouth. "You're so pretty … Is that what he tells you?"

I spit on his face.

I don't know where I found the courage, and I immediately regret it because he slaps me and then cups my chin harshly. "You will obey, whether you like it or not. Your body will submit and do as its told."

He pushes my head away and walks off, and I grind my teeth, not wanting to cry out.

"I told you what would happen if you didn't listen to me. No more nice guy," he says as I keep trying to loosen the chains keeping me down.

However, something begins to buzz between my legs, right on that padded part of the sawhorse. And it's vibrating through my body, awakening a part of me I didn't want Graham to see.

"Be ready," he says, and then he leaves and slams the black door shut.

The vibrations continue their unrelenting assault on my body, making it impossible for me to concentrate on anything other than the thumping between my legs.

In front of me, a black television screen turns on and shows a man and a woman fucking like rabbits. He rams his cock into her like he's trying to come in all her holes. Mouth, pussy, ass, one after the other, and then all at the same time with two other men. It's like one giant orgy with toys and cum everywhere. I don't want to see this, but I can't look away because I can't turn my head. I'm completely powerless.

I hate this. I hate it so much, but I can't fight my body's response to the vibrations and the images in front of me. I feel myself getting wetter and wetter, my pussy feeling as if it's about to explode with need. I don't know how much time has passed since he tied me up and turned the vibrator on, but I can't fight the desire anymore. I don't have the will to ignore it any longer. I feel the incredible need to come.

So I do.

I let myself go to the sensations and let the orgasm ripple over me, a desperate moan escaping my mouth.

Not soon after, I hear a clicking noise, and I know the door behind me has opened.

It's like Graham knows exactly when to open the doors … which means he's really been watching us all this time, keeping an eye on us.

Which makes me wonder … what else has he seen or heard?

I can't think about it right now, though, because Cage has entered the room and slammed the door shut behind him.

I can't turn my head, no matter how desperately I try—to the point of straining my neck. The vibrations are still going strong, making me want to scream, but I can't. It feels so wrong, especially with him watching like that.

He's circling me, contemplating it, wondering what this is and why I'm here. I can't bear him seeing me like this, so … indecent, yet for some reason, my body can't stop yearning for that same moment I had with him last time.

That connection of pure lust, where our bodies almost seemed to melt into one.

I want that more than anything right now, and it scares the hell out of me.

The moment I feel his hand sliding my dress farther up my ass, the buzzing causes another orgasm, and I quiver from the waves flowing through me. I know he can see me unfurling, but I don't care anymore.

I just want this to be over.

***

CAGE

Strapped to a wooden device, she seems to be convulsing over and over again; her body has reached its limit. Sweat drips down her back as she pants against the soft fabric covering the wood, her eyes closed, her mouth opened wide. I grab her face and make her look at me.

"This?" I smack her ass with a flat hand, and her eyes pop then roll to the back of her head.

She sucks in a breath and moans when my finger slides

down into her crevice, feeling the wetness pooling between her legs. She's dripping, her pussy wide open for me to use. When I stick my finger inside her, she bites her lip, so I tip her chin up and say, "Yes?"

She nods softly. "Yes …"

I know she's still mad at me for picking her instead of the other girls. I'm the one who caused her to be here, but is that really such a bad thing? Being trapped with me?

I know she wants me—I can see it in her eyes—but she's conflicted, just as I am. The need feels sinful. Wrong. But undeniable.

She wants to fight this because my father wants this badly, and she refuses to make him happy. I understand. He's her captor. But there's more to this than just his wishes. There are my desires too … and my desire for her is stronger than anything I've ever felt before.

Especially when I look at her like this, bound to a post in a perfectly fuckable manner. I'm guessing Father wanted her ready for me. The vibrating machine below her body made sure of that.

The images of people fucking are plastered all over the wall, but I pay no attention to them. I'm only interested in one thing … her pussy wrapped around my cock.

I take off my shorts and grab my shaft, rubbing it until it's hard. With my free hand, I grasp her chin and kiss her hard on the lips, making her taste my greed and giving her what she needs so badly … peace.

Her body immediately relaxes as I claim her mouth, inside and out. Only when she's out of air do I stop. I smile briefly, and she seems less worried as I walk to the back of the device and perch myself behind her.

"Wait …" she suddenly mutters.

I stop right as my tip touches her entrance.

"Please … I don't want to … get pregnant," she mumbles, blushing.

Pregnant? But I want my seed inside her womb.

I frown. "Baby," I growl, and I rub myself against her pussy again.

"Cage!"

The way she says my name makes me stop immediately. She sounds mad.

"What then?" I ask, raising a brow.

"Not … there …" she whispers, visibly constrained by her own request.

I frown, not understanding her, but then she says, "Look down." So I gaze at her ass and every delicious part of her until I finally realize what she means.

She has more than one hole in her body. And all of them belong to me.

I can take them right now. She's even asking me for it.

Begging me to.

But I am apprehensive. I want her to carry my seed … I don't want to throw that all away.

However, the pleading look in her eyes as she strains herself to the max just to be able to look at me has me convinced this is the right move.

Besides, I've learned from all those tapes he showed me how to give a woman pleasure. There's more than one way … more than just one hole.

So I step away and walk to the closet to grab some lube I know is stashed away there. Once I have it, I spray it on my length and drizzle some on her ass, letting it slide down.

I push my cock along her slit, spreading it everywhere and making myself even harder.

We both know we need this. I need to claim her, and she needs to feel me inside her to make her whole again. So I push just the tip into her asshole until she squirms.

I place a hand on her back to hold her down and brace her for what's to come. I know I'm huge, and I know this is going to hurt, but she'll have to push through the pain to find the bliss.

Every inch causes a loud moan to escape from her mouth, but I don't give up. Not even when she's panting do I stop. And boy ... does it feel good to bury myself deep inside her ass. She's so tight. I wonder if it'll be just as good when I finally take her pussy.

I bite my lip and sink into her completely, causing her to moan again. When I pull out, she's much wider, and I thrust back in again to keep it that way. Her ass is getting used to my length pretty quickly, the lube still letting me feel the friction of her skin against mine.

Grasping her waist, I speed up the pace, pounding into her with my balls slapping against her.

I love how she feels around my cock, how she's totally given in to my needs, how she's still clenching her legs as if she's afraid to let go. But a quick finger has her pussy exploding again.

A smirk spreads on my lips as I watch her fall apart, and I use the opportunity to smack her ass to jolt her up again. Her head tilts back, and I reach for her hair, fisting it tightly, slamming into her even harder.

When I come, I roar out loud; my cum jets into her ass, filling her to the brim. I keep thrusting until every single drop has left my body and I feel sated. When my cock is flaccid again, I pull out and let it stream out of her. Claiming my woman is the prettiest sight there is.

With a content smile, I walk to her front again and grab her face, making her look at me. However, she can barely keep her eyes open and her head lifted. When I grab her hand and squeeze, she can't even squeeze back. She looks and feels too weak. Too drained to even keep breathing if she stays like this.

So I immediately search for the release button on this damn thing, but all I can find is a button near the vibrator, which turns it off. She lets out a gasp, but her body is still tied to the wood, so I keep searching, desperately trying to free her.

When all else fails, I grasp for the rope that's also in the closet and wrap it around the metal. I tug so hard, my muscles feel like they're about to give way, but I manage to wedge the metal loose enough to free her hands. I do the same to her feet, not giving a shit that it feels like I'm burning inside.

When she's completely freed, she almost tumbles down the device, but I catch her in my arms and hold her tight to my body. She looks exhausted as she squints at me. I smile and press a kiss to her forehead.

"Mine."

***

Ella

Mine.

The word means so little in the real world, but in here—in this glass prison where there's only two of us and nothing else really matters—*mine* means everything.

And when he speaks that word to me, my body lights up like fire burning through my veins. I can't describe it, and I'm not even sure I want to understand why I feel the way I feel. I just do.

When he looks at me with those warm, caring eyes, I think he just wants to hold me tight until I fall asleep. He'll take care of me, protect me … die for me.

I'm not even sure I could ask him if push came to shove.

He presses another kiss to the tip of my nose, and sparks of lightning shoot through my body. I smile but not because I'm happy. I smile because I'm proud.

Proud of myself for conquering my fears and doing what needed to be done for the sake of our survival. Even though I was tied up, I feel like I protected myself from a worse fate. I gave him my body, but I didn't give him my free will. Cage couldn't take me without my permission, not even if he tried. I had to say it out loud for him to agree, and even then, he still listened to my request.

He's not an animal. Not anymore.

I tamed him.

I sigh as I rest my head against his firm chest while he waits for the black door to unlock. The screen goes black first, and then I hear the familiar click.

Cage brings me back into my room and places me down on the bed. For a moment, I almost wish he'd lie down with me and cuddle with me until I fell asleep.

I'm so tired.

I never knew how exhausted coming again and again would make me. How him fucking me in the ass would seem like a relief in the face of hours on that sawhorse. I needed him to fuck me to free me from my bonds.

It was the only way.

But God ... did it feel wrong, and it hurt so badly at first. It was hard and painful, but I told myself to push through it and just accept it. When he was finally completely inside me, ramming in and out, it eased up, and pleasure replaced the pain. It felt so full but so good. I'd already felt so much of it that I needed him to fill me. I wanted to feel sated and wanted it to be done.

And now that it finally is, I'm glad I still gave Graham exactly what he wanted without sacrificing my freedom. Because if I ever get pregnant in here ... that's the end of it.

No one, and I mean no one, would want to get pregnant in a place like this.

That's cruel beyond words.

So I opted not to even make it a possibility. I begged him to take my ass so he wouldn't take my pussy instead. I knew there was no other way, but still ... the moment he ripped through me, I felt invigorated. Alive. As if I could finally let go, and it would be okay.

Cage pulls my blanket up and tucks me in then sits down on the bed and picks me up again. He pulls me into his embrace and cradles me as he leans back against the glass. I'm so sleepy; I don't even bother to ask him why. It feels nice to have his warmth envelop me, to make me feel as if I'm not alone on this night.

He plants a kiss on my forehead and whispers, "Mine."

Goose bumps scatter on my skin as I nuzzle his chest and feel the energy leaving my body.

"Rest now," he whispers, holding me close to his body.

And I do. For the first time in a long time, I fall asleep without the fear that's chaining my mind to this cell and dream of the green grass and bright sun again.

EIGHTEEN

Ella

I wake up in his arms. I don't know how long I slept, but I can tell he did too. There's sleep in his eyes, and he has circles under his eyes. But he's still beaming as he looks at me, blinking softly as I yawn. He smiles, and I smile back, feeling his arms envelop me like a warm cocoon.

And then he does the most peculiar thing.

His finger reaches for my cheek, caressing me softly before he leans in and kisses me.

And I let him.

I don't know why I do, but I don't want to resist.

I'm too tired to say no, and after weeks of no human contact, I crave his. If this is something to be ashamed of, then so be it. I'll gladly accept his affection because I need it more than anything right now. His mouth on mine makes me feel alive.

"Oh, my lord ... you're kidding me, right?"

Syrena's voice makes me pull away from Cage, and my cheeks flush red the moment I notice she's caught us.

Well, shit.

"Making out like teenagers in your cell?" she scoffs. "Really?"

I quickly unfurl from his arms even though I know she can't even see us. She's blind, obviously, but apparently, she could still hear us. I don't want to give anyone the impression that I'm into it even though I am.

"Relax," she says, laughing. "I get it. You fuck each other a couple of times, and you're smitten. It happens. Regularly, trust me," she says. "You lovebirds go right ahead. But please, keep it quiet, I don't like to hear someone fuck."

"We're n-not—" I mutter.

"No need to deny it, honey," she says. "It's cool. Just don't throw it in my face, okay? It makes me jealous because I wish I had a hunk of a man like you have," she jests, chuckling again.

"Hunk?" I say, cringing from the word.

"Don't pretend you're not totally into that body," she says, raising a brow.

Her comment makes Cage smile at me, and that makes me want to hide behind my pillow. God, I hate it when I'm exposed like that.

"Y-you discuss it like we're n-not trapped in a c-cage, fighting for s-survival," I reply.

"Oh, I know, but we all need distractions and fun. Plus, it feels nice, right? I can imagine. I only have my hand." She holds up her hand to show me.

"Ew ..." I mumble.

She grins. "Don't pretend you didn't do that at home. Stop being a prude."

"I'm not," I say.

"What?" Cage asks.

"Nothing," I say, burying my face in my hands. "Please, can we discuss something else?"

"Sure," Syrena says. "I'm curious, though ... Is he your first?"

"Yes."

With a dropped jaw, I glare at Cage who just spilled the beans like that. He gazes back at me with a shrug, apparently not aware of what the fuss is about. To him, that's the best part, when to me, it was quite embarrassing. Especially considering *who* he really is.

"I knew it," she says, shaking her head. "How does it feel? Good, right?"

"Shut up," I growl.

"Well, look at you. Got your voice back and you're already swearing," she muses. "Good for you."

"Thanks t-to you," I say, giving her a face.

Although, I do have to agree. My voice has been getting better every day.

Suddenly, the door opens, and I stumble up from the bed in shock.

"What are you doing in her cage?" he screams.

I never expected Graham to come in now, looking pissed as hell. Just seeing his face makes me clench my fist.

He drugged me, tied me up to that … thing. I did what he asked even though it went against every fiber of my being. And now he comes in here yelling?

He marches over to my cell, completely ignoring me as he barks, "Get back in your cage!"

Cage's face sours, and he immediately turns around and waits for the black door to be opened by Graham. When he rummages in his pocket and presses a button, the door opens, and Cage swiftly disappears through it, coming out on the other end into his cage again.

I can't believe he actually listened. No wonder his name is Cage … That's how Graham addresses him all the time. Does he even have a different name? Why would anyone do this to his son? How could anyone be this cruel?

"Couldn't do what I told you to do?" Graham rages.

Cage just stares, his nostrils flaring with anger, but he doesn't reply.

"No matter, I'll deal with you later," Graham hisses at him, and then he concentrates on me. "You think you can outsmart me, girl?"

I shake my head, but I know the damage is already done. I can tell just by looking into his eyes. He knows. He's been watching.

"You made him fuck you in the ass," he spits.

"Of course, she did," Syrena says, but he completely ignores her.

"I told you to behave. I told you what would happen. You want this, don't you? You want to get on my bad side." He points at me, pushing his finger so hard onto the glass I feel like it might break. "You … you'll pay for this."

"No," Cage says, slamming his fist into the glass.

153

"Yes. I told you what would happen if you didn't do what I said," he growls. "Now you'll both face the consequences."

"She did what you asked," Syrena says.

He still ignores her every word; his eyes painfully focused on mine.

"You … you think you can keep this a secret from me, don't you?" A wicked smile forms on his lips. "Think you're a clever girl? Think I can only see the images on the camera? There's a microphone too."

My eyes widen, and my heart stops beating for a second.

He could hear us.

Which means he knows I spoke to Cage.

How long has he known? It must've been longer than just today. There must be cameras here, surrounding the prison, too.

He's known all along yet he never said a word, never gave away his knowledge. Until now.

Until he could use it against me … to teach me a lesson.

My own cleverness has brought my destruction. By going against Graham, I sealed the deal.

He rummages in his pants again, pushing some buttons.

Suddenly, the sound of gas spilling from the ceiling makes me stop breathing.

I pull away from the glass, grab my blanket, and wrap it tightly around me, hoping to keep it at bay.

That's when I realize the smoke doesn't surround me.

It's entering Syrena's prison instead.

"No!" Cage yells, smashing his fist into the glass near her, but she quickly falls to the floor.

"Help …" she squeaks, grasping her neck as she rolls

around on the floor.

It's horrible to see her like this, and I know for a fact how it feels to suffocate in the smoke. I want to scream, but my throat feels clamped shut. I watch in horror as Graham walks into the black door and goes into her cage. I can only bang on the glass with every ounce of strength I have to make him stop. But nothing holds him back from dragging her lifeless body out of there, all the way through the room and out the black door.

Tears run down my cheeks as I realize what just happened.

The only person who I could talk to who knows what it's like to be free … is gone.

I watch her slowly fade into oblivion, knowing the last thing she knew was this cell … and the people inside it that caused her demise.

NINETEEN

Ella

For days, all I can do is stare at her cage, punch the glass, and bite my lips. I continue until both my lips and knuckles bleed. I don't feel the pain. None of it matches the gut-wrenching hurt I feel in my heart since Syrena's been taken.

I don't know what Graham did with her.

I try to ask every damn time he enters this room to bring us food, but nothing comes from my mouth no matter how hard I try to yell. So I keep tapping the cage, hoping to draw his attention, but he's ignored me ever since he took her.

He won't acknowledge I exist even though I'm begging

for him to answer me.

I need to know ... need to know if she's okay.

I'll never forgive myself if she's not.

As I stare, praying for her safety, I swear to myself that I will see her again. And that I will make Graham pay for everything he's done.

The food he brings spoils in the box as I refuse to touch it. I'd rather starve than make him happy. I know he needs me alive, so not eating is my only leverage. And right now, I'll grasp anything I can to regain what little control I have over my life.

Because I owe it to Syrena. Her spirit gave me hope, and now I will do the same in return. I won't give into him, not until I know she's safe.

Cage has been looking at me for the past few hours. He's tried to distract himself with workouts, but he keeps coming back to circling his prison, trying to get my attention. It's not working. Whenever he opens his mouth to tell me how much he likes me, or how sorry he is about what happened to Syrena, I just shrug it off and ignore it.

I don't care how he feels about anything right now. This is not about him. He should've stopped Graham. He could've fought. He could've *not* listened to him. Anything.

But he didn't.

And I do partly blame him for it.

Even though Syrena being taken was partly my fault, none of this would've happened if he hadn't chosen a girl in the first place. He could've refused. He could've told Graham he wasn't interested in anyone, so no one would be captured.

But instead, he was selfish. He chose his own needs over

those of another person.

No one has the right to do that. *No one.*

How could I not be mad at him?

So I'm just going to wait it out until Graham feels compelled to tell me what I want to know. And until that happens, I'm just going to sit here and pretend I'm a ghost.

***

CAGE

Not hearing her voice is painful.

But not being able to see into her eyes is killing me.

Every time I try to make her look at me, she turns her head without giving me the slightest chance.

I know why she's upset. I didn't stop him. I could have, but I didn't because … that's just it. I don't know why. I just do as I'm told because that's all I've ever done. I don't know any better.

That's no excuse; I know that.

I have none, to be honest.

She says I'm fearless. But even fearless men have their weakness.

Mine is her.

I don't want her to get hurt.

I'll do anything and everything in my power to prevent that. Even if it means going against her wishes. Even if it means listening to my father, who she despises so much.

She's right if it makes me a bad man. I never claimed to be anything else. I'll give my life if it means she's safe.

However, I understand if she doesn't see it that way. But

by not eating and not sleeping right now, she's endangering herself. I don't know why she's doing it. Maybe to defy my father, to get her way … because I know she wants Syrena back. Hell, even I want Syrena back even though she always nagged me about things I didn't have the answers to.

I don't want to see her hurt either. However, if it comes to choosing between Syrena and Ella … the choice is simple to me. If that makes me just as evil, then so be it.

I will protect my woman.

No matter the cost.

"It's time," his voice booms through the boxes.

Sighing, I grab the gauze and tape he gave me a few hours ago through the box and wrap my hands with them. Then I stand in the circle on the concrete and wait until it lowers me into the ring again.

I try to catch a glimpse of Ella, but she still won't acknowledge me. Even when I'm about to walk straight into a fight that could kill me. Even when I know she cares.

I've seen the way she looks at me. She can't deny it. She feels something for me, which is why it annoys me when she refuses to acknowledge me.

I press a kiss to my lips and point it in her direction, staring at her until I catch at least a hint of her gaze. It's not enough, but it'll do … for now.

The elevator goes down, and soon she disappears from my sight.

***

The wait seems eternal, but the ring finally comes into view. I step out. Cheers are audible from the sidelines. I

159

don't pay any attention to the guests clapping as they see me walk up. I couldn't give two shits about who's watching right now. I just want to get this over with.

I step inside and nod at my opponent then prepare for the fight. Father talks to me from the sideline, giving me more of the same advice he always gives, but I don't even listen to him. All I can think about is Ella, and how disappointed she is in me.

I don't want her to give up on me, but that look in her eyes … filled with tears … just cut me like a knife. No wound to my body compares to the pain I feel inside my heart when I see her like that.

When the fight begins, I try hard. I punch and kick, but my muscles don't seem to apply the same strength they usually do. I can feel my energy waning quickly. Everything around me feels fuzzy. I don't know why, but I can't focus.

My face feels hot and bursts with pain after a fist lands right on my cheek. Blood flies everywhere. I bite my lip, and the metallic taste of blood fills my mouth.

None of it matters.

A bell rings.

My opponent pulls back after applying a final kick and pushes me to the ground. Panting, I get up, sweat dripping down my forehead. I barely feel as if I put up a fight. I didn't. I'm losing because I lost the will to care.

"What the fuck are you doing?" Graham yells.

He made his way up to the ring, and he's right up in my face right now.

"Are you trying to lose?" he spits.

He's right. I feel like I am. Maybe I don't want to win if it means I'll lose her.

"What's your problem?" he asks.

"You," I answer.

He grimaces and growls, "What?"

"You," I repeat. "You ... Ella ... Everything."

"You're worrying about that now? Win this motherfucking fight." He slaps me hard on the back. "If you lose, you die, and I am not fucking letting you die, so get to work."

When he turns his back on me, I growl back, "No."

He glances over his shoulder, tentatively stopping his tracks and turning around. "What did you say?"

"No." I stay headstrong, like her.

His nostrils flare, and he stomps toward me, pointing at me with a sneer. "How dare you defy me!"

"She's unhappy," I say, remaining steadfast.

"So? What does that girl have anything to do with you fighting to win?" He shoves me with one hand. "I don't train losers. You win this goddamn fight, hear me?"

"I don't care." It's the truth. I don't care if I win or lose if I don't have her smile.

"You want to die?" he asks, grinding his teeth.

"I want *her* ..."

He shakes his head, chuckling. "I can't believe this." He sighs. "You won't fight because she's mad at you?"

I nod. He knows damn well what he's done. What he made me do. I refuse to be her enemy.

"What do you want me to do about it, huh?" he snarls.

"Fix ... it ..." I growl back, not backing down.

His nostrils flare again as he glares at me, contemplating it for a second. "If you'll win this fight ... Fine."

Grinding my teeth, I reply, "Done."

I don't care what it takes. As long as she's happy again, I'll bash any motherfucker down that I can find.

Before he walks away, he holds his hand up high in the air, and the bell rings again. My opponent starts closing in, and Father gets out of the ring just before the first punch lands.

I don't take it to the face this time, though. No, I capture it with my fist then punch him right back in his guts.

He heaves, and I kick him in the jaw, throwing him to the ground.

The men in the seats go wild for me, but some are screaming because their champion is about to go down, and it isn't me. I'm not willing to stake my life as long as I have her.

She's my beacon of hope. My sole reason to survive.

I briefly gaze up to the hole in the ceiling through which I know she's watching. I can see her eyes blink as she stares, frozen, wondering how I know she's there watching me.

I've always known.

I thrive on knowing she's watching me.

Like a guardian angel from high above.

Smirking at her, I brush the blood off my knuckles and jump on my opponent, ready to strike my final blow. I kick and punch as hard as I can, shoving my fist up his face and stomach until he's coughing up blood. And even then, I don't stop. The animal in me has come out in full force, ravaging my enemy until nothing's left.

When I'm done, his soul has left his body, and all that remains is a floppy, bloody mess, his eyes staring lifelessly up at the ceiling. I spit on the ground and get up, roaring out loud at the people on the stand.

They stare in silence, and it takes minutes before the sound of victory echoes in the hall. Bells chime, and Father runs up to pat me on the forearm.

"You did well. I'm proud of you," he says.

Proud.

Does it even mean anything anymore?

I used to live for this moment, for his approval. But now? All I can do is gaze upward into the cell above, wanting her to see every ounce of desire I'm firing back at her with just my eyes.

God, I want her so much, it's making me crazy.

I push Father aside and march toward the elevator, not giving a shit whether the men in the seats want to celebrate my victory or exchange the money they bet. Not even Father shouting at me, asking me where I'm going, fazes me.

I just want to get to her and her alone.

And not even Father can get between that.

TWENTY

Ella

I watch him come up from the ground below, his body covered in blood. I don't know if it's his or his opponent's, but I do know he put up one hell of a fight. I'm still mad at him, but I can't stop looking. Something about a man covered in blood commands attention ... demands respect.

When he went down there, the first thing I did was gaze through the circular window in my floor. How could I not? I had to know if he would survive. I know they fight to the death down there, and I don't want him to die.

Despite hating him for not resisting Graham, I don't want him dead.

I just had to know, had to watch him fight. And it was

painful … every single strike. He took them again and again, seemingly not caring about whether he'd get hurt. He didn't defend himself, and it made me want to scream. Why was he giving up?

Graham was there, but the way they talked made it seem like they were mad at each other. But at what? What happened is a mystery to me. It was unlike him … but then he threw me that look.

I couldn't look away and neither could he.

For some reason, just me being there, watching over him, made him change his mind.

Just like that, he found the spark he needed to fight once again.

I could see it in his body, the primal fire blazing within him as he beat his opponent to a pulp. He's not just fighting to survive. He's fighting … for me.

For the right to claim me.

I couldn't stop watching him do it. Couldn't tear myself from the glass until the fight was over and he stepped out victorious. Like a true champion.

And still … I can't stop looking.

He unfurls the wraps around his hands, revealing the bruises underneath, but the pain doesn't seem to move him. Instead, he takes off all his clothes like he always does and walks into the spot where the shower immediately turns on.

For a moment, I'm struck in awe at his presence … the power that scorches from his body.

I envy his ability to see through all the suffering and focus on the beauty alone.

He's like a young man stuck in an adult's body, seeing the world through a hazy lens.

I wonder if it'll ever change.

Whether we get out of here or not, this man is no ordinary man.

The door bursts open, and I get up from the bed, wondering what Graham is doing here. He's marching to my cage in an aggravated manner as if I did something wrong even though I haven't. I face him without fear and without emotions blinding my observations. I don't need them anymore when there's nothing to care about. Nothing to look forward to.

I wait until he says what he has to say, but he catches me completely off guard when he plasters a piece of paper against the glass.

It's a photograph ... of Syrena.

Made just days ago.

I immediately head to the glass, not giving a shit about whether I'm in his face and throwing everything I just promised not to do out the window.

It's her ... it's really her. And she isn't bruised or cut or bleeding. She's ... alive.

"I sold her, but she's unharmed," Graham says, frowning.

I can't stop looking at the picture, though, but then he pulls it off the glass. I feel like he just gave me a shot of heroin and then took it all away again.

However, he saunters to the box and tucks it inside, shoving it my way.

"Keep it. It's yours," he says.

I snatch the picture before he can take it away again. He'll have to claw it out of my dead hands before I ever give this back.

"If … you behave," he adds, raising a brow.

I make a face at him, refusing to use my voice for someone as disgusting as him.

"You want more perks? Act like an adult," he says. "And maybe … just maybe … you'll see the outside world again."

Outside world.

Did he just say that out loud or did I dream it?

Images of the green bushes and trees around my house flash through my mind again—the bright sun and blue sky, birds flocking together, the sounds of nature, animals, quacking, crickets chirping, my mom's voice.

I almost tear up again, but I push them away.

I want to go there but on my terms. It has to be my choice, not his.

So I clench the photograph between my fingers and stare him down until he gets the message. I'm not going to be easy. I'm not going to be good. I'm going down loud and with my pride intact. He might use my body, but he'll never break my soul.

When he's gone, I sit on the bed and stare at the picture in my hands. My eyes tear up again at the sight of her face. She's pretty. They must've noticed that too, so they finally bought her. I don't know where she is or if she's happy … but all I can hope for is that she's safe. That the man who bought her will make her whole again.

Cage has been watching me from his corner, staring at me while under the shower. He's fully nude, but as always, he doesn't seem to care. But I'm not focused on him as he's used to. I'm homed in on the picture and all that it entails.

This was a gift from Graham … that he felt compelled

to give me. But why?

Was it because I'm refusing to eat?

Or is it because of something else?

I look up at Cage and ask, "Did you do this?" I hold up the picture.

He steps out from under the shower and grabs a towel, drying off as he walks closer, still completely naked. I don't let it get to me even though his body is to die for.

He nods briefly then points with his fingers at the picture.

I wonder why.

Turning it around, I notice scribblings on the back that I'm not prepared for.

Fight. Live. Love. Never give up. You will be free.

It's her, but it isn't her handwriting. It can't be. She was blind. Her buyer must've written this on the back for her. Maybe as a last request.

I smile, tearing up. Her last minute here, with her freedom still belonging to her, was spent trying to give me a message of hope. My heart fills with gratitude and joy, wishing I could thank her for what she's done.

I won't give up.

She's here, watching over me through her picture, reminding me of what's at stake. Reminding me of what this world owes me. The freedom to live how I want.

"What does it say?" Cage's guttural voice blocks out all the voices in my head.

"That I shouldn't ever give up …" I mumble, licking my lips. I pause for a second then gaze up at him. "Thank you."

"I didn't …" He swallows, unable to finish his sentence.

"I know you asked your father to do something," I say. "Down there …" I point at the carpet under which the circular window lies.

He nods again, rubbing the back of his head, still completely oblivious to the fact that he's naked. And buff. And … hot.

Jesus, why am I thinking this right now?

Blushing, I place the picture down on the bed and sigh out loud, telling myself I can do this.

I need to do this. If I ever want to see the outside world again, I need to give Graham what he wants.

And what he wants … is for me to fuck Cage.

It's fucked up, but there's no other way.

I'll throw away my dignity for the sake of my freedom.

Anyone would.

So when the shower turns off, and the door emits that familiar click sound again, I don't panic. I don't flee. I stay put and wait until he comes to take me.

TWENTY-ONE

Ella

He makes his way through the room and opens my door. He looks like a walking sex god. Like a bear, he stalks toward me, but carefully, as if he doesn't want to scare me. But I'm not afraid. Not anymore.

I don't believe he could hurt me. He wants me too badly. He likes me too much to ruin me.

At least, that's what I hope.

When he's close, I suck in a breath as he inches toward me, eyes closed, and sniffs me again. He does that every time as if he savors my scent ... or maybe it makes him hard.

He grunts, and when his eyes open, he tips my chin up

and presses his lips to mine.

I go meek like a lamb, completely soft in his arms as he wraps them around me. I can't help myself anymore. I'm falling … falling for the giant protector in my prison.

His tongue runs along my lips, nudging them apart. He claims my mouth with fervor, licking the roof of my mouth and tasting my tongue. I kiss him back just as hard, incapable of holding back. His mouth is just too delicious … too sinful.

His hand snakes around my waist and pulls me closer against his rock-hard body. I'm no match for his strength as he grabs me. At first, it frightened me, but now, it makes me feel safe. Loved.

I gulp down my nervousness as he stares hungrily into my eyes. He presses a greedy kiss against my jaw, his lips drawing a line all the way down my neck. I cock my head, letting him get closer, and he takes it as an invitation to slide his hand up my body and grasp my breast.

I moan into his mouth as he cups my breast and squeezes while pressing sweet kisses just below my collarbone. When he does this, I can almost drift away from this place. So I let him… I let him take me away.

He swoops me up into his arms again, and I wrap my arms around his neck. With my feet tucked behind his body and his hands on my ass, he carries me back to the room with the velvety bed. It's already down on the floor again, and Cage places me on the soft sheets, immediately locking his mouth with mine again. His kisses feel rampant. As if he couldn't stop even if he wanted to.

Hovering over me, he presses sweet, heavenly kisses all over my body until he reaches my breasts. With one hand, he inches up the pink dress I'm wearing until I'm naked, throwing it off the bed.

For a moment, I feel self-conscious, wanting to wrap my arms around my body and curl away, but his ravenous eyes and the way he licks his lips at the sight of me makes me feel good. Makes me feel wanted. Proud.

He grabs my wrists and firmly pins them above my head, pressing another kiss to my lips before going down. His lips roam freely across my chest, and he groans when he reaches my nipples. Suckling them one by one, he takes his sweet time to treat them well. Heat rises through my body as need crawls through my veins.

I should feel embarrassed for letting him take me like this, for being so easy, for letting go of my inhibitions. But then I remember it's my only way out of here.

And when he sucks and licks me like that, it makes my eyes roll to the back of my head.

I can't deny that it feels good, and I can't say no because I don't want him to stop.

I quiver underneath him as his hand slithers down my body and between my legs, cupping my pussy. Wetness pours out against his palm as he claims my breasts with his mouth. He's like an animal wanting to devour me, and I actually want to give myself up to his needs even though he's my first.

My first ... ever.

And it's about to happen.

Oh, God.

The panic rises again, but when his fingers start to thrum and play with me, I lose my mind again, forgetting why I was afraid in the first place.

It feels so good. Everything he does with his fingers, his mouth, his hands ... everything feels like it was made for me, and only me.

His mouth covers mine again, and I moan into his mouth as he explores my pussy. I can't help it. I want more, so much more, and he gives me exactly that when he lowers himself between my legs and licks me down there again. His tongue expertly rolls around my clit, making it thump. I want to run my fingers through his hair, but I'm frozen to the bed with my hands still above my head where he left them.

I scrunch the sheets with my fingers and suck in a breath when his mouth cups my pussy, sucking hard. The pressure he applies changes rapidly, his tongue circling around like he wants to eat me and then some.

I'm amazed he's doing this instead of pleasuring himself. I expected him to immediately want to come, but instead, he's focusing on me. Like he wants to ease me into it. Make me happy. Make me his.

It's working, all right. He's twisting me around his tongue and pushing me to the peak of ecstasy. When another hungry groan leaves his mouth, I fall apart in sweet bliss. He captures me with his mouth as I buck below him, wanting his mouth everywhere, all over my body. God, I want it all.

By the time he's done, I'm panting, and I feel so dirty, but he makes all the bad feelings go away with that tempting smirk of his as he leans up to peck me on the belly.

He works his way up again, all the way to my mouth, claiming me with that same tongue that gives me so much pleasure. I can taste my own sweetness on his lips, and it turns me on even more to the point of moaning into his mouth.

He responds with an equally eager groan. Then he wraps his hands around my waist and attempts to flip me around. I can feel his hard-on poke my thighs as he prepares to enter me. I brace myself against the bed and hold up a hand.

"Wait …" I mumble.

He frowns, confused as he's gripping his own dick by the base, wanting to take me right now.

I place my hand against his ample chest and push back just a little to make him inch back. He's on his knees, and I use the opportunity to crawl closer and straddle him.

If this is going to be it, I want it to be on my terms.

So I push myself onto his lap and lower myself onto his length until I feel it inside me, filling me up. I don't stop, not until I'm all the way down to the base. It feels huge and thick inside me, throbbing with greed as I adjust to his size. He smiles and nuzzles me then presses a gentle kiss to my lips, after which we begin to rock.

At first, we go slow so I can get used to feeling his length inside me, thrusting up and down. I decide how fast we go and how deep. But I can't help but take him all the way. I'm that infatuated, that lost in him, that I let myself go.

His firm hands wrap around my waist and back, holding me tight, pushing me up and down. Faster and faster until I'm bouncing up and down on his cock, his warm pre-cum making it slippery smooth. Each time my nipples brush his solid pecs, the friction causes them to stiffen. I blush as I look down at him. He won't look away. He's completely enthralled by me, and I can't stop gazing into those lustful eyes.

I let him use me, let him fuck me raw like the beast he is.

My head tilts back as he presses a kiss to my neck and thrusts inside me hard and deep, filling me up. He grunts, and I can feel him pump inside me, releasing his seed. Jetting warm cum into me, he keeps going, fucking me until he's sated.

And even then, it's still not enough.

Still inside me, he rolls me off him and lies on top of me. He's still hard and fast, fucking me like there's no tomorrow. Like there's nothing but him and me.

In and out. Hard and fast ... and so damn deep.

His hand wraps around my neck, and he squeezes, holding on tight.

Fear engulfs me again as I feel the air leaving my body, but when he collects a kiss, I feel my body calm under his touch. He controls my body's every need, my mind's every thought, and I let him. He's the only one I'd trust enough to choke me, knowing he would never go too far. I trust him ... with my life.

That's why my voice is here whenever he is.

He is the storm in my calm world.

The thunder in my clouds.

The sun in my darkness.

Right now, he is everything I need to know.

Like an animal, he pounds into me, cupping my thighs, his fingers digging into my skin. The pain makes me hiss, but he claims my mouth to stop me from feeling the pain by turning it into pleasure.

He keeps going, groaning like a beast. It feels so good; something inside me feels like it's about to burst. To the rhythm of his thrusts, I come again, unwinding hard and with a moan. He tenses and goes in deep then pulls out and jerks himself off right on top of me. It squirts everywhere, coating my body in his cum as he comes undone.

Panting, he rubs his dick off on my pussy, rubbing it in deep, spreading it everywhere like he wants to get it all over me. Like he wants to mark me.

"Mine …" he growls.

There it is again.

That one word that unlocks my heart.

For a moment, all we do is stare at each other. Then he pounds down on me like a predator, but the kisses that follow are sweet and gentle as if he wants to tend to me, nurture me … take care of me.

He lies down next to me and wraps my body with his arm, tucking me into his fold. He's huge, encompassing, but I feel safer with him than anywhere else in this place. I can hear his heart beat as he lies on his side, my face pushed against his chest. Listening to it reminds me of being human in a place where my humanity has been stripped from me.

"Sleep …" he mumbles, snuggling into my hair.

Goose bumps scatter over my body as he holds me tight. I couldn't move if I wanted to or even if I tried. The calmness he exudes causes me to close my eyes, and I fall into a deep sleep with a smile on my face, knowing that I fulfilled my purpose here … And that Graham might finally let me go.

TWENTY-TWO

CAGE

Waking up with Ella feels like a dream. We're still in the bedroom on the soft bed, my hand still wrapped around her. She's turned around in her sleep and huddled close to me, curling up against my chest. Heat flows through my body looking at her naked skin, her sexy curves, as I think about how I laid claim to her yesterday.

She's my woman—completely mine—and I adore every inch of her sweet body and that beautiful smile.

However, when I gaze down to admire each little nook, I notice a red stain on the sheets. My eyes widen, and I lean up to inspect it, trying not to wake her. It's right between and below her legs too.

Fuck.

I nudge her away to take a closer look and dab the sheets with my hand. It's wet ... and it looks like blood.

"Ella," I say because I wonder if she knows what this means.

Her eyes open slowly, the salt still in her eyes as she blinks. I point at the blood pooling underneath her. She doesn't seem entirely awake, so I grab her shoulder and look deep into her eyes. "Pain?"

"What?" she mumbles.

I point between her legs again. When her eyes follow and see the blood, they widen and she sucks in a breath.

"Shit!"

She clambers out of bed as if she's seen a dead body, almost falling over her feet to stagger away.

I throw off the sheets to reveal more blood that has seeped through. If this came from her... she must be wounded.

Fuck.

Was I too rough? I wanted to go slowly, ease her into it, but I couldn't stop myself from ramming into her with all my pent-up lust. Did I go too far this time?

Fuck!

It's my fault. It has to be. Just thinking about it makes me want to punch the wall, so my fist instantly responds.

Ella jolts back from my sudden outrage, and I immediately regret my decision. I try to approach her, but she leans back. I hate when she's fearful of me because I will never, *ever* harm her.

"Come ..." I say, wanting to inspect her for injuries.

She shakes her head and looks down at her own legs covered in blood. "Shit."

"Blood," I say, and I look at the camera in the corner. "Come, now!" I growl at it.

I know he's watching, so I'll keep yelling until he comes. I want him to look at her and see if she's okay.

"No," she says, shaking her hands. "Please, don't call him."

"You're bleeding …" I growl, and I shout back at the camera again. "COME HERE!"

My voice is so loud it makes Ella inch back again until she reaches the door. It clicks open, and she rushes through, back into her cell.

I know I'm scaring her, and I know she hates Father, but I need to know if she's okay. It doesn't take him long to get here, though. I follow her through the black door, which closes behind me just seconds before Father arrives.

He barges into the room and screams, "What happened?"

I point at the red stain on Ella's legs.

His eyes follow, and soon it clicks. A smile slowly creeps onto his face. "Well, I'll be damned."

He reaches into his pocket and takes out a device with buttons. I know just what it is, and the mere sight of it makes me do a double take.

"No," I say.

"You know it's necessary," he says. "Get back into your cage."

The black door opens again, but I want to go to Ella instead. I hold out my hand. She doesn't budge, despite me trying to get her to come with me. "Come," I say.

She shakes her head, her eyes alternating back and forth between me and Father. She doesn't understand that I want to protect her … and right now, I don't know what he's going to do to her if she stays.

"Come. Now," I say, wanting to grab her hand, but she flinches.

"Get back into your cage!" Father yells, and he shows me the device. "Or do you want me to press *that* button?" His finger hovers over the one that makes me stop in my tracks. The one that causes immeasurable amounts of pain. The one I want to avoid at all cost.

I swallow and slowly step away from Ella.

"Get back …" Father says, pointing at the door.

I creep toward it, never taking my eyes off Ella, wishing she'd come with me. But she's frozen to the floor as he forces me to back away from her.

"Go," Father emphasizes, and when I finally enter the door, it quickly snaps shut in my face.

Fuck.

Reluctantly, I go back to my cage and stand near the glass, watching his every move and keeping an eye on her. I don't want him to touch her. I don't want him to do anything to her, but I have no choice in the matter.

I'm just as much of a prisoner in this place as she is.

He gazes at her with too much interest.

"Don't," I tell him, but he ignores me completely.

Then he presses the button and gas fills her room again.

"No!" I yell.

"Silence!" Father screams. "Don't you dare forget your place."

"She's mine!" I growl, pounding on the glass, but I can't break through, no matter how hard I punch.

She shivers as she struggles to breathe. Soon she begins

to cough, and it doesn't take long for her to fall to the floor. He walks out of the room and comes back with a wheelchair. I watch helplessly as he goes into her cell and picks her lifeless body up from the floor, stuffing it in the chair like a puppet before pulling her out of my sight.

"Why?" I ask.

"Because she's bleeding, that's why," he answers then goes through the black doors. When he comes out again, he stops to say, "Make no mistake … this girl is my property, and I *will* take care of it as I see fit. I brought her here, just as I brought *you* here. *Don't* forget that."

I grimace and lean away from the glass, fury raging through my body as I watch him wheel her away. When she disappears from my sight, I roar out loud, feeling the loss of my mate to the bone.

***

Ella

When I wake up again, the first thing I feel is a pang in my belly. The bright light above my face makes me squint. Where am I?

Music blares in my ears, making me want to plug them. A radio is playing "Don't Worry Baby," and the sound is what pulls me back to reality.

I can feel cold metal beneath me, and leather straps run across my body, making it so I'm unable to move my limbs. I look around and notice Graham standing near a desk with a computer on it. I don't recognize this room, though. It's not the one I was in before. This is much bigger ... and it looks like a lab.

"Oh, you're awake," he says. "Good." He picks up a tube and stares at it then shakes it. He grabs two thin photographs and plasters them on the wall. Only then do I realize they're not photographs ... They look like ultrasounds.

"I bought my own equipment. Beats having to go to the hospital every time. Neat, don't you think?" He smiles as if he's actually proud of his accomplishment. As if it's not at all an invasion of privacy.

The stinging sensation inside my belly—and between my legs—interrupts my thoughts.

"If you're in pain, I can give you painkillers," he muses. "You're probably experiencing some irritation due to the swab that went up there."

Swab. Up there.

My eyes widen.

Did he ... perform a pelvic exam on me?

Bile rises in my throat as the tears spring into my eyes.

I suffocate on my own emotions; the horror that I feel bursting to the surface. But no matter how much I try, I can't move. I can't bring myself to fight and scream.

"Relax," he says. "Otherwise, it'll only hurt more." There's that wretched smile again. I want to punch him. Cut him. Stab him. Kill him.

I've never had these thoughts before, but now I definitely have them. He took something from me that I never wanted to give away. And for what?

He can't even look me in the eye as I fall apart. Instead,

he's busy looking at the ultrasound pictures stuck to the wall. "So ..." he mumbles. "The good news is, everything seems to be working perfectly, which I'm thankful for, seeing as how that other girl was completely useless."

Other girl ... does he mean Syrena? Or the ones who came before me?

Not knowing eats away at me, but I have no time to think about it because he keeps telling me more. And every little bit of information is crucial right now.

"The bad news is ... well, I suppose it's not exactly bad news," he says, chuckling as if any of this is even remotely funny. "But the blood is normal. You're on your period."

Period. The idea seems so farfetched if I think about it because I used to get that at home. In the safety of my own bathroom. I wasn't examined by some creepy man or kept in a dark, damp hole. Periods meant pain, but I could live with that pain. In fact, I'd do anything to have just *that* pain.

After being through so much in this depraved prison, I never even thought of my monthly calendar, let alone actually *having* a period. That I'm still able to bleed surprises me ... I guess nature doesn't give up as easily as I had hoped.

But then I realize ... why does this even matter to Graham?

I look up and watch him take down the ultrasound pictures. He sighs and says, "I'll give you some pads and underwear along with a disposal bag when you go back to your cell."

Despite trying so desperately, I stammer, but no words come from my mouth. I don't want to go back into that glass cage. Anywhere but there. The small space is killing me.

"Oh …" A vicious smile spreads on his lips. "Are you trying to talk?" He laughs. "How amusing to watch you struggle."

That bastard. Laughing at my expense.

"What is it that you called it? Selective mutism?" he muses, watching for my reaction.

I try to stay calm—I honestly do—but that look on his face brings me terror unlike anything I've ever experienced before. I knew he was watching us through the cameras … I just never realized the extent of it. How often? How much? Does he listen in to every conversation?

Of course, he'd never tell me. That'd be like giving away his hand, and he plays to win. I'm just a chess piece on the board I've yet to understand.

However, when he opens his mouth, it uncovers itself.

"Well, no matter," he says. "I know all I want. You're not pregnant. We'll try again when possible."

Pregnant.

The keyword that unravels me.

The chess piece that beats them all.

"What? Is that a surprise to you?" he asks, closing in on me. Shaking his head, he says in a condescending voice, "You should've known I wanted you to have sex with him for a reason. You're not just a prize he won."

My lip quivers as he brushes my face ever so gently, the mere touch of his skin on mine making me want to puke.

"You're so pretty, so thin and curvy at the same time … perfect … for conceiving."

No amount of breathing can provide the oxygen I need right now. I feel lightheaded. Sick to my stomach. On the verge of passing out.

"You're not just here for him. You're here for me," he says with a low voice. "So his sperm can create the perfect fighter for me to make money off of ... over and over again."

TWENTY-THREE

Ella

A chill runs down my spine.

Babies. That's what all this was about. It's why I was taken. Why I was put in that glass prison. Why he made me fuck Cage ... so I could make a baby that grows up into a fighter worth lots of money.

I'm breathing heavily as panic shoots through my body, making me want to run.

This can't be happening. I can't become pregnant. Not in this place. Not now.

When he approaches me, I can feel the fire running through my veins, forcing me to act. I can't lie here and be silent while he takes what little I have left of my humanity. I won't allow it.

When his fingers undo the leather straps around my body to put me in the wheelchair again, I'm still weak from the drugs, but I can feel my nerves awakening. A burst of strength flows through my body from sheer willpower, and the moment my feet are unlocked from the binds, I kick him.

Hard. Right in his face.

I roll off the table, trying to land on my feet, but I end up on my knees. Pain shoots through my body, but I ignore it as I grasp the first thing in view: a metal tray. As he comes back up, raging out loud, I smack it against his face.

He topples down to the floor, and I scramble away through what seems like a door. I still can't make out everything around me, as my vision is still hampered, but I won't let it hold me back.

I have to flee. Have to get out of here.

The urge to dash is stronger than the pain, stronger than anything I've ever felt before.

I glance behind me for only a second to determine whether he's out before I make a break for it. Still half-intoxicated and completely wobbly on my legs, I make my way through the door and down seemingly endless halls.

I don't know how much of what I see is real and how much of it is my imagination running wild, but I have to focus in order to get out of here. So I home in on all the doors and pick one then go down a set of stairs, almost tumbling over the last few.

Despite my lungs feeling as if they're on fire, I run and run. I pass a room with an elevator and a black door with a numbered padlock on it. I pause for just a second, realizing this might just be where he keeps us. Behind that door ... could be Cage. And I'm leaving him there. I'm abandoning him.

But I have no other choice, do I?

If I don't run now, I might never have this chance again. Graham will be coming to his senses soon, and when he does, he's going to follow me. And that numbered padlock makes it impossible for me to unlock the door. I don't know the code. It would take hours, maybe days to decode, if I had that time. But I don't.

Graham's on my tail. There's no time left.

I have to take this chance. Have to flee before it's too late. Before he captures me again.

So I sprint away from the door and down the stairs in the far-right corner. I feel terrible for making this choice because I know Cage will still be there, all alone, waiting for me to come back. But the will to survive is too strong, too powerful to ignore.

I continue down a long hallway and past a set of windows that allows me to view the boxing ring Cage fights in. Up ahead is another door, and when I pass through it, I come through a dark room filled with red lights with a whole bunch of cages and podiums. One girl's cleaning up the floor on her knees, her neck locked in place with a thick chain. I shiver, but there's no time to help her.

Because I can already hear Graham's screams behind me.

I bolt, not giving a shit where I run next. I'm going to escape this place. I need to, so I keep going until I find more doors, more hallways ... and then ... light.

Searing light.

Like a burning star right in front of me, scorching the very skin off my bones.

But I know for a fact it's the drugs playing with my mind because what I see in front of me ... is the warmth of the sun blinding me.

Making me cry tears of joy.

But there's no time for elation, no time to stay and feel the breeze or smell the air because he's coming. Fast.

My legs move me even though I can't feel them anymore. I just know I have to keep running to stay ahead.

Through the red, scorching sand that lies in front of me.

Because literally nothing is around me ... except for a desert and the burning heat of the sun.

My tears instantly dry up. I have no clue where I am or where I should go to get help. In the distance, I think I can see a dirt road, so I make my way toward it.

I glance behind me to see Graham emerging from the compound.

I have no idea where I am, and I don't have a clue how to get away from here, but I will keep trying. I can't let him take me again.

I'm bolting on pure adrenaline now, my body shaking as I rush through the biting sand that gets between my toes, but I can't stop. I won't stop. Giving up is for the weak, and here... outside ... I'm no longer weak.

This is my home. My world.

The clouds above me protect me from losing my courage, the mountains in the distance providing me strength. I am human. I am frail. But I will not give up.

A pang shoots through my back, right into my spine, and I sink to my knees. I force my feet to get up and walk, but they don't listen to me anymore.

Instead, I drop farther to the ground, my body incapable of anything but flinching. With the last bit of my energy, I touch my back ... only to find an arrow stuck in my skin.

I pull it out.

Too late, the tranquilizer has already entered my system, poisoning me from the inside out. Within seconds, my body stops flailing, stops functioning entirely, except for my breathing and heartbeat.

A single tear rolls down my cheek as I come face to face with my captor again, staring right back at me from above.

***

While I was out, Graham dragged me back to the compound and pulled me all the way back into the room where he keeps the wheelchair, putting me inside. I don't even know where that is as the drugs coursing through my veins makes it impossible to focus.

All I can do is cry as I realize my only chance at escaping this hellhole was futile.

I'm back in his claws ... going straight back into the glass prison.

As he straps me to the chair, I groan, feeling the drugs pour into me. I feel horrible, and it makes me want to puke.

I can see him watching me from the corner of my eye, judging me.

He leans over me and says, "You dirty little bitch ... thought you could escape, huh? After everything I gave you ... I told you, you might see the world again if you'd behave, but now you've really messed up." He laughs, waving his finger at me. "Trying to run from a snatcher. Good one."

"S-na…tcher?" I mumble, doing my best to get the word out even though it's hard. I've never talked in front of someone I don't trust, but the need to know more outweighs my fears right now. I need to learn every detail I can if I ever want to try to get out again. It's my only hope. So every time I open my mouth, I pretend I'm talking to my mom, picturing her image in my head and her sweet voice talking back to me when I do.

He cocks his head. "What … you thought I was alone in what I do?" He chuckles. "Oh dear, you're so sweet, so innocent."

His words make me feel nauseous again, and they sound like poison coming from his mouth.

"Yes, I'm a snatcher," he says. "Part of a company that deals in … well, you know. People." The smile that follows makes me sick.

"S-sell …?" I ask with trouble. How many has he sold, and how long has he been doing this? How big is this company, and how many people are involved?

"You're pretty smart, aren't you?" he says, nodding to himself as if he thinks it's clever. "But yes, we sell them. At least, I did until recently." He taps his foot and rubs the back of his neck. "Damn Vladim disappearing on me like that … makes it hard to do business. Snatchers live for cash. I'm lucky I have my fighting ring as a side business. The bets bring in good money. But I want more." He balls his fists.

"Why m-me? W-why C-Cage?" I ask, my voice hoarse.

"Cage was created for fighting; it's in his veins, his blood. *My* blood," he says, grinning.

"Which is why I want him to spread his seed," he

muses, letting his mouth run wild. "Everybody needs powerful, well-trained fighters in their ranks. They sell like crazy, but they're so hard to make, considering what you need. Good genes, fighter DNA, a womb." He clears his throat as he realizes he's telling me too much. More than is good for him. "Not that it matters to you. You're just an incubator." He inches closer again. "Don't think you're useful for anything else here, girl."

A mere touch of his hand on top of mine makes my skin crawl.

"You can try to escape, but you're much too valuable for me to let you succeed. Good try, though. You're not the first, believe me."

I shake my head, wanting to get away, but I can't. I'm trapped, locked in place by his heinous greed.

"Do you want to know what I did to the other ones who tried?" he asks, raising a brow.

I don't respond, but he answers anyway, sliding a finger across his throat.

Bile rises again, and I have to swallow to keep it down.

He grasps the wheelchair's supports, inching eerily close to my face, his breath smelling like death. "You know you deserve it, right?"

I try not to react, but it's hard when my breath hitches in my throat. He grins when he hears.

"So are you going to be a good girl from now on?" he asks.

I nod vehemently, not trying to get killed.

He pauses, leaving me in agitated anxiety.

"You're lucky I'm nice. Because you fucked my son and actually did what I asked, I'll give you the benefit of the doubt, but ..." He holds a finger right up in my face. "Don't think you can ever do that again without losing a finger or two."

He turns and walks to a cabinet, plucking out a syringe, which he tucks into his pocket. Then he takes out a packet of pads and throws them on my lap. When he approaches me, I lean away, desperately trying to avoid getting stuck with a needle again, but he doesn't attempt to stick it in me. Instead, he goes behind me and starts to push the wheelchair back through the corridors ... back to the hole again.

I try to fight, try to struggle, but no matter how hard I try, the relaxant poisoning my muscles makes it impossible. I'm helpless as my captor brings me back to the place I never wanted to see again.

To that cell ... where I left *him*.

The only one I can talk to even though he's his son.

The moment Graham opens the door, I see him gazing at me, the look in his eyes feeding my despair. I feel guilty but, above all, sorrowful because I didn't make it outside. That I now have to face his wrath as he realizes I abandoned him.

I feel terrible knowing he was in there when I wasn't. That I betrayed his trust and left him even though I care about his fate too.

I wonder if Graham already told him what I've done.

Does he know I tried to run?

Does he hate me for doing it?

I won't blame him.

I can't.

I made this choice. Now I have to live with the

consequences.

But as Graham carts me back into my cell, I can't help but feel knots form in my stomach at the mere idea of being stuck in there again with the only man who even remotely cares about me in here.

He places the wheelchair down in the center, forcing me to look upon the man I left behind. He leaves the room for a second, only to come back later with a bunch of underwear, probably taken from the closet.

He places them on the bed and says, "That should be enough."

He approaches me again and places a chilling hand on my shoulder. That's when something sharp enters my neck. The needle.

I try to reach for it, forgetting I was tied up, so I'm unable to defend myself.

My body goes weak again, and I can barely keep my eyes open. The straps are untied, and he pulls me out, hoisting me into his arms. Then he places me on the bed and rolls out the wheelchair.

The last thing I hear is his ominous whistling before passing out completely.

TWENTY-FOUR

CAGE

I've been staring at her ever since she came back. She hasn't flinched, let alone move from the bed since she was put back into her prison by Father. I wonder how she's doing and if she's hurt. If she's sleeping ... and what she's dreaming about.

I wonder where she went. She was gone a very long time, and he seemed quite upset. He was even raging at me, despite the fact I didn't do anything to cause him to get angry.

I think she may have done something irrevocable. Something no one can take back.

Why else would he walk away without even speaking to me?

When she groans, I perch up to see if she's awake. Her muscles tense, and she takes a deep breath, coughing right after. I check for blood but see none. He must've fixed her up like he always does with me when I get hit too many times by my opponents.

She leans up on her elbow, so I get up from my bed and walk toward the glass, placing a hand against it to let her know I'm here. The moment our eyes lock, she frowns and looks away. Something watery sparkles in her eyes, and the drops begin to roll down her cheeks again.

"What happened?" I ask, my voice low because I'm anxious, but I don't want to upset her further.

She doesn't respond, just shakes her head and buries her face in her hands. She stays like that for minutes maybe, and when her face appears again, it's completely red and covered in wetness.

I swallow away the lump in my throat, trying to shake the uneasiness from her sadness, but it won't go away. I wish I could pull her into my arms and hold her tight. Tell her everything would be all right.

But she's there ... and I'm here ... separated by impenetrable glass.

I hate it.

Licking my lips, I cock my head and gaze at her legs. There doesn't seem to be any more blood but best ask just to be sure. "Blood?"

She shakes her head again. "It was my period."

"Period?" I frown. Never heard of that before.

"It happens every month ... to girls."

Every month? To girls? She's not making any sense to me. Father never told me about this.

When she sees my confused face, she opens her mouth again.

"We bleed from the same entrance you use to ... have sex," she says, clearing her throat and rubbing her arms. "It's to prepare us for having babies."

Babies. Now that word I do know. Father always hammered on about how he wanted me to make them, but I never understood how. Just that I was supposed to fuck the girls that came in, so I do. Ella and I did, so does that mean she will get pregnant now?

"I'm not pregnant," she says, looking up at me with despair.

Does that mean my fucking didn't work? Or did something happen? Was it the bleeding? Or was I too rough?

"It's not your fault. This is natural." She shrugs. "Sometimes girls get pregnant; sometimes they don't."

She sighs out loud and pulls her legs up to her waist, clutching them tight as she sits on the bed. She seems to be inside her head, but I want to know what she's thinking. I want to know what Father did to her if the bleeding is natural. Why he had to take her.

"Explain," I say, sitting down on the floor in front of the glass.

"What? The bleeding? I just did."

"Father took you," I say.

Her lips part, but nothing comes out. Instead, her eyes go back and forth between me and the floor until she can't hold it in any longer. "He wants me to become pregnant."

I nod.

"You knew?" she asks, her brows drawing together.

197

I nod again. Father forbid me from telling her anything.

She closes her eyes and shakes her head, rubbing her forehead. "Of course. You just never understood why and what it means."

"What did he do?" I ask her.

She ponders it for a moment. "He ... probed me on the inside." She swallows.

I can tell it's difficult for her to discuss. If she means what I think she means, it means he touched her in a way that made her feel bad. In a place only I'm supposed to go.

Just the thought of it makes me ball my hands into fists. How dare he do that to her.

"I ... I'm sorry," she mumbles.

I look up, shaking off my anger. Did she just say she was sorry? "What?"

"I ..." She bursts out into sniffles again, and I don't know what's wrong.

"Tell me," I say, cocking my head, hoping to catch her attention.

"I tried to run," she says, barely able to look me in the eyes.

"He was mad ..." I say, frowning, only now realizing why.

He wasn't mad at me. He was mad at *her* for doing something he didn't want her to do.

"I fled. Outside," she says.

"Outside," I mumble, remembering she said that word before. I only know the 'outside' of this cage. The few rooms that are here and beyond. But I get the feeling she means far beyond that. The bigger world ... where she came from.

Did she try to go back there?

"Why?" I ask.

A harshness boils up inside me that I can't put into words. A kind of ... betrayal. If she fled, that means she wanted to get away from here. Away from ... me.

"Away from me?" I ask, my voice changing in pitch because it hurts me to know this. To know she was almost gone, and I wouldn't even have had the chance to say goodbye. That she wouldn't even think of taking me or even telling me.

"I'm sorry ..." she mumbles again, her cheeks stained with wetness. "I wanted to ... I wanted to take you with me, but I didn't have any time."

I cross my arms. "Don't want to go."

She stares at me for a few seconds before bursting out into a strange laughter, followed by headshakes and more wet drops rolling down her cheeks.

"Of course, you'd say that," she says. "You don't know any better."

"Better?" I ask. "That world better than me?"

She licks her lips, her face contorting with guilt. "Look ... I don't know anymore, okay? I like you, I honestly do, but I like ... my world too. I miss home."

Home. I know that word. This is my home. The place I was born. The only place I know. It's where I feel most comfortable at. Maybe she misses that. Comfort.

And I believed I could give her that comfort. That I could give her anything she'd ever need. Guess I was wrong.

I look away and get up from the ground.

"I'm sorry," she repeats, but I don't know what to do with her words.

I don't know what it means to be with her when she wants to be somewhere else. Does she even like me as much as I like her? Could she ever want me the way I want her when she never chose to be here in the first place?

No.

I chose for her to be here.

It's my fault she's here.

That's why I fight so desperately for her acceptance. For her to crave me back.

Because once I stop fighting for that, once I give up ... all that's left is the guilt deep inside my heart, knowing it was my choice to bring her here.

I picked *her*.

And I bear the weight of that decision.

"Please ... don't go ... don't ... please talk to me," she says, still sniffing, reaching for the window. "I can't be alone, not in here. Please. I need you."

Her pleas break me. Force me to turn around as I sit down on the bed and gaze at her, wondering how I can fix this brokenness that I feel inside me.

"Tell me ..." I say with a low voice, unable to push myself to speak louder. "Do you want me?"

"Yes," she says. "No ... I mean ... yes, but I don't know." She sighs and shakes her head. "It's so confusing."

"Yes or no?"

"It's not as easy as that. Liking you has nothing to do with being out there in the real world." She slams her hand down on the floor. "I wish I could explain the concept of freedom to you, but I can't. Dammit."

"Freedom ... is outside. Without me. You want that?"

"No ... of course not." She shakes her head. "Listen,

Cage … I like you, but it's not right."

I make a face. "Not right?"

Is she saying she doesn't want me anymore?

"That sounded harsher than I meant. I'm sorry," she says, sighing again. "God, why does it have to be so hard?"

"It's not," I reply.

"Yes, it is. It's not a question of liking you or not. It's not as simple as a yes or no question."

"I don't agree," I growl.

She raises a brow at me. "Really?"

I shrug and rub the back of my neck. I really don't understand why she's making it so difficult. She can either like me or not, but she's in here, stuck with me. There is no choice. I took that away from her.

Sighing, I clutch my hands together and let my head down. That's just it, really. That's why she's so upset. It's my fault she's stuck in here. I picked her.

"I'm sorry …" I mumble.

"What?"

I look up at her shocked face. "For choosing you."

She licks her lips, and her eyes fill up with water again, but she brushes it away. Nodding, she bites her lips. "I understand. You made a choice. It's as simple as that. You didn't know what you were doing," she says. "Or at least, that's what I keep telling myself in my head."

She lets out a pitiful laugh, one I've come to expect when she's uncomfortable.

I don't want her to feel that way.

"It's okay," I say, smiling softly.

She smiles back. "Thanks."

It's quiet for a moment before she begins again. "I really

didn't want to leave you here, you know. I know it's not fair to say that, but I didn't want to abandon you. But you … you like it here, right? It's all you know. This is your home. He's your father."

I shrug. I understand what she means, but Father isn't all that either. I used to look up to him, used to make him want to be proud. But now? After sharing a cage with her for so long, I finally learn there's more than one side to him. That he can be unkind to anyone who gets between him and his target. Even if it's my girl, my Ella. And I'm not sure I'm going to allow that to ever happen again.

Because deep down in my heart, I can feel the burning fire that I feel whenever I look at her. Think of her. Dream of her. I feel that *only* for her. And nothing he does can get close to that.

I want her. I want to keep feeling that, and I'll do anything in my power to keep it.

Even if it means going against him.

Maybe I am at a point where I have to make a choice. Just like she did.

She made the choice to run, and even if he did catch her, she still ran away without me. That was her choice. I wish she'd stayed, but that's my feelings toward her. I can't force her to feel the same.

But still, I can't help but wonder … why didn't she think of me?

"You left me?" I ask.

She licks up some of the drops rolling down her lips. "There is a padlock on the door, Cage."

I narrow my eyes, confused at that word. Padlock? Never heard of it before.

"It's a lock, like on the black door, you know? It can't be opened without knowing how."

Now I understand. She couldn't open the door from the outside because only Father knows how.

"He's the only one who knows how to open the door. He knows the code; I don't. I couldn't ... I couldn't take you with me. I'm sorry," she repeats.

I lift a hand. I don't want to hear that word anymore.

Enough is enough.

I understand. She followed her instincts. I do the same when it comes to her. It's only natural.

After all, this place would turn anyone into a beast.

Even the most innocent of all.

TWENTY-FIVE

Ella

More than two weeks have passed since I escaped. I'm sitting on the floor directly across from him against the glass. With pictures drawn with lipstick and more words, I've explained my world to him in great detail. When I stop, he asks me to continue. It's been like this for days. I like talking about the world I know because it brings me back there. To the snowy mountains I saw on my travels, the deep rivers, the far ocean, to the animals, the life ... the people. Cities and technology are a little hard to grasp for him, but I guess that's understandable, considering he's never seen any of it.

But still, it's nice to discuss it because it helps me

remember it still exists. It's not just there in my head, but it's real too, and it's waiting for me to come back.

"Can I see too?" he asks when I tell him I've seen it all.

I sigh, tucking a strand of hair behind my ears. "If you want ..."

He nods slowly.

"But we'd have to escape this place first."

A frown appears.

I knew it would be difficult for him. To comprehend there is no both ... there is either being in here or being out there.

"We could—" I mumble.

"Impossible," he says, interrupting me.

"It's not, if you're willing to try," I say.

His eyes narrow, and he just looks at me for a moment without saying a word. Then his eyes slide to the pieces of toilet paper that I wrote on again, and he mumbles, "Teach me."

"What?" I ask, picking up one of the pieces. "To write or read?"

"Both," he says.

I smile, realizing he's finally making that first step into becoming more than just a caged animal. He honestly wants to try his best, and I applaud that. Even if he may never see the sun, at least he learned a little bit about what it means to be human.

I draw each of the letters on the papers and show them to him then pronounce the sound. He follows and tries to redraw the shapes on the glass with his finger, and I guide him every step of the way.

Soon, he's even reading some simple words I write

down like glass, bed, and paper. When he tries his hand at them himself, it doesn't take him too long to grasp how to write the letters. He's a quick study, and I imagine he would have done well in a real school. I'm not a great teacher, so doing my best is all I can do to help.

We sit like this for days on end—talking, learning, teaching. I love his responses, his reactions, and the smile on his face whenever he succeeds or discovers something new. Like a young guy with adult needs and desires. And a very adult body.

I grin as I catch myself glimpsing at his pecs, which flex every time he moves. It's hard not to, with him being all up in my face, demanding every single second of my attention. But I don't mind. I actually like talking to him. Getting to know him. Feeling like I'm more than just a womb and he might be more than a man with seed. That he might be more as a person to me, too.

Suddenly, the black door clicks open, and we both turn our heads toward our own door leading to the bedroom. When his head turns back around and he looks at me, I bite my lip, wondering what he's going to do. He gets up from the floor, and I expect him to rush through that door to grab me. But he doesn't.

Instead, he places a hand on the glass and cocks his head, gazing at me with eyes that are so full of love, they undo me.

I briefly smile as I get up, and I place my hand on top, watching the joy spread on his face.

It's so simple, yet it means so much …

This connection we have is undeniable.

A voice blares through the speaker in the far-right

corner of the room. "It's time. Get her."

Cage doesn't even seem fazed by Graham yelling. Instead, he leans his head against the prison and smiles back. It's almost as if he's looking for my approval.

"You know what I said ..." Graham growls through the speaker. "If you don't do it, I will make you. Choose."

I swallow and rub my lips together before nodding at Cage.

"You sure?" he asks.

"It's the only way if I ever want to see the outside world again," I say, trying not to cry.

He nods, and I blink away the tears as I see him turn and walk through the door ... only to come out again in mine.

It's strange to see him this close again. Every time feels different, as if we're not the same people, even though we see each other every day. But something has changed ... me.

I'm not longer that scared, innocent girl. I made my choice ... and I choose him.

***

He stands in the doorway with his hands beside his firm body and his muscles bulging with need. He's tense ... and I know why. It's been too long since we last touched each other. I've been keeping count of the days. The longer it took, the more agitated he became. And now I can feel the electricity zing through the air.

Still, he doesn't move. He's waiting ... waiting for me to stand by my decision and be true to my words. He doesn't just want to claim me ... He wants me to choose it.

So I approach him, touching his fingers with mine as I slowly pass him. The brief contact has me shivering with need, and goose bumps spread across my body as I saunter into the bedroom. I can hear him turn and follow me, shutting the door behind him.

Standing in the middle of the room, I turn and watch him step closer. Towering above me, he gently tips my chin up and leans in for a kiss. His lips turn me into mush again, and I can't help but moan into his mouth when his tongue dips out to lick the seam of my lips.

He responds by grasping me by the ass and pushing me against his body, making me feel his hard-on. I don't mind … In fact, it only turns me on.

I'm past the stage of feeling guilty, past the stage of caring. Fucking him is my only way out of here … and now, it doesn't even seem like punishment anymore. I'm falling for him. I'm falling, and I don't want to stop, no matter how close I am to crashing. Even if it kills me, I can't stop kissing him back.

Can't stop wanting him. Can't stop letting him put his hands all over me.

His roughness shows when he spins me on my heels and shoves me against the door, kissing me madly. His lips are all over my neck and collarbone, his hands squeezing my breasts. With his knee, he parts my legs and rubs it against my pussy, making me warm and wet. I actually whimper when his hand reaches down between my legs, and he touches me.

He smiles at the sight of me falling apart.

That smile is the only thing keeping me alive in this place.

He curls up my dress and pulls it over my head, throwing it to the floor. He cups my breasts and licks my nipples, alternating between the two until they're peaked and my body craves him.

With two fingers, he slides down my slit, spreading my wetness all over before circling my clit. I suck in air as he pushes inside—exploring me, probing me, owning me.

He cups my mouth with his, claiming my breath too. I reach for his pants and rub his length through the fabric, feeling it throb under my touch. He's eager ... so eager, he grunts against my skin and thrusts his fingers inside me just as he would when he fucked me.

Curling my fingers underneath the fabric, I push down his pants until they drop to his feet, making his cock bounce free. It bobs up and down as I start rubbing it, just as hard as he's rubbing me.

It doesn't take long for him to lose control.

Groaning like an animal, he grabs my ass and shoves me high up the door. I clutch my legs around his waist and wrap my arms around his neck. I can't take my eyes off him as he slowly lowers me onto his length, the tip penetrating my entrance.

I gasp when he enters, pushing in until the base. My eyes almost roll to the back of my head, but I try to keep it together because I don't want this to be over yet.

I've gone without his touch for too long. I want to enjoy it, savor it, because it could be over with the snap of a finger. One fuck, and he's spent ... and Graham will pull us apart.

All because we're his toys, and he plays us like we're fools.

I can't let his control over our situation be the only reason I'm doing this, and it's not. When I look into Cage's eyes, feel his skin against mine, I know there's more to this than just sex. I can feel it inside my body ... my heart.

We don't just fuck ... we meld together.

He belongs to me, and I belong to him.

TWENTY-SIX

CAGE

I thrust into her with everything I have, wanting to claim her so badly. From the way she looks at me with those lustful eyes, I know she wants me just as much even though she'll never admit it.

That's why I was so angry about her trying to run away without me. She broke me, and now I have to heal that wound. I do it by pounding into her, letting my rage out into fucking her hard, showing her just how much she belongs to me.

Our hot breaths mingle as we lock mouths, desperately clinging to one another. Sweat drips down my body as she tightens around me, her body quaking with need. After a few thrusts, I feel her muscles clench around me, and she gasps then lets out a moan. She falls apart in my arms, and I can feel her squeeze my length, making me come.

Burying myself deep inside her, I fill her with my seed, releasing myself inside her with a roar.

But I'm not done yet.

Still hard and inside her, I carry her to the bed and flip her over. On her knees, I grasp her hips and drive into her, all the way to the base.

Her moans sound more like she's surprised at what I did, but she didn't realize just how much I missed her. Every damn day I'm not able to touch her is another one too many.

Running my hand over her back, I enjoy the sight of her naked body lying in front of me, ready for the taking. She whimpers at my touch, and I grasp her ass and spank it hard as I thrust into her.

She rocks back and forth against me, just as eager for my shaft as I am for her pussy. Her wetness pools between her legs, making it so easy to slip in and out of her.

She glances over her shoulder and looks hungry for more, so I reach between her legs and start fondling her again in the rhythm of my pounding.

She loves it, her tongue dipping out to lick her lips as she struggles to stay put as her body quivers with need. With my dick deep inside her, I wrap one hand around her hair, fisting it tightly and pulling back. She doesn't seem to mind me taking control as I flick my finger and watch her come undone.

I groan when I feel her tighten around me again and I come too. Hard.

Jetting my cum inside her, I release my grip on her hair

and grasp her ass, forcing myself into her until the base. I slap her ass again as I yank out, my cock still dripping, just like her pussy.

I love the sight of it … love the sight of her crevice covered in my seed … exactly how it should be.

"Mine, " I growl, pressing a kiss on her ass before she falls down to the bed.

She smiles and gently pats the bed, beckoning me to lie down next to her.

So I do … I lie down on my side right next to her, gazing into her eyes, marveled by her beauty and that precious smile. I can't help but caress her cheek and tuck a strand of her hair behind her ear.

I lean in to give her a kiss on the nose, and she curls up close to my body. I can feel her warm breath against my skin, her body folded into mine. Her hair tickles my neck, but I appreciate every single itch.

I don't want anything else but this.

If I could have this every day, the rest of my life, I would be happy.

But I'm not alone in here.

She has needs and desires too … and they don't always align with mine.

I know she wants out. Even though she probably also wants me, I know she wants to be back home even more. It kills me to know I'm the one who took the one thing she desires the most away from her.

I don't want to be that person. I want to be better.

Even if it means I'll lose her, even if it means I'll never see her again, I don't want to be the reason she's not where she wants to be. I can't live knowing she's not happy right here by my side. If that's the case, I need to fix this.

I sigh. "Are you happy?"

She looks up at me with furrowed brows. "Why do you ask that?"

"Freedom, home ..." I mumble, knowing it's always on her mind.

Her face contorts, and I know she's thinking about it again. That place she calls home.

Biting her bottom lip, she nods. "I do miss it."

I understand. It must be hard not to be where you want to be. In a place where you're not treated the way you're used to. To be stuck in a place ... with an animal like me.

"What if I get pregnant, Cage?" she mutters.

"You are?" I ask, hopeful that she is.

I want her to have my baby. I don't care where or how or when. All I care about is her, me ... us ... a family.

I never had a real family, but I do want it more than anything.

"I don't know, but what if I have a baby, right here? In this cell? Is he supposed to grow up in here? Locked up without anything that resembles the real world? Doesn't he deserve freedom?" she says.

I think about it, wondering where she's going with this.

"What will that kid's purpose be, Cage? A fighter, just like you?"

There's nothing wrong with being like me, though. Is there?

Is it so wrong to be a fighter?

To kill?

Maybe it is. She said life could never come back once it's gone. Maybe that's why she's so worried. She doesn't want

214

our kid to take away life.

"Me …" I mumble, realizing she thinks I'm a killer. A monster.

"You're not bad, Cage. But I don't want to condemn another person to this life," she says, grasping my face. "Do you understand? I can't raise a kid here, let alone create one. Not in this place."

My heart sinks into my shoes. "So no baby … with me?"

She snorts and smiles at the same time, shaking her head. "No, silly … I mean … not … here." She blushes. "I never said I didn't want one with you."

She clears her throat. "I just mean that it's not right. We can't make another soul suffer. We can't do that, right? Tell me I'm right. Please."

She doesn't want to have a kid here in this cell. Doesn't want it to become me, which I understand, a little. Blood and killing are in my veins, but should it be in my kid's too?

That kid will be hers too. It will have her blood too, and she *loves* the outside world. She craves freedom. She's so different from how I am. What if he was more like she is? I couldn't even imagine her fighting, let alone a kid who's like her. No, I can't do that. She's right; it's wrong.

But what can we do? Run?

"You want to leave?" I ask.

She twists and places her hand on my face, cupping me, caressing me. It feels so good … my whole body fills with warmth and need for her to touch me more like that.

"Don't make me say that, please," she mumbles.

I place a hand on top of hers. "But you do …"

I know it's the truth. She doesn't need to say it, but I

just want to be sure. I want to know, so I can decide.

"Yes," she says, sighing. "But it's not that easy. I like you too. I don't want to leave you."

"Right," I say. I can tell she really does care about me, but it's tearing her in half. I can't let it happen.

"We go together."

Her lips part, and she frowns, her eyes widening. "What?"

"We run," I say.

She puts a finger on my lips and then looks around at the cameras. "Don't."

"Why?"

She glances back and forth between me and the camera a couple of times. "It's too dangerous. What if he finds out?" she whispers.

"He won't," I say. "He doesn't care."

I know because I asked him about it once. He told me he only looks through it to see if I'm doing what he wants me to do. He rarely listens in, maybe once or twice a week. Doesn't like the sounds.

She sighs and sits up straight, clutching the edge of the bed. "I don't know."

"You want this?" I say, putting a hand on her back.

"Yes," she says, smiling at me. "More than anything."

I nod. "Yes."

"You mean … you want to make a plan? To escape?"

I nod again. If that's what she wants, I will do it. Anything to make her happy.

Her face lights up, and she jumps on me, wrapping her arms around my neck and hugging me tightly. Only after a few seconds do I wrap my arms around her too. I didn't expect her to be so … grateful. So sweet and kind. So welcoming to my devotion to her.

She whispers in my ears, "Let's do it."

TWENTY-SEVEN

CAGE

For a few hours, we talked about how to do it until we'd made up our minds. We're going to trick Graham into coming into the cell and then trap him inside while we run. It's not a good plan, but it has to work. It's the *only* plan we have.

To make it work, he has to come here, though, and there's only one way to make him come. He can't gas us both and put us both in that single wheelchair, so we have to be in the same room for this to work. He has to feel like there's no other way.

There's one thing Ella doesn't know, though. He put something in my body a long time ago. If I ever misbehave, he'll just push the button and electrify me. I've felt it once before when I tried to save a girl from his grasp. It was excruciating, and I don't want to ever feel that again. So I'm going to make sure that once he's here, he won't be able to use it.

I'll tackle him and snatch that thing out of his pocket, breaking it into a million pieces. I'm done listening to and following his words as if they're law. I want more. I want the things she's shown me. I want to see the world with my own eyes. Experience what she's experienced. I want it all.

With her.

I nod as I try to visualize the plan in front of me. She'll go with me into my cage and protect me from him by holding me. That way, he won't use the device because he doesn't want her hurt in the process.

If he actually tries to gas us both, it won't work. I've already punched a hole into the ceiling above my cage and ripped out the wiring that causes the gas to flow inside. We even searched for a way for us to exit through there, but the tubes are so tiny, there's no room.

So our plan is the only plan.

It's not great, but it's worth a shot.

I'd rather try than not try at all … and have her be unhappy for the rest of her life.

No, I'm not willing to sacrifice her happiness. Not for anything. Not even for my own needs.

So now, we're lying on my bed in my cell, waiting for him to come.

It doesn't take long.

I know he watches every now and then, and he hates it when things don't go exactly as planned.

Within five minutes, he's rammed the door open,

making her jolt up and down in my arms, but I shush her to calm her down. Everything will work out. It has to. For her sake.

"What are you doing?" he screams. "I told you to go back to your cage immediately!" His face turns red as he approaches us. "Get back there, now!"

He's pointing at Ella specifically, and the buzzing sounds of the doors opening echoes in the room. But I won't let her go.

"No …" I growl back, holding her tight.

"What?" His nostrils flare, and his eyes widen. "Do as I say. Now!"

I ignore his demand and just glare at him, wrapping my arms more firmly around her body. I'm not letting him take her from me.

"She's mine …" I growl.

He breathes from his mouth, grinding his teeth. I can tell he's tempted to use the device, but her being in my arms stops him. He knows the electricity could hit her too, and neither of us wants that.

So he marches to the door, exactly as planned.

He enters the bedroom, and we quickly rise from the bed. I position myself behind my cell door. She stands on the other side. I nod at her, signaling I'm ready.

When he opens it, I jump him.

I quickly snatch the control from his hand and throw it away. It flies into the glass pane, shattering.

"Run!" I scream at Ella, and off she goes, bolting through the door.

Father and I struggle on the ground.

"Get off me!" he growls, smacking me in the face.

I punch back, but not as hard because I don't want to hurt him badly. He's still my father, and deep down, I still want him to love me. I don't want to kill him.

I refuse to use all my strength on him. I just can't.

From the corner of my eye, I see Ella making a run for it through the room and into the hallway. She's at the door when Father overtakes me and rolls on top of me, beating the shit out of me.

He's not holding back. His fists rein down harder on me than anything he's ever done before.

"You think you can do this to me?" he spits in my face. "I'm your fucking father!"

I try to fight him off, but he's outwitted me, using filthy tactics to stay on top, like poking my eyes and ramming his elbow into my stomach.

"I fucking made you!" he shrieks. "Fuck you!"

I can hear Ella's screams from afar. "Cage! Get up! Fight him!"

Her voice gives me the power to overwhelm him with a punch to the gut, and I quickly turn the tides by sitting on top of him and pounding on him. Quickly glancing back at her, I shout, "Go!"

She shakes her head, visibly upset, her lips quivering. She's still waiting at the door … waiting for me. But I don't want her to be stuck here against her will. If she has to go without me to be free … then so be it.

"LEAVE!" I scream at her, her eyes filling with water at the sight of me.

It's hard, but I know it's for the best. She nods.

Then she pulls the door handle, but it won't open.

He locked it from the inside.

"Cage ... Shit! I need the code!" Ella yells as she's banging and smacking the door, pulling it as hard as she can. "It won't budge."

"What's the code?" I yell in his face.

At first, there's nothing but silence, but then he begins to laugh maniacally. "You think I'm going to give that to you? Not a chance. I'd rather die in here than let either of you escape."

He's cruel. Beyond cruel. And I want none of it.

My limit is gone, and I punch him so hard, blood spurts from his mouth.

However, I'm not prepared for the surprise attack to my gut with something sharp ... a knife. The pain is instant ... gut-wrenching.

I grasp for it and try to pull it out, but he shoves me aside and tackles me to the floor, choking me.

"You motherfucker ... think you can get away with that? Huh? How dare you betray me!"

Ella's still trying to get the door open, smashing her fingers onto random buttons that don't seem to work. "No, no, no!" she yells, droplets streaming down her face. "Open, goddammit!"

Before I realize it, Father's pulled something else out of his pocket and rammed it into my skin. A needle filled with fluids.

"No!" Ella screams, watching in agony.

I hate that she has to see this. Hate that she has to watch him play dirty. That she has to witness me lose a fight.

I twist and turn, trying to get him off me, and I even shove my hand in his face, tugging and poking at everything, but it doesn't work. I'm losing my energy, losing the control over my limbs, and soon, every inch of my body fails to respond.

I watch in misery as he gets up from me and rushes through the doors on his way to her. I'm completely powerless as I watch her struggle with him to the very last inch of her strength. He overpowers her too, ramming a needle into her body as well.

Not soon after, she collapses to the ground.

Water fills my eyes and rolls down my face as I slowly fade out of consciousness.

I've failed her. Our plan is ruined, and now I've doomed us both.

TWENTY-EIGHT

Ella

When I wake, my head hurts, and my vision is blurry. I feel like I've been smacked in the head a million times ... or dragged down a staircase.

I try to move but can't. Something completely restricts my limbs ... but I can't tell what. It's something thick and bristly and pokes into my skin. Like rope.

And I'm sitting on something hard ... brown ... It must be a wooden chair.

When I look around, all I see is bright lights and more rope, and a stage right in front of me. The fighting ring.

My eyes burst open, and I force myself to wake up. Sounds from people sitting in the stands come from the left and right. They're watching something … something going on inside the ring.

Two people fighting … or three … no, more.

I can't tell because everything is still blurry, but I know this … One of them is Cage.

It's his towering shadow right in front of me that discerns it. I scream.

The people in the stands don't react. They're still watching the fight, throwing their fists into the air and cheering on the fighters. I don't know who's who, but I can tell they're not rooting for Cage. All the fighters inside the ring must belong to them, each one of them having an owner just like Cage.

Pets fighting over the same prize.

And I'm a powerless spectator to this debauchery.

"So this is the beast …" one of the men yells, laughing right after. "I want to see more!"

I feel like he's talking about Cage because they're all looking at him—at the way he moves, ducks when attacked, and slides across the stage like an agile warrior.

But something's wrong. His body quakes after each blow, and I can clearly see rivulets of blood running down his body.

He's still wounded … from the knife Graham stuck between his ribs.

It's an unfair battle, and they're all enjoying his pain. How ugly.

One of the men flicks his fingers, and someone in the corner of the hall steps up and enters the ring. It's a three-way fight now … except both men only throw punches at Cage.

"I wanna see how much he can do ..." one of the men in the stands says.

"Yeah, let's see how hard he is," another one says.

They all laugh, and I hear Graham speak up. "Great idea! He needs to be punished anyway."

"Why not add more then?" One of the men shrugs.

"Yeah." Graham bites his lip. "Let's get more fighters in the ring. I want him to sweat and bleed. He needs to learn his lesson."

Graham turns around, briefly glancing at me before yelling, "Get into the ring. One by one. Let's go!"

More men step up from the shadows and get onto the stage.

No. No. No!

That means they'll keep pouring in until Cage can't take it any longer. He might die. But he can't ... he *can't* die!

A burst of energy overcomes me, and I start moving the chair up and down and sideways, trying to get their attention. They have to know he's hurt and that this isn't a fair fight.

But the more I move, the more Graham's face begins to sour. I know he's onto me. It won't be long until he shuts me up. So I open my mouth and try to scream.

What comes out is a vague attempt at putting up a shriek, but it works.

They're all looking at me now.

"Who's that?" one of the men asks.

"H-help!" I scream, my voice hoarse, but it feels so good to let it out.

"Oh, she's the girl I chose to carry his kid. What do you think?" Graham mumbles, and my jaw drops.

"Nice. Looks fragile, though," one of them says.

"Oh, yes, but she puts out well enough," Graham says, and they all laugh, making me want to scratch their eyes out. "Not that it matters," he adds. "As long as she gets pregnant, I'm happy. Any offers?"

"I haven't seen enough of what he can do yet," one of the men says, and he cocks his head. "Show me more."

I can't believe what I'm hearing; none of it makes any sense in my reality.

But this is their world ... their domain ... where everything wrong is the norm.

These aren't people ... they're monsters.

"More!" Graham shouts, beckoning more fighters to step forward. Soon, Cage is overwhelmed, fighting as well as he can, but he's losing. He can't beat that many people at the same time. Does Graham actually want him to lose? Bring him to the point of death before releasing him from his pain?

How could he?

I keep jumping up and down in my chair, trying to shake these ropes off, but it's no use. I don't stop making a ruckus, trying to get them to stop. However, none of them seems to give a shit about me sitting here tied to a chair, watching the dirty fighting game in front of me.

Cage is barely hanging on, and his face wears a look of utter defeat. He's almost ready to lay down his life. But I don't want him to die. It would kill me.

"Cage!" I scream. "Don't give up!"

Everyone's looking at me again, but I don't care.

I just want him to push through all of it and come out victorious.

He didn't give up on me, so I won't give up on him. We can make it. We can pull through. Together.

***

CAGE

My ears catch the sound of her voice. From the corner of my eye, I see her sitting on a chair, but I can't look for more than a second because I'm already brutally smacked in the face. Fist after fist, it just keeps raining down on me, and I can barely keep up. A hook from the left from mystery man one then a kick to the knees from mystery man two.

I don't know why we're fighting or what the point is, but I don't have the time to ask either. The hits just keep coming, and if I don't dodge them, I'm down on the floor. Once that happens, I'm a goner, so I can't let it happen.

But fuck … it's hard.

I keep shuffling, defending myself even though my body shakes with adrenaline.

Blood pours from the wound between my ribs, and it hurts … but I bite through the pain and keep fighting.

That's all I can do. Keep fighting … Keep fighting to live.

I don't know how long this has been going on, but it feels like ages. Father put me here after our struggle. I woke up on the floor with a man staring right back at me. That same man just threw a punch at me, which I barely dodged.

Father wants me to fight them all. Not for money but as punishment. But why? He keeps adding more. I can't beat all of them. Does he want me to die? Does he hate me so much that he wants to get rid of me? All because we tried to escape. Maybe it was a stupid idea.

However, the moment I hear her scream and see her twitching in the chair, I know we did the right thing by standing up to him. It's what she wanted, and I'd rather have her be proud of me than him. I don't care anymore about what he thinks or wants. All that matters to me is her.

And if I can't have her—can't give her the freedom she deserves—then what's the point?

Another hit to the chin makes me go down, and I struggle to get up. They kick me in my stomach, and I cough up blood.

Her shriek goes through marrow and bone, but the sound wakes me. Pulls me from my misery, from my self-loathing … and I get up and fight again.

With her here, watching me, there's no fucking way I'll ever go down.

Why? Because I refuse to let her see me defeated.

To make her watch me die.

No.

However, my body is tired from the drugs and weak from the wound, unable to fight as it usually does. The men in the stands laugh at my pain and her squeals, and it makes me wanna lash out. So I grab one of the men by his waist, topple him, throw him over my shoulder, and toss him out of the ring.

That gets their attention all right.

"Stop!" one of the men barks, and everyone stops fighting me.

Father seems furious. He stands up and screams, "You

think you can act all fucking proud? No fucking way."

"Why not let him fight for the girl? Have the men try to attack her. Should be fun," one of the men suggests.

My gaze immediately goes toward Ella whose eyes widened the moment she heard those words. They intend to throw her to the wolves.

Use her as bait.

TWENTY-NINE

CAGE

Father smirks then whistles. "Boys, get the girl. Put her in the center. Let's amp up the stakes."

"No!" I growl, but it's too late.

While five men hold me back, two others walk out of the ring and grab the chair, lifting her into the air. She's trembling in place, her eyes watery as they carry her back into the ring while all I can do is watch.

"NO!" I growl again, but then I get punched in the face.

"Now, boys ... fight fair ... place her in the center," Father says, clapping his hands. The grin on his face is devilish as he looks at his guests and then at me. "Let's make this fun, shall we? We all want better fighters, so let's make the next generation a powerful one. Here's your true prize, gentlemen. The first to grab the girl wins the right to fuck her."

No. Fuck no.

I immediately pull myself loose from their grasp, roaring as I punch my way through the men.

I will not let them put their hands on her.

I'd rather die than let that happen.

She's my woman. My Ella. And I will do whatever it takes to protect her.

***

Ella

"Go!" The moment the bell rings, all the men pounce on me, and I close my eyes, ready for the downfall. I can't handle the intense emotions pouring into my veins, making me want to lash out even though I can't.

Who will grab me? The one with the facial scars? The one with the missing toes? Or the one with the missing eye? All of them are vicious monsters, and I don't want their hands on me.

But I have no choice. The moment any one of them grabs me, I'm theirs.

Graham doesn't make any random bets. He wants money, so he'll give me away to the winner just so he can make a kid quicker. It's cruel. Inhuman. But he doesn't care about any of that.

All he wants is something he can sell, and a warrior ....

That he can sell.

It doesn't matter to him who made the kid or who lives or dies.

As long as he has his toys, no one can stop him.

But the longer I keep my eyes shut, the more I keep waiting for something to happen. For someone to touch me … to take me … use me.

But nothing does. Not a single finger touches my skin.

All I can feel is the wind rushing past me as the men fight over who gets the right to fuck me. And when I squint to see who it is, the only thing I see is Cage towering over me.

Protecting me.

From everything and everyone around him.

Like a beast, he plows through the fighters, warding them off. He growls and spits, slashes and scratches, throwing punches like a madman. One of them goes down with just one kick to the head while the others keep coming.

Cage doesn't stop.

He's fighting like an animal, raging over anyone who dares to come near my chair.

And I'm helplessly watching, wishing I could run. Wishing I could save him from this pain … from knowing I'm about to be taken away from him. His most prized possession … given away to a random winner who gets to fuck me.

But he won't allow it.

No matter how many times they try to approach me, he keeps fending them off. One of them comes so close I turn my head to prevent him from grasping a strand of my hair. Cage head butts him and kicks him in the nuts, causing him to buck and heave.

He punches another one in the face, and then another one in the gut, keeping up his fighter spirit. I don't know how he does it. His veins are bulging, sweat drops rolling down his body, blood everywhere, but he doesn't give up.

I can tell his body is drained, yet he refuses to step down. Even though it could mean his end if he keeps going like this.

I can't imagine anyone fighting this many enemies at the same time and surviving.

Especially with a wound like his.

It must hurt so much, and still, he doesn't give up.

Another one approaches. Cage's nostrils flare, and he delivers an uppercut to the guy with seemingly superhuman strength. All I can do is watch in awe at the raw power he exudes.

It's as if me being here, offered up as a prize, has only emboldened him … given him the fury he needs to overcome his opponents.

I wonder if Graham knew this would happen, but by the look on his face, he seems surprised. They all do. Every one of those men up there is silent and seems highly concentrated as they watch the fight below … the fight around me.

It's a spectacle of unknown proportions, and I'm at the center of it all, watching it unfold right in front of me. Fist after fist lands, and still, Cage does not surrender.

He fights as if it's his last day on earth. As if he's giving his last breath.

Giving it all … to save me.

To stake his claim on me forever.

And it brings me to tears.

"Don't give up!" I yell at him, bolstering his spirit. "Fight for me, Cage. Fight!"

This seems to only make him growl and punch harder. Opponents being pushed back like they're being struck by the horns of a bull—that's how hard he pushes back. No matter how close they get, he always seems to push them away, ramming them with every inch of his anger.

I feel so powerless as I watch him, wishing I could do something to help.

One of them sticks his fingers into Cage's wound, causing him to growl in pain. They're all over him—climbing onto his body, latching onto his legs, and punching and kicking him to the ground.

But he can't give up. He just can't, because of us.

We have to survive.

"Live, Cage! Please! I need you," I scream, teardrops rolling down my cheeks.

One glance is all he gives me, but it's enough. He roars and bites one of the men on top of him, tearing off an ear. Then he elbows one of the others and takes his arm between his body, twisting, tearing until it breaks. A shriek is audible, and he continues pulling and twisting limbs until some of them are partially severed.

All I can do is watch as blood and skin cover the floor, body to body, everybody being ripped to shreds.

A neck cracks, twists, and the body flops to the floor. Another one approaches, and his eyes are poked out. One on the floor tries to pull him down, but Cage steps on his arm, breaking it. Then he jumps on his face and breaks that too.

This savage killing is happening right in front of me.

And I can't look away.

Covered in the sweat and the blood of his enemies, Cage grabs the face of the final man standing and smashes it into the ground until there's nothing but pulp.

After it's done ... no one's left standing but Cage.

His body moves in rhythm with his breathing, his muscles twitching, still tense from the battle that just took place. But he is victorious ... and his roar is louder than a lion after claiming his mate.

All I can do is stare in awe at the animal in front of me.

The *man* who just won because he didn't want any other man touching me.

Because he's my man. And I am his.

But my man ... my man ... is looking at me with an intense gaze before his eyes roll into the back of his head and he collapses to the floor.

"Cage!" I squeal.

I want to get up; I try, but the ropes prevent me from getting closer even though I desperately want to go to him. He's bleeding everywhere.

"What? They're all dead?" the men in the stands yell, some of their jaws dropped.

Another one stands up. "This is an insult!"

"Calm down," Graham barks. "You all agreed to this. You even begged for it, so shut up."

"I never agreed to get my man murdered," one of them hisses back.

"A bet is a bet," Graham spits. "Those are the rules. Take it or leave it. Now, the winner is obviously my boy, so he gets the prize, and then you can all buy a new fighter from me once I have them. Okay?"

All the men seem sour after his speech, but none of them are even paying attention to the fact that Cage is lying here in the ring, practically dying.

"Please!" I look up at Graham. "P-please, h-help us."

The men laugh, repeating what I say with a high-pitched, fake voice as if somehow any of this is funny.

It's not. It's tragic. We're human, but we're all just entertainment to them.

The only one who seems remotely interested in Cage is Graham, who hasn't sat down since the fight began. He cocks his head, checking out Cage who's still lying flat on the floor, unmoving. I'm beyond worried right now. I don't want him to die.

"P-please," I repeat.

"Aw, look at that little girl beg," one of them muses. "He won, didn't he? Get up then."

Graham holds up a finger, and it silences them all. "He obviously fought hard." He clears his throat. "Gentlemen, this game is over. I'll see you again next time."

And with that, he walks down the stands and approaches the rings. I lean back away from him as he comes closer. "You ..." he mumbles, placing his hand on my shoulder. "Are one lucky girl."

The devilish smile that follows makes me want to spit, so I do. I spit right in his face.

It doesn't even faze him.

He just wipes it off and smears it on my leg before turning around and calling out to some henchmen standing in the corner of the room near the doors.

"C'mon. Help me get them back to their cells."

THIRTY

Ella

We're carted back to our cells, but I don't even care. All I can focus on is Cage, whose lifeless body is hanging by a thread. The men who put us back in our cells don't even seem to care. They release me from the chair, cutting the ropes, and place me on my bed. I can't do anything; my body is still numb from the drugs.

None of the guys seem to care about our well-being. They're henchmen of the men Graham was entertaining, so they're quickly whistled back when the men start to leave. Graham sends them off with an amicable goodbye as if he enjoyed their time together. Meanwhile, his son is practically dying in the cell beside me.

When the drugs circling through my system begin to wane, I lift my head and call out for Cage. He doesn't respond. He just lies there on the cold, harsh floor, completely still, covered in blood. So I turn my head toward Graham who's about to leave the room. "W-why won't you d-do something?"

He cocks his head and squints as he gazes at me. "He has to learn his lesson."

"He'll die," I say, swallowing away the lump in my throat. "If you don't h-help him."

He smiles briefly. "Hmm ... care about him that much, do you?"

I don't answer; I don't want him to know my feelings for Cage. He has no right to them or me or him.

He nods. "Fine. I'll bring some bandages and a first-aid kit." Then he turns around and leaves, closing the door behind him.

It's eerily silent when he's gone, and I'm left with a Cage I no longer recognize. His body is completely torn with gashes and bruises everywhere. Blood stains the floor, and he still hasn't moved.

I'm beyond worried right now, tears welling up in my eyes.

Why did this have to happen?

We should've never tried to escape. It's all my fault. I put the idea into his head.

"Cage ... don't give up," I mumble, tears running down my cheeks. "Please."

I hope his soul can hear me because I'm begging for him to survive.

The time it takes for Graham to come back is

excruciatingly long, and when he does, I jump up from the bed and cling to the glass. "P-please, let me s-see him."

I don't care what I have to do to make it happen; I'll do anything he wants me to.

Just as long as I get to see him. I have to see if he's still alive.

"I'll help you," he says, taking something from his pocket. My heart swells, but then I notice the item in his hand. "If you pee on this stick."

It's a pregnancy stick, but I'm flabbergasted he cares more about that than his own son.

"Well? Tick, tock. He's dying, remember?"

"Okay, f-fine," I say.

He raises a brow, pushing me to the brink of despair.

"P-please," I beg as Graham comes closer to my cell.

"Good girl," he muses, tucking the stick into the box and pushing it my way. "Pee on it. Then I'll give you the first-aid kit."

I nod and snatch it out of the box, marching to my toilet. I don't even give a crap that he's watching; I just want this to be over quickly.

When I've done my business, I hold it up to show him. "D-done."

I watch as he tucks the first-aid kit and bandages into my box and shoves it my way. "You know ... begging suits you well," he muses, and then he turns and leaves.

"W-wait!" I call. I still can't get to Cage.

He shoves his hands in his pocket before opening the door.

Suddenly, I hear a clicking sound right behind me, and I know the room is open.

Brushing my tears away, I quickly grasp the items from the box and run through the black doors to Cage's cell. I slide down on the floor next to him, throwing everything I'm carrying beside me. While Graham exits the room, I focus my attention on Cage. I place two fingers on his neck and feel a very faint heartbeat. I lean over to hear a soft breath. It's there ... but barely.

I pull him toward me, laying his body on my lap. I throw open the first-aid kit and dump the contents out in front of me. I'm struggling to find what I need. I'm not a nurse, but there must be something I can do.

When I look at him from up close, the slashes in his skin draw my attention. They're thick and deep ... blood seeping out. Especially the knife wound is deep. Gashes on his face and mouth are bleeding the most, so I dab them with a wet piece of cloth to make it stop.

I grasp a few pieces of cotton and dab them into a bottle of alcohol to sanitize the wounds. Then I wrap the dressings around them, tying it up. It's not great, but it's something.

Some of his wounds are too deep, though, so I grab a needle and thread to suture it up, trying to finish as quickly as possible before he can feel it. I don't want to hurt him even more. When it's done, I grab the cloth and hold it under the faucet until it's soaked. I wipe him off to get rid of the blood and then wrap more bandages around him.

I'm struggling to contain the tears, but I fight through them as I patch him up as best as I can. I lift him off me and softly place him on the floor before getting up to grab a cup of water. He needs to hydrate quickly, so I sit down beside him again and try to wake him up.

"Cage?" I whisper. "Please ..."

I hold the cup to his lips but no success.

Another tear rolls down. I can't believe I'm crying right now. Maybe I really do care more about him than I could ever imagine. Him dying is the worst possible thing I could imagine right now. Worse than being stuck in this cell forever.

"Please … don't leave me here alone," I whisper.

A soft groan comes out, but the sound elates me, electrical currents shooting through me when I hear him. He's alive … for now.

I pull him into my arms and hug him tight. "You fought so hard …" I whisper into his ear. "Now it's my turn to take care of you."

When I pull away again, his eyes slowly open into little slits, his frown showing his pain. He coughs, and more blood comes out. I dab another piece of cloth against his lips.

"Don't push yourself," I say. "Take it slow."

He licks his lips and squints again, groaning. He tries to move, but I hold him down.

"You're hurt badly. Take it easy," I say. "No need to move. Just let your body heal."

He turns in my arms. Even though he's already bleeding through his bandages, he doesn't care. His hand reaches up for my face, his thumb brushing my cheek.

"Ella …" he grumbles from deep down his throat.

My eyes fill with tears, but I blink them away as I place my hand on top of his. "I'm here."

"My Ella …" he says, barely keeping his eyes open.

"It's okay. We're together," I say. "You won."

He groans, but I swear I can almost see a hint of a smile

242

right after. "Of course."

I grin at his arrogance. I kind of love him for it.

Yes … Yes, I realize it now. I do love him. I love how he is. So beastly yet so innocent and pure. And he's got a heart of gold.

I press a small kiss to his forehead. "I love you …"

I don't fear saying the word. Not anymore.

He made me forget about the guilt that ate away at my heart. He made me love the power of my own words again, and for that, I'm not just grateful … I'm in love.

He coughs but then smiles again, leaning into my touch. "Love …" he repeats. "I like that."

I can't stop smiling, but I'm worried if he moves too much he might make the wounds worse.

"But I can only love you if you keep living," I say. "So stay still and rest."

"Hmm …" He rubs his lips together.

"Water?" I ask, holding the cup close.

He sips eagerly, choking on half but swallowing the rest. "Easy, easy," I say.

"Thank you …" he says. I've not heard him say those words before. It sounds nice when he says it. I could get used to it.

I put the cup back down again, but he keeps looking at me like I have something on my face. Not that he should be concerned about that. He needs to heal, not focus on me.

"What?" I ask.

He grins. "I love you."

I pause. Did he just say he loves me?

He coughs again, and I dab the cloth against his mouth to remove the blood.

"I love you," he says again, his eyes focusing on mine. No matter where I look, he follows my eyes.

"I love you," he repeats. He keeps saying it until I laugh.

"Okay, I get it," I say. "You love me."

"Yes," he says. "Forever."

He leans up, groaning, but when I try to push him down, he refuses. He persists until he reaches me and grabs my face ... and then he kisses me hard.

And it feels so damn good ... I kiss him back just as hard.

Because at this moment, I realize I could've lost the chance to ever kiss him again.

When our lips unlock, he murmurs, "Mine."

There's that word again. That word that creates butterflies in my stomach.

I finally understand it now. It's his way of saying 'I love you.' His pledge to me.

"I'm yours," I say, leaning my forehead against his.

"Safe ... you need to be safe ..." he mumbles, and he places a hand on my belly. "For the baby."

I don't know why he thinks I'm pregnant. Maybe he's just hoping I am because it's the only thing that keeps him going. I won't take away that belief, even if neither of us truly knows. But that still doesn't change anything about our situation inside this cell.

"I'll never be safe in here," I say.

"Escape," he says.

"We tried that already, and it didn't work," I reply.

"Try again." He looks up into my eyes. "Don't give up."

I can't believe he's using my words against me. He's getting smart on me.

Still, even if I did try to escape, I couldn't bear to leave him here. "But what about you?" I ask.

He shrugs. "Leave me."

"No," I say, making a face. "I can't and don't you bring that up again."

"You," he says, clutching my head. "Be safe … so the baby is safe."

"Baby? You keep saying baby. Why?" I ask.

He points at the stick lying on the floor. I forgot I even brought it with me when I rushed into his cell.

However, when I pick it up to look, my jaw drops, my whole body shaking.

I'm … pregnant.

THIRTY-ONE

CAGE

I feel terrible from the fight, my body hurting on all sides, but I still can't help but feel happy because she's pregnant. She's finally having my baby. Our baby.

The stripes on the stick show that she's pregnant. Father taught me how the stick works, so I can alert him. But now I don't want to … I don't want him to know.

I place my hand on her belly again, wanting so desperately to feel our little one inside her.

However, the look on her face makes me doubt she's as happy as I am.

Biting her lip, she shakes her head. "This can't be happening."

I know why she's upset. Being in here means being

subjected to my father's whims and that includes the baby. I can't let him do the same to our kid as he did to me. She has to get out of here.

I nod. "You will escape." I grab her hand. "Whatever it takes."

She nods too, her face darkening. She finally understands what must be done.

She has to leave me here.

It's the only way.

Father only takes her out of this room without me, so that's her only shot.

"I'm not giving up on you," she says, placing a hand on my face. "I'll get us both out of here. I promise."

I place my hand on top of hers, forcing myself to vividly remember her touch, so I won't forget once she's gone.

I know she means best ... but I know my father better.

He values his business more than anything in the world. He'd never, ever let me leave.

Suddenly, I hear a clicking noise, and we both look at the black door. That sound means it's open again ... but more important is the reason.

Father's voice booms through the speakers. "Get back in your room."

He's talking to Ella, but she's reluctant to go, still holding me tight.

"Go. I'm fine," I lie, but I don't want her to worry.

Right now is not the time to defy him. Not yet. It won't work if we're both stuck in the same cell. He'll never come in here. She needs to go to him to make it work.

"But—"

I place a finger on her lips and whisper, "Escape."

I want her to be safe. For our kid to grow up somewhere good instead of in here. She knows how important it is to me because she nods, biting her lip.

I pull her in for another deep kiss before releasing her from my grip. "Go."

She slowly gets up, grabbing all the items from the box, and then walks backward out of the door, taking everything with her. When the door closes, I sigh, but even that is painful. My body aches with every inch of movement, but I don't want to show her weakness. Not now. Not ever.

For her, I will be strong, no matter how difficult it is.

Because I owe it to her … for bringing me something no one else could.

Compassion.

***

Ella

I go back into my cell and sit down on the bed, watching Cage carefully from where I'm seated. I don't want to go, but I know Graham will come to get me. It's only a matter of time until he knows I'm pregnant. Maybe he already knows.

I can't let him have this baby. Nor can I have this baby inside this cell. Cage is right. I have to escape, no matter the cost.

I stare at the camera hanging in the corner, wondering how long I have to wait. It's the first time I'm actually prepared. Why? I took the small scissors from the first-aid kit and tucked them below my dress, right between my thighs with the sharp end pointing down, of course.

I'm hoping the mess I created when I patched up Cage covered it up. If not, I always have plan B.

The moment the gas turns on, I move into action. I quickly wrap up the sheets, douse them in the water from the faucet, and wrap them around my head. Then I lie down on the floor and start fake coughing.

Cage watches me from his cell with a worried look on his face. He attempts to reach out to me, but the pain stops him halfway through.

I nod at him, and he does too. I know we're thinking the same thing.

It's okay. I'm going to be okay. *We're* going to be okay.

Soon, the gas stops. I breathed in enough to feel drowsy and weak but not enough to pass out. It's just enough to fool Graham into thinking I'm incapacitated.

So I wait and wait until I hear the door creak open. Graham steps out, tentatively checking on me and his son.

"Learn your lesson?" I hear him ask.

I can't open my eyes for fear of discovery, so I just listen.

Cage groans, the noises going through marrow and bone, but I have to stay still. Have to surrender in order to win.

"Good," Graham says. "Now behave while I examine her. If you do as I say, you'll be fine. I'll have doctors come and visit you. Agreed?"

"Yes," Cage grumbles, immediately coughing afterward.

Graham walks past my cell, and I hear him enter the

black door. I quickly take a peek at Cage, who's gotten up from the floor and is now stumbling to his bed. He lets himself fall onto the soft bed, groaning out loud again, clearly in a lot of pain.

I hate the sound of it, but I know I have to ignore it. This moment is my only chance. My last shot at freedom. I can't waste it.

However, I can definitely feel the gas take effect, causing my body to feel numb again. I can't move any of my limbs, and the moment Graham lifts me from the floor, I feel like a ragdoll. He pulls the sheets off me and chucks them onto the bed and places me in the wheelchair. Then he rides off with me while I pretend not to be awake to witness it all.

When the door closes behind us, I know I've left the room I shared with Cage. A button is pressed. A beeping sound ensues. We go in. The elevator goes down. Another beep. The door opens, and he pushes me out again. We go through some hallways, which feel endless, but I refuse to open my eyes because I could out myself.

So I keep them shut until Graham lifts me up again and throws me down on a metal table. Just like the one from before when he took the ultrasound pictures pictures.

I wish I could run, but my body doesn't respond to any signals except for a few twitches. I try not to flinch as he firmly ties the straps around my body, locking me in place. I hate being tied up, but I'll have to sit it out and wait until my body regains the strength it needs to fight.

Suddenly, the radio is turned on, and I hear that awful song again, "Don't Worry Baby."

"So … pregnant, huh? Let's have a look," he mumbles, and I hear something like a chair roll across the floor.

I don't know what he's doing, but he's quiet for a few seconds while he taps on some kind of device. Maybe he took the pregnancy stick with him. I can't tell, but the sound freaks me out. I hope to God he won't start probing me while I'm awake. Anything but that.

When he comes closer, I tense up as he starts taking my temperature and swabs the inside of my mouth with a cotton. The second time he comes back, he pushes a needle into my skin, forcing whatever liquid inside my body. It could be anything, poison for all I know.

But he wouldn't do that now that I'm pregnant, right?

He wants this baby more than I do.

He needs it to be safe, so everything he's doing right now is probably beneficial to my health. At least, that's what I hope.

This probing and stuffing and checking goes on for about half an hour until he's done all the tests he can. My body has already begun to get rid of the numbing agent inside my veins, as everything tingles. It's not long before I can move my fingers and lift my arms properly again.

"I see you're waking up," he mumbles, smiling. "Well, you're all checked up and pregnant indeed. Finally."

"Why …" I mumble back, hoping I can finally make the words I want to say come out of my mouth. "Why m-me?"

"Why you?" He laughs. "We already went through this. My son chose you. How? With pictures, obviously. But you know this. You've seen them. Why are you asking me again?"

"How d-did … you f-find me?" The words feel like they're stuck in my throat.

"I already told you I was keeping my eyes on you. You

251

were one of the candidates, and when he picked you, I went to your house and pried open the lock. It wasn't that hard. Wasn't the first time I've done it either."

I don't even care how he got in. All I can focus on is that one word … *Candidates*. That must mean all the girls on the pictures were supposed to get pregnant too. Did he pick us because of our disability?

"It doesn't matter. What does matter is this baby inside you. It will grow up here, and you will stop trying to escape, or I will make all your lives a miserable hell."

But he said that if he had what he wanted I would be free again.

"What?" I mumble. "B-but you s-said …"

"I said *if* you behaved … but you did not. You and Cage betrayed me." He grabs my arm, squeezing so hard it hurts. "You think you're the first who tried? Think my son is going to run off with you? Like he could live in the outside world? Bullshit," he growls. "Cage isn't my first experiment."

Experiment. Not the first.

I'm overwhelmed with information that I can't place.

"F-first?" I ask.

"Yes," he says with a smug smile on his face. "I had another son."

Another son. Cage has a brother?

***

"B-brother?" I repeat, shocked.

"He was the first to grow up in that same cage, and I gave him everything he needed. Everything he could ever want. When he was good, I'd let him go out into the real world as a reward. First, just a couple of minutes to look around and then hours to see the cities. Then days to explore, but I always told him to stay away from the people. Soon, it became a week. I even taught him how to drive because he kept asking me to." He snorts. "I didn't care as long as he fought the fights I wanted him to fight. I should've stopped myself and him before it was too late. Now he's ... gone. I haven't heard or seen from him since the day he escaped."

Cage had a brother ... who was out of the compound ... but came back?

It's too much information to process in one go. I don't even know why he's telling me this, but maybe he feels like it's his duty to inform me ... now that he's decided he's going to keep me.

"He was a good son and listened to me in ways Cage can't seem to do. Although he wasn't great socially, he was very smart. He was born much earlier than Cage was, and I kept them away from each other. But he had a taste of the real world, saw what it had to offer, and he wanted more." He chuckles as if it's funny, even when it isn't. "Do you think Cage would ever be satisfied with his cell knowing what was out there? Of course, not. And you want to repeat all that with Cage?" He shakes his head. "I'm not going to make the same mistake."

"M-mistake?" I mumble, trying to make sense of it all.

Cage never mentioned a brother. Maybe he doesn't even know he exists.

Graham creepily smiles at me. "The outside world, honey. It was a forbidden fruit. Something he could almost grasp ... but never taste." He sighs. "Which is why Cage can never go outside."

Graham turns around, sliding his chair toward his desk again, and he leans over as if he's contemplating something. It's silent for a few seconds, and I wonder what he's doing. He's … looking at something in his hands.

"What h-happened?" I ask.

When he turns around, I catch a brief glimpse of the thing in his hand. My heart stops, and my lungs forget how to breathe for just a moment.

It's a picture of a man.

The same man … who killed my sister.

THIRTY-TWO

Ella

"He ... ran away from me and never came back," Graham says, but I can't focus on anything he says.

My ears are ringing. Voices in my head screaming at the top of their lungs.

"After he killed a little girl too," Graham mumbles.

Little girl.

My sister.

"Well, I assume he was the one who killed her. I don't know what happened. I wasn't there. I just saw the ad in the newspaper asking for tips on the killer along with a sketch of him. But I know in my heart he never meant to kill her. He was always just looking for someone to talk to. Like a pet."

He puts the picture away, but I can't stop staring at it.

Can't stop the tears from rolling down my cheeks without my permission.

Can't stop feeling like my world just came to an end.

"I still don't understand why he refused to listen when I told him talking to people on the outside wasn't a good idea. And look what happened. All it takes is one little girl who actually talks back to him without fear, and then he took her. He just wanted a friend. He was never the killing type." He clears his throat. "Not that it matters. He's long gone, and I learned from my mistake. Cage isn't going anywhere, and neither are you. I've got him chipped, and you're pregnant as can be." He smiles at me. "See? Works out perfectly."

He rolls my way again and places a hand on my leg, squeezing. "Oh … I just remembered something … wasn't that girl your sister?"

My eyes widen, and he cocks his head to see my reaction.

But I can't. I can't respond to this. Can't describe what I'm feeling right now.

Can't feel anything … but rage.

The look on his face changes from curiosity to pure malevolence as he squeezes harder and leans in toward me. "That's right. She was your sister. That girl is the reason I started following you. You lost your voice because she died, didn't you?" he says, grinning. "Maybe that's why I took you … because you're so quiet, and you've been a perfect victim from the start."

My breath hitches in my throat.

No matter how badly I want to breathe right now, I can't. I can't breathe.

"So actually, I'm glad he killed your sister. Because it allowed me to keep an eye out for you … watch you grow until you were the right age… and now I have you here right where you belong."

My sister got killed because of him … because he let his son out of the cage … and he's glad?

I shudder when he takes his fingers off me and starts pulling the straps loose.

"Let's get you back to your cell," he mutters. "Before the drugs wear off."

But I'm not listening anymore.

All I see is black and red dots in front of me.

Rage, like a fiery volcano … boiling inside me.

And the moment he's unleashed the straps around my body, I reach between my thighs and take out the scissors.

Without thinking twice, I ram them into his neck.

I can feel the sharp blade entering his flesh. It cuts through like butter.

He gulps as I pull it out.

Blood gushes everywhere.

Delicate skin ruptures so easily … I'll never forget how it feels.

And I want to feel it again.

I stab him once more until the scissors become stuck inside his throat.

I watch him suffer. Every second of the way, I watch the pain seep into his bulging red eyes. I watch … because I want to feel every ounce of pain he's experiencing right now. Because it's the same pain I've had to endure all these weeks. Because I want him to know he caused his own end.

Blood spurts out of his neck, dripping down his shirt,

and he stumbles back. He tries to grasp anything to hold, but fails miserably. Tools and supplies tumble to the floor, after which he falls too.

I slide off the metal board and watch him struggle on the floor.

He's scrambling for air, reaching for the scissors and desperately trying to pull them out.

All the while he's keeping eye contact as if he can't believe I did this to him. Or he's pleading for me to help him.

How ironic.

With a slow, steady stride, I walk past him, leaving his bloody body on the floor behind me.

I don't care if he dies from suffocation or if he bleeds to death.

I just want it to last an eternity.

But before I walk out, I grasp every photograph he has on this desk and take them with me. One of them is of Syrena. The moment I saw it, I knew I had to take it. I have to find her and make sure she's all right. All these pictures will serve as evidence, as a testament to what Graham's done. I'm not going to let him get away with this.

At the sight of his squirming body on the floor, I turn and make a run for it. I can still hear his gurgles.

The more steps I take, the more my body begins to shake. My fingers too, and I can barely hold the pictures. Every time I blink, I see his face in front of me ... and the scissors I rammed into his neck.

I try to shake it off, but the farther I get away from him, the harder it becomes. I'm painfully aware of the blood splatter on my hands, and I get the sudden urge to scrape it off with a knife.

I don't know why I have these violent thoughts, so I quickly make my way to a faucet and rinse it off as best as I can. The blood stinks so badly that bile rises up, and I puke. When my body has cleansed itself of its demons, I wash my face too and wipe everything off.

The blood still stains my skin, even if it's less than before. I can still smell his scent on me. I can still hear the gurgling sounds in my head, and I want them to stop.

I wish everything would stop, but my head just keeps spinning, and my heart is beating out of control.

You're not alone.

Cage.

Cage is still locked up in his prison. All by himself.

I have to let him know I'm okay. I have to find him and take him home.

I rush through the building, through the unknown corridors of which I have a vague memory of from the last time, and through the open doors. No one's in the dark room with the red lights this time … it's completely empty as if that girl was never there.

So I run up the stairs and through the doors and hallways until I get to the familiar elevator room again. The same room with that door … behind which Cage is being kept.

I sprint toward it and bang the doors. "Cage?"

"Ella!" Hearing his voice makes my heart skip a beat.

"I'm here!" I yell.

"You're safe."

"Yes," I reply. "Are you okay?"

"No, but I manage."

I swallow. "Hold on; I'll get you out of there."

I jerk the door with everything I got, putting all my strength into it, but it won't budge.

"I can't open it," I shout.

"The code," he says.

Right. There's a box right next to the door, and when I open the lid, there are nine numbers I can press. But which ones and how many? I never got the code from Graham. I couldn't open my eyes when he was wheeling me out because then he'd know I was awake.

And now he's dying, if not already dead.

What if, by killing Graham, I sealed his fate to be stuck in this prison forever?

A horrifying shiver runs up and down my spine, but I ignore it and focus on my ability to think.

"Cage, did Graham have any special dates?"

"Dates?"

I push my ears against the door, trying to hear him better while shouting back. "Birthdays, deaths, marriage."

"No … Marriage?"

I sigh. Of course, he doesn't know what that is. "Never mind that. Did he ever mention any specific date?"

"No," he says again.

"Anything that involves numbers? Did he ever mention anything?"

"No …"

The more he says no, the harder it becomes to swallow.

Tears fill my eyes, but I blink them away because I just remembered something. "I'll go check his office and see if I can find the code there. Okay?"

"Go," he says, and I immediately rush off.

Back to the small office. I can hardly remember where it is, but when I find it, I immediately start searching.

I literally open all the drawers, pull out all the notes, and throw everything off that's not what I'm looking for. In one of the drawers, I find more pictures of the girls he once took, so I grasp them and find a bag to tuck them into. A blue duffel bag will do, so I chuck out all the contents and throw the pictures inside. I add a flashlight I found along with a bunch of keys. I don't know what they open, but any keys will do if I want to get out of here.

But no matter how hard I search, I can't find a code anywhere. Nothing that looks like a lock combination. Nothing.

The longer I comb through his stuff, the more I come to realize that I won't find anything, no matter how hard I try. My pulse begins to race, and my breathing becomes ragged as I make my way back to the room where Cage is.

I bang on the door. "I can't find the code, Cage!"

It's silent for a while, and I worry something might've happened to him while I was gone.

"Go," he suddenly says.

I suck in a breath as I hear the word over and over in my head.

"No!" I shout, my eyes filling with tears. "I am *not* leaving you here."

"Escape, remember?" he yells back.

Of course, he'd say that. Tempt me with my memories and my desire to be back home.

But I don't want to go back without him.

I don't want to be home knowing he's still stuck in this hellhole.

How could I?

"No, I can't!" I scream, trying to rip open the door, smashing any numbers on the keypad, but nothing I do works. "*Please* ... no."

"Ella." His stern voice breaks my panic. Breaks my heart into pieces.

"Go!" he barks. "Be free!"

I shake my head and yell back, "No!"

"LEAVE!"

His voice is so loud, it makes me jump back a little.

As a tear rolls down my cheek, I lean my head against the door and place a hand against it, wishing I could touch him one last time. Wishing I could change the course of our lives. Wishing ...

But not every wish comes true.

I know that now.

With my eyes facing the thick door, I run through every scenario, every room once more, and come to a grim conclusion.

I don't know where I am. I can't call for help to tell them where we are. I already checked every inch of the office, even the computer, and there doesn't seem to be any internet, so I can't find my location either.

I have only one option ... Run.

It's the only way to make it back to civilization and find help.

But it requires leaving Cage here. Alone. All by himself. In a prison without food. Where no one can reach him.

He'll lose his mind.

Tears stream down my face as I stare at the door, knowing I have no other choice.

Even if I don't want him to be, he's right.

I have to leave him.

Abandon him.

My heart shrivels up and sinks into my shoes as I face the impossible choice.

"I'll come back for you," I say. "I promise. Tell me you can hear me. Please."

"I hear you," he replies, his voice as calm as the night sky before a storm.

"Good. Don't you die in there, you hear me?" I shout. "Promise me you'll live."

"I promise," he says.

This choice is eating away at me … The one he's already made for me.

Because that's just who he is.

Even when he knows he'll be alone, without food, stuck in a prison for who knows how long … Waiting until I come back … if I ever come back …

And he still wants me to go.

I'll be safe even when he isn't.

I could never make this decision by myself, so now he's taking it away from me by commanding me to leave. To save me. To save *our* baby.

At the cost of his own sanity.

"Thank you," I say, the words barely forming on my lips as I struggle to breathe.

When the last teardrop falls to the floor, I turn around and run.

THIRTY-THREE

Ella

The sun is hotter than I remember. Seeing the birds fly over my head feels bittersweet as I burst out from the compound and leave the damp prison behind me.

The salty smell of the dense desert fills my nostrils as I suck in the first breath of fresh air in a lifetime.

I look around, wondering which way I should go. To my right is a truck, so I run toward it and stick my keys into the ignition, hoping this will take me where I need to go.

If I can get to a city with a vehicle, it'll be much quicker to come back too, so this makes me feel a little less restless. A little less guilty about leaving Cage behind.

The mere thought of leaving him here chokes me up,

but I try to ignore it as I stuff the bottles of water I snagged from the kitchen into the bag.

However, the moment I press the gas with my foot, nothing happens. The truck sputters, trying to run, but the engine doesn't actually start. I push the gas again and again. "C'mon!" I growl, frustrated with the car.

The more I turn the keys and ram the pedal with my foot, the angrier I become until I start slamming my hands onto the wheel. I have to get this truck to start, have to make it work. I have to. I have to … for Cage.

My eyes fill with tears again as I stop trying, realizing it's not going to work.

What's the point of having a truck if it doesn't drive?

Nothing.

There's no point.

No point … to any of this.

Defeated, I roll out of the truck and slam the door shut in annoyance. With my bag slung over my shoulder, I kick a rock in front of me and start walking.

I don't look back.

I keep walking, into the sun, into the blistering heat, knowing this could be my death sentence.

But what other choice do I have?

None.

There is no choice … No saving grace.

Nothing except my legs putting one foot in front of the other.

The sand bites as I go through the desert, far beyond the distance I imagined I could ever walk. I keep going in a straight line, hoping I might eventually find a road. But in the middle of nowhere, the chances are grim.

The road I saw when I escaped before was a lie.

A sham, conjured up by my mind.

There's nothing but dirt ahead, and I have no choice but to keep moving.

My water bottles are already halfway empty when the sun above me moves position. The only thing that allows me to keep track is the shadow cast on the breast-shaped mountains to my left. The wide nothingness around me tenses me up, but I ignore the knot in my stomach and keep going.

I've done it before. Back when I found my sister ... and had to carry her all the way back through the woods to the road. Then I had to wait for a passerby in a car to call for help. My sister's body was heavy but so was my heart, and I needed to bring her home.

I didn't give up then, and I'm not going to give up now.

There's no time to think about the pain in my muscles.

No time to think about how I'm ever going to find my way back home.

No time for anything but walking.

Just walking ... so I can save Cage.

I can't let him die a lonely, miserable death in there.

I just can't.

So I keep going, way past my limit, way past the distance my body is willing to carry me. The sun has caused my red skin to blister, and my vision has become blurry from the heat. My water bottles are completely empty now, and even the last drops from the inside of the plastic don't provide enough to quench my thirst.

Still, I don't give up.

I can't give up.

I can't give up for Cage.

For this baby. Our baby.

I *can't* give up.

Not until my feet become numb. Not until my throat is as dry as the air, and my skin and lips cracked. Not until my body refuses to move another inch and collapses to the ground.

And even then, I crawl.

Through the thick, scorching heat across the endless desert.

When even my fingers feel like they're burning, I stop, my body needing the break before it breaks down.

Turning on my back, I gaze above me at the bright blue sky, thinking about the last time I saw it and wondering if this will be the last time.

Vultures are already circling above my head, waiting for the last of my spirit to leave my body. Waiting for me to give up.

I'm tempted. So tempted to just let it all go.

I'm already free. Free as a bird to roam the skies if I wanted to.

My sister's waiting for me up there in the clouds.

I reach for her, wanting to get closer, hoping I can touch her. Hoping she can see I put up a fight. I didn't go willingly. But I went with pride and honor.

I went on my own terms.

In freedom.

***

Lights circle me, and I wonder if I'm in heaven. It's so bright and welcoming but very cold. Colder than I expected. The thirst is still there, but it doesn't burn in my throat as much as it did before. I wonder if everyone experiences heaven this way, or if it's just because I'm still on the way there. Floating up into the sky ... that would be a sight to behold.

"I've got vitals," a voice echoes close to me.

I wonder who it is. Could it be God? Or maybe it's my sister ... I can't wait to see her again and hug her tight. However, the moment I try to picture her, all I see is a man, calling me from down below on the ground. A beastly man ... roaring like a lion.

Cage.

He's still alive. I can't die. I can't die, knowing he's still in there. I'm not going without him.

I blink, forcing my eyes to open, forcing myself to continue living even when my body refuses to do so.

My limbs buzz, and the ground underneath me shakes. But that ground feels much colder than I remember it being and much harder too.

Something blocks the bright light above me, a shadowy figure.

"What's your name?" There's that voice again. It's so warm and unlike anything I've heard in weeks.

My chapped lips part, but no sound leaves my mouth as I try to talk. My throat clamps up, and I cough.

"Take it easy," the voice says.

When I squint harder, I can definitely make out the figure of a man but not one I recognize.

"Do you know what day it is?"

I shake my head, but my muscles barely move, still tensed up from the battle I fought against Mother Nature herself.

"July third," he says.

July… I count out the weeks in my head.

That means I've been locked inside the compound for more than seven weeks.

Seven weeks … of my entire life.

I was gone … gone from the surface of the planet.

No one knows where I am.

And no one knows how to find us … where to find Cage.

I almost shoot up into a seated position, but something keeps me down. Straps around my body, tight and suffocating.

I shake my head, my eyes searching for a way out. I feel a hand on my arm, and the voice speaks again.

"Calm down. You're not going anywhere but the hospital right now."

Hospital? How?

A minute ago, I was lying on the ground in the blistering heat, and then the next, I'm in this cool, compact thing with a man I don't know.

"You were in the desert, remember?" he says, cocking his head. "You're lucky a passerby found you while driving along the road. She called us."

Us?

I look around and notice the medical equipment, the badge on his shirt … and then I hear the sirens above me.

I'm in an ambulance. A real ambulance. With real people.

"We're lucky she made you drink from her water bottle, or you might've died."

I try to swallow, but everything hurts, and it's so hard to comprehend what's going on.

It feels like minutes ago, but I know now that isn't true. My mind is playing tricks on me. Just as it did when I thought I was dying ... when in fact I'm being saved.

Rescued by honest and good people bringing me to the hospital.

A hospital in a real city where I'll finally see the real world again.

Where I can see my parents again and hug them.

Where I can ... go home.

Without Cage.

Because he's still stuck inside that compound, probably screaming out my name, not knowing when and if I'll ever come back.

I grasp the shirt of the man who's sitting in front of me and say, "Cage ..."

"What?"

A tear wells up in my eye as I realize the task that lies ahead. "I have to save him."

THIRTY-FOUR

Ella

Taking my first breath feels like a rebirth.

The first since I've awakened in the warm cocoon surrounding my body.

Soft fabric rests on me, and I clutch it tightly as I open my eyes.

It hurts to look. Everything hurts.

My muscles feel tight and weak. Around me, everything is white. It reminds me of the cage I spent weeks in; the cage I left behind in search for home. Freedom.

I'm free.

I remember my walk through the scorching desert, the blistering sun razing my skin. I remember the suffocating pain I felt in my lungs when I sucked in the much-needed oxygen, the burning sensations in my throat from lack of water, and the endless red soil underneath my feet.

All of that has been replaced by pristine white warmth, but the color feels colder than that prison cell I came from. That glass prison where I left a piece of my soul.

Where I left … *him*.

In a burst of energy, my body shoots up from the bed, wires and all, and I scream. "Cage!"

In my mind, his image is as clear as day.

The beast of a man … Cage.

He's still stuck in that dark, damp hole while I'm here … wherever that is.

I look around and see the tubes going into my body, dripping some kind of fluids when I pull it out. It hurts a little but not enough for me to care.

I tug the tiny tubes from my nose that provided oxygen and throw the blanket off me. When my feet hit the cold, hard floor, I shiver, and when I get up, I almost fall again.

My body is still weak from the ordeal, but I manage to walk to the door, clutching the sink on my way.

I might be fragile, but I'm not about to give up.

The moment I remembered I left him there all by himself, I knew I had to go find him.

I don't care how; I just know that I have to. No matter the pain in my body.

This is nothing compared to what I felt all those weeks in that glass prison, being hungry half the time with no privacy, no lights, no nothing … except him.

The man I came to trust.

The man who stole my heart and locked it away in the

cell he calls home.

I will show him the light of the sun. I will make him see the world through my eyes. I will give him a new home.

My home.

I stumble through the door and out into the hall, blinking a few times. My vision is still a bit hazy, but I can clearly make out the signs that say EXIT, so I head that way.

A lady in a blue suit stops me halfway there. "What are you doing out of bed?"

I frown, trying to push her away, but all I manage is a soft nudge.

"No, no, back to bed," she insists, wrapping her arms around my shoulder. "Where were you going anyway? You're not well enough to go home yet."

I open my mouth, but only a scratching noise comes out.

"Don't try to talk or exert yourself. Your body is still recovering," she cautions, guiding me back into my room.

But I don't want to go there. I want to search for Cage. I need to find him.

I turn toward her and grasp her arms, parting my lips, but again, nothing but a faint, throaty sound leaves my mouth. Dammit. Why do I have to be selectively mute? Out of all the time it's present, why does it have to be now?

I wish Cage was here.

I can talk to him; I trust him.

Tears well up in my eyes as the woman directs me back to bed and forces me to sit then lie down again.

"There, there. Now don't get out of bed again." She chuckles as she reinserts the IV and puts the tubes back in my nose. The oxygen gives a much-needed boost to my breathing, though, and I suck in a breath.

I cough, and the woman walks toward the sink and pours a cup of water, handing it to me.

"Thirsty?" she inquires.

I nod and gladly sip. It feels strange to have liquids running down my throat again as if something was blocking it or it was burned.

"It might feel funny for a little while. You were quite dehydrated." She raises her brows and makes a weird face. "And that's an understatement. But you're in the hospital now, and you're taken good care of." She smiles and shows me her name on the ID card attached to her nurse scrubs.

"Name's Jenny. I'm your nurse. If you need anything, you can press that button over there." She points at a device hanging from the wall. "And I'll come right away to help you. Okay?"

I nod and lick my lips, tears welling up in my eyes.

I know I'm in the hospital. I know I'm safe.

But what about Cage?

Is he in pain? Is he even alive?

Not knowing is what hurts the most.

Jenny smiles at me. "Now, you just rest, okay? If you need anything, just call." When she's about to leave, I grasp her shirt and force her to stop. I try to signal with my fingers that my throat is incapable of producing the sounds needed to talk properly.

She pauses and frowns. "Wait. Hold on." She walks off, out of the room, and comes back a few minutes later with a notepad and a pen. She hands it to me and says, "Here. Write what you want to say."

Can't Talk. Selective muteness.

"Oh, okay," she says as she reads the words. "What's your name? We couldn't find any identification on you."

Ella Rosenberg. Please contact parents.

I write their number, too, along with their address. When she's read it, I immediately tear the page and continue to write frantically.

CAGE. Have to find him.

I hold up the notepad and show it to her, watching her eyes read the words as I clench the notepad tight. Please understand ... please.

"Cage? Who's Cage?"

I turn the notepad back around and pen down the words as if my life depends on it.

I was in a prison. Compound. Desert. Not alone. Others. Victims. Cage.

I write as few words as possible, wanting to cram everything that happened to me in a small, confined space and hope she understands. There's no time to be precise or to expand on the details. No time for anything because Cage is still stuck there, this very instant. He has no access to food, and the water might stop running too. He could be dying.

Her eyes widen, reading the words I penned on the paper. "Is this true?"

I nod vehemently and grasp for the pen again.

CAGE. Still there. Find him. Police.

She nods. "You're saying you were taken by someone into a cell? And that you weren't alone; there were others? Someone called Cage?"

I nod repeatedly until she understands the gravity of the situation.

"All right. I'll call the cops and have them take your statement. It'll probably take until tomorrow, though."

I pen down more words.

No time. Now.

Underlining them both.

She grimaces and bites her lip. "I'm sorry, honey, but I can't force them to come based on a statement alone. A missing person case takes time, and you have to have patience. But I promise you, I will do anything I can to get them here quickly, all right?" She pats down my blanket and tucks me in like a good nurse would when all else fails to make me happy.

Because that's just it.

She wants to take care of her patient when her patient doesn't want to be here at all.

It's a tough situation neither of us can change.

Please.

I pen down the word as a tear rolls down my cheek.

"I'll do my best, honey. That's all I can promise you. I'll call them today," she says.

I nod a thank you.

"I'll call your parents too," she says. "So they'll probably visit later today. You should rest now."

Mom. Dad. I can't believe I'm going to see them again.

It feels like ages.

And I'm not the same person they remember me as.

I wonder how I'm going to tell them what happened to me.

I don't want to break their hearts.

***

Later that day

The moment I see their faces as they enter my door, I burst into tears.

Mom does too as she rushes toward me and wraps her arms around me, hugging me tightly. For the first five minutes, no words are exchanged. All we do is hug each other and cry. Even Dad can't keep it dry.

I clutch Mom and Dad's clothes, wishing I could hold them forever. It feels so unreal to be able to touch them again. I can't imagine what it must be like for them.

To not see your daughter for weeks, and then for her to suddenly turn up at a random hospital. It must've been like lightning striking the earth in front of you.

It's a stroke of luck that I managed to escape. If I hadn't … they would've probably never seen me again.

I shiver at the thought.

Mom releases me from her grasp and cups my face, caressing my cheeks and brushing away the tears. She smiles and hugs me again.

"Oh, honey …"

Dad grabs my hand and squeezes it tight as he sits down beside me on a tiny chair. Mom sits down on the bed and keeps touching me. I don't think it's weird. I think I would've done the same if I were in her shoes and had almost lost my daughter.

My daughter or son … that's right.

I'm pregnant.

I look down at my belly, wondering if the baby is still

there.

If there's still a heartbeat.

"Mom … Dad …" I mutter, my voice sounding hoarse.

But it's so good to hear it still works.

Only with them … only with people I trust.

And with Cage.

Cage … poor Cage.

"I'm …" I choke on my own words. How do I begin to tell them my story? How does anyone find the words needed to describe the horrors they've endured?

It's impossible.

"Take your time," Dad says, cocking his head as he places a hand on my shoulder and gently squeezes. "Take all the time you need."

THIRTY-FIVE

Ella

Telling them about being taken by Graham, my time stuck in the glass prison cell, and all the horrible things that happened there takes time. But it feels like a cleansing; as if a waterfall is cascading down my shoulders, rinsing my soul.

It's strangely purifying as I unload the weight I've carried for so long. The moment I tell them about my sister and the connection with Cage's brother, they both start to cry. It's hard to see them in pain, but they needed to know about her fate.

We hug again and I continue my story, leaving nothing out. The more I talk, the more I calm down, feeling a sense of awe at what I've accomplished. That I'm free again, on my own terms, by my own volition.

That I did what no one else could. I survived and escaped.

And now we're here—in a clean, sterile hospital far away from the worst place on earth.

But I'm not happy. I fake my smiles whenever my parents gaze at me as they try to understand what I've been through. But deep down I know ... I could never be happy without *him*.

Cage. Where are you? How do I find you if I don't know where to look?

I swallow away the lump in my throat as I tell my parents about the man in the cell next to me. About all the things he was ... and all the things he could never do. Being born there makes him unique. Makes him a beast.

Would they understand the kind of love we have?

The moment I tell them about the seduction and sex, they grimace, and I realize it's impossible to explain. Feelings are unique from person to person. Even if you share them, you can never understand the depth to which they go.

And my feelings for Cage are ... definitive. Pure.

There are many shades to what we have, but I choose to only see the positive.

I don't blame him for anything that happened. I only wish I could've taken him with me to the real world. To show my parents love comes in all shapes and sizes.

Even if they don't understand right now, they will if they see him.

It's okay. They will ... once we find him.

"So you ... made love to this man?" Dad asks, still stuck on the part where I told them about the bedroom.

I nod, and Mom squeezes my hand tight. "It's okay, honey. You don't have to say anything you don't want to say."

"But I want to. I want you to know everything. I'm not ashamed of what happened. Even if my imprisonment wasn't by choice, I choose to love Cage for who he is. I know he's the son of my captor, but I also know what he feels for me and what he did to free me from that hellhole."

"And you're saying he's innocent?"

I nod. "Completely. He doesn't know any better."

Dad frowns and averts his eyes, clearly having trouble with the notion that a human can be like that … unknowing … living in ignorant bliss.

But Cage didn't ask for any of it. It's not his fault. He was born that way.

"Do you love him?" Mom asks.

"Yes. With all my heart," I say, wondering how they feel about it.

"As long as you're happy with him, I don't care," Mom says, and we both smile and begin to cry again. I'm glad she accepts it. I don't know what I would've done if she hadn't. I can't bear to lose my parents too.

Dad shakes his head, but he's smiling too. "If that's what it takes to make my little girl happy, then so be it."

We all hug each other again, and I'm genuinely relieved it went the way it did.

"But don't think I'm ever going to think you being locked up in there is okay. Someone's gotta pay," Dad grumbles.

That's when I realize I haven't even told them I killed Graham.

I'm not sure I even can because the moment I think about it, knots form in my stomach and bile rises in my throat.

I quickly grasp a bucket below my bed to hold in front of me as I throw up.

"Oh, honey, let me go grab some napkins for you," Mom says, getting up quickly to wet some paper towels. I gladly take them, wiping everything off while she empties the bucket.

"Thanks," I say when she comes back. "Sorry about that."

"Ah-ah, I don't wanna hear it," she responds, holding up her finger. "You're allowed to feel sick after what you've been through." She sighs as she grabs my arm again. "You know I'm here for you, always. No matter what."

I nod, but I know I haven't told them the complete story yet.

There's something else … something growing inside me … something precious I don't want to get rid of. What if they ask me to do it? Or worse, what if it's no longer there?

I went through hell and back to get out; what if the baby didn't survive the ordeal?

"What's wrong, honey?" Mom asks, but I struggle to answer.

Panic bubbles to the surface, and I press the button that the nurse told me to press.

She walks in moments later.

I open my mouth, but again, nothing comes out, so I reach for the notepad and pen which are on the bedside table.

Baby. Alive?

I pen it down as quickly as possible and hold it up to her.

I can't believe I only asked about it now. It's been hours since I woke up. I neglected to even think about it, let alone ask. How terrible.

She squints and then nods. I sigh in relief.

"Yes, it's alive and well. We checked with an ultrasound when you were under," Jenny confirms, and I clutch my chest and close my eyes for a second.

"Did you need anything else while I'm here?" Jenny asks.

"No, I think we're fine," Dad responds for me, and she promptly leaves.

When I open my eyes again, the looks in their eyes terrify me.

"Please ..." I shake my head, tears forming in my eyes again. "I didn't want you to find out this way."

Mom pulls me close again, her warm hands enveloping me as she murmurs, "It's okay, honey. We love you. We will always love you."

"Are you ... *pregnant?*" Dad sputters, inspecting the notepad with a dumbstruck look on his face.

I nod softly, not wanting to feel his judgment.

But then he does the most peculiar thing.

He actually starts crying.

I pull him in for a hug again, together with Mom, and we cry some more.

I guess that's all you can do in a situation like this where everything is out of our control.

It happened, and there's no way around it.

I know they're sad for me ... but I'm not. I don't feel

anything but protective about this baby.

"Do you want to keep it?" Dad asks after a while.

"Yes." There's no hesitation in my voice. No reluctance. I'm all in.

I don't care what I have to do or what it takes, I'm having this baby.

This baby is my only connection to Cage. The only remnant of *him*. His baby lives inside me. His blood will live on through me even if he doesn't make it.

How could I ever want to get rid of that?

"You're sure? Even though the baby was conceived in that … place?" Dad clears his throat as if he's having trouble with the word 'prison.'

I understand because the thought of that place still gives me the chills.

"Yes, I'm sure. A hundred percent. No doubts," I say, looking them in the eyes.

"All right. I won't say a word," Mom says, the corners of her lips gently tugging up into a smile again.

"Thank you. Your support means a lot to me," I say, and they both squeeze my hand. "I just wish you could meet him too. You'd understand."

"Maybe someday," Mom says.

I nod, but desperation sinks into my heart again when I think about the glass prison. "Cage is still stuck there, Mom. I have to find him."

"We will, sweetie. We will," Mom assures. "Did the nurse call the police yet?"

"Yes, they should arrive any minute now," I reply. "I have to tell them about Syrena too."

"Syrena?" Dad asks.

"Another cell mate," I say. "She disappeared, and I assumed Graham had sold her."

"Sold …" Dad makes a fist with his hand. "I can't believe this is still happening in today's world."

"It is, and we were all oblivious to it. But I'll find her. I have to. Just like I have to find Cage. There's no other way to save them," I say, swallowing away the lump in my throat at the thought of the enormous task ahead of me.

"Right. And we'll help you every step of the way," Mom says. "Right, Hank?" She gazes explicitly at Dad.

"Right. Whatever you need, hon. We're here," Dad says, smiling at me awkwardly. "I'll punch my way through all of them until we get to your Cage, okay?"

"Thanks, Dad," I say.

A knock is audible, and we all turn our heads to watch the nurse stride in. "Sorry to disturb you, but the police are here to take your statement."

"Great," Dad says. "Let them in."

The nurse swallows. "Ah … I'm sorry, but they want to speak to her alone. Is that okay?"

My parents are silent for a moment before my dad says, "Yeah … sure."

They seem a bit dumbfounded, but I guess that's only natural. After all, they've just been reunited with their lost daughter, and now, they're being asked to leave. I'd be reluctant too.

Luckily, they agree, and Mom kisses me on the cheek and whispers, "We'll be right back, honey."

"I'll be okay, Mom," I say, smiling as she kisses me on the forehead.

Dad kisses me too and says, "We're here for you. Just

around the corner."

"Thanks," I say. "Go get some coffee and a snack."

I chuckle as they leave the room, but deep down, I still feel uneasy.

I don't think that feeling will ever go away. Not as long as Cage is still locked away.

THIRTY-SIX

Ella

When the police officers enter the room, I have a slight panic attack. I'm really going to have to tell strangers what happened to me. But I guess there's no other way.

"Hi, Ella, I'm Officer John Nelson, and this is Larry Stevens. We're here to take your statement."

I nod as John sits down on the chair my mom sat on.

"You can tell us everything. Don't be afraid," one of the cops says as he clicks his pen.

I nod and write on the notepad.

What if it's bad?

One of them licks his lips, reading my words.

"We won't judge. Nothing leaves this room unless you

want it to," Larry says as he sits down on the chair my dad just vacated.

I nod and then tell them the same story I told my parents, using the notepad and the pen. I tell them everything from beginning to end, leaving nothing unmentioned. From describing the inside to the outside of the compound, I even tell them what all the men who came to watch the fights look like, as well as Graham, and that I stuck a pair of scissors in his neck.

They don't seem at all fazed by my admission. Maybe they expect it ... After all, a captive will do anything to get out and be free. Maybe even kill.

However, him penning down literally everything I say has me on edge.

"Don't worry," Larry says as he gazes up into my fearful eyes. "As I said, we're not judging. A victim is usually cleared of any and all blame if he or she attacks the captor in order to escape. No one will charge you for it. You can relax."

After I let go of the breath I was holding, I continue with my story, telling them about Syrena, our purpose in those cells, and my pregnancy. And I tell them about Cage. I tell them anything and everything they want to know, hoping they can do something with it. Hoping it will spur them to act, to try to find Cage by any means necessary.

But the more I talk, the more I come to realize they're there to play the same game they always play. Listen and write it down ... maybe process it in a week. Or a month, who knows.

But I don't have that time. There is no time.

We can't wait.

I hold up the notepad.

Cage could die.

"No, ma'am. I promise you; we'll do everything we can to get him the help he needs."

I frantically write more words.

Don't know where he is. How?

The cop looks up at me after reading. "The lady who dropped you off at the hospital left her phone number too, and she's already been asked where she found you. We can send a search unit over tomorrow."

I blink as tears fill my eyes.

Please. Find him.

"But ma'am, he …" The cop clears his throat. "The nurse told us you're pregnant. I'm so sorry about that. I think it's a wise decision to talk to a counselor. It will help you get through this, and it will also help you with decisions. You know."

Annoyed, I pen down more words.

Know what? I want to keep the baby.

I hold it up in anger, right in front of his face.

"I'm not saying you shouldn't, ma'am," he remarks, and he looks over at his partner, who jumps in.

"We think it's best to talk to a counselor anyway because we see this happen to victims in every case like this. We want to make sure he's not …"

I don't want to hear it.

Cage is good.

I write the words while the tears run down my face.

Don't you dare suggest otherwise.

He holds up his hands. "Ma'am, listen, we're not saying he isn't. We're just saying it's a good idea to talk to a counselor about your ordeal. They might be able to help. That's all we want. To help you."

Then find Cage.

I underline the words, tapping on the paper.

"We will do our best, ma'am. As I said, there will be a search party. But it's in your best interest to remain calm and focus on your recovery, okay? Let us handle the searching."

I fold my arms and look away at the window, wishing I could just jump out and run.

I don't think the urge has ever been this strong. Not even when I was inside the glass cage.

John tucks his notepad away. "I think we've got enough. If you remember anything else, feel free to give us a call. We'll include everything you give us in the file."

Then I remember the pictures I took, and I scramble to find them. Of course, the nurse tucked them all into the plastic bag she stuffed my clothes in too.

I pen down more sentences.

Wait. I have something for you. Pictures, in that bag.

The officer points at it, and I nod, so he grabs it and opens it.

Girl on the picture: Syrena. Please find her too. Graham sold her.

"We'll do our best, ma'am. However, we're going to have to take this as evidence," the officer says, tucking the picture into an air-tight plastic bag.

Will I get it back?

"That depends on the investigation, ma'am. I can't promise anything, sorry."

I sigh. I suppose there's no other way. If I want them to

find her, I have to cooperate.

I nod as one of them shakes my hand.

"Thank you for the information, ma'am. Good luck on your recovery."

I mouth them a thank you as they leave the room.

Not soon after, Mom and Dad step back inside. Seeing them cheers me up instantly. Especially when I notice the Cup of Noodles in my mom's hands. She sits down beside me and hands it to me.

"Thought you might like it," she hints, winking.

"Thanks, Mom." God, I'm so glad I can talk again.

Not being able to talk in front of strangers is really annoying sometimes. I never get used to the feeling of my own throat clamping up the moment anyone but my parents step into my room. Or Cage. I don't know why I had the ability to talk in front of him ... but I did, and I'm grateful for it.

I gloat as I gobble down the noodles, the spiciness setting my mouth on fire. It's delicious, and the mere taste makes me want to cry.

"Oh, you don't like it?" Mom asks.

"No, no, I love it," I reply, slurping up some more. "It's just been so long ... Too long since I had some actual *good* food."

"Well, in that case, I'll prepare all your favorite meals when you get back home," she says, patting my leg. "Did the doctors tell you when you can go back home yet?"

"No, not yet. They wanted me to recover first."

"And you should," Dad chimes in. "You'll need plenty of rest. Especially if we're ever going to go outside and face that damn crowd."

"Crowd?" I say with a frown, wondering what they mean.

Mom makes a face. "Yeah, I don't know …"

"What crowd?" I ask her.

"A bunch of reporters out front are asking about you. It's all over the news already," Dad grumbles, and my jaw drops. "Apparently, some staff member couldn't keep their trap shut."

"Hank!" Mom snaps.

"Sorry, sorry," he says, and it makes me snort. "But I don't think it's professional. At all."

"Well, we can't do anything about it now," Mom says, clutching her bag. "Only thing we *can* do is keep *our* mouths shut at the very least." She sneers at Dad, making it impossible for me to eat the Cup of Noodles without laughing.

Someone knocks on the door again. This time it's not a nurse, though. It's Bo.

The moment I see him, my mood lightens, and I put the noodles away.

Bo clears his throat as he holds a small bouquet in front of him. "Sorry if I'm bothering you guys; I can wait."

"It's fine," Mom says. "Come in."

"Uh yeah, your mom and I should go get another cup of coffee. Get a little caffeinated before we face the storm of people outside." Dad laughs and beckons for Mom to go with him. "Let's go."

"You sure, honey?" she asks me. I nod, and she gives me another peck on the cheek. "All right."

When they've left the room, Bo approaches and smiles awkwardly.

"Hey …"

I sign to him. **Hey.**

A long time ago, I taught Bo sign language. It was only because he asked, of course; otherwise, I wouldn't have bothered him with it. But he wanted to learn so he could at least understand a few of the things I wanted to tell him. So we could actually communicate properly.

I don't know why I can't talk to Bo. He's the only person other than my parents who I interact with on a weekly basis. But it just never happened. Not since my sister died.

I swallow away the lump in my throat as he sits on the chair where my mother was and holds out the flowers again.

"I brought you some flowers," he says.

They look nice, I sign. **Thank you.**

I smile as he puts them down on the bedside table and mumbles, "I'll go find a vase for them later." He smiles. "So … how are you?"

I shrug.

"Not good, huh?" His head lowers, and he gazes at the floor as if he regrets every single word coming from his mouth. "Sorry, I just … I don't know what to say."

You don't have to say anything, I sign.

"But I do. I do, Ella. You were gone. God, you were gone so long …" He runs his fingers through his blond locks and sniffs. "I can't believe you were actually missing. I thought you'd never come back." I can see the hurt in his eyes. "I searched. God, I searched for so long. What happened to you, Ella?"

I don't know what to do, but I can feel his pain inside me, tearing me apart. So I hold out my arms and pull him in

293

for a hug. He stays there for a while, and I can feel the droplets run down my neck. He doesn't make a sound even though I know he's crying. He probably doesn't want me to know. Doesn't want me to see his weakness.

I recognize the feeling. I used to feel the same thing back in the cage.

But now? Now all I feel is the strength and determination to continue—to fight—for my future and for everyone else's.

"I thought I lost you, Ella. I thought you'd never come back," he whispers. "Just like your sister."

The mere mention of her makes my heart stop.

He pulls back. "I'm sorry. That was insensitive of me."

It's okay, I sign.

He was never good with words, but he has a heart of gold.

He always blamed himself for her disappearance, thinking he could've changed the course of history if he'd only gone along with us that day instead of playing computer games with his other friends. But it's not his fault, nor is it mine.

Like Cage said … you can't change the past.

You can only work toward a better future.

He sits back down on the chair, and it's quiet for a few seconds before he speaks again. "I don't know what to ask. What to say. I don't want you to feel uncomfortable."

I'd prefer not to discuss it, I sign. *I don't want you to think less of me.*

"I won't ever think less of you," he assures me, frowning. "*Ever.*"

I nod and sign, *Thank you.*

And I decide then and there to tell him everything. From the beginning to the end, nothing's left unmentioned. I discuss the prison and the men, Syrena, Graham, Cage, and even his brother. At first, I feared his reaction, but I'm met with only compassion and understand, and it makes me hug him tight.

After explaining everything that happened to me, he thanks me for sharing it with him, and he hugs me again. But I didn't tell him one thing. The most important part.

I rub my belly and grasp his hand, placing it on top.

"You're ... pregnant?" he mutters, licking his lips.

But the moment I nod, he shows no happiness. No smile.

Nothing ... but regret.

THIRTY-SEVEN

Ella

Sitting in a wheelchair, I'm carted out of the room. Dad had already gone outside to pull the car up to the front door. My body still hurts but not as much as it did before, and the doctors have given me the all clear to go home. I'll still be taking medicines for the pain, of course, and we agreed it was in my best interest to talk to a counselor starting tomorrow. Even though I hate how the police officers treated me and my story, they were right. I need help to process what I've been through.

After the hospital staff have wheeled me out, I thank them and say goodbye, and greet my mom who's waiting outside. It's then that I realize how big my story really is.

Ten, maybe even thirty journalists are all lined up outside the doors, huddling close, screaming their lungs out to get my attention. Flashes of light nauseate me, and I cover my face to prevent them from blinding me. Questions are being fired at me from all directions.

"Ms. Rosenberg, can you tell us who kept you prisoner for all this time?"

"Do you know why he took you?"

"What happened while you were inside the cell?"

So many questions … but my lips do nothing but sputter.

I don't know why they're here or why a staff member would tell the reporters without me saying it was okay. I'm a story now. A sick enjoyment for others to watch. I'm sure my face will be plastered all over the news.

"Please, get out of the way," Mom asks nicely while the nurse keeps pushing the wheelchair.

We try to go through the crowd, but they keep following us, jumping on our tail and practically making it impossible to get to the car. Going home was supposed to be easy … but this? Being scrutinized by strangers, knowing the whole world will soon know what I've been through? That's the true ordeal.

"Ms. Rosenberg, is it true you weren't alone in that cell?"

I try to ignore the questions, I really do.

"Ma'am, is it true that you're pregnant? Is the captor the father?"

That.

That's the moment I break.

The moment I turn and gaze at the woman who asked

297

about my baby, wondering why someone would ask such a thing.

Whether I'm pregnant is none of their business.

I wish I could tell them to shut up, but all that leaves my throat is a measly squeak.

"No comment," Mom growls at them.

"I'm sorry, honey," Mom says to me as we walk to the car. "I told them to get out of here when we walked into the hospital, but they refused to move."

"It's okay, Mom," I say, rubbing my belly with my hands.

"They don't know the real story," she says, bending over to my height. "They don't know what you've been through. Let them talk." She smiles and pecks me on the forehead.

Then she and Dad help me get into the car, and the nurse brings the wheelchair back inside.

We drive away from the hospital and back home. Along the way, I can't help but stare at every single house we come across, all the trees beside the road, and the birds high up in the sky. I feel like a kid again, witnessing the wonders of the world all over again.

When we arrive at my home—not my parents' home, *my* home—Mom turns around in the front seat and asks, "Are you sure you don't want to stay at our place? Maybe this place has bad memories; I don't know."

"I'm sure, Mom," I say, smiling. "I just want to be home again."

Smiling, she nods and steps out of the car. Dad turns off the engine and steps out too, and they both help me get out. I can walk, but I'm just not as stable as I once was. The doctors say I should regain my strength in a few days.

298

While I walk inside on my own, Mom and Dad grab all the stuff they brought for me to the hospital, like clothes and toiletries, and bring it inside. When I step through the door, I take a long whiff, inhaling the scents of my home. The wood still smells the same. Still creaks the same. Nothing's changed.

Except me.

It's been long … too long.

And I don't think I've ever been this happy to step foot inside my home.

Gosh, the memories.

Especially considering I live so close to the forest where I lost my sister.

I chose this place for a reason … Because it gives me peace.

"Hey, guys." Bo walks in too. "Sorry, I just figured … maybe you could use some help?"

"Well … sure," Mom muses. "That'd be lovely. You can help clean up the house a little. Vacuum's in the closet."

"Ah, sure," he says, rubbing the back of his head.

Thanks, I sign as he grabs the vacuum from the closet.

"I'll start upstairs then. Give you guys some time to adjust," he says with an awkward laugh. Then he runs upstairs.

I can't stop staring out the windows at the beautiful grass in my backyard. The flowers are in full bloom.

I think I'll go for a run outside when I'm fit again. I want to feel the grass underneath my toes again.

"You okay, hon?" Mom asks.

"Yeah, of course." I take in a gulp of air. "You don't have to ask every second."

"I know, I know." She shrugs. "I can't help it. I'm naturally worried."

I laugh as I walk through my home, flabbergasted at how much it looks exactly the way I left it. Everything, including the couch, the TV, the kitchen. Even the hallway and the staircase.

I stare up at the floor above me. "Do you mind if I …?" I mumble.

"No, no, go right ahead," Mom replies, winking. "I'll take care of everything down here and cook up something delicious. You just wait." She giggles.

"I'll drive to the store, get some groceries and stuff," Dad says. "Be right back."

"Thanks, Dad," I say, hugging him before he leaves with the car.

I take off my shoes and slowly but steadily climb the stairs, feeling the soft carpet tickle my toes. I always loved how it felt, and I still do, but now it's even more special. It feels like home. Like the place that calmed me.

However, the longer I spend roaming my own house, the more I come to realize how empty it's always been. Devoid of any sign of life.

I used to love the silence. The loneliness soothed me.

Now it only serves as a reminder of what I left behind in that cage.

My Cage.

I take a deep breath and walk up to my room. Clutching the doorpost, I gaze inside, my heart racing in my throat. There's the bed … the bed I was sleeping in the moment I was taken. The sheets are still undone, the pillow on the ground.

Mom cleaned up downstairs a few days before I came home because she has a key, but I guess she forgot to check this room.

I pick up a broken frame containing a picture of me and my sister. Looking at it makes me smile even though the floor is littered with glass. Graham must've knocked it off the dresser as he pulled me through the door.

I glare at the glass in my hand, the sharpness of it almost cutting into my skin.

The pain … feeling like a long-lost memory.

"What are you doing?" The sudden sound of Bo's voice makes my heart do a backflip.

I clutch the shard as I turn around. *Nothing,* I sign.

He frowns. "You sure? There's something in your hand."

Picture broke, I sign.

I shiver and quickly discard the shard in the trash. Then I clean up the rest of the shards and throw it all into the bin. I place the broken frame on the dresser, making a mental note to go to the store to buy a new one tomorrow.

The store. Another place I haven't seen in such a long time.

Gosh, it's as if I'm reliving the entire world all over again but through a different lens.

There's the me before … and the me after.

And I'm okay with that.

I'm okay with who I've become.

Still, seeing my room untouched and left the same as before makes my smile disappear.

"Are you sure you're okay?" Bo asks as he watches me like a hawk.

I nod even though it's a lie.

I don't want him to worry.

Bo always worries about me. It's been like that since Suzie's death. He feels responsible for me now, and I get it. We're friends. He doesn't want to lose me too.

He almost did, though.

For weeks, I was gone. He didn't know if I was alive.

It must've been tough for him.

I walk to him and give him a big hug. He seems a bit stunned but accepts it anyway, placing a hand on my back too.

"If you need anything, let me know, okay?" he says, caressing me softly.

As I pull back, I nod again, and I sign, *Shower.*

"Of course. I'll just be up here cleaning." He winks.

I turn around and enter the bathroom, locking the door. Tearing off my clothes, I swallow when I see my own body in the mirror's reflection. My breasts are plumper, nipples enlarged and darker, but my stomach shows no signs.

I prod myself and stand sideways to see a bump, but there isn't any. Still, I rub my belly, knowing something's in there. Something … human. Like me. Like Cage.

Despite being a beast of a man, he was innocent in it all.

Licking my lips, I turn away from the mirror and turn off the light. Then I step underneath the shower and turn it on, letting the water cascade down my body. I shower in the dark because then I don't have to see myself in the mirror.

The warmth and pressure of the water don't equate to the shower inside the cell. It's so different from what I've experienced for the past few weeks that I can't help but let the memories filter back in.

I think back to the small cell, the hard bed, and the shower I had. The shower right next to Cage's. The shower where I first saw his naked body and that arrogant smirk of his. And how he used to look at me with such hungry eyes it was impossible for me to look away.

Those memories are just that ... memories.

None of it exists anymore.

All that is left is me, standing under a shower, alone in the dark.

I force myself to gaze down at the water pooling near my feet. I don't want to see myself in the mirror because that girl I saw ... isn't happy. And it's so clearly visible, anyone could see.

I don't want to see.

I don't want to know how sad it makes me to listen to the water drops rolling down. I don't want to realize the impact this had on my body. I don't want to feel the tears well up in my eyes and stream down my face, mixing with the water. I don't want to remember who I used to be and what I've lost. I don't want to know anything.

All I want is Cage.

He makes me happy.

But he isn't here.

How can I be free when he isn't?

How can I enjoy the life I've been given when he has none?

I can't live like this. Not while knowing there's still time ... still time to save him.

My fists clench, and I realize there's only one way to get him back.

I have to go search for him myself.

No one will do anything if I don't act.

The police will take their sweet time to set up searches, but it's time we don't have.

I'm not willing to risk it, so I'll go to them once I can and demand they start the search party and offer to go with them.

No ifs. No buts. If they refuse, then so be it.

I'll go out there into the desert alone if need be.

Anything … to save him.

THIRTY-EIGHT

Ella

The first thing I do when I step into my garden is fill my nostrils with fresh air. No matter how many times I do this, I can never appreciate it enough. After having smelled only the damp, stale scent of the prison I was in, the outside world is so much better.

My counselor said this would happen. That my emotions would fluctuate and that I'd probably experience everything on a much larger scale right now, due to being deprived for so long … and because of the pregnancy.

But talking to her in several sessions has really helped me deal with what happened to me and my emotions regarding my situation. She helps me put it away into a corner of my mind where it doesn't consume me anymore.

Even the part where I stuck a pair of scissors into Graham's throat. I've finally accepted that what I did was only a natural reaction to being locked up. And I can finally forgive myself for it.

After breathing in and out for a while, I lie down on the grass with my camera around my neck and make butterfly motions, letting the bristles of the grass flow through my fingers. I love how it feels. How the sunrays gently warm my skin. How I can hear the chirping of the birds, their songs invigorating me.

I grab my camera and take quick snapshots of everything that catches my eye. Bugs crawling on the ground. Birds chirping in the trees. The clouds in the sky. Everything and anything … because it's at these moments I find my short-lived happiness.

Placing the camera on my belly again, I sigh. I close my eyes, letting the wind wash over my face. I can't let my mind go, can't force my body to relax. Not even when I'm in my own garden, my favorite place in the world.

And I know exactly why.

"What are you doing?" Bo leans over me, gazing at me with a weird look on his face as if I'm doing something I'm not supposed to.

I shrug and get up off the ground, brushing off my pants and shirt. I feel much better now that I've had time to recuperate. I feel like I could take on the world and then some. Now is the time to act, so I march back inside and put on my coat. Then I open the front door and go to my car.

"Where are you going? I thought we were going to stay at home for a couple of more days. At least, that's what your mom told me," Bo says as he follows me around.

I pause and turn my head, beckoning him to come with me.

"Where to? You wanna go shopping?" he asks.

I shake my head.

Find Cage, I sign.

His face immediately darkens. "You want to go search for the man who was stuck in a prison with you?" he blurts out, and I nod. "No, you're still recovering."

Fine, I sign.

But I get in anyway and shut the door behind me.

He quickly opens the passenger side door and climbs in too. "What are you doing? The doctors told you to take it easy."

I shrug and sign, *I'm going to find Cage.*

"Why not leave that to the cops? I'm sure they've started a search party by now."

Because they don't know him. I do.

But no matter how much I sign, he doesn't seem to get it, so I just put the keys into the ignition and start the car.

I'm going. Choose, I sign.

He sighs out loud. "Fine, but I'm coming with you. No way am I letting you do this on your own."

I smile and step on the gas, seeing his panicked face.

Lucky for him, I'm dropping by the police station first because I want to know how the investigation is going. And as I look at Bo's face, he seems pretty okay with me driving there. The moment he realizes where I'm going as we drive up the parking lot, he relaxes a bit.

"You could've just told me you were going to the police," he says.

307

I shrug and grin, shutting off the engine and jumping out. I don't care what he or anyone else thinks. I'm not that fragile, meek little girl I used to be. I feel stronger, more capable, as if I could climb a mountain. Maybe this baby inside me is giving me the strength. It's part of Cage after all … He's a fighter and so is my baby.

"So … got a plan?" Bo asks as we walk up the steps and into the police station.

Nope, I sign.

"What?" He grabs my arm, forcing me to stop. "You can't just walk in there without a plan."

Why not? I want them to find Cage. That's it. I'm not leaving until they do something, I sign.

I jerk free of his grip and push on, determined to get them to help me. I don't care what it takes.

"Wait," Bo says as he walks after me.

I don't stop until I reach the front desk. I quickly grab the notebook along with a pen from the bag I brought with me and start writing.

I need Officer John Nelson. Urgent.

The woman at the front desk gazes at the note and then at me for a second, sighing before she turns and walks away. A few minutes later, John walks up to the desk.

"Ella. I didn't expect to see you here. You were discharged from the hospital already?"

Search party. Cage.

I write the words as quickly as possible.

He raises his hands the moment he reads them. "Listen, they're already out there doing their best. It's across state lines, you know."

Where?

I hold up the notebook.

"Nevada. I have no jurisdiction there. It's out of my hands."

Nevada? We were in Nevada? But that's more than eight hours away from here.

Where did the woman find me?

I write as fast as I can.

"Valley of Fire Highway."

My eyes widen. The red sand. That must be it.

But that place … is scorching hot.

I can't leave Cage all the way over there by himself.

Are they looking there? Scouting the area right now?

He makes a face. "I'm … sorry, Ella. I don't know. It's out of my hands. You're going to have to contact the Las Vegas bureau if you want more information, but I doubt they'll tell you anything. It's still an ongoing investigation."

Annoyed, I grimace and tear my notebook off the counter, storming back outside again.

"Ella!" Bo yells, rushing after me. "Ella, wait!"

I'm not waiting. I've waited long enough.

I don't care what state I have to drive to. I'll find him.

"Where are you going?" Bo asks as I get into the car.

Finding Cage, I sign.

And I crawl behind the wheel and put the key into the ignition. However, Bo jumps into the passenger seat again.

He looks me dead in the eye. "If you're going … then I'm going too."

***

We drive to my house only to gather a bag with supplies and clothes before we get back on the road again. I didn't want to waste too much time on packing because every single second counts right now.

Bo's in charge of the food and drinks while I drive us down the interstate, passing through several cities. We stop to take a pee break and to buy some sandwiches, but that's it.

I keep driving, no matter how many times Bo gives me that look ... that look of 'when are you going to stop this madness.' But I won't. I won't stop ... not until I've found Cage.

Not until I know he's safe.

Soon, it's getting dark, and my eyes are getting weary.

"Okay, stop. Enough," Bo protests.

I shake my head.

"You're tired; you can't drive safely. We need to rest," he says.

I shake my head again, refusing to give up. We're not there yet. I won't stop until we're there. I don't care about cops or jurisdictions or the fucking fiery sand. I just want Cage back.

"Ella. Stop. Please," Bo pleads, looking me straight in the eyes.

Those wistful, sad eyes of his are begging me to listen, and it's killing me.

I sigh and then stop alongside the road and cock my head at him. However, he's already opened the door and jumped out of the car. I frown as I watch him walk around it. For a second there, I'm almost inclined to believe he might refuse to go any farther.

But then he opens my door and beckons me to step out. "I'm not asking you to stop," he adds when I glare at him with a raised brow.

Mulling it over for a second, I think about my options. Continuing like this isn't really a problem except for the fact I can barely keep my eyes open. But I don't want to go to a motel. I don't want to sleep.

Bo clears his throat and beckons me again. "C'mon. You're in no condition to keep driving."

He does have a point even though I hate that he's right. I guess there's no other way.

Letting out a long breath, I step out of the car and walk to the passenger's side in defeat. He gets behind the wheel and stares at me while I put on my belt.

"I'll drive," he says.

I sigh, *Are you taking us to a motel?*

"I should. It's the smart thing to do," he reasons, smiling. "But we're not here to be smart. At all."

So he's going to help me? Thank God.

Thank you, Bobby, I sign.

He smiles in appreciation. "Don't thank me yet. Thank me when we find him," he says, winking, as he pulls the gear into position and drives off. "But," he adds after a while, "don't call me Bobby or our deal is off."

I grin and sign, *Got it.*

THIRTY-NINE

Ella

I'm feeding Bo snacks and drinks while he drives, making sure we only stop when necessary. I even texted Mom because she was freaking out when she found me missing from the house. It took some convincing to tell her I was fine, and she almost wanted to come and get me herself. But that's just it ... I don't need anyone to take care of me anymore.

I want to do this on my own, and I don't want her to be there. Not because I don't appreciate it or because she'd be in the way, but because I don't want her to see the true horrors of where I've been. I want to spare her the grief.

It takes hours to get to our destination, and I can't help but doze off every so often. I can't help it; my body is too tired to keep going.

However, right when I'm about to step into my dreams where I'm together with Cage again, Bo shoves my shoulder.

"We're here," he informs, waking me up abruptly.

It takes me a while to come to my senses, but the moment his words connect in my brain, my eyes fly open.

I immediately jump out of the car and gaze at the horizon.

Red sand ... as far as the eye can see.

This is exactly the place I remember; the same desert I fought my way through to get back to the land of the living.

But where do we even start looking?

Bo steps out of the car too, locking the door before he comes to stand beside me and gaze at the scene in front of him.

"This is where they found you?"

I nod.

"How did you even manage to get here? That desert stretches for miles and miles. No one could survive that."

I don't know. I guess I had an angel watching over me, I sign.

He smiles. "Or maybe you're an angel disguised as a human."

I roll my eyes, but his comment did make me grin. Bo's always had that effect on me. He manages to defuse tension with the snap of a finger—even though it isn't always appropriate. But I don't care; I like him the way he is. Just your average Joe ... or Bo, in this case.

"Okay, where do we start?" he asks.

I narrow my eyes and gaze at the road we just drove on, trying to find a point of entry. Something that could lead me to my trail. Something remotely familiar.

"Do you recognize anything?" he asks.

I shake my head.

"Maybe not here … but what about out there? Any rock formation that looks familiar?"

I stare ahead. In the distance, I see a set of breast-shaped mountains that looks odd but reminds me of something. Something I saw when I was struggling to walk, struggling to even breathe.

I point at it and mouth, "There."

"Okay, let's go," Bo says, and he immediately runs back to the car again.

I sign at him as he gets behind the wheel, *What are you doing?*

"Bringing us there," he states. "Jump in."

***

We drive as fast as humanly possible through the desert toward the mountains I described. My heart is racing in my throat as I watch them creep closer, though not nearly fast enough. I wish I could catapult myself from my seat and land near the compound, but that's wishful thinking. Who knows how far it still is. Even if we get to the mountains, there's no way it's that easy to find the compound. That's just the start of the trail.

I sit back in my seat anxiously, chewing my nails while urging Bo to hurry up. I know he wants to drive safely, and I do too, but my mind is going in circles right now. Cage is locked away somewhere deep inside that compound in the middle of fucking nowhere, and he's injured. Maybe even dead.

Shivers run all down my spine.

I hope not.

I pray to God he's still alive.

When we get to the two breast-shaped mountains, Bo stops the car, and I immediately rush out into the open terrain. Rubbing my forehead, I try to get a sense of where I am, but I have no clue. Nothing seems familiar except these two rocks.

Far away, near some other rocks, I can definitely see a bunch of cars, though ... and a whole row of people talking to each other. People in black suits with a smidge of gold.

Police officers.

My eyes widen, and I turn and sign at Bo, *There!*

He follows my finger as I point and gazes into the distance, mumbling, "Are those ... cops?"

I don't even wait for his response before I jump behind the wheel and beckon him to get inside.

"Coming," he says, and he quickly jumps in before I drive off.

I'm much faster than Bo is when it comes to driving, and it seems to scare him a little because he's holding the handles and his seat like his life depends on it.

"Slow down," he stresses. "The car's gonna flip."

I don't think it will. His fear keeps him from ever doing anything reckless. Not for me, though. I've been through hell and come back alive. I can handle rough terrain. Especially one so familiar to me.

The closer I am, the more amped I get, at which point I begin to honk. Some of the police officers turn their heads, mumbling to each other. They must wonder what I'm doing here. But I don't care about the looks I'm getting. All I want is for Cage to be safe and to come home with me. That's all I want, and I'm not leaving until I have him.

I park my car right next to a police car and jump out, throwing my door closed without even waiting for Bo to get out too. I march toward the police men with Bo chasing after me.

"Ella! Hold up," he says, but I can't wait.

"What are you doing here, ma'am? This terrain is off the tracks you're allowed to go on," one of the officers says.

I quickly take out the notepad I brought with me and write.

I'm Ella Rosenberg. I was a prisoner in the compound in this desert. Are you searching for Cage?

Some of the police officers talking amongst themselves have turned around and started walking again before I even have the chance to show them my words. Damn.

I hold it up quickly to one of the few remaining officers.

He frowns and says, "Ella? You're *the* Ella? The one from the news?"

I nod. Apparently, I'm notorious already.

"Okay. Interesting." He makes a face. "And you came all the way out here to what ...?"

"To help find Cage," Bo says, coming to my aid.

"No need, ma'am," he states, "We've already found the bunker."

My eyes widen, and I struggle to contain myself as I quickly write more words.

Where is it? Is Cage there? Is he alive?

"We don't know if he is, ma'am. We're preparing to go inside, but you have to stay here." He holds up his hand.

"We can't allow you to go inside."

"Why?" Bo asks, beating me to it.

"We don't know if it's clear for entry yet. We'll search the compound and bring out any captives. But you're not allowed to go any farther than this. Let us handle this," he says.

His radio sounds, and I can clearly hear the men saying they're going in. My heart skips a beat. The man replies, and this back-and-forth conversation goes on for a bit. Trying to peek over the man's shoulder, I'm chewing on the inside of my cheek, hoping to catch a glimpse of what's going on, but apparently, they want to keep it under tight wrap.

I await anxiously for what's going to happen next. I keep a hawk-eye on the man in front of me, who's still talking to the other officers through his radio with his back turned against us. My heart beats in my throat, and the only thing keeping me from running over there is Bo's firm fingers latched onto mine.

"Status update," the man in front of me says.

It takes a while for the other group to answer, making me almost chew my lip off.

"Nothing, sir."

My eyes widen.

"Nothing?" Bo asks.

"Everything's clear," the police officer replies.

What?

What does that mean?

How can everything be clear?

That doesn't make any sense.

"Did they find him?" Bo asks.

The man in front of us turns around again and makes a

317

face. "No, it appears the compound has been abandoned."

My jaw drops, and I sign, *No, that can't be true.*

I jerk free of Bo's grip and start running. Past the man, past the rocks. No matter how much they shout, I won't turn around. I won't go back, not until I find him. He has to be here. There's no other way.

Cage is in there; they just haven't found him yet.

When I get over a hill, the compound is in clear view, and it makes me take a gulp of air. Still, I push on, unafraid of the place that was my prison for so long.

I rush to the big, iron doors and go inside, letting them slam shut behind me. The lights flicker and there are cobwebs everywhere. There are also dirty footprints on the floor—black ... or maybe even red.

I push on and go through the corridors, through the red room, up the stairs, and through more corridors. I know exactly where to find him. I don't have to look anywhere else.

I can hear the police men downstairs. Through the small windows, I can see them walk around the fighting ring area, but no one else is there. They won't find a thing down there.

I also know why ... They're searching in the wrong place.

I quickly open the door in front of me and run straight for the iron bolted door with the keypad next to it. I smash my fists onto the door screaming, "Cage!"

It's the first time in hours that I hear my own voice again.

Except, no matter how hard I call for his name, he doesn't respond.

"Cage, please!" I plead with him, hoping, begging he's

still alive.

Tears well up in my eyes as I smash the door with my fists, wishing I could break through.

After a few minutes, the police officers enter this room, pointing their guns at me. I put my hands in the air and beckon them toward the door.

"Move!" the first one yells, and I step aside.

Another one grabs me and pulls me with him into the small chamber that used to be Graham's office, but now it's littered with paper and thrown aside furniture because of me. Because of my escape.

"What are you doing in here? Are you one of the captives? Or did you get in another way?"

I nod and shake my head, walking to the desk so I can grab a piece of paper and a pen and write.

I used to be locked up in here. Ella Rosenberg. Cage is in there, behind that door.

I hold it up to him and point at the door, which the other officers are breaking open right now.

They stick a small explosive to the back of the door and yell at each other. The one guy inside the office with me shuts the door and holds me close. A bang ensues.

I struggle to breathe.

Did they get it open?

I can hear them walk. The metallic door makes that familiar creaking sound.

I quickly free myself from the man's grasp and rush through that same door and into the room where I was held for weeks.

But I am not prepared for seeing the glass prison with my own eyes again.

Not prepared for the bloody stains on the windows and walls. Handprints.

Drops all over the concrete floor.

Cage is nowhere to be found.

FORTY

CAGE

Days ago

With every ounce of my strength, I throw the broken piece of metal that I ripped off the bed against the glass. It doesn't even leave a scratch. It bounces off the glass like it's made of the same material as my bedding.

I groan and move to the bed again, ripping off another piece. Every inch of my body hurts, but I need to keep going. Need to keep trying.

For Ella.

For me.

For *my* freedom. *My* life.

I need to be with her. I promised her I'd live. And the only way to make that happen is to break this prison surrounding me.

So I fling another piece of metal at the glass, hoping it'll stick, but it clatters to the floor like everything else I've thrown at the cage.

Why can I not break through?

No one is as strong as I am, yet I still cannot get through this fucking cage.

It doesn't make any sense, yet in some fucked-up way, it does. Because Graham intentionally made it that way. He made it so strong that even I couldn't break through. So he could keep me in here forever.

I spit on the ground and pick up the metal and start ramming it into the ground, hoping I can maybe dig a way through, just as Ella described when she talked about digging holes in the dirt when she was younger. I don't know what dirt is or what it feels like, but if it's anything like this concrete ground, it means she pulled off something even I can't do. Because no matter how many times I strike the ground with an object and with as much ferocity as I can muster, it still won't leave a mark.

What do I do?

What would she do if she were in my situation?

She'd exploit it and run. Of course, but how?

She's so smart, and I'm … me.

When my strength fails me like this, I have nothing left to turn to. And it pisses me off.

In a fury, I roar and pick up the entire goddamn bed, ripping it from the bolts in the concrete ground, and I chuck it at the glass cage.

The metal sounds screech as half of it falls apart.

However, the other half has made a clear dent in the

window.

A small fracture, as tiny as a hair.

I narrow my eyes and stare at it for a second, wondering if I can do anything with this. If this is the cage's weak spot, I wonder if I'll be able to smash it to bits.

However, the pain in my stomach makes it so hard to raise my arm to even try, so instead, I close my eyes and wait, hoping the pain will subside.

I can't give up.

She wouldn't.

And I said I would never give up on her either.

When I open my eyes again, I wonder if I'm asleep.

Because the door just opened … and my father is stumbling in.

Blood follows wherever his footsteps go. His entire body is covered in it.

My eyes widen.

He's alive.

Since Ella escaped, I assumed he was dead or gone.

But this? I never expected this.

He clutches his throat tightly as he pulls something from his pocket and presses it. A clicking sound is audible. I turn around. My door was opened.

With an unsteady hand, he beckons me, and I walk out of the door immediately, not even thinking about staying inside the cell.

Even if it's my home, I won't miss it. Not even for a second.

I move through the bedroom and out into the main area where he is.

For a split second, I think of attacking him. Of biting

my way through his flesh and pulling out his tongue. Of ripping off his head and cracking his skull against the concrete wall.

But then I realize … he's the only one who knows how the outside world works.

If I'm going to survive there, I need him too.

As I approach, he pulls a knife from his pocket and points it at me with a shaky hand as if that's going to do anything. He's wounded. He's no match for me.

I narrow my eyes at the sight of his throat. It seems punctured … severely.

With his hand, he beckons me to come, and he turns around again, barely able to walk. He's not going anywhere like this.

So I quickly catch up to him and nudge my shoulder under his arm, supporting part of his weight. I hate I have to do this—hate it with every fiber of my being—because I want nothing more than to pull his hand away from his neck and let the blood gush out.

But that wouldn't be of much help to me right now.

I need to think like Ella. Be smart. Calculating. And when needed … vicious.

She was smart to have stabbed him and escaped.

Now the smart thing to do is to let him guide me.

I can always kill him later when I see fit.

He groans and sputters as we walk out of the room and into the hallway. I help him get through the hallway and carry him down the stairs. He points at a room I've never been to, but I go in there anyway. There must be a reason he wants me to. However, when I go inside, I'm momentarily fazed by the strange bed and equipment lying around the room. Sharp, metallic objects are everywhere, needles, and straps.

Is this where he kept her?

Where he did things to her that made her want to kill him?

It must be.

However, there's no time to think about it. We have to get out of here.

Father points at something lying on the desk, a set of keys, so I snatch them. Then I help him walk out again. As we pass the area where the food is prepared, I quickly grasp a cloth I see hanging from a rack and I hand it to him so he can cover his wound.

As he wraps it around and keeps pressure on it, we make our way outside.

A blinding light forces me to stop.

It's so hot and yellow that I cringe and take a step back.

"What *is* that?" I growl, wanting to cover my face and my body.

"Sun," he gurgles, shutting his mouth right after. It must hurt to talk with a hole in your throat.

I can't stop looking at it. Can't stop wanting to get closer and let it burst onto my skin with heat. But Father grabs my arm and drags me along to the back of the compound to a shiny, metallic thing. I recognize it from the pictures Ella drew. A truck.

He opens the door and gets inside, urging me to get in too. But the moment I sit down on the empty seat, I feel overwhelmed. This thing has a wheel and more odd shapes on the floor near my feet, and I have no clue what to do with them.

Father jams the keys into a slit and twists it. Something begins to rumble. Then he smashes my knee down on the pedal, and the truck suddenly moves forward. It bobs back and forth, stuttering as I try to adjust to the feel of driving this thing. That's what Ella called it. Driving. Does she know how to do it? If so, she's even more impressive than I thought.

As we cross the red ground, I wonder where I've ended up. Seeing the outside world for the first time is menacing. I never expected it to be this ... red. And dirty. And rocks are everywhere.

Where is the green grass Ella told me about? The luscious trees and the rippling rivers? Where are the animals, the plants?

All I see are seemingly dead shrubs, twigs, and the occasional bird flying high in the sky.

The rest seems ... awfully dead.

Is this just part of the world? Will there be more? I hope so.

I love the sky, though. It's just as pretty as Ella described it to me with the white clouds contrasting the stark blue.

Still, I don't know where we're going, and I don't know how long it will take. Judging by the blood-drenched cloth bound around Father's throat, he won't hold out much longer.

I need to know where to go. Otherwise, I'll never find Ella.

"Where?" I growl.

He just waves his hand toward something in the distance.

Something flat and concrete-like. A road?

I make my way toward it and drive the truck as fast as I can, despite the rocky terrain. When we finally get there, the sudden flatness of the road surprises me. It's a lot different from the strange, red ground. Ella once told me a lot of people use these roads to travel from place to place, but I don't see anyone. Where are the people?

I keep driving in the direction Father pointed at, not knowing where I'm going. I've never felt this lost in my life, but it doesn't matter as long as we get where we need to be. He's the only one who knows how to get to where the people are. Where Ella might be.

He points at a sign on the road with letters that spell out Las Vegas, so I'm assuming he wants me to drive there even though I have no clue what it means.

The drive takes ages, and the more time that passes, the more that bright thing in the sky goes down. I wonder if it'll go out completely because it's getting less hot in here too.

That's a good thing, considering the fact Father is barely awake. His eyes open slowly, and his mouth seems dry and his face white. As long as he doesn't die before we get to where we need to be, I'm good.

In front of me, a huge mountain of buildings like the compound comes into view but much bigger. So tall and wide that my eyes widen at the sight of them. They're plastered with colors, bright, flashing lights, and quick moving images like the ones my father used to play in the bedroom but with clothes.

The closer we get, the more cars like ours become visible with lots of different colors and sizes too. And people are driving them too, going back and forth across the many roads. It looks complicated and messy.

I wonder if I can even get through them without hurting anyone.

"Sign," Father mumbles, spurting blood from his lips. "Hospital."

He keeps pointing at something on the boards we pass that are standing alongside the road and hanging above, so I assume he wants me to follow them.

We're lucky Ella taught me how to read, even if it's only a little bit, because I can definitely recognize the word 'Hospital' plastered on the signs.

I drive as slowly as possible to get a sense of where I'm going because this entire thing—this city or whatever Ella called it—is so damn huge and I panic if I think about it. So many different things are happening at once. Music coming from all directions, honking and screeching noises coming from cars, people yelling and screaming, flickering colored lights everywhere. It's dizzying, but I won't give up trying to find my way through. Not now, not ever.

I might not understand a thing about this world, but that won't stop me from trying.

I drive through the lanes and across some grass parts until we get to a building with an 'H' on the top, and I park the truck somewhere close.

Father pulls the keys out, opens the door, and stumbles out.

However, he doesn't get far.

Three steps and he's already flopped down face first onto the concrete.

So what do I do now?

FORTY-ONE

Ella

Present

I sit in the car with Bo's arms wrapped around me, but I still feel cold and alone. I don't know how to cope with what I'm feeling right now because the emptiness in my heart is too big a hole for him to fill. Even though I'm thankful Bo is here right now and supporting me, it doesn't take away the fact that I feel so lost.

Everything I've done the past few days was for this moment. This entire journey was so I could see Cage again. But he isn't here. Where do I look if I don't know where to start? My hope is starting to wane.

I dab my eyes with his shirt and shake my head, signing,

Sorry.

"It's okay. Cry all you want," Bo says, petting the back of my head.

I nod and smile, looking up at him. I don't know what to do now. Where to go. Should we go home? Should we drive around the country to look for Cage? How far could he have gone?

I wish I knew, wish I had some sort of clue, but there's nothing.

Nothing apart from the fact that the second vehicle that was apparently behind the compound, which I completely missed when I escaped, is gone. The police officers knew it was there because they found tire tracks. However, the farther they tracked them into the desert, the more they disappeared in the shifting sand. The wind caused the tracks to vanish, and now we have no lead. Nothing to go on.

I didn't even get time to see if anything was left of him or my time in that cage. The moment the officers grabbed me, they brought me outside, refusing to even answer the most basic questions, like how Cage even managed to escape.

I don't know what to do with myself now that he's gone.

All I can do is sit here and think ... think about what to do next.

"Wanna go home?" Bo asks after a while as I look up into his eyes.

I nod, but before I can respond by signing, I clutch my stomach. It suddenly hurts so badly, as if a sharp knife has been thrust into my belly and pokes around my insides.

"What's wrong?" Bo asks, but I don't even have the energy to talk right now; the pain is too intense.

What's happening to me?

I never felt anything like this before.

"Ella ..." Bo says, his voice stern and calm at the same time. "Tell me what's wrong."

I pull my hand away from my stomach and lift my shirt, but nothing is there.

Until I lower my eyes to my pants ... and find the bloodstain.

My eyes widen.

"Fuck," Bo hisses, gazing right at it. "You're bleeding."

Shit.

He's right.

I'm bleeding.

Oh God, is it the baby?

I rub my stomach again and hold it tight as Bo turns in his seat and twists the key, starting the engine. "I'm taking you to the hospital," he says.

I nod, but everything hurts, so I try to focus on my breathing. I have to relax, have to give my body time. I can't lose this baby; I have to do everything I can to avoid that.

This baby is my only ... no, my *last* connection to Cage.

I clutch the dashboard as Bo drives off, rushing through the unkempt desert and crossing the wobbly terrain. The pain shoots up and down my body, and I tense up, trying to fight it, trying to fight for this baby.

But the longer it takes, the more blood I see pooling in my pants.

I'm beyond worried right now, but I can't do anything but sit and wait, hoping this baby is still alive by the time we get to the hospital.

So I focus and put all my energy into surviving.

Because that's all we can do in times like these … survive.

***

When we get to the hospital, Bo brings me inside, and two nurses immediately come to our aid with a wheelchair. They wheel me to a bed in the ER, and a doctor inspects my body and the blood. Before my pants are taken off, they ask Bo to leave the room.

I'm afraid, so afraid. I can't stop grasping the railings of my bed and the sheets below me, trying to hold something, anything as they inspect me.

They probe me with tools. I don't know what it is, but it feels horrible, and it makes me cry. It reminds me of what happened at the compound, but the second I think about it, I shut out the memories, forcing myself to think of a happier place. My garden, my house, the town. Anything.

Someone does an ultrasound of my baby. Another one inspects my pants and cleans up the bloody mess. I hear some words spoken, but they barely register. My whole body is shaking.

Tears roll down my cheeks as I hear the news.

Relief washes over me. I'm still pregnant.

The baby is still alive.

But it was a close call.

Just like that. With the snap of a finger, he or she could've been gone.

My body stressed out to the point it almost gave up. Stressed out … because of me. Because I focused so much on finding Cage and forgot to focus on my baby.

With a flat hand, I rub my belly and hum, hoping the baby can hear.

I'm sorry. I'm so sorry.

I neglected myself, and I almost paid the ultimate price.

But the joy I feel knowing it's still alive makes me sure of my choice. Sure of Cage.

I want him, and I want this baby. More than anything.

The nurse says everything is okay, but that I need to take it slow and get some rest. She asks me if I'm in pain and whether I want some pills. I shake my head and close my eyes, lying down on the bed. She nods and cleans everything up while I lie there clutching my shirt.

She says it happens a lot with stressed-out women. That it's normal. That there was nothing I or anyone else could do.

As if that makes it all better.

I came so close to losing my baby. I'm terrified.

Terrified it'll happen again.

That it'll just fall out of me somehow. It's ridiculous and totally ludicrous, but I still have this fear I can't shake off. I have to be more careful.

The nurse hands me a wet towel to clean myself with while she grabs a bag to put my dirty clothes in. She brings back a new pair of pants that Bo probably got from my bag and places them on the chair. Then she puts a big paper towel over my lower body, covering it up. She wants me to take the time before I put on the fresh pair of pants. Give my body some time to recover.

She wipes off the blood from the bed and chucks everything away. The room is pristine clean again as if nothing happened. Then she leaves me alone.

I hug my body, hoping the baby can feel my love. The last sliver of Cage is living inside me and growing. I don't want it to stop.

Shivering, I turn around on the bed and curl up into a ball, crying to myself from all the pent-up stress. I stay, unmoving. My body feels crushed by the weight of my heart.

A creaking noise makes my eyes fly open, but I don't turn around. I can't find the will.

Soft footsteps come my way. A warm embrace follows. Someone sat down on my bed and arms wrapped around me. Bo.

I don't even care that he can see me, that a thin sheet of blue paper is all that covers my lower body, and that my face is red and tired.

I need him.

I need someone to hold me, someone to take this fear away. Someone who understands what I'm going through and won't judge me.

I turn around, and he pulls me into his embrace. I hold Bo for the last shred of dignity I have left. I cry into his shirt. I cry and cry until my tears dry out. Until my heart has finally let go of the sadness and fear that strangled it for so long.

After crying my heart out, I look up into Bo's eyes and sign, *Thank you.*

"The baby?" he mutters, looking concerned.

I smile softly and sign, *Alive.*

He closes his eyes and lets out a sigh. Then he pulls me in for another hug.

"You gave me quite the scare," he says.

I nod.

I gave myself quite a scare too.

But now that it happened, I've finally come to terms with the fact I'm not alone. I have his baby, and I have Bo. He's the most amazing friend I could ever wish for, and I know he'll help me take care of this baby even if I never find Cage again.

But I won't ever go back on my promise.

I will keep looking.

No matter how long it takes.

I'll find him.

FORTY-TWO

CAGE

Days ago

I was dragging my father's body toward the building with the H on it when a bunch of people came out to pull him away from me. They put him on a moving table and drove him inside, and then they pushed me inside too. They separated me from him and brought me into a room with a bed.

I wanted to leave, but my body felt so weak, and I could barely move. The wounds on my body weighed me down, and I wasn't able to stay upright.

So I lie down anyway, despite my mistrust of this place.

I didn't know what a hospital was, and I was incredibly

confused when they started to tear off my clothes. At first, I was angry because no one should touch me that way except Ella. Until I saw the familiar cotton balls and alcohol being pulled out of a drawer, and I realized they were going to fix my wounds.

They sewed up the open wounds and put on some stinging substance that probably cleans it. Then they wrapped me up and had me put on new blue clothes, which are surprisingly thin.

I was told I needed to stay a day or two to heal, and that if I needed anything, I should call. I had no clue how things worked, so I waited until they came to feed me. After about two days, I felt strong enough to walk again, and I decided it was time to leave.

The nurses were so busy with the other people, and I didn't want to bother them, so I walked out on my own. I didn't need help with that, but what I did need help with was finding my father.

But no matter how many times I asked a woman at some desk, she refused to answer. She kept telling me no one with his name was in the hospital, which didn't make sense. And she kept looking at me like I was asking the strangest thing, so after a while, I just left. Just in time because some beefy dudes were headed my way, probably to throw me out. Not that they would've ever won in a fight with me, but I don't want to hurt anyone if I can avoid it.

Especially since Ella asked me not to injure anyone if I didn't have to.

And now I'm here, in the middle of some city I don't know, with so many people, and I don't even know who to ask for help.

There are too many people, too many noises around me, and I'm panicking. Like I want to get out. I've never seen this much before, taken in this much information, and it's too overwhelming to cope with.

I need to get out of here. Fast.

***

I march toward the nearest car I see running and bark at the owner who's sitting in the driver's seat playing with a strange device in his hand. "Drive me to Ella," I growl.

"What?" The guy looks up at me with furrowed brows. "Who the fuck are you?"

"I need Ella," I say. "You know where?"

"Fuck, dude, what the fuck do you want from me?" the guy snaps, and he tries to slam his door shut, but I keep it open. "Get your hands off my car."

"No," I say, bending over to take a good look at him. "Take me out of here."

"Fuck no. Get a cab, motherfucker." He slams the door shut.

I jump away from the car as he immediately drives backward, the tires almost running over my feet. Before I can even say a word, he's already driven the car off the parking lot.

Well, fuck.

Are all people like that?

I hope not.

I try again with someone else, an older lady who's packing things into the back of her car, and this time, I cut to the point. "I need a ride," I say.

She turns around, looking confused. "Sorry?"

"Take me out of this city?" I ask.

"Well ..." She frowns. "Couldn't you call a cab for that?"

"Cab?" I repeat. What is that, and why does everyone keep saying it?

"You don't know what a cab is?" She smiles. "Oh, honey. Where are you from?"

"Red sand."

"Red sand?" She gives me a funny look. "Well, all right." She closes the trunk and walks to the front. "I'll make this my good deed for the day. Get in."

I nod and immediately walk to the wheel, but she stops me before I get there.

"Whoa, where are you going?"

"Car." I point at the front seat.

"No, no," she replies, laughing again. "I'll drive. It's my car."

I shrug, not understanding what the problem is, but all right. I walk around the car and sit down in the other seat. As she perches herself behind the wheel, she says, "But you'd better not try anything with me, or I'll use my pepper spray on you, got it?" she muses, holding up some kind of can. "I also know three different styles of Kung-Fu, just so you know."

I don't know what any of that is, but I don't care. I'm not looking for trouble.

I hold up my hands. "No fight here."

"Good," she says, nodding and then tucking the can into her purse. "Now where do you want to go?"

"Out of this city," I say.

"But where to?"

I think about it for a second, but then I realize I don't even know the answer.

Ella never told me where she lived.

The only thing I remember is her talking about the many trees and the green grass and rivers. But when I look around, there are no rivers or green grass. So it has to be somewhere else. Somewhere less hot with much less red sand, probably. She never mentioned any sand.

"Forest," I say. That's where I need to be. Somewhere with lots of trees.

"A forest?" She giggles again. "Boy, you don't make any sense. There are tons of forests, but none of them are in Nevada. You're outta luck, kid."

"Nevada?"

"Yeah, the state?" she says. "Gosh, it's like you crawled out from under a rock or something."

Maybe. I did come out of the compound in the desert, which was very rocky.

"So what forest do you need to go to? I might be able to help you out if you're specific."

I shrug, not knowing the answer to her question.

"Sierra National Forest? Eldorado? Plumas?" She keeps naming stuff I don't recognize. It's all names, but nothing comes to mind when I think about them. Ella never said anything except that it might be somewhere close to a creek.

"Creek. Trees," I add. I definitely remember her saying something about a creek ... and some type of tree. A willow. But I don't know what it looks like.

"A creek? Hmm ..." She ponders it for a second. "Well, California has a ton of creeks. Although not all of them have that many trees if you're talking about a big forest." She snorts. "Must be somewhere up north."

She's probably right, but that doesn't make it any easier to know where I'm going. Are there so many places in the outside world that even the people living there have no clue where I need to go?

"Tell you what, I'll just drive you to the border, and then you can find a different ride from Primm. That's where I'm headed anyway," she says, starting the engine. "My girls from the bingo club are waiting for me there. We're gonna up our game a little, try out the slot machines at the casino and maybe even the blackjack table." She grins, looking my way, as if I'm supposed to know what that means.

She waves. "Ah, forget it." And then she puts the car in reverse and drives off the parking lot.

***

She drives us all the way to Primm as promised where she jumps out of the vehicle to go to the big building, leaving me stranded outside. She invited me to come along with her, said she enjoyed my company, but I don't want to waste any time in a place I know Ella isn't going to be.

I have to find her; that's my number one priority right now.

The old lady gave me a hint, saying I should go to the hotel on the other side of the road and ask for a cab there. They would be able to help me. So I did exactly what she said, but the people at the front desk kept looking at me as if I was some kind of monster.

Maybe it's because I'm wearing some clothes and shoes

341

the old lady bought for me back in Las Vegas. She kept saying I needed to change because I still had a hospital outfit on, but I didn't mind. It was nice and breezy. But the old lady wouldn't take it, so I ended up changing into some bright blue shorts and a pink shirt.

I don't care what I'm wearing. I just want to get where I need to be.

But boy … people sure are making it difficult.

When I finally get a cab, I hop inside and tell him I need to go to the next nearest town in California because that's apparently where we are, according to what the old lady said.

We drive all the way to Barstow, but that still doesn't have trees or rivers, so I tell him to keep driving north, exactly to where the old lady said I should go.

We don't stop until we get to an area that has more trees and grass in it, but it still doesn't look like what Ella described. However, the driver refuses to go any farther, so I get out and start walking.

He rolls down the window and shouts something about money at me, but I don't know what that is, and I don't have it. So I keep walking until the cab is out of sight and I'm closer to the trees.

I don't care how far I have to walk or how deep I have to go.

I'll keep going until I find her.

Until I find my Ella.

FORTY-THREE

Ella

Present

I've flown home. Bo didn't want me to go home by car because it would take too long, and I needed to rest in a safe place. The only place I trust—home. The people at the hospital agreed, so I reluctantly agreed.

Bo drove the car all the way back without me. It took him two days because he had to stop on the way to sleep, or he would've been a danger on the road.

Meanwhile, I contacted my parents and told them about everything that happened. Of course, they came straight to my house after our conversation.

Mom didn't want me to be alone while I went through

all the stress, probably worried just as much as I was that I'd lose the baby. Dad was his usual non-talkative self, which was fine because he preferred to work with his hands. In this case, he cleaned my garage and picked up groceries for me, while also helping Mom clean the house again.

I apologized profusely for putting them in this situation, but Mom wouldn't accept it. She just told me to stay in bed. Even brought me soup and hot drinks to spoil me.

I'm grateful they're so understanding and helpful.

When Mom comes up again with more bread and a homemade stew, I smile and roll over in my bed.

"Hey honey, how are you feeling?" she asks.

"Better after smelling that," I muse. "Looks yummy."

"Made it especially for you," she replies, setting down the plate and cup on my nightstand.

I sit up straight in bed, perching a pillow behind my back, and then spoon some stew into my mouth. It's delicious. Exactly how I remember it from way back when. A taste of childhood and forgotten dreams. Good dreams. Good memories.

I narrow my eyes when I see her staring at me, grinning. "And?"

I knew she only made this to take my mind off other things … like my baby … or Cage.

Because we can all lie about it and say I don't think about him at all, but that's not true. I think about going out there every single day. This fragile body of mine carrying another life is the only thing stopping me.

"It's good, Mom," I say as I put the stew down and pick up the bread to take a bite. "Best you ever made."

She chuckles. "Oh, you don't have to shower me with

compliments."

"I do," I say.

She holds up her hand. "Don't be silly."

"Because you're here, helping me," I add.

She grabs my hand. "You're my daughter. I don't even have to think about it. Helping you is second nature."

I smile. "Thanks, Mom."

For a second, we stare into each other's eyes, then she comes closer and pulls me into her embrace. "You know I love you. Always."

I blink away the tears in my eyes. "I know. I love you too."

"And I'll help you with whatever you need. Anything. Just let me know, okay? Don't go off on your own again. Please."

I pull out of her arms and shake my head. "I can't do that. I don't want to be stuck in this house all day. I want to go out into the world."

"But can't you … I don't know, do something safer? Like taking your pictures?" She points at the camera lying on my bedside stand.

I haven't touched it in days. I know I'm supposed to take photos and send them to my editors so they can include them in the magazines, but I'm just too tired. Too restless to work.

Luckily, they've given me some much-needed time off, but it still doesn't help when Mom points it out. I know I can do something else, but the thing is … I don't want to.

I want to find Cage.

"Taking pictures won't help me find Cage, Mom," I reply. "I have to keep searching."

"But you can't. The doctor said you needed rest," she cautions, cocking her head as she gazes down at my belly.

"I know, but that's not going to be forever. I'm not going to lie in bed for nine months. I feel much better already, so I don't think it'll be long before I'm up on my feet again," I say.

"And then you're going to go out there to look for him again? How? You said it yourself that you don't know where he is," she says.

"I don't know." I frown. "I'll figure it out. But I'm not giving up. I'd rather search the rest of my life than live with regret. Than live … knowing I didn't give it my all."

The words fall so hard that I struggle to breathe, so I cough.

She licks her lips, soaking in my words before opening her mouth again. "Then let me come with you. Let me help you."

I smile as she pulls me in for another hug. "I know you want to help, Mom, and I appreciate it." But I don't want to make any promises I can't keep. Especially not to her.

This is my burden to bear, my responsibility. I can't ask her to come along. She's old and even more fragile than I am. I can't do that to her, but I can't say no either.

I hope she won't be mad at me for too long if I suddenly decide to get up and leave to go search again.

She'll just have to forgive me.

***

The next day, Bo comes to visit me. I'm already up from the bed, putting away some clothes after folding them, when he knocks on my bedroom door.

"Hello?" He holds up a basket of fruit that he brought. "Thought I'd bring a gift for the sick young lady."

I grin and sign, *Thank you. Those look delicious.*

"So how are you feeling? Better?" he asks as I put away the last of the clothes and sit down on the bed.

Better, I sign. *Good enough to go out again.*

"Out? Where?" He folds his arms as he leans against the door.

Searching for Cage, I sign.

He frowns. "Whoa, hold up. You just came back from trying to find him, and now you wanna go out there again?"

I shrug. I'm doing it anyway whether he likes it or not.

"You're serious?" he adds as if he still doesn't believe it.

I nod. I've never been more serious.

In fact, I've already started packing.

"No, wait up. You can't do this," he protests, holding up his hand. "The doctors said you needed rest."

I need to find him, I sign fast and heavily.

I don't want him to get in my way, but I get that he's worried. Still, finding Cage is more important to me right now.

"Please, Ella," he says, perched against the door like he's going to stop me from going. "You have to stop this."

No, I sign. *I refuse to give up.*

"But it's dangerous."

Cage is in danger too, I add. *I won't abandon him.*

When I try to leave, he blocks the door.

Please move, I sign.

He just stands there and stares me down. "Please don't do this, Ella."

347

I make a face.

"You think I'm messing around, but I'm not. I care about you. I thought if I went with you and helped you that you'd be safe, but you're not. You still want to put yourself in danger. I can't let you do this," he says.

It's not up to you what I do, I sign.

Bo's face darkens. "And you're willing to risk your life for a man you don't even know beyond the walls of a prison cell?"

I know Cage, I sign. *He's a good man.*

"Good?" Bo scoffs. "He got you pregnant … while you weren't even free."

I frown. Is he saying what I think he's saying?

"Call it what you want, but to me, getting someone pregnant in a cell means it's—"

I place a finger on his lips and sign, *Don't use that word.*

I know what he was about to say. I won't allow it.

"Isn't it the truth?"

I shake my head and sign, *I love him.*

Bo grimaces, his body tensing up. "After mere weeks? This is insane, Ella, and you know it."

I don't want to listen to this. I don't want to hear it. *Let me through,* I sign.

"Are you being forced or something? Is that it?" he asks.

No, I sign, shaking my head vehemently. *Leave.*

His posture loosens, and he steps away from the door.

"Fine, if that's how you feel about it …"

I don't respond. I just march out the door, not even caring if he stays inside or not.

Whether or not Bo agrees, I'm going to find Cage.

FORTY-FOUR

Ella

As I sit in my car, I contemplate what to do and where to go.

Cage could be anywhere. He doesn't know the world as I do; he doesn't know how it works. How to make use of it.

For all I know, he could still be stuck in Las Vegas. But that would be unlike him. He'd never sit and wait for me ... He'd come looking for me. He'd walk all the way here if he had to; I know it.

In fact, I think he might already be in this state too. But where? And how do I start looking?

There has to be something ... something he knows. Something I told him.

Something that makes him think of me.

The forests.

I mentioned them a lot.

And the river. The creek.

I know I mentioned my town to him somewhere in our conversations, but did he remember it?

My heart beats faster with every thought that rushes through my head.

I feel like I'm so close, I could almost grasp him. If only I knew where to start. It's like a hidden trail, and all I have to do is find the first clue.

It has to be the forests. If he remembered them ... and if he only remembered the word creek ... he has to be somewhere close.

At least within a two-hundred-mile radius. It's the only thick forest around, and I'm sure he must've asked someone for directions to a forest.

It's the only way.

He has to be here. *Somewhere.*

And the only way to pinpoint his exact location is by asking the locals if they've seen something.

So I make a plan. At the local print shop, I get a few thousand copies of the same message. It's a note with a question about whether anyone has seen a man who calls himself Cage and might be injured. I describe his features and even drew a picture of him from my own memory, hoping it'll suffice. All that, along with my email and phone number on more than a thousand papers.

One by one, I stick them to the poles alongside the road, and I ask stores if they can hang up one of the papers on the front of their shop. Everywhere I go, I ask people if they've seen someone like him or heard anyone else discuss anything that sounds familiar.

For some reason, a few vans have been following me on my journey for the past few hours. I'm guessing they're news reporters because they sometimes jump out of their vehicle with a camera and microphone in their hands, but I've quickly learned to outpace them.

Back when I first came home, they were on the property so many times, it was ridiculous, and the only way to deal with them was to shut them out completely. Ignore and they'll go away, so I'm applying that same mantra now.

I continue my search, driving through all the towns and visiting every store and every home. I don't care how many doors I have to knock on, or how many wooden poles I have to staple, or how far the news crews follow me. I don't even care about rain falling from above as the thunder cracks open the skies.

I'll keep searching, completely soaked if I have to.

Water can't hurt me and neither can trying as hard as possible.

Besides, the reporters are staying inside their vans now that it's raining, which is a plus for me even though they're still following my every move.

Out of nowhere, a bike suddenly appears, and it's racing toward me. Bo's on it, and he stops in front of me. "Ella."

I don't turn. I keep walking, ignoring him completely. I have no time for this. He can try to persuade me to go home all he wants, but I won't. He'll be wasting both our time.

"Listen," he says, walking next to me with his bike in his hand. "I ... I wanted to say I'm sorry."

I pause and gaze at him.

He licks his lips. "About what I said earlier ..." His eyes

dart to the ground, afraid to even look at me. "It was stupid, and I wanted to apologize."

It´s hard to keep ignoring him if he's sorry. He followed me all the way out here just to say he was sorry. How could I not forgive him?

I place a hand on his shoulder and lower my head to look into his eyes, and I mouth, "Thank you."

He smiles tentatively. "You're not mad at me?"

I raise a brow, a half-smile forming on my lips.

Maybe not. As long as you don't tell me to stop looking for Cage, I sign.

He throws his helmet onto his wheel and nods. "Okay. If this is really what you want … I'll help you look for him."

I frown. **Really?**

He nods "Yeah." Then he places his bike against a pole and chains it to it.

I sign, **How did you know I was here?**

He shrugs. "I just went from town to town until I saw your car."

It's impressive even though he makes it seem as if it's no big deal.

"Give me some flyers and I'll start handing them out," he says.

I appreciate him changing his mind, though. And I get that he wants to make it up to me, so I hand him a stack of flyers to begin with.

"Thanks. I'll start posting these around and handing them to all the shops. I'll start here and go west, okay?"

I nod. **You're okay with the rain?**

"Yeah, of course." He grins, but I sense a deeper undertone I can't quite put my finger on.

The moment fades, and he clears his throat, adding, "Well, I'll get started then."

Thank you, I sign. **I really appreciate it.**

"It's no problem. Really. I wanna help," he says, winking. "Well, let me know if you hear anything." He briefly holds up his cell phone, indicating I should text him, before tucking it back into his pants and turning around to walk away.

I do too, starting at the east of the town, going from house to house. No building is skipped. With my notebook and pen in hand, I ask people questions, showing them the flyers I printed. None of it works.

The longer I keep searching, the more I'm starting to lose hope. I've lost count of the number of towns I've been to already. No one I speak to has ever heard his name or seen the man I described. Everyone gives me weird looks as if I'm searching for a needle in a haystack. And that's okay because I am. But no one could possibly understand how valuable that needle is to me.

When it's almost evening and my stomach is growling, I pause and sit down on a bench not far from my home. I'm too hungry to keep going, and I have to think of my own body too for the sake of the baby.

So I munch on a sandwich that I bought at the local coffee shop and watch the people walking in the streets, clutching their raincoats and umbrellas tight. They gaze at me as if I've lost my mind as I sit in the rain, enjoying the drops falling onto my face. I don't mind. It's hard to explain what it feels like to feel rain again after being stuck in a prison cell for so long. Nothing feels more right. More welcome.

My body comes alive in the pitter-patter, the spats cascading down my face, the dark sky a gentle reminder that I'm free again. There's only one problem left to solve before I'm complete again.

Suddenly, I spot a little girl standing right next to me, frowning as she cocks her head at me.

She squints and asks, "What are you doing?"

I hold up my sandwich.

"But it's raining."

I shrug.

"Do you talk at all?" she asks after a while.

I shake my head.

"Oh … so you can't or you don't want to?" she asks, sitting down beside me.

I mouth, "Both," to her.

She nods. "Interesting. I've never met anyone who can't talk."

I smile at her, but I do wonder what she's doing here. Isn't she supposed to go to school or something?

When I hear other girls giggling, I peer over my shoulder and notice they're all looking at this little girl. Gossiping about her. Maybe they were even making fun of her. No wonder she walked off.

"Ignore them," she says. "They're mean."

I nod slowly. I can see why. I used to have those girls at my school too. Always teasing others. It's a vicious cycle that never ends, no matter how old we get.

As I finish my lunch, the girl points at my bag and asks, "What's in there?"

Taking a deep breath, I grasp one of the papers in my bag. Maybe this little girl can help me. It's worth a shot.

I hold up the paper to her and point at all the questions at the top so she understands what it says.

"Are you looking for that man?" she asks.

I nod again.

She bites her lip and narrows her eyes, and I expect her to say those familiar words that I've heard all day long. No, she hasn't seen him, or she doesn't even know who this is.

But when she opens her mouth, my heart stops for a second.

"Oh ... I think I know where he is."

My eyes widen, and I immediately grasp her shoulders, mouthing, "Where?"

I'm almost shaking her—that's how eager I am to know where he is, how much I want for her words to be true. But she seems overtaken by my enthusiasm, her lips parting, her eyes growing big with fright.

I try to relax, focusing on getting her to tell me, so I look her directly in the eyes and make a hand motion to ask for more information.

"Uh ... I think I saw him going into the forest. I was playing outside after school, so I don't know for sure because I wasn't paying a lot of attention ..." she mumbles.

I quickly pull out a pen and a notepad from my bag and write.

Where did you see him?

After reading the words, she turns on the bench and points straight behind her.

"There."

I grasp her and hug her tight, mouthing, "Thank you," before I jump up from the bench and run straight for the woods behind the school.

On the way there, I text Bo, telling him I have a lead. I direct him to my location using a picture and a compass point. Meanwhile, I keep running, my pace increasing with each heartbeat, desperate to get to his location in time.

I don't even try to take the car because the forest is far too dense. I'll have to go on foot.

But I know how to run.

I knew it the moment I ran from the compound; I am ready to give my life for my own happiness.

To save the person who cannot save himself.

Cage.

I'm coming.

FORTY-FIVE

CAGE

With a piece of wood, I've managed to skewer the bunny I found and clean its insides. I stripped off the fur and laid the meat out on a stone in the sun. After a few hours, it's tough and dry enough to eat, and I rip through it with my teeth, chewing on the salty meat. It's not the best food there is, but it's something.

I stare up at the scorching sun as I eat and fill my stomach, wondering how much time has passed since I escaped the compound. I've traveled so far up north that I don't even know where I am, but I'm not going out there to ask either.

I tried asking—again and again—but the people in this world are not what I thought they would be. They're angry and constantly wary as if they don't trust anyone who approaches them. And then there's me—a dirty, unkempt brute who marches into their space. They can't help but feel threatened by my appearance.

One or two words usually have them trembling even if I only ask for something. I'm not trying to scare them away. I'm not trying to be full of rage. But I can't help their response to seeing me either.

Whenever I ask for food, they turn the other way or tell me off. Other times when I asked for a bed, I've been met with a closed door. After trying too many times, I just gave up.

I just can't seem to do it. Not without Ella here to help me.

Walking and living in the wild is my normal now. I'm on my own now, and that's fine, because I still manage to survive. I know how to catch an animal, and I know how to find herbs and berries. Sometimes I resort to stealing— although that's only when I'm really, really hungry. I don't want to make people more upset, but I can't continue with a hungry stomach either, and sometimes there's no other way.

I don't have money. I don't have a house. I have nothing. So I live off nature instead.

However, the more time I spend out here in the wild, the less I feel like I could ever go back.

Like I could ever fit into the society beyond the forests, beyond the mountains.

The cities and their people are just so different … so different from me and what I'm used to.

I don't think I can ever adjust.

I prefer the outdoors—the smell of the grass and trees, the damp morning air, and the restless animals of the woods. Humans ... they make me anxious, especially their technology. I guess I'm more in tune with nature than I thought.

Besides, I'm still trying to find Ella, and I won't give up the search. Ever. I promised her that she'd be mine, and I'm sticking to my word.

However, the moment I swallow the last bit of meat, I hear a familiar voice calling out my name.

"Cage!"

It's loud and clear.

Like the song of a bird, so beautiful.

It's mine.

My Ella.

***

Ella

When I enter the forest, I can see Bo's not far behind me, just a few blocks, but I can't wait for him. I need to get to Cage before he runs off again. There's no time to waste, none. Who knows where he could be. I could miss him again, and I don't want that to happen.

My legs tremble, but I keep running, refusing to give up.

I run as fast as I can, past thick trees with branches scratching my skin. I ignore the pain as I tread through the thick forest, barely able to see a thing. Wet, fallen leaves and soil stick to my shoes and pants, but I don't care. The ground below me is wobbly and overgrown, rocks and dead trees everywhere, but even that won't stop me from running.

I know what the doctors said. I know I need to take it slow for the baby; I know I need to be careful.

But I can't stop myself. I can't stop wanting to find him …

I *need* to find him.

He's here; I know it.

He's so close; I can almost taste it.

So I scream.

For the first time in ages, I scream out his name again.

"Cage!"

The wind carries the sound of my voice, and it echoes against the trees like a gong. I look around. Birds fly up high, probably frightened from my voice. Then a twig snaps.

I spin on my heels and run in the direction of the sound.

"Ella?"

The moment I hear his voice, I stop.

My feet feel nailed to the ground as my own name resonates in my ears over and over again.

Tears well up in my eyes.

Cage.

He's really here.

He's right there.

Just beyond that ledge.

As if the wind itself is carrying me, I sprint toward the ledge, stopping right in front of it.

There, in the distance, a man stands between the bushes. His hair and beard wild and bristly. Clothes completely soaked, body covered in blood. Eyes boring into mine.

That one look is all it takes …

It's him.

It's really him.

He's here; he's really here. In the flesh. Alive and well.

Tears stream down my face as I tentatively walk past the trees, closer to him, around the ledge. He doesn't take his eyes off me, not for a single second as I approach him.

The only thing that separates us is a few thick trees and a curtain of rain clashing down on the earth.

My heart's almost beating out of my chest; that's how excited I am.

I don't even know what to do with myself the moment I see him.

The closer I get to touching him, the more afraid my body becomes.

Afraid of the consequences.

Because once I do, there's no going back.

I am his, and he is mine.

But the closer I get to him, the more I realize … I already crossed that line long ago.

***

He's completely frozen in place as I stand across from him, mere feet away. I'm shocked at the state he's in, but all that fades compared to the relief I feel inside my heart.

Finally, I found him, after all this time.

I don't stop walking.

My feet carry me toward him, unrelenting, unable to stop running.

Running into his arms.

Against his chest.

Inside his warm embrace.

His arms wrap around my wet body, and I clench mine around him, feeling his body for the first time in too long.

I cry, but they're tears of joy as I hug him tight, praying I'm not dreaming. In my mind, I thank God for staying with me, for granting my wish, and for giving me the best gift in the world.

I feel so much; I can barely handle the emotions curdling inside me, bursting out into tears and smiles.

I bury my face inside his dirty, wet shirt and take in a long breath, smelling his scent. Taking in all that is him and more. I'm not alone as I hear him sniffing close to my neck.

Feeling his skin against mine is not enough. I want him; I want him so close to me that I can't breathe. I want him to take it all and then some.

As the tears subside, I gaze up into his eyes and look at the bloodied face of the warrior who saved me.

Behind me, I hear Bo's voice, calling my name over and over again. It stops abruptly after I hear a few crackling noises behind me, and I know then that he's seen us—seen *me*—completely soaked in the middle of the forest, in the arms of the man who took my body and soul and chained it to his heart.

But I don't care about any of that. I don't care that Bo's watching, or that there might be reporters on the way, or that I'm completely soaked and dirty.

All I care about is *him*.

Cage.

My man.

With two hands, he cups my face and smashes his lips onto mine. It's a kiss I've been dreaming of for ages, and it finally happens. It's the best feeling in the world.

I don't care about the metallic taste of blood, or the dirt on his face, or the rain pouring down from the skies above. His lips are on mine, his tongue twisting around mine, claiming my mouth. Owning it.

Because I am his.

Completely and utterly his.

I always was.

From the very beginning, I never stood a chance.

In him, I found the man I needed to become whole again. In that cell, I lost a part of me but gained so much more in return.

Cage …

I didn't fulfill my promise to him, but I didn't have to.

He saved himself.

And now he's finally found me too.

FORTY-SIX

CAGE

The moment she jumps into my arms, I feel like I'm finally home again.

She's here, right here in my arms. I can smell her, taste her, kiss her.

Fuck, how hard I kiss her ...

I missed her so much it hurts inside. I can't describe what I'm feeling the moment I see her again and feel her body against mine, skin to skin, face to face.

I want nothing more than to hold her close for the rest of my life.

I'm finally where I belong.

My Ella ...

My woman.

I'm here.

I can't stop kissing her, can't stop wanting to grab her and take her with me. It doesn't matter where to as long as I can completely own her.

It's been too long, far too long since I last touched her.

And now she's finally here in my arms.

"I'm sorry," she mumbles, sniffing. "I'm so, so sorry."

I brush away the drops rolling down her cheeks and shake my head. She has nothing to be sorry about. I don't care how long it took us to reunite because we did.

"I left you ..." She sobs, shaking her head. "It's not right."

I smile, frowning as I cup her face and make her look at me. "You did what you had to."

"No," she says, shaking her head. "I could've tried harder, could've been there sooner. Could've—"

I silence her with another kiss, tired of her trying to find excuses to blame herself.

None of this is her fault. I told her to go, told her to escape. I demanded she save herself because I couldn't live with myself if she was in danger. If she'd still be unhappy, there, in that cage.

But she's free now. Free of the burden of the compound. Free ...

Yet she still came looking for me.

Does that mean she needs me just as much as I need her?

"You came," I say, surprised she actually found me.

Because, to this day, I still don't know where I am, or where she'd be.

I only knew I had to be in the forests and near the rivers. But I still don't know where she lives. Where her home is.

"Of course, I did," she says, and I can hear the pain in her voice. She hugs me again. "How could I not?"

A warm electrical current runs through my body when she holds me so tightly.

"You didn't have to," I say, looking down at her. "You were free."

"Being free means nothing ... without you," she mutters, gazing up into my eyes.

Her words undo me. Strip me of all the weight and sorrow I've been carrying since she left. Leave me naked and vulnerable, but stronger than ever before.

She places a hand on my cheek and caresses me softly, and I lean into her hand.

"I missed you so, so much," she murmurs, smiling back.

I place my hand on top and say, "Me too."

She nods. "I was so afraid ... that you'd ..." She can't even finish her sentence before choking up already, and I pull her against my chest for another tight hug.

"I'm here," I say. I know she was terrified, but she no longer has to be. I'm alive and well.

"Your wounds?" she mumbles, raising my dirty shirt to look at them.

I flinch and hiss when she touches them.

"Sorry ..." she says, lowering the shirt again.

"It's fine," I say.

"Looks painful but someone has redone the stitches, haven't they?"

I nod, but I don't care about my wounds. I care about hers. What happened to her while she ran? Did she suffer? Crossing the red desert must've been painful. I can't believe she made it out unscratched.

I place a hand on top of her belly and whisper, "Baby?"

She nods softly, and it puts a grin on my face. With one swoop, I drag her toward me and kiss her again, this time even harder than before.

When I take my lips off hers, I notice a stranger standing behind a tree. He's watching us.

With furrowed brows, I stop and push her behind me. If this person wants to harm us ... or her ... he'll have to go through me.

No one touches my woman.

The stranger clears his throat, and his eyes widen as he realizes I'm staring straight at him. He takes a step back, so I take one forward.

However, Ella immediately jumps in front of me, blocking me from chasing after him as he runs.

"No," she objects. "That's my friend."

"Friend?" I make a face. I don't understand.

"Someone I like," she says, still holding out her hands. "His name is Bo."

"You *like*?" That word only makes me more enraged, and I point at myself and say, "You *like me*."

She snorts and shakes her head for a second. "No. Yes, I like you too, Cage. But I like you in a different way. I *love*-like you. I *need* you, physically." She tilts her head down. "I don't *love*-like him and don't need him physically."

Her words only confuse me more.

She sighs out loud. "Just don't hurt him, okay?"

She grasps my hand and squeezes. Her small hand cradling mine feels so natural, so good... I don't want to ever let it go. It calms me down and makes me realize she

367

really is mine.

As if she's saying I don't need to fight anyone off because she will always belong to me, no matter what.

"C'mon. Let's go home," she says with a smile brighter than I've ever seen before.

The sun cascades on her hair as white as the moon in the sky, and her body still looks so appetizing even without a dress. Was she always this pretty? This beautiful in the light of day?

I wonder if things are going to get better now that I've finally found her again. Now that I'm finally going to see her home.

With a soft hand, she pulls me through the woods. Halfway through, we come across that same guy staring at us from a distance. He's leaning against a tree, watching us as we appear from the woods. He seems agitated, his muscles tight and clenched. I wonder why.

If she likes him and he likes her, does that mean he's nice to her?

Did he protect her while I was gone?

Did he take care of her when I couldn't?

Or is there more that I simply don't understand?

As she pulls me closer, I can feel her hand squeeze mine harder until we reach that guy named Bo.

She makes weird symbols with her hand. I don't know what she says, but he seems to understand.

"I figured it was him," he says, and then he gazes at me. "So ... you're *the* Cage." He sticks out his hand. "Name's Bo. Nice to meet you."

I stare at his hand and wonder what I'm supposed to do with it.

Is this what people always do when they just meet?

"Okay …" He clears his throat and lowers his hand again.

Ella makes some more strange gestures with her hand, even grabbing his arm, but he leans away. With furrowed brows, he keeps nodding.

"Got it. I'll just … leave you to it then," he retorts, turning around and walking away with slumped shoulders.

"What's with him?" I ask after he's gone.

"He's …" She sighs. "It's complicated."

"How?"

She glances at me and then gazes at the ground again as we saunter through the woods.

"People don't know how to act around you. They've never met anyone quite like you before."

What is that supposed to mean?

"Why?" I ask.

She shrugs. "I don't know. They're just not used to someone who doesn't know how to… act. How to behave, socially. And Bo's a sensitive dude. He … he …"

I stop and grasp her arm as her cheeks begin to turn red. "He what?"

"Well, he always took care of me, you know? And he's always worried about me."

"Worried … like me?" I say.

"Exactly." She licks her lips. "And I think he may … have had a crush on me."

"Crush?" I frown.

"Love. He love-likes me," she says. "I don't know how to explain it. And I don't know for sure. It's just a hunch."

Love-like? She just said that was only between her and

369

me. But now he wants her too?

I make a fist with my hand.

It's not happening. Not on my watch.

I'll punch his guts if I have to, but he's not stealing her away from me. No one can.

"I saw it," I growl.

"You saw what?"

"His need."

"Need?" Her eyes widen. "No, no, not like that."

"Yes."

It's exactly what I saw.

The same hunger I felt when I couldn't touch her because there was a thick glass separating us. That same look ... and he gave it to her.

"Did he touch you?" I ask, holding both her arms.

"No, of course not. Cage, don't get angry, please," she pleads, placing a hand against my stomach and pushing me away. "Especially not at him. He can't help it. We don't choose who we fall in love with."

"I chose you," I say.

She pauses and a brief half-smile appears on her lips as she blushes again.

"I know you did. But most people ... don't. Bo didn't. Bo ... Bo's always taken care of me ever since I was young. And I guess he must've thought he had a chance." She rubs her forehead. "No wonder he was so upset when I kept looking for you. I should've seen it coming."

He did have a strange look in his eyes ... as if he was sad about something.

She gazes at the leaves again and kicks a rock away. "Why didn't I see it sooner?"

I place a hand on her shoulder. "Not your fault."

She rubs her lips together, mulling it over for a second. "Let's just go home. I don't like talking about it."

"And Bo?" I ask.

"I'll talk to him later. Or rather sign," she says, grasping my hand again. "Let's go."

FORTY-SEVEN

Ella

I bring Cage out of the woods and onto the streets, holding his hand so he won't feel the need to run. I hope I don't run into too many people. I just want to bring him home, get him to safety, and worry about getting him used to my world later.

It's too soon for him to be exposed to this much of our world. He can't handle it.

He hid in the woods, covered in blood and dirt, looking like a savage for a reason. He was probably scared of the people ... or maybe he didn't even know how to properly talk with them without sounding like a drunk on steroids.

But we're out of luck, it seems.

A few steps are all it takes to alert the people in the vans to our presence. The camera crews that were following me now jump out and run toward us as we make our way down the hill and back to the town.

A reporter jumps out too, complete with microphone and an earpiece that she shoves into her ear right before she marches our way on her thick heels. The closer they get, the more I clench Cage's hand, hoping we can walk fast enough to avoid them.

However, they keep adjusting their course as I do, relentless in their pursuit to get us to talk to them. The more we come closer, the more my stomach begins to curl into itself. My blood boils at the sight of these people, rushing to get their next big story.

Because that's why they followed me around.

They know I'm the girl who escaped the compound.

And now she's somehow miraculously found the guy she was looking for.

I saw it in the news, the other day, people photographing me in that red desert with a caption of "What is she looking for?" and other newspapers mentioning more captives.

It's sick how they manage to spin a story without me even giving them a single word to go on.

It's like they've been following me from day one, knowing there was more to this story than just me escaping.

And now they know.

Cage is here, and he's not going anywhere but home.

They know; I can see it in their vulture-like eyes, the hunger for his story.

But they won't get it.

Not now.

Not ever, if it's up to me.

As they bombard me with questions while we pass them on the way down, I ignore them completely. I gaze beyond them, holding Cage tight. He's my anchor, and I'm his guiding light. Together we stay strong; we go against the tide. I don't care what they say or what they write. Let them make up their stories. I know mine.

"Ella, we know you've been searching ever since you escaped the compound. Is this the person you were looking for?" the woman with the microphone asks, but I lift my head high, refusing to even answer with a smile.

"Ella? Is this him?" she asks again, following us with her camera crew.

"Ella? Please talk to us. The world wants to know your story."

Still, I don't respond. It's easy when you haven't been able to talk to strangers for over a decade.

I march toward my car with Cage trailing behind me, holding my hand.

I glance behind me to make sure he's okay. His whole body is tense, and he keeps checking his surroundings as if he doesn't know where to go or whether he's safe. It's sad and infuriating to watch him so insecure of his surroundings, and these people not giving a shit about any of that. Don't they understand their presence will only make him more agitated? More inclined to lash out?

I don't want him to get angry because then the first thing the world will see of my Cage is his rage …

And that can never end well.

"What's his name, Ella? Were you two in the compound together?" the woman asks, almost tripping on her high heels as she strides through the grass.

I don't even look at her as she keeps trying to step in front of me to block my way.

"He's covered in blood, any news about that?" she asks.

I don't even know the answer to that myself, but I don't care either.

He's a good human being. He wouldn't hurt anyone unless he had to.

"Are you two a couple?" she asks.

Now they're even trying to dig into my private life.

I don't understand these people. How unconcerned for a person's well-being they can be. How much they care more about the story they can tell than the people behind it.

They can lie for all I care.

I just want to get home.

When I'm finally at my car, I quickly open the doors and direct Cage to get in on the passenger's side before going to the driver's side. The camera crew is still there, trying to butt in, but it doesn't faze me anymore. I pretend they don't exist as I slam my car door shut and start the engine.

"Ella! Tell the world your story. They need to know," the woman yells through my window.

One stern look ... that's all she gets from me before I put the car into reverse and drive out of the parking lot.

On the way home, we hold hands, only letting go so I can shift gears. I like touching him, feeling him beside me, and knowing he's there now. Looking at him never gets old. Not even with all the dirt and blood. I can see past all that ... all I see is the beauty of the beast underneath.

***

CAGE

I can't keep my eyes off her, and I don't even try. That's how in love with her I am.

With the sunlight scattering on her skin, she's even more beautiful than I could possibly imagine. Outside the glass prison we spent so much time in, she comes alive. I can see it with my own eyes now; that smile on her face is more vibrant than ever.

Her eyes grow watery, so I ask, "What's wrong?"

She shakes her head. "Nothing. I'm just happy." I smile back, but her lips part again. "How did you even find this place?"

"Maps. And people," I reply. It wasn't easy, but I managed.

"And you walked all this way?"

I nod.

"Wow ..." she murmurs to herself.

I don't understand what's so impressive about it. I just wanted to go to her, so that's what I did. I tried to find her as best as I could ... even though she found me first.

"How did you survive on your own for so long?" she asks.

I shrug. "Hunting. Foraging."

"So you didn't steal from anyone?" she asks.

I frown. "Sometimes ..."

I don't like to think about it because it wasn't right. I don't want to take things that don't belong to me when other people might need it, but I couldn't stop myself.

"You only did it because you were hungry," she says, placing a hand on my lap. "It's okay. No one will punish you for it."

I nod, hoping she really sees it that way. I don't want her to think of me as some kind of monster.

I don't want to see her hurting.

I love her. I need her more than anything.

I hope she needs me just as much.

With my palm, I gently caress her cheeks, unable to stop myself from touching her.

If I'd known being free would have such an impact on her ... I would've tried harder, sooner, to get her out. I would've gone to the ends of the world if I had to. Just to see this smile.

I don't know how long it takes to get to her home, but I don't care either. Every second I get to spend with her is another one in pure happiness.

I'm right where I'm supposed to be. With her. My woman. My Ella.

And our baby.

I place my hand on her belly and feel the smoothness of the small bump, her warmth radiating through her clothes. I'm here for her ... and our little one.

But as I feel her body under my hand, I can't help but slide it down to her leg, desire swelling inside me. It's been so long since I last felt her around me, since I last took her body and made it mine.

Too long.

And from the look in her eyes, I can tell she's thinking the same thing.

The hunger ... it only grows.

I can't wait to dig in.

However, as we drive up a road and along the trees, a house comes into view. She tenses as she gazes at the people standing on the stones and grass outside. They're holding big mechanical things that look like the cameras my father installed in our cells. There are so many of them, I lost count by the time we arrive.

As Ella parks the car, the hoard of people approaches us, and I immediately sink back into my seat. The hairs on the back of my neck and on my arms stand up straight as the people hold the cameras against the windows. Shouting ensues. I don't even know what they're saying because they're all talking at the same time.

"Shit," Ella growls. "How the hell did they find out so quickly? That woman must've called and told them. Shit!" She pulls the keys out. "I can't believe they actually followed me back home."

"Who are they?" I ask, wanting to throw stuff at the window just to make them back off.

"Reporters," she says, but when she sees my confused face, she adds, "People who want to know everything about you and where you came from. Our story."

Our story? But we aren't even finished with it yet.

"I don't want to tell them," I say, making a face at one of the females glaring into the car, trying to get a good look.

"Me neither. Let's just go inside," she says, smiling at me. "But before we do … I have to warn you. They'll try to ask you stuff, personal stuff. Whatever you do, don't respond. Don't even react."

The way she talks about it reminds me of Father prepping me for a fight. Is this like that? Going outside is like going into a ring? If it is, I should prepare.

I rub my knuckles and say, "Got it."

"Ready?" she asks.

I nod.

She opens the door on her side, and I open mine. However, I'm not prepared for the barrage of flashing lights directed straight at my face. They blind me, and worst of all is the instant influx of voices making me want to lash out.

I immediately pull the car door shut again, sitting back down on the seat.

Fuck. I thought I could do this, but I can't.

I've never been around that many people in my life, not even in the ring.

How does Ella deal with this? How does she march through the crowd, seemingly oblivious to the people around her bombarding her with questions? Or does she shut them out?

She walks over to my side of the car and leans over to gaze through the window.

"C'mon," she says.

But when I see the people behind her, all I wanna do is growl.

I want them to go away and leave us alone.

Ella gently opens the door and pushes her hand through. "Grab my hand," she coaxes. "I'll take you inside."

Sighing, I take it, and I let her pull me out of the car into the mass of people. Their screams and yells and the constant flashes of light and cameras shoved in my face make me go insane. Ella's hand squeezing mine is the only thing that keeps me from going wild.

"What's your name? Were you in the compound with

379

Ella Rosenberg? Are you her boyfriend? Were you one of the captives? You were in the woods together; did you live there?"

Countless questions and I don't want to reply to any of them. They come way too close for comfort. How do they even know all this?

However, as Ella pushes through the crowd, one of them almost breaks us apart.

"Is she pregnant with your child? Was it conceived in captivity? Was she a willing participant?"

Willing? Of course, she was.

How *dare* they even ask that question.

The moment one of the cameras touches my skin, I lose it.

I grab it and roar out loud, right into the camera, silencing each one of them.

"Cage!"

Her voice brings me back to reality, back to her.

I glance over my shoulder at her worried face, and I realize I almost went over the edge there.

I was this close to grabbing the cameras and smashing them into the crowd of people.

But Ella told me I shouldn't respond or react in any way.

That includes wanting to use my fists.

"Don't do it," she stresses, shaking her head as she clings to my fingers tightly.

I nod and lick my lips, closing my eyes so I no longer have to face these people.

I let her be my guide.

The moment I give in to her, the questions continue,

but I try to ignore them as best as I can. Maybe it's already too late. Maybe I already ruined it by even growling at them. I should've listened to her and let them talk.

But it's so fucking hard ... I don't understand why it's so easy for her. Have these people been following her all this time? If they have, and she's been resisting all this time ... Fuck, she's strong.

I always knew she was strong, but I never realized just how much.

As a door shuts behind me, the noises from outside dampen.

"You can open your eyes now," she says, placing a soft hand on my chest. "We're here."

Here.

Right here ... is home.

FORTY-EIGHT

CAGE

When I open my eyes, my body relaxes, and I look around for the first time. The walls are close together, but the room is bigger than the cell we were in. There are even stairs leading upward.

She grabs my hand and pulls me in to the part she calls a living room. There are windows everywhere, just like our prison, but some of them can actually open. Behind it is green grass and trees, exactly as she described it. It's pretty … and so light.

I never knew the outside was this bright.

And this place … this is her house, her space, her home. It's beautiful.

I can see why she missed it so much.

As I stare outside and place a hand on the window, wanting to go there, she goes to her knees right in front of me and starts to unlace my dirty shoes. I can't stop focusing on the fact she's at the exact height she was at when she first wrapped her pretty lips around my cock, though.

That is one memory I'll never forget, no matter where I am.

Now that we're both free of our prisons, I'll get to see her do it many more times.

And I intend to make it happen very soon.

"Let's get these out of the way," she says, pulling them off and chucking them onto a small rug right in front of what looks like a door to her garden.

It's strange not to stand on a concrete floor. The wood on the floor in this room feels … nice.

"Hungry?" she asks, and I cock my head, smiling.

"Very …" I can't stop myself from practically groaning because my mouth is already watering at the sight of her.

But she turns and walks right off into a different space in the living room that has lots of little doors with tables on top and things I don't recognize.

As she pulls open a door, I recognize some food sitting on the shelves, so I walk toward her and smack it shut again. She seems surprised, but I grasp her face with both hands and say, "Not that kind …"

A hint of a smile forms on her lips, and it looks so appetizing that I bend over and kiss her on the mouth, claiming her again as I did before in the woods.

She giggles in my mouth, and it makes me pull away for a second. "Oh …" A blush appears on her cheeks. "I get it."

I smirk. "You do?"

She closes her eyes for a brief second, smiling like crazy. "C'mon ... let's go upstairs."

I frown. "Upstairs?"

I wrap my arm around her waist and pull her close to my body, wanting her to feel every ounce of my lust for her. "Why not here?"

I kiss her again, this time parting her lips with my tongue, wanting to taste every inch of her.

"Because you're dirty," she retorts, grinning against my lips as I stop kissing her.

"So?" I don't see the problem.

She rolls her eyes and pulls away from my embrace, but she still holds my hand. "Follow me."

She pulls me along again back to the place where we entered and then up the stairs. The softness underneath my feet feels strange, but I like it. It's soft and delicate ... like her.

We pass a few doors and enter the one in the back. Squares stones are on the floor, but none like I've ever seen before. In front of me is a sink with a mirror above it and a small cabinet filled with towels beside it. In the back of the room is something that looks like a shower.

Ella closes the door behind me and slides around me, curling her fingers underneath my shirt to pull it over my head. She looks at me, her eyes reflecting the same need as in mine.

I know what she wants ... I want it just as much, if not more.

***

Ella

I can't help but to stare at his muscular pecs as my eyes travel downward to the V that leads me to the hardest bit of his body. I can see it grow in his pants as I gaze at it. It's already stiff, just from us exchanging looks.

I lick my lips, almost tempted to go down on my knees again and suck him off.

But he's still covered in blood, still dirty, still ... a savage. It wouldn't be right. Not when we just came back from the woods where I found him.

When I gaze up into his eyes again, he's not looking away either, and I find it hard to even breathe around him. I know he can sense my desire from the way my skin flushes around him.

He towers above me, but as I undo his pants and slowly push them down, he still doesn't move an inch. I bite my lip as my hands run down his firm ass, which I can't help but touch. As the fabric drops to the floor, all that remains is his naked body ... and my eyes ogling his ample length.

It looks even bigger in the light of day.

He tips up my chin with his thumb and whispers, "Mine?"

Goose bumps scatter all over my skin.

God ... it feels so good to hear him say that right now.

I nod, and he leans in for a mind-numbing kiss, putting all my senses on high alert.

I place a hand on his chest, pushing him away before we jump into things again. Still, my eyes can't help but draw a line downward again. I suck in a breath, gazing at his shaft, wondering how good it would feel to have him inside me.

But I shake my head and force myself to remember we only just came home. He needs to get used to this place first. Used to being free. Used to me.

So I grab his hand and pull him with me into the shower, turning it on as I step away so I don't get wet too.

The water cascades down on his naked body, washing away the blood and dirt. He's quickly clean again, and I can't help but stare at the rivulets forming down his abs. My tongue darts out to lick my lips, eager to lick them off his skin, but I quickly stop myself again and clear my throat.

"Let me know when you're done," I say, turning around and walking off.

However, right before I manage to slip away, he grabs my wrist.

"Stay." The guttural, throaty voice has me shivering with need.

I stop and glance at him … That was a mistake.

Those eyes.

God, those eyes.

They're sinful.

How can I resist when he looks at me like he's ravenous?

It's impossible. I already lost the fight the moment he kissed me.

He doesn't let go … not until he's raked me in like a prize on a hook. And I let him twist me close to his body, despite my clothes getting completely drenched from the shower.

I don't care anymore.

I'm done resisting. Done fighting the desire to let him take me.

So I let him take me into his arms and kiss me hard.

I'm completely his.

***

CAGE

She might think she can run, but it's too late for that. She was mine the moment she stepped into my prison, and she is still mine now. Nothing changes the fact she belongs to me. Not a glass prison or a wooden home, nor the dirt or the blood washing away with the water.

I want her … I don't care what I have to do, but I will get her on her knees.

I don't know why I feel so riled up, but I am … I want to stake my claim on her, show her she's mine. No one, and I mean no one, can come between us.

Not those people outside, not my father, not her friend … no one. Not even her.

I won't allow her to run. Not this time.

Once was all I could take, but I want her in my arms and on my lips … And I want that sweet pussy around my cock again.

It's been too fucking long.

Living like a savage in the outside world put my senses on high alert. Being alone for so long only made my desires stronger, my lust for her growing by the day.

And now that she's finally in my arms, I'm not letting

her go.

No fucking way.

She wraps her arms around my neck as I pull her into the shower with me, not caring if she gets completely soaked. Clothes don't matter; they can dry. What matters is finally releasing this pent-up need inside me ... and inside her.

Because from the way she latches onto my mouth with equal greed, I can definitely tell she's been holding her desires for far too long.

I kiss her back just as hard, taking her tongue with mine and circling around. My hand slides down her neck to her tits, squeezing tight, twisting her nipple with my thumb and index finger. Her sweet moan makes my cock rock hard, and I pull her against me to make her feel it.

I want her. I need her so badly—it's almost inhuman the way my body aches for hers.

My fingers curl around her shirt, and I pull it over her head, tossing it away. Her nipples peak against my skin, and I bend over to cover them with my mouth, sucking hard to make them even more taut.

With my other hand, I release the button of her pants and force them down. My hand immediately dives between her crevice, wanting to feel her pussy clench around my fingers. She moans into my mouth as I flick her clit and thrust a finger inside. I've missed the sound of her moans, the wetness inside her. I want it all, and I *will* have it all.

However, she unlatches her mouth from mine and pulls away from me.

"What—"

She places a finger on my lips, smiling deviously. Then

she goes down on her knees.

I stand in awe at her beautiful, pristine eyes gazing up at me while she perches herself against the wall … right in front of my dick.

Her tongue dips out, and she latches onto it.

I immediately tense up, not used to the feel of her hands and mouth around my length. Fuck, it's been too long since I last felt her there.

I focus, trying not to come right away as she licks me. It looks so good from up here with that sweet little mouth wrapped around my cock. She's so innocent yet so dirty … and completely mine.

My woman, my Ella. I'm finally here to make her feel good again, and instead, she chooses to give me the ultimate pleasure. How could I not smirk when I see her kneel between my legs?

However, when she takes me into her mouth, that smile quickly turns into a groan, and I struggle not to shove it in farther.

She sucks and licks so wonderfully … making me want to come right down her throat.

I grab a fistful of her hair and hold it tight as she moves forward and back across my length. My balls tighten as my veins pulse; my dick releases pre-cum onto her tongue, but she doesn't even seem fazed by it.

Instead, she takes it even deeper. All the way to the base.

Another groan escapes my mouth. My whole body tenses as the tip touches the back of her throat.

She gulps, coughing as I pull out again, not wanting to hurt her … but fuck me, her choking sounded so good. I want to do it again.

So I wrap my hand around her face and pull her back over my cock again. She doesn't resist me, so I push on, thrusting in and out. She lets me take control, lets me fuck her mouth against the wall despite her struggle to breathe. I can see it in her eyes; she's begging me to do it, begging me to fuck her mouth and come all over her tongue and down her throat.

She's perfect, too perfect, and it makes me roar out loud and thrust in all the way to the base again. My balls tighten, and I roar as I release my seed inside her mouth. I jet inside her, holding her down, coating her tongue with my thick cum. Her tongue moves against my length, swallowing it all down.

As I pull out again, she wheezes, gasping for air.

I bend over and kiss her on the forehead, wanting her to know how much I love her. She greedily accepts it, glancing up at me like a little angel as I tip up her chin and kiss her on the lips. The sweet, salty taste makes me remember how much I've missed her ... and how much I enjoy having her be mine.

With my help, she rises to her feet, wrapping her arms around my neck again. My cock is still hard, still eager for more, so I push her against the wall and let my tongue roll down her body, along her nipples, suckling on them.

I lift her up, and she folds her legs around my waist, her eyes on me. I don't break our gaze. Not even when I lower her onto my shaft and grunt with pure need. She's so wet ... All this from just having me in her mouth?

It's the best gift she could give me right now, and I'll gladly accept it.

I bury myself deep inside her until her mouth forms an

o. I start rocking up and down, fucking her hard, our eyes never unlocking. Every thrust goes deeper and every moan is louder.

I bang her hard against the stone shower wall, not giving a shit whether it's right or wrong. I need her now more than I need oxygen to breathe. I can't take my eyes off her, can't take my lips off her skin, and don't want this connection to break. Ever.

"Mine?" I growl, nibbling on her lip.

"Yours," she mewls as I thrust even harder.

A smirk spreads on my lips, and I ravish her some more.

"Come," I growl, wanting to feel her tighten around me.

And she does. Right as I say it, her eyes roll to the back of her head, and she comes undone. Her body quakes, but I stop her from falling, holding her body close to mine. Her pussy squeezes my cock, and I groan with her, allowing my seed to spill into her again.

We rock up and down, her body wrapped around mine while I coat her insides with my cum. She's glowing, glistening from the hot shower, her body covered in sweat and water. I swipe my tongue along her skin, wanting to taste every inch of her skin.

Partially sated, I pull her under the shower with me.

But it doesn't cool me off.

Far from it.

But after a quick kiss, she insists on grabbing some bottle and squeezing the contents out on my body and rubbing it all over me. So I go along with it, smearing the soap on her body too, getting to run my hands all over her again.

Of course, by the time she's rinsing off the soap, I've

already grown another hard-on just from looking at her.

She chuckles, hiding her laughter behind her hand.

"What?" I ask.

She steals a glance at my shaft before looking straight at me again.

I raise a brow. "Hungry for more?"

The smile that appears on her lips is enough of a yes for me, so I put my arms around her waist and underneath her legs and lift her up into my arms, making her squeal.

FORTY-NINE

Ella

We're still completely wet as Cage marches out of the shower. I quickly reach for a towel in the cabinet before he walks us both out of the bathroom.

"Wait, we need to dry off," I mumble as he kicks open all the doors one by one until he finds the one with my bed in it.

"Later," he says as he sets me down on the bed and crawls on top of me.

"But the whole bed will get wet," I murmur as he lowers himself on top of me, kissing my collarbone and neck. God, he's so hard to resist when he does that.

He looks up and quips, "So?"

I suck in a breath as he draws a line all the way down to

my pussy, burying his face between my legs. His licks are eager, almost desperate for more as he laps me up. I moan with delight as he works my clit and circles around with his tongue. It feels like he's loving every single inch of my skin, and I don't want him to stop.

Two fingers are pushed inside, and I gasp for air as he continues to eat me out. Delicious shocks roll through my body as he probes inside, taking his sweet time to wrap me around his finger, almost literally.

I bite my lip and clutch the sheets as he works me, his mouth tantalizing and hot on my skin. God, I've missed this so much. Him. His touch, his mouth, his body … everything about him.

I feel like I've died and gone to heaven, flying on a cloud as he keeps going, never stopping to take a breath.

His tongue knows exactly what I like and keeps swiveling along with his fingers until I fall apart in his arms. My whole body quakes and shivers with delight as I release the pent-up need, moaning out loud.

Flustered, I bury my face in my pillow and giggle.

He quickly pulls it away and lowers himself on top of me, smothering me with more kisses. It's the best feeling in the world.

We don't stop.

Not for hours.

We cuddle and have sex and cuddle some more. I can't stop touching him and neither can he. We're addicted to each other. Addicted to the closeness, the warmth, the excitement.

The sex is hot and feverish as if we're catching up for all the time we lost. He keeps coming, just as I do, and covers me in his cum. He rubs it into me, on my skin, inside me, as if he wants to mark me as his territory. And I'm okay with it. In fact, I love it.

I love him.

Still, I wonder if he could live like this and be happy. In this place—this big, open world—without a glass prison to contain his needs. With so many possibilities, it could overwhelm him. Maybe he doesn't want to be out here.

As I lie on top of his chest, basking in the afterglow, I murmur, "Do you miss it?"

"What?"

"The cage …"

"No." He turns his head and looks at me, plucking at one of my loose strands of hair to tuck it behind my ear. "Never."

I prop myself up on my elbow."How do you know for sure?"

He plants a finger onto my chest and taps. "Because I have you …"

Love. That's all I feel. His boundless love and greed for me.

His devotion to me and our baby as he places a hand on my belly and kisses it.

He's perfect in every way … perfect for me.

I just hope others will see it that way too.

***

CAGE

It's only a few days after my arrival, and I've already gotten used to life inside her home. I love her bed. It's very soft. But I love her most of all. She takes very good care of me.

She even bought me new clothes. Half of them don't fit properly because she didn't know my size, but I'm still thankful. These clothes make me feel more human and less like a beast.

I've also finally gotten used to how the mechanical devices work in her home. At first, the microwave and toaster scared the fuck out of me when they randomly dinged out of nowhere, but after using more than half the loaf of bread into both, I finally understand how they work. There's a timer on it.

Much like some other items in her house, such as the electric kettle, which she uses for a strange brew called tea. I've tasted it, but I don't find it interesting even though she seems to love it. The other one, a coffeemaker, that one … oh yes, now that I can drink. The moment I tasted coffee, I knew I had to get more. I don't even know what it is, but it pumps me up.

But she keeps laughing at me when I drink it and want to do my jumping jacks right afterward. Apparently, it's something a lot of people drink. I could definitely get used to it.

Ella thought I'd have the most trouble with the television, but it's not that different from the videos Father showed me. Except that nobody is naked, and they're not having sex. It's just … people doing stuff. Fishing. Cooking. Cleaning. And arguing … they argue a lot on the television.

The only thing I can't get used to is the outside. The world. How green and blue it really is. The vibrant colors and the liveliness of it all. The first time I went outside since coming here, I lay down on the grass and stared at the sky for hours, maybe more.

I can't help it. It's fascinating beyond words.

However, the moment something buzzes in my ear, I quickly get up and rush back inside. Ella just put food on the table, and it smells delicious. It's those pancakes again that she made yesterday. They taste amazing.

"C'mon, sit," she says, pulling out a chair to sit on too.

I do what she asks and gobble down some pancakes. She can't stop watching me while I do it, and it makes me feel weird. As if I'm supposed to say or do something. I don't know why she keeps looking at me while I'm eating.

"What?" I ask.

"Nothing," she muses.

Always that same answer.

"I just like watching you," she adds.

Of course. I nod, smiling. Now I understand. She's like me, except I couldn't stop looking at her when we were in the prison, my cage, my home … This is her home. She's watching me adjust and see the world through her eyes.

"So what happened?" she asks out of nowhere.

"Where?" I look up, my face still covered in this delicious sauce she covers the pancakes with. I don't know what it is, but it makes me want to lick the entire plate, so I do, and it makes her giggle.

"Outside," she says. "You ran in again."

"Oh … that." I put down my plate. "Something buzzing …" I point at my ear.

She makes an o shape with her mouth. "A bee?"

"Bee?"

"Your father never taught you about bees?"

"No. Only things that mattered," I reply.

She nods a few times, narrowing her eyes. "Interesting." She picks up the empty plates and carries them to the kitchen. "Well, I guess we're gonna have to take you on a trip to the zoo then."

"Zoo?" She keeps saying these words I've never heard before.

"Yeah. It's where all kinds of animals live but in cages."

"Cages?" I grumble, folding my arms as I lean back. "No."

She sighs and cocks her head. "It's not a cage like yours. It's a good cage with everything they need. It's for their own good. They keep them alive in there. And they can educate people about them."

Oh … well, in that case, I might be tempted to find it a little bit interesting. Okay, a lot, but I won't ever say that. Not when it comes to cages. I've seen enough prison in my life to know it only leads to pain and suffering.

"Let's go there. Today. What do you say?" she asks.

I raise a brow, not sure what to do with her suggestion. "Okay?"

Her smile seals the deal. "Great." She walks toward me and gives me a kiss on the cheeks. "But first, we're going to meet my parents."

***

398

The moment her mother and father arrive, she immediately runs out to greet them. She's much more vibrant out here than she was in the cage, and it only adds to her personality. I love how sweet she is, and how well she's treated me since I came here. I wish I could've returned the favor when we were still in the glass cages. Sometimes, I still think back to that time, wondering if I'll ever be able to be what she wants me to be. Out here … the world is different. More difficult. I've got a knot in my stomach just from wondering whether I'll fit in. If people— or more importantly, her parents—will accept me for who I am.

However, I don't have any time to think about it because her parents have already stepped through the door.

I turn and step into the living room, waiting until they enter the room. I scratch the back of my neck, not knowing how to respond as her mother enters the room. She looks just like Ella, making me wonder what her father looks like. I don't have to wait long, though, as he barges into the room after giving his coat to Ella.

"Is this him?" A mouth is talking, but I can't even see it underneath that bushy moustache. "This is the guy who got you pregnant while you were in that cage?"

How am I supposed to respond to that?

He makes it sound so … bad.

Even though I never had bad intentions.

I just wanted her, my girl … my Ella … to be the woman to carry my child.

It's all I knew how to do, all I was taught. I know now she has more dreams and wishes, but that doesn't take away from the fact I care more about her than I care about my own life.

I'd jump through fire if I had to just for her.

If that isn't good, I don't know what is.

I clear my throat and approach them both, holding out my hand as Ella showed me. Her mother smiles as I take her hand and shake it, saying, "Nice to meet you." Exactly as Ella taught me.

I don't like all these social rules, but I can see why they do it. It's already reduced the tension by the time I've greeted her father.

"What a nice young man you are," her mother says.

"Thank you," I reply, smiling too as Ella runs into the kitchen.

"Coffee, anyone?" she calls out.

"Of course," her father says.

"Coming right up!" She gestures for me to talk to them.

"Uh … right …" I sigh. "Wanna sit?" I point at the couches, which are very comfy.

"Sure." Her mother immediately props herself down with a pillow.

I flop down on the other end of the couch, and I feel like I've landed on a cloud each time I do. I don't think I'll ever get used to these things. I wish I could've had one back inside the compound.

"So tell me … what was it like being in that … prison?"

"Mom!" Ella shouts from the kitchen. "I thought we talked about this."

"Yes, yes, I remember," her mother says, blushing. "I'm just a very curious old lady. Sue me."

I laugh, which makes her blush. "It's fine."

"See? He's okay with me being nosy." Her mother leans over the couch to stare at her father. "Don't you want to say anything?" He's still in the kitchen, avoiding me, probably.

"No … I can listen." He folds his arms.

"Dad …" Ella mumbles.

"What?" Her father shrugs.

"Oh, it's all right," her mother muses, gently nudging me. "I'll do the talking."

"What do you want to know?" I ask.

"Well … I have so many questions; I don't even know where to start."

I shrug. "The beginning."

She narrows her eyes. "You're right … So tell me, did you really live in that place all your life?"

I nod, and the shocked face that follows makes me feel strange. To them, it's not normal… but to me, it was. I don't know any better.

"So you've never seen the real world? Where you are now? This is the first time ever?"

I nod as Ella puts down the cups of coffee.

Her mother immediately grabs hers and takes a long sip, still staring at me.

"Dad? Come sit with us," Ella says as she pats the chair next to her after sitting down herself.

He reluctantly agrees, sighing as he joins us, but he keeps staring at me as if I'm some kind of dangerous animal that could pounce on him at any moment.

"It's hard to believe," her mother mumbles. "But if you've never experienced life outside a cage, does that make you a … savage?"

Ella almost spurts out her coffee. "Mom!"

"What? I'm just pointing out what it looks like."

I chuckle. "It's okay."

"It's not." Ella gazes directly at me. "He's not a savage. Not anymore." A moment of silence and appreciation is exchanged between us, and I can't help but smile at her when she keeps looking at me like that.

Only after a few seconds does she avert her attention back to her parents. "He's just a man who went through a bad time. It's not his fault; none of it is. He had no choice. And he's here now, with me … and we're together." She picks up her coffee and takes a sip.

"As a couple?" her father asks.

"Yes," she replies.

"And he's taking care of you?" her father asks. "And the baby?"

"Always," I reply, and now they're all looking at me. "I love her."

It takes them a while to process my words, which is strange as I never say many. But her mother immediately turns and hugs me, surprising me. She pats my back and says, "Oh, I'm so glad you said that."

"Uh … thank you?" I mumble, unsure of how to respond.

"You're welcome, honey," her mother says, placing a hand on my shoulder. "And you should know that as long as you're here for her, I'm happy. I don't care who you are or where you came from; as long as you can give my little girl everything her heart desires, I'm happy."

She turns her head and looks at her man. "Hank?"

He was in the middle of taking a sip of his coffee, but he stops and puts his cup down, clearing his throat. "Yes, yes … I agree."

"So you're okay with him being … my boyfriend?"

Ella's entire face turns red the moment she states, "And the father of my child?"

"As long as you love him and he loves you and your baby. Of course, I will."

Ella immediately jumps into her father's arms, hugging him tightly. "Thank you."

"Aw, don't thank me yet. He'll have to prove it." Now he's glaring at me again. "You'll take good care of my girl? Give her everything she needs? You know what happens if you don't."

I actually don't know what will happen, but I'm guessing it has something to do with violence. He couldn't win by a long shot, but I wouldn't try to fight him. It's her father, after all, and I understand how she feels about him. So I'll keep it civilized. Besides, he's not asking much.

Loving her is easy.

I nod. "I will."

It's a promise I don't take lightly … and it's a promise I intend to keep.

FIFTY

Ella

We spend the first part of the day talking with the police, so Cage can give his statement. Since he was part of their official search, we needed to visit them personally to verify he was actually found. Plus, they want his contact information so they can contact him for further details about the investigation. I'm fine with giving them what they need because I want them to be able to do their job properly.

Some of the female officers wanted me to press charges because he got me pregnant while I was still in captivity, but there's no way I'll ever pursue that. He doesn't deserve it. I just want us to be left alone so we can be at peace.

However, it's proving to be difficult as the reporters are still following us wherever we go. Even as we go to the zoo for a day so I can show him all the animals, they still track down our car and chase us all the way to the entrance.

I can't wait until the interest dies down, and I can go back to my life as it used to be. With Cage, of course.

We hold hands as we stroll past the cages, and I point at all the animals inside, telling him about their origin, their movements, and their sounds. He's captivated by all of them, no matter how big or small. From monkeys to insect and birds, he's enthralled by watching them play and eat.

It's immensely rewarding to watch him explore this part of life, to interact with the animals and actually see them up close. I take pictures of him and the animals while I'm here, knowing I could sell some of them to the magazines I work for. None that involve Cage, of course, because he wouldn't be able to cope with all the attention. But also because he's like my own little secret. He's like a big kid stuck in an adult body, experiencing the world for the first time.

"Is this all of them?" he asks as we stroll through the open bird cage, admiring the birds flying freely across the enclosure.

"Nope. There are many, many more all around the world."

"Wow …" He can't stop gazing around him, marveling at their colors and beaks.

But the strangest thing is that they all seem to flock toward him. He doesn't even need to lure them in; they just walk in front of him, perching on his shoulder and even on his head.

I giggle as one of them taps his little feet, digging his

nails into Cage's shoulder.

"Does it hurt?" I ask.

"Nah."

Nothing hurts to him. Not when you've been hit by men a million times before. I guess pain doesn't faze him anymore.

He pets the bird even though it's not technically allowed, but I'm around, so I'll supervise. I just want him to know what it's like to live with them, and that he doesn't have to fear them. In fact, he seems quite loving around them. Very different from the primitive man he was in the cell … and the brute he is in bed. I love how unapologetically dirty he can be, but I can get used to this side of him too.

He's even grown to like the insects, which surprises me, considering how he kept rushing back into my home whenever they'd land on his arm or crawl over him. I guess you have to get used to the tickling sensation of their little legs.

However, the moment Cage comes face to face with the tigers and lions, he's sold. Instantly. I giggle as he roars at them and they roar back, and he smacks his own chest like he wants to impress them or something. People keep glaring at him as if he's lost his mind, but he doesn't even care about any of that. He's completely focused on the tigers and lions. He's found his animals, that's for sure. Which shouldn't surprise me at all, considering their strength.

"I like their teeth," he says as he watches one of them yawn.

"I'm sure you do," I say, chuckling. "But they'd defeat you in a fight in no time."

"I'd love to try …" he muses.

I wrap my arm around his shoulder and say, "Better not. The zoo won't be happy about that, especially not when they have to rake your insides off the grass."

"Who says I'd lose?" he asks.

"I do." I grin.

He raises a brow. "What did you say?" He pulls me off his shoulder and immediately starts tickling me all over, kissing my neck along with it as he captures me in his arms. I'm helpless, completely left to his mercy, and I'm loving it.

"Say that again?" he growls, still showering me with kisses while alternating it with tickles.

"Okay, okay, you win."

"See?" he muses. "Easy."

"You won … me," I say, and he kisses me on the lips.

"Only prize I want …" he murmurs between kisses.

"But you're still not going to fight the lions or tigers," I say, leaning back as our mouths unlatch. "I won't allow it."

"Oh, really?" The smirk on his face is so irresistible.

"Yes." I cross my arms. "They're dangerous. They could kill you, and I'd prefer to keep you alive, thank you."

"Hmm …" The guttural sound from his throat makes goose bumps scatter on my skin, especially when he looks at me like he's hungry for more. "I like this."

"Like what?" I mumble.

"You … feisty." He leans in and presses a kiss to my neck, only for his tongue to dip out and draw a line all the way up to my jaw. "Mine."

God, that's all he has to say to make me melt into a puddle.

He's the damn lion, and I'm the lamb in his cage,

waiting to be devoured.

And I don't even regret it. Not even once.

***

The moment the front door is closed, Cage immediately grabs my ass and pulls me toward him, smashing his lips on mine. I giggle, but his lips cover my mouth quickly, preventing me from moving. He holds me tight and groans against my lips, pushing his half-hard dick against my thighs.

I can't believe we're doing this again so quickly, but I guess his appetite is never-ending. That's what you get for shacking up with a beast ... you get fucked, a lot.

But I'm not protesting, not one bit. Not even when he spins me around and shoves his fingers down my skirt, fingering me without holding back. Right here, in the hallway, where everyone could still see us because my door has a tiny window. But I don't even care. All I want is his fingers and lips all over me. And oh, boy ... does he know how to work magic with that tongue of his as he plants kisses right below my ear.

"Mine ..." he grumbles, making my blood rush through my veins as lust fills my body.

"Yes," I mewl, wanting to give in to him completely.

However, when I open my eyes and come face to face with Bo staring at us, I shriek.

Cage pulls his hand from my skirt and steps back as I clutch my body, embarrassed.

What the hell is Bo doing here?

The paper bag of groceries he was carrying drops to the ground as he stands with his jaw gaping.

My eyes widen the moment I see the pain in his eyes, cutting into my heart.

He spins on his heels, leaving the groceries spilled on the ground as he rushes off.

I don't think twice. "Wait here," I say to Cage as I open the door.

"Need help?"

"No, I got it," I say as I run after Bo.

I have to catch up to him before he leaves. I can't let him walk away like that. Not after seeing what he saw. I'm mortified. It was horrible that he had to see that, and I feel guilty … I have to fix this. I have to talk to him.

I sprint as hard as I can, reaching Bo just before he jumps on his bike. I stop him, through, placing a hand on his wheel so he can't leave without giving me a chance to explain.

I'm sorry, I sign.

But the hurt is too big. It shows on his darkened face, his posture, everything. Even his body is tense.

"Please don't," he rasps.

Please, I sign, *I don't want this to get between us. I'm sorry you had to see that.*

"Get between us? You mean that guy shoving his hands down your skirt as if he owns you? In front of the whole world?" he shouts.

Hearing it come from his mouth only makes it sound even worse.

But I never wanted him to witness that.

If I'd known you were coming, I wouldn't have done that with him, I sign.

He turns and puts a foot on the bike. But if he leaves

now … I might never see him again.

I quickly sign, *Please, don't go. We can discuss this.*

"What's there to discuss?" he barks. "I know what I saw. End of story."

No. I shake my head. He's being mean just to hurt me, and I get it, but it still hurts.

"He's the father of your baby. I get it," Bo says. "But other than that, what does he give you? Can he provide for you? Does he work? Does he do anything at all other than act like a caveman?"

I grimace. I understand he's upset, but he's taking it out on Cage now.

That's not fair, I sign. *Cage didn't choose any of this.*

"Yes, he did. He chose you," Bo says.

What? No, it's much more than that, I sign. *We chose each other. I trust him and he trusts me.*

He nods, but the look in his eyes feels like a sharp dagger. "You trust him, yet you never even told him anything about his brother. But you told me. When were you going to do that? Never? How can there be trust when he doesn't even know the full truth? I don't understand."

My lips part, but nothing rolls off my tongue. All I can do is gasp at the realization that Bo just talked out loud about Cage's brother … and that I still haven't told him.

I know I haven't. I was waiting for the right time. The right moment. If there ever is any.

But that has nothing to do with how I feel about Cage.

Bo puts on his helmet. "Whatever. I'm done."

Please. Don't do this, I beg him with signs.

"Do what?" he snaps. "All I wanted to do was help."

And you did. Thank you for that, I sign. *And for the groceries.*

He makes a sour face. "Really? The groceries? That's all that matters?"

No, of course not, I sign.

"All these years, Ella," he scoffs, shaking his head. "Why can you talk to him but not me?" he growls. "You feel safe to use your voice around him but not me? A guy you've known for years?" His eyes are red and turn watery. "A guy you met in a *cage* and you trust him more than you trust me?"

I clutch my chest, my heart feeling like it's breaking into tiny pieces.

I shake my head, not knowing how to respond.

It's not true, I sign. *I trust you.*

I just don't know any better. Signing is how I've always communicated with Bo. After my sister's death, there ... didn't seem to be any voice left in me except when I was around my parents. But Cage changed that. He changed me.

And when I finally escaped and came back home, I reverted to my old self around Bo.

I didn't use my voice because it didn't feel necessary. I'd been signing to Bo for so long, I didn't know anything else, so that's what I kept doing. Because it felt safe.

But I never imagined it'd hurt him so much ... especially to see me talk to Cage.

To see me ... being kissed and touched by him.

Tears well up in my eyes. *I'm sorry,* I sign.

"Don't," he hisses, getting on his bike. "Just don't. I wanted to help you, but I can't. I just can't fucking do it anymore. You want to be with *him?* That ... *animal?*"

The word animal sets me off.

Turns a switch in my brain that I didn't know existed.

Before I know it, I've already slapped him … right across the face.

I immediately pull back and put my hand in front of my mouth.

Bo just stands there idle, staring at me with pain in his eyes.

I can feel it to the bone. It scrapes and scrapes at me until nothing's left but chiseled off dust. It makes me want to wish I could shrivel up and die.

I shake my head as he touches right where I slapped him with two fingers.

After a silence that feels like an eternity, he spits, "Fine."

And then he bikes off quickly before I have the chance to say something … anything.

Speak.

That's what I should've done all along.

Let him hear my

voice.

Tell him how and what I felt.

So there wouldn't ever be this hurt inside my heart and his.

"B-bo!" I call out his name as he drives off.

It's the first time ever that I've yelled out his name.

And it makes him glance over his shoulder … just before he disappears out of view.

FIFTY-ONE

CAGE

I've been staring through the window, watching them from afar. They're fighting, but I don't know about what. I can hear him discuss me and trust.

But then I hear that one word ...

The word that makes me question everything about my existence.

Brother.

I gasp, placing a hand on the door as I get closer. Did he really say ... I have a brother?

And Ella knew all along?

Why didn't she tell me?

As Bo bikes away, she sinks to the ground, and I open the door, stepping outside. When she glances at me over her shoulder, I can see the pain in her eyes, and it's killing me.

"Cage …" she mumbles, drops rolling down her cheeks.

I frown. "I … have a brother?"

She nods.

So she did keep it from me.

I make a fist with my hand and look away.

"I'm sorry," she says as she gets up from the ground. "I'm so sorry; I should've told you."

I go toward her and grasp her hand. "Come back inside." I pull her, and she comes along willingly back into her house.

"I'm sorry," she repeats. "I was trying to find the right moment to tell you, but I couldn't. I didn't want to hurt you, and if you knew what had happened to him …"

I place her on a chair and scoot it my way while I stand in front of her with folded arms, waiting for more.

"Where is he?" I ask.

She shakes her head, biting her lip. "I don't know. Your father didn't know either. I just saw him hold up a picture and recognized it."

"You recognized *my* brother?" I ask, wondering what he looks like. "Where's the picture?"

"The police took them for their investigation," she replies, sighing.

I grind my teeth. I don't understand what all this means. I have a brother, and I never knew about him. Father didn't say a word. Why would he keep this from me? And where is he now?

"Where'd he go?" I ask.

"He …" She lowers her head. "He ran away from your father and then … he took my sister and she died. Right now, I don't think anyone knows where he is."

My brother killed her sister?

"Oh …" I mumble.

But how? And why would he do that?

She didn't deserve that.

When she grows silent, I go to my knees in front of her and make her look me in the eyes. "He killed your sister?"

She nods.

I can't believe it. No brother of mine would hurt the sister of the girl I love.

That's not right.

I shake my head. "Then he isn't my brother."

She furrows her brows, gazing back at me with a confused look on her face.

So I add, "Brothers don't kill …" I look up at her. "I'm sorry. For what he did."

Her expression relaxes a bit, and she places a hand on my cheek. "Oh, Cage … You don't have to say that. I know what happened; my sister died, but it was a long time ago. I don't blame him and neither should you." She smiles briefly. "I'm really sorry about not telling you sooner."

I place a hand on top of hers. "Why?"

"Because I was afraid of how you'd react." Her eyes are watery again. "And because I was selfish in my needs for you … And I'm sorry."

I lean in and wrap my arms around her, hugging her tight. I don't care that she didn't tell me. I just want this bad feeling to go away.

"I'm sorry," she mumbles again. "About everything."

"Shh …" I silence her, pressing a kiss to her cheeks. "Not your fault."

"Yes, it is. He's your brother, for God's sake. I had no right to keep it from you. God, why am I so stupid sometimes?"

"You're not," I say, looking her directly in the eyes. "You're the smartest girl I've ever met."

She snorts. "You haven't met a lot of girls."

"Don't need to. I know what you're worth."

Her blush makes me smile, and at that moment, all the bad feelings go away. Her happiness does that to me. It soothes me and calms my mind. Makes me forget about all the pain inside my heart.

She's here, right in my arms ... and that's all that matters.

The rest will come later.

"Your brother—"

I place a finger on her lips. "No. Tell me about Bo."

I can see her hurting. I want to fix it.

"Bo? He ..." She swallows away the lump in her throat. "He said some very mean things."

"What?"

"Well ..." She frowns. "That you couldn't provide for me financially, but that's stupid. I already said I'm fine taking care of you."

Providing for her ... financially?

Like paying for things? The house? The food?

He's right.

I'm supposed to take care of her and give her everything she needs, yet I can't. I don't have any of that money the people here always seem to have. I don't have anything to offer but my love. Except that's not enough. She needs stability. Someone who can give her more in this world.

Something I can't ...

"He's right," I say, grimacing.

"No," she stresses, clutching my face, "Don't say that. It's not."

"Yes." I take her hands and pull them down. I don't deserve her affection if I can't give her the same in return. What kind of man can't take care of what's his?

"I want you. But I'm not good enough."

"Stop," she says, "I don't want to hear those words."

But what am I supposed to do about it? How do I give her what she needs if I don't understand this world? Maybe she *is* better off with Bo. He can provide for her.

"Bo can—"

"Shh," she says, placing a finger on my lips. "I don't want to hear it. It's not true. Bo might be able to provide, but he can't give me what you're giving me. I don't want Bo the way I want you." She cocks her head. "Love."

"Love ..." I repeat. Is that all that matters?

But love doesn't provide. I can't take care of her with just love.

"How do I provide?" I ask her, desperately wanting to know how I can be what she needs me to be.

Her eyes are all watery again. "No, you don't have to."

I grab her hand and squeeze. "I *want* to. Tell me."

"Well ... we could find you a job," she mutters. "But that would be hard. We'd have to find something that fits you. Something you can do that's easy to understand." Her eyes narrow. "What are you good at?"

"Good?" I shrug. "Fighting."

She bites her lip. "Well ... I guess we could search for something that has to do with fighting. But anyway ... that's dangerous."

"Fighting. I can do it," I say.

Her brows draw together. "Are you sure?"

I nod.

She smiles. "I appreciate it, but you really don't have to. I don't want you to get hurt."

"I want to," I say, and I place a hand on my chest and make a fist. "To take care of my woman."

She laughs again, but I don't know why. It's not meant to be funny. I'm dead serious.

"So ... Bo? What else?" I ask.

"What?"

"Tell me more." I point outside. "What else happened there?"

"Um ... He said you were an animal, so I slapped him."

At first, I stare at her, but then I can't stop the grin from spreading on my cheeks.

"Why are you laughing?" she asks.

"Because it's funny."

"It's not."

"It's the truth," I say, shrugging.

"What?" She makes a face. "No, you're not an animal. You're a guy, just like him."

"He wishes he was me," I say, raising a brow.

She shakes her head, snorting too now, but it's the truth.

"Maybe that's why he's so upset," she says. "He really is jealous of you."

"I'm sorry," I say. I don't like the guy because he's trying to make her his, but I know she likes him, and I have to accept that.

"I should've been more clear with him ..." she

mumbles.

I tip up her chin. "Not your fault." I smile, cocking my head as I lean in. "You're pretty. Smart. Any man would want you." I press a slow and gentle kiss onto her lips. "*Mine.*"

She giggles softly, and I place more kisses below her lips on her chin and neck.

"Soft … and delicious …" I groan, letting my tongue roam freely across her skin.

"You know I can't say no to this," she murmurs, but it sounds more like a moan. "But we got caught the last time."

"No one can see you here …" I whisper into her ear, nibbling on her earlobe. "Except me."

"So what does that mean?" she mumbles, tilting her head back to allow me access.

But I wrap my arms around her waist and pull her up from the chair, setting her on the table with her legs entwined around my back. I push my body against hers, making her feel my hard-on to remind her what's going to happen next. And I growl, "This."

***

Ella

A few days later, we found the perfect job for Cage. A local fighting ring is looking for more trained participants. When they first saw me and Cage, they laughed a little, probably thinking I was joking when I told them he didn't have any previous experience. At least not in a fighting ring like the one they have here.

They don't have to know he's been part of an underground one all his life. And that he was taught to kill.

Luckily, when he unrobed and showed off his muscles, they were quick to give him a chance. In the locker room, he prepares with a new set of hand wraps we bought. I can't stop biting my lip as I watch him do it, though. It reminds me too much of the ring below the cage.

That place ... was his personal prison.

"Are you sure you want to do this?" I ask.

He only briefly glances up at me before continuing with the wrap. "Yes."

I'm worried he might be pushing himself too far for me.

So I grab his hand and stop him. "If you don't want to do this, tell me now," I say, making him look me in the eye. "You don't have to do this for me. I'm happy as we are. You don't have to fight for me."

"I'm doing this for me." He finishes wrapping his hands, sticking it down with tape. Then he turns my way. "I *want* to fight."

He grabs me with both hands and presses a kiss to my forehead. "Stop worrying."

"I know," I mutter. "I just don't want you to get—"

"Hurt?" He laughs because the idea alone is funny to him.

I smile, shaking my head. "You're not a god, Cage. You can still die."

"You've seen me fight. You think I'll lose?" He raises a brow.

"No, I'm not saying that," I say.

He tilts his head down and growls, "Then trust me."

I swallow away the lump in my throat and nod.

He kisses me again, this time on the mouth, taking the last of my worries away with those godly lips of his.

When he takes his lips off mine, I whisper, "I trust you … but don't kill anyone, please."

He snorts. "I won't."

"You sure? Don't break bones either. Just … put in half of your strength."

"Half?" An arrogant smirk appears on his face.

"Yes," I say, playfully punching him. "Now go out there and kick some ass."

"Kick his ass? Sure." When he walks off, I grab his arm one last time.

"It was a figure of speech."

"What's that?"

I roll my eyes. "Never mind. Just don't do it. Just … be nice."

"Nice … while punching? Okay."

I laugh. "Exactly."

He nods and then smacks his own palm with his fist. "Ready."

***

I follow him as he walks out of the dressing room and into the fighting ring where a bunch of guys are already waiting for him. Everyone watches as he and some other beefy guy climb into the ring together. I stay behind, near the dressing room, not wanting to get close to so many muscled up men. They kind of freak me out—except for

Cage, of course. The calmness he exudes is enthralling to watch as he circles his opponent. Even though the other men have contempt for him, I know they'll be blown away by his performance. All they have to do is watch.

When the moment arrives and the fight starts, the beefy guy starts punching right away, immediately rushing at Cage. However, Cage expertly dodges every single one of his strikes, including the dirty tackle the man almost gave him.

Cage keeps glancing at me, watching me like a hawk as he bounces around on his feet. Like me watching helps him concentrate. But the more I look at the way he moves, the less anxious I feel. It's not like before, back when we were still imprisoned and he had to fight off all those men. Those were pros … and there were a ton of them attacking him all at once.

But this? This is just one guy using whatever means necessary to hit Cage … and it's not even working. It's like he wants to prove a point. That he's untouchable. That he really is the super human I believed he was when I first saw him fight.

He's still that same man from inside the cell.

Only now he's uncaged.

I watch in awe as he shuffles across the ring with the men behind him shouting and cursing, telling him to quit playing around. But that's just it … He's toying with the guy. Playing with his mind until he loses it.

One misstep and then … Cage pounces on him.

One hit to the face is enough to knock him out.

His body drops flat to the floor … just like everyone's jaws.

He wasn't even competition.

Cage cracks his knuckles and jumps right out of the ring, leaving the man KO'd on the mat. He makes his way toward the main man who's sitting in a plastic chair in the corner of the room, completely flabbergasted like the rest of them.

"And?" Cage asks.

The man stammers for a second as he looks Cage up and down. A broad smile appears on his face as he's probably seeing dollar signs. "Fuck yes, you're in."

FIFTY-TWO

CAGE

A few weeks later, and I'm already a regular in the ring. Once they got a whiff of what I could do, a lot of them were willing to throw money at my face to have me fight for them. I let Ella do all the talking while I just accept whatever she tells me to do. I don't know what it means or what the rules are; I just listen to her because I trust her to make the right decision.

And boy, did she.

I'm fighting like crazy, one after the other, every single week. It's only gotten crazier since I started. Apparently, more spectators are there since I've been fighting. The news of me appearing out of nowhere to join the ranks of the fighters has somehow brought about a load of people who want to see me.

I don't mind. I can fight, and whether they're here or not, it doesn't matter. I focus solely on my opponent, finishing them without trying to actually kill them. It's much harder than I anticipated, though, as my hits are fast and unpredictable, too strong for the regular untrained body.

But I have to do it for her. For Ella. I must keep my strength under control and only fight with what's needed.

It helps that she watches every fight. With her eyes on me, I keep calm and stay in control over my fury. I've learned to channel my anger over what my father did into these fights, though. And it's caused me to win ... again and again and again.

Just like now, when my opponent is barely able to stay standing, breathing heavily through his mouth while I'm still hopping around. My fists are eager to hit him again, but I know he can't take much more, and I refuse to kill him. Ella said they could take me away and lock me up if it ever happens, so I must avoid it at all cost.

With Ella cheering me on from the sidelines, I deliver my final punch, and my opponent drops to the floor like a wooden plank. The crowd erupts in chants and clapping, and I can't stop myself from doing a victory roar, the same one I always do. For some reason, the people watching me have come to expect it, and they roar with me, almost as if they're trying to connect with me. I don't know why they do it, but it does make me smirk proudly.

The referee calls the fight, and I stop and jump out of the ring. My manager immediately jumps on my neck, yelling, "You did it! Fuck, Cage, if I'd known you were this big of a moneymaker, I would've searched the entire country to find you."

"Really?" I doubt that's true, but whatever. I'll take it. Fighting for him means I'll get paid, and with money, I can support my Ella. I don't know how much it is or what the value of the small green papers really is. To me, it's just paper, but to the rest of the world, it's everything, so I understand it's important. It gets stuff done. Still, the money doesn't faze me. Only her proud face as she gazes at me from the corner near the dressing room.

"You're gold, man. I'm serious. You earn me so much cash; I've never had this many people come to see a fighter before. And Jesus, do you know how many bets were made? We'll be millionaires together." He holds his hand up high and waits, staring at me, but I don't know what he wants from me.

"Uh ... okay," he says. "No worries. I'm happy either way. Can't wait for next Saturday. I'll see you then? Ready to ruin twice as many?" I nod at my manager who keeps yapping in my face, but I don't care about any of that. I don't care how many guys he wants me to fight, or how much money he wants to earn now that he has me.

All I want is her. I'm only doing this for her.

My Ella ... And now that I've won, she'll be my biggest prize.

***

Ella

I clap as he approaches me, wanting to press a kiss to his cheek, but when he marches toward me, I think I'm in trouble. The expression on his face is wild and hungry—as if he wants to eat me alive and then some. I swallow, not sure what to expect as he bolts toward me, muscles still bulging out of his shirt.

With one hand, he grabs my face and forces his lips onto mine as his other hand snakes its way down my ass to hold me tight. I melt in his arms, unable to free myself from his grasp, but I love it. I love how greedily he kisses me. As if he wants to taste every inch of my mouth and more. I can sense his arousal, especially when he rubs himself against me.

When our lips briefly unlock, he growls, "Come."

My pussy thumps from his voice alone, and I let him drag me along into the locker room. He locks it from the inside out as I stumble backward, almost falling over a bench. I'm that shaken up from watching him fight like that up close. The raw, animalistic energy he exudes is impressive … dangerous … and it's turning me into a willing prey.

Just that look he gives me as he turns around is enough to make me freeze.

"In here? We can't; they'll hear us."

"Don't care," he growls. "I want you. *Now.*"

He approaches me and smashes his lips onto mine again, grasping my face with both hands this time. The groan that leaves his mouth sets my body on fire as his hands drive me crazy with lust.

He quickly spins us around and marches toward the showers with me still in his hands. I'm helpless to fight it. I don't want it to stop even though I know it's wrong because we're not even at home. Everyone knows what's going on in this locker room, yet I don't even care.

All I want is for him to take what belongs to him ... me.

I kiss him back with equal intensity, wanting to taste him on my tongue forever. If this isn't bliss, I don't know what is.

He pulls my top over my head and throws it in the corner and then frantically undoes the button of my pants, ripping those down too. With his teeth, he roughly slides down my panties and immediately starts licking my pussy.

Not stopping to breathe, he immediately dives in to lick me. I struggle to even stay standing against the shower wall as he laps me up like an animal. He's that aggressive; sucking hard, pushing his tongue inside me, and making me all wet and wobbly.

My fingers tangle in his hair as he groans against my skin, making me want to moan too. So I do; I let myself go in his hands, which firmly grasp my ass. He's buried between my legs; his tongue draws circles around my clit until my legs part even farther, allowing him to shove two fingers into me.

I love every single thing he's doing even though I know people might hear. I'm more enamored with the fact that this is what he chose to do after his victory. Of all the things he could've done to celebrate ... the first thing he did was grab me.

His woman.

So he could lick me.

God, if that isn't sexy, I don't know what is.

I accidentally turn on the shower with my back, and I giggle as the water rushes down on us, but he doesn't even seem fazed. Not even as the water completely soaks him. He hasn't even taken off his own shorts yet; that's how eager he was to take me. He just jumped on me and took what is his, and I don't even mind.

I'm lost in desire and pure need, pushing his head in farther, wanting him to do it harder, faster, more. Everything. I've never been this easy, but with him, it comes naturally. It's like sex is our way of expressing ourselves. Like it binds us together in ways talking can't ever do.

His lips have ruined me, and I openly embrace my own demise.

He's my catalyst; the thing that sets me off and makes me tick.

The one person who knows how to push my buttons and turn me into a lover of all things dirty.

He knows it all too well … what he does to me with that tongue.

I can see it in his eyes as he glances up at me for a second, a smirk on his face as he watches me bite my lip. I can't help it. He's that good.

His groans and growls push me to the edge, and I suck in a breath.

"Come," he commands.

His gruff voice is all I need to collapse.

My eyes roll to the back of my head as I clutch him. He holds me steady as I feel the waves of ecstasy flow through my body, again and again.

When my orgasm subsides, he licks up my wetness and sticks his tongue inside me, grunting like a beast. *My* dirty beast.

He quickly rises again and immediately smashes his lips onto mine again. I can taste myself in his kisses, but I don't mind; it only arouses me more as he explores my mouth. His hand is all over my breasts, squeezing both and twisting my nipples until I moan into his mouth.

A grin spreads on his lips as my hands slide down his wet pecs and abs, along every hard ridge down to his V, and I fantasize about licking up all the droplets of water. My fingers curl around his shorts, and I push them down until the waistband finally moves over his bouncing cock. It's huge, and it still makes me do a double take every time I look at it.

However, I don't even get the chance to grasp it or lick him because he immediately flips me around and presses me against the shower wall. Water from the shower rushes down my back and drips down his hair as he roughly pins me to the wall and grasps a fistful of my hair. I moan as he pulls my hair to tilt my head, and he claims my mouth once more. The tip of his length pushes against my ass, and I welcome it greedily.

I'm not even afraid of what's going to happen or where he'll put it. I just want it inside me. I'm completely his, and he knows it. In fact, I can tell he enjoys it, just from the soft grin on his face as he spreads my legs with his knee.

He swipes his cock up and down my slit, making my body arch to get closer to his. He places a hand on top of mine, our fingers entwining as he slowly pushes inside my pussy. I gasp as he buries himself completely inside me, all the way to the base. I can feel it tighten, my clit thumping with need, desperate to come again.

He starts thrusting, slowly at first, savoring each one as if it's his last. The last inch makes my jaw drop and my eyes roll to the back of my head. That's how good it feels.

After a few thrusts, he increases his pace. However, a sudden finger pushing into my ass makes me squeal. With his other hand, he covers my mouth as he probes around inside me. His finger and cock enter me at the same time, causing an overload of sensations.

It feels like fireworks go off inside me. I never imagined I'd be this filthy, but he makes me want it so badly. I'm consumed by lust. But I no longer feel any shame. I feel only our desires melting into a single need ... fuck.

His body is so close to mine that I can feel his droplets rolling onto my back, the heat rising between us as we get closer and closer to euphoria.

I let him take control as he fists my hair and rams into me with fervor. He plunges in deeply, taking me roughly, not the least bit soft. He's lost his ability to be gentle; still raging from the fight, he's taking out all his pent-up rage on me. But I don't mind it one bit. I know he'll be good to me, and I'll be good to him.

I mewl when his grip tightens and his veins pulse inside me. He howls out loud and then I feel it ... the warm jet of cum inside me, filling me up. I almost drool as he buries himself deep inside me, coating me with his seed.

When he pulls out both his dick and finger, I struggle to stay standing, but his hands keep me upright.

"Mine ..." he growls, and he grabs my ass and spreads my cheeks.

Without warning, he pushes the tip of his length into my ass. I gasp and a high-pitched sound leaves my mouth as he pushes in, still hard. Need mixes with pain as he starts to move—deeper, faster—claiming my ass too.

I feel so dirty, yet the more he thrusts, the more I like it.

I'm smashed against the wall, being fucked into oblivion, and I want nothing else than him. My body rocks along with his, rubbing against his as he slams into me. He's unrelenting as if he has the energy to continue for days and then some. I succumb to the desire as his hand slides between my legs and grabs my pussy. He toys with me, circling my clit with his fingers, pushing them inside me when I'm at the very edge.

As I come, so does he, and I can feel both his fingers and cock inside me. He pulses, releasing himself inside my ass once more, and I can feel it fill me to the brim. Together, we moan and grind until we're sated and completely undone.

And as he pulls out, he captures my body in his warm arms and pulls me into his embrace. The water of the shower rushes down on his back as he stares into my eyes and places one soft, sweet kiss on my lips, sealing our bond.

And I can't help but hope that it can stay like this forever.

Just me and him … together.

But something still nags at me, something I can't shrug off.

Fear … fear that in one quick swoop it could all be over. I just hope I'll see it coming.

FIFTY-THREE

Ella

After a few more days of not responding to any of the questions thrown at us, the reporters have finally backed off. The property around my house is empty again now that they realize they won't get a blip of information out of me. Which means we finally have everything to ourselves again.

I smirk as I sit down on his lap with a bowl of fruit in my hand. As he tries to reach for the fruit, I quickly hold it up high, stopping him from grasping any.

"No, no," I say.

He raises his brow in response.

"This is for a test," I say.

"A test?"

I grin. "Yup. I say a word, and you spell it out."

I've been teaching him to spell, write, and read slowly over the past couple of weeks, but he's gotten the hang of it so quickly that I needed to up my game and think of something to challenge him. So I'm going to tempt him with delicious sweets if he does it right.

"And then?" he asks.

"Then you get a piece of fruit ..." I stick out my tongue when he narrows his eyes.

A smirk appears on his face. "Okay."

"Ready?" When he nods, I say, "Strawberry."

He spells it out slowly, saying each letter one by one like they don't go together, but he actually pronounces them right. I smile when he gets to the last letter.

"Great." I grab a single piece of strawberry, knowing it's something he's never tasted before. "Close your eyes and open your mouth."

When he does what I ask, I gently place it on his tongue. He chews it softly and swallows.

"Hmmm ... sweet."

That groan makes me meek, but I have to focus on his education first. Even though the dirty grin that follows almost tempts me to kiss him. When he tries, I push him away and say, "No, learning first."

"Fine. More of those?" he asks, peeking over my shoulder at the bowl.

"There are more strawberries," I reply. "But you're only getting them if you spell the words. Plus, other fruit is in there."

"Just as sweet?" The way he licks his lips makes me zoom in on his tongue, and I have to hold myself back from jumping his bones. Damn, why does he always have to make things so hard… and *be* so hard.

"As sweet as you?" he adds, making it even harder for me to resist.

"Maybe." I grin. "Words first."

I grab a book I placed on the table and open it to a random page, pointing my finger at the first difficult word I can find. *Captive*. Perfect. "This one. Spell it out and say the word."

He does it again, speaking every single letter like it's the first time he's ever done it, but it works. He's memorized the things I've taught him well.

"Captive," he says after finishing the sequence.

"Good!" I say when he's done.

"Now I get my prize …" he growls, tipping my chin up, but I quickly grab another strawberry and hold it between us.

"Not me … fruit, remember?"

He purses his lips. "Why?"

"Because I say so, and it's fun," I say.

"Bossy …" he jokes, smirking again. "I like it."

He steals the strawberry from my fingers and stuffs it in my mouth. Then he surprises me by smashing his lips against mine. When I close my eyes, he bites the strawberry in half, sucking on it as he pulls away, leaving me breathless again … and with half a strawberry in my mouth.

"Hmm … delicious." He groans, winking and melting my heart again.

"Okay, okay … I get it," I say, smiling as I put the bowl away. I place a hand on his chest right as he reaches for my face to try to kiss me again. "But we don't have time for fooling around; you have another fight in an hour or so. We need to get you there and prepare."

"Really?" he protests.

"Yes, really. You wanted to fight, remember?" I say. "If you want to stop, just say so."

"No," he says, grabbing my wrist. "I want to provide." He pulls my hand to his face and kisses the top of my hand. "For my woman."

A blush spreads on my cheeks, and I quickly crawl off his lap before I lose control again. As much as I want to have sex with him, his scheduled fight comes first. We made this choice together, so he can help out and feel useful, so we have to put in the effort to get him there on time.

I quickly crawl off his lap before things get too hot and heavy. I run to the hallway and grab our coats and the car keys, yelling, "Coming, Cage?"

"Oh, yes ..." he grumbles, and the way he says it makes me chuckle.

There was a definite double meaning to that.

***

CAGE

When I step into the ring, the crowd erupts in screams and cheers. According to my manager, I've become the recent favorite of many, and I made him a lot of money. It doesn't matter to me because all I want is to make *her* happy. That girl sitting in the chair at the front of the line, not too far away. With Ella's eyes on me, I know I won't ever lose. I won't allow it. I'll beat my opponent to a pulp to prevent that from happening. But I won't kill him. I'll just punch him until he gives up.

The moment the referee starts the fight, I bob up and down on my feet, awaiting his move. I don't know the guy and don't care to. I'm only here to win. However, from the look on his face, I can tell he's thinking the same thing. But I doubt he has the same experience as I do.

Nothing will make a man stronger than literally having to fight for his life ... and that of his woman.

A smug smile spreads across my lips as I watch him shuffle with his fists up in the air as if he thinks he can surprise me. I'm one step ahead of every one of his.

When he strikes, I dodge, and when he tries to kick, I jump.

All I can do is grin as he gets more and more worked up. The crowd is going crazy with chants as they watch our fight, and I know my manager will be pleased if I manage to draw it out as long as I can, so I have to be careful not to punch him too hard.

However, the moment I prepare for a jab, I notice something from the corner of my eye.

A set of eyes drawing attention by only focusing on me.

One glance is enough to distract me.

It's a face I've not seen in weeks ... and it strikes me to the core.

It makes me want to leap out of the ring.

Suddenly, knuckles ram into my jaw, catching me by surprise. I stumble, falling backward onto the mat. The crowd turns silent in shock. I blink a couple of times and stare straight at the spot.

But he's gone. Completely disappeared.

And I'm left questioning whether what I saw was real or if it was all in my head.

Am I losing my mind?

"Cage!"

Her voice wakes me up and pulls me back to reality. I immediately follow the sound and see her distressed face the moment my opponent towers over me in an attempt to strike me down again.

I can't let him win.

No fucking way.

Not on my watch.

So I quickly throw my foot up, right into his crotch. He groans, grabbing his nuts as I swiftly get up on my feet again. One heavy fist to his face and he's flipped around and falling down right on his face, knocked out.

The crowd erupts into cheers, but I can't enjoy it, can't focus on the sound of my victory, because of what I saw.

I immediately jump out the ring and storm out through the entrance with my manager and Ella on my tail.

"What are you doing?" my manager calls out. He stops following me halfway through as he probably realizes I'm not stopping as I march out that door and onto the street, still in my fighter gear.

"Cage!" Ella's voice makes me glance over my shoulder briefly. She places a hand on my back and asks, "What happened? You let him hit you. You never get hit." She swallows. "What did you see?"

I look around, trying to see if I can find him, but no luck so far.

Was it a dream?

Or did I really see him?

But as I come face to face with my worst nightmare, I realize I haven't even told her yet. She doesn't know how I got out.

"Father. I saw him." Her face fills with terror as I turn around and grab both her arms. "He's here."

FIFTY-FOUR

Ella

A chill runs up and down my spine the moment he says those words.

His father ... is here?

No, that can't be.

He has to be dead.

I stabbed him; I remember it. Twice, even. The memory still makes knots form in my stomach. I never felt like I could completely rinse off his blood. As if a part of him stayed with me even after I'd fled.

And now that turns out to be true. But how?

How is it possible?

I shake my head. "But I killed him," I say, not wanting

to believe it.

I'm desperate. Anything but him … I can't take it. Not again. If he's really here, then he's after us, and we'll never be safe.

"I saw him," Cage admits.

"Are you sure?" I ask.

He nods.

I keep shaking my head, my entire body trembling as I come face to face with my own prediction. Something would ruin us … but it wasn't me.

It was him.

His father was dying when I left him.

But for some reason, he's still alive, and that can only mean one thing.

Cage … he helped Cage get out …

"You … let him live?" I ask as I take a step back, horrified. Cage tries to grab me, but I jerk my arm free. "No. Answer me!"

He licks his lips, looking defeated. "Yes."

The admission alone makes the hairs on the back of my neck stand.

I can't believe this.

The man who caused my sister's death … who took me and put me in a tiny cell … who made both of us his puppets and used us for his own sick, twisted games … is still alive. And Cage set him free.

"Why?" I mumble. "Why would you do that? I thought he was dead."

"He helped me out," Cage says. "Without him, I'd never—"

"No! We could've saved you!" I shout, unable to keep

441

my emotions at bay even though we're standing on the street. I don't care anymore. "Do you know how far I went to search for you? We drove for hours on end to get back to the compound. I spent days trying to find you, and the officers did too, and when we finally found the compound, you weren't even there." I sniff. "Do you have any idea how that made me feel? How lost I felt? If you were there, we could've saved you."

He just nods and listens, and it makes me only want to lash out more.

"He could've just died! But you let him help you, and now he's still alive!" I say, pushing Cage, but he won't budge.

No matter how much I try to get him to move, to do anything, to yell back, he refuses.

"Why?"

"He brought me to a hospital," Cage explains. "Without him, I'd be nowhere."

"Don't you say that!" I make a face. "He never did anything good for you. *Ever.* The man is evil, and you know it."

It feels like my blood is boiling; that's how mad I am. Why would he keep this from me? All this time, he knew; he knew his father was alive because Cage drove them to the hospital. And he didn't even tell me. Not how he escaped or got his wounds fixed. Not any of it. And now I understand why ... because his shoulders are slumped, and he can't even look at me.

"I'm sorry," he mumbles.

It breaks my heart in two.

"I thought ... I thought we trusted each other," I reply,

442

choking up.

"I do," he says. "*We* do."

"But you didn't tell me. You kept the worst man on earth alive … and for what?"

"I didn't," he rasps, grimacing. "I wanted him dead."

"Then why did you let him live?" I ask.

"He was gone," he answers. "Disappeared."

My eyes widen. "From the hospital?"

He nods. "I was too late."

It's silent for a few seconds as I think about what just happened, and everything I just learned. I can't believe he's still alive. The mere idea makes me want to puke. But if it's really true, we can't stay here and wait until he comes.

Because if I know one thing, it's that Graham will do whatever it takes to get to us.

Whether it's for revenge doesn't matter.

He's coming for us. For Cage, for me … for my baby.

I immediately clutch my belly, wanting to protect it at all cost. "He'll come for my baby," I mumble.

Cage immediately places his hand on top of mine on my belly. "No. I will protect you and the baby," he growls.

"But what about the cell? What if he takes us back?" Just the thought of going back there makes me cold and shivery.

"I won't allow it," he replies sternly, gazing straight at me. "Ever."

I nod, worried that Graham might appear at any moment and take us again.

I'm still mad, but I understand Cage is only trying to look out for our best interests. Now is not the time to fight.

Cage did what he had to do to survive. I get it even

though I'm upset he never told me. What's done is done. We have to focus on not getting caught now because Graham could be anywhere.

But what do we do?

"Let's go home," Cage says, grabbing my hand.

"But your gear. Your clothes. The fight," I stammer.

"Don't care," he growls, dragging me along with him back to my car.

I don't fight his grip. I let him take me because I know that right now it's my safest option.

Only one thing's on my mind, and that's keeping the baby safe. Whatever the cost.

If Graham's back, then so be it.

But I'd rather die than let him get his hands on me or my baby.

I won't go back into that cell.

Never again.

We hop into the car, and I immediately drive off, not even caring about the fact that I'm being reckless. I just want to go home, lock the doors, and hide in the attic. Is that crazy? Yes. But Graham is much, much crazier than any of that.

I'm sure he'd kill us before he'd ever let us be free.

I can't let it happen.

We must prepare for his vile schemes. Must be one step ahead of him.

However, the moment I arrive at my home, I already feel my own courage sink into my shoes.

This is the place where I first met the man of my nightmares.

Where he swept me off my bed and took me.

The place where it all started.

A pit forms in my stomach as I gaze at Cage, biting my lip. I don't know what to do. I wonder if we should keep driving, to the end of the world if I have to, just to stay safe.

But Cage places his hand on top of mine and promises, "I will protect you."

I nod and open the door, slowly creeping outside.

I wonder if Graham's in my house at this very moment, snooping around and waiting to ambush us.

He knows how to enter my house without a key. He's done it before, so he could do it again.

With fear, I wait until Cage has jumped out too and walked over to my side. With his strong arm around my waist, I feel safer than on my own. But it still doesn't feel right. It's too quiet, too suspicious, and I wonder if that's just me. If my own terror is setting me off.

I wonder if it'll ever go away while I know the man is still alive.

I shiver.

What will we have to do to finally be rid of him?

To be able to live in peace?

He won't stop coming after us. Not unless we put an end to it.

I grasp his hand and squeeze tight as we go to the door and I push the key into the lock. As I open the door, I stare for a while, looking for something, anything that'll tell me he's here.

But I find nothing. No scratches, no footprints, no knocked over tables. Nothing.

With a calmer mind, I place the car keys on the cabinet in the hall and tread forward. Cage pushes ahead and says,

"I'll go first."

I nod and follow him into the living room, circling as we check each room. But nothing seems off. Everything is still in place as if he was never here.

"Upstairs," he says, and I nod.

"I'll go."

"Together," he says.

"No, you check the yard. Otherwise, he'll catch us off guard." I point at the glass door while opening a drawer in the kitchen to grab a knife. "This will help."

"Yell if you see something," Cage instructs.

"You too," I reply, making my way to the hallway.

I carefully walk up the stairs, trying not to make a sound. I don't want to alert him to my presence if he's there. One creak makes my heart jump, but it's my own feet causing the noise. Once I'm upstairs, I search every room, pointing the knife forward to attack anyone who I might come across.

However, the more doors I open, the less my heart pounds. Nothing's out of place, and no one's there. I checked every room, under the beds, behind the curtains, and even the shower. Nothing.

Then I hear a roar.

It's outside.

Shit.

It's Cage.

I rush down stairs as fast as I can, still holding the knife. When I jump down the last step, I see *him* ... right there ... next to my car.

Graham.

He wasn't in the garden.

He was right outside ... waiting for us to come.

And he's pointing a gun at Cage.

My hand shakes as I approach him, still holding the knife.

"Don't do anything stupid, Ella." His voice alone causes the bile to rise in my throat.

"C-Cage ..." I say, still walking toward him, unafraid. "Give h-im b-back."

Graham's eyebrows twitch, and a vicious smile appears on his face. He begins to laugh uncontrollably. Then he switches off the safety on the gun and points it directly at Cage's head. "Don't. Move," he hisses, adding under his breath, "fucking bitch."

I stop in my tracks, still holding the knife despite my hands shaking. I won't let him do this to us. I can't let him hurt Cage. Not again.

He spits on the ground. "You fucking did this to me." He points at the scars on his neck. "It took weeks for me to recover. You almost fucking killed me, you know that?" he growls.

I don't answer, but I secretly wish I had the balls to tell him straight to his face that I hoped he died.

"What do you want?" Cage seethes at his father.

"You know what I want," Graham hisses. "You two, where you belong."

"I belong with Ella," Cage says.

I shake my head at him. I don't want him to say anything to set his father off and make him do something bad.

"Fuck, no. You're *mine*. My fucking fighter," Graham growls in his ears. "*My* boy. And you owe me your fucking life."

"I owe you nothing," Cage spits. "You lied to me."

"Lied?" Graham snorts. "I gave you everything you needed, and then you go around and betray me like that?"

"I have a brother," Cage shouts.

This momentarily shuts Graham up, but it doesn't last long. "Lock is none of your fucking business."

Cage's eyes widen the moment he hears his brother's name. "Lock?"

Graham wraps his arm around Cage's throat. "You think you could escape, did you?" he growls. "That you could do this to me and get away with it?"

I shake my head, mumbling, "P-please …"

"No! You RUINED me!" he screams, his face red and bulging.

I fear for Cage … His life is on the line, and Graham's sick in the head.

He could pull the trigger just like that.

And then he'd be gone.

I can't allow it.

"You took *everything* from me!" he spits. "My job, my money, my fucking house. Even my best fighter …" He grinds his teeth, pushing the gun into Cage's head. "And even the goddamn baby."

"P-please don't d-do this," I mutter, desperately trying to get him to see how bad this is for all of us. "You n-need us."

I don't ever want to say those words, but if it means it'll stop him from killing Cage, then I don't care what I have to say. I know that's why he's here. We were his sole income. The fighter and the girl who could carry his baby. And he wants them back.

"You … It's all your fault," he hisses at me.

I know it is, but I don't regret it. Not even for a second.

"Leave her," Cage growls all of a sudden, his body rigid like a rock. "Take me."

"No!" I scream. "Don't you dare!"

I don't care if he wants to protect me; if it means I'll lose him, then it's not worth it.

Graham starts to laugh again. "You think I want *you*?"

My eyes widen, and I suck in a breath, realizing what he means.

He stares at me, completely ignoring Cage's pleas. "Get in the car."

I shake my head. "No."

"Do it!" Graham snaps. "Or I'll blow his head off."

"You n-need us both," I reply, trying to remain calm even though I'm screaming on the inside.

"I need a fighter, but he's already wasted. This world has tainted him, so I need a new one. A better one." The intense look he gives me and my belly makes me grab myself with my free hand.

"No!" Cage growls. "Stay away from her."

Suddenly, Graham knocks Cage on the back of the head with the gun so hard he falls to the ground.

"NO!" I scream.

"Get in the fucking car!" Graham hisses, pointing the gun at me now. "Or I'll fucking kill him."

I believe his threat now. He already smacked him down, knocking him out. I know he'll do anything to get his hands on this baby. Even kill his most prized warrior.

"Drop the fucking knife," Graham instructs.

I nod, and my lips tremble as I drop the knife on the

ground.

Cage is still unmoving as I move past him, wishing he'd get up and do something. But he doesn't. Not as I approach the car. Not as I get inside and wait for my fate. Not as I hear my own keys jingle in Graham's hand.

Not even when he gets in behind the wheel … and starts the engine.

And as he puts the gear into reverse, I turn around in my seat and scream as loud as I can, as hard as my lungs will let me. "CAGE!"

FIFTY-FIVE

CAGE

The sound of her voice pulls me back from the nether. My head aches, but I ignore the pain as I crawl up from the ground and roar out loud. The car is driving backward ... with my woman, my Ella, inside it. Stuck to a window, she screams my name. The terror on her face fills me with rage.

I pick up the knife she dropped and run.

I run as fast as I can.

I know the car will be faster as it drives off, but I don't care.

I'm not going to stop trying to chase them.

I still have a chance as long as the car is still accelerating.

As fast as I can, I bolt across the street, giving it my all. My muscles strain, but I refuse to listen to my own limits. I go beyond them, way past human capacity, but I don't fucking care.

He has my fucking Ella.

My woman.

No one takes my Ella.

No one.

Not even my father.

Sweat rolls down my back and forehead as I force my muscles to their limit. I'm almost there, and Ella screams my name, but he's still holding a gun to her head, forcing her to behave. I won't let him hurt her or take my baby. No fucking way.

So I jump on the back of the car, holding the top of the roof ledge.

The car swerves but manages to stay on the road as I pull myself up to the roof. With crawling motions, I slide forward to the front where the glass is.

Without thinking, I jam the knife into the driver's side window.

My move makes him jerk the wheel so hard I almost fly off the hood, but I manage to hold on by grasping the knife. Half my body lies on the windshield now, covering his vision.

"Let her go!" I growl, smashing my fist into the glass as hard as I can.

He can barely stay on the road, and his face looks as if it's about to burst as he screams, "Get the fuck off!"

"No! Give me back *my* Ella!"

"Motherfucker, just DIE!" he screams, jerking the wheel again, trying to shake me off.

I refuse to let go. Not when she's looking straight at me

with that same terror in her eyes.

She's afraid ... not for her own life, but for mine.

I won't allow my father to do this to her.

I'm going to keep my promise. I'll keep her safe.

With all my fury, I kick in the glass until it's completely shattered. His face and my body are covered, but I don't give a damn. The car almost drives off the road and the gun drops from his hands as he tries to keep the car steady.

Roaring, he reaches out to grasp me, but I quickly use the knife and slash him. The blade hits his cheek instead of his neck. But the vehicle is unstable, and I know I can't keep this up for long.

He groans and grunts in pain, trying to grab the knife from me and the wheel at the same time.

However, I immediately jump back out onto the front and go up to the roof of the car again, then quickly move to Ella's side. With one fell swoop, I rip open her door and growl, "Jump."

She shakes her head. "It's going too fast. It'll hurt the baby."

I hold out my hand. "I'll grab you."

She nods, still unsure, but she crawls out of her seat anyway.

"You're not fucking going anywhere!" Father screams, and he tries to grab her by her shirt, but my grasp is stronger and faster. I wrap one hand around her waist and pull her up to me on the roof of the car.

I press her close to my body. "Ready? Hold on."

She nods, burying herself in my chest, wrapping her arms tightly around my neck.

I make the jump, right into the forest beyond her house.

The ground is course and rough, scratching across my body as I roll out.

But I hold her for dear life, not wanting to let go of what's mine.

I'll protect her from the pain by being her cushion.

There's a loud bang up ahead, but I let it pass. First, I need to know if my woman's safe.

Twigs leave bloody gashes on my back, but I'm alive. And when I look down and see her pretty eyes, I know she is too.

My eyes turn watery and so do hers as I ask, "Baby?"

"I think we're okay. No pain," she says as we crawl up from the ground. But then she sees the wounds on my back and chest. "Cage! You're hurt."

I shrug. "Don't feel it." I brush off the leaves.

She immediately reaches into her pocket and pulls out her phone. "I'll call the police. And an ambulance. We need help."

I nod.

Then I glance over to the place I heard the loud bang.

It's the car ... smashed into a tree not far up ahead.

And I watch as seconds later, *he* runs out and into the forest.

***

"Fuck!" I growl, immediately chasing after him.

"Cage! Don't do it! What if he still has the gun?" Ella yells after me as I run as fast as I can, but I don't care about any of that right now. I'm not gonna let him get away with it. Not this time.

I slide down the ledge into the forest, rushing through the woods across the many fallen leaves. I can hear him run, the sound of crushed twigs pointing me in the right direction.

I follow him and roar, "I'll kill you!"

I want him to know I'm here.

That I'm not going anywhere, and neither is he.

I want him to face what he's done … and accept the consequences.

I *want* him to know he's going to die. Today.

My lungs fill with air as I catch up to him, my muscles taking me farther than I thought they would. I don't fucking care what I have to do, but I will see his death with my own eyes.

It's the only way to make him stop.

As I run, I can see him beside me, only a few trees away.

Our eyes lock, and he raises the gun.

Bang.

Bang.

The bullet bounces off the trees, scaring the birds away.

But me? I'm fearless.

He can't hurt me anymore.

He didn't chain my body in that prison … He chained my mind, and Ella set it free.

I can see the fear in his eyes as I get closer and closer.

He shoots again.

The bullet narrowly grazes me, causing a burn on my skin.

It doesn't even faze me. Nothing will stop me from hunting him.

But then he suddenly disappears.

A loud cry and a thud follow.

I stop in my tracks and gaze around, sniffing, wondering where he went.

However, my eyes catch something mere inches away from my feet.

A ledge.

Below me is a huge drop-off.

I lean away, barely able to save myself from falling. A close call.

I turn to my right and go toward the place I last saw him, still gazing over the edge.

That's where I find him.

On the ground below, limbs twisted, eyes red, blood pouring from his mouth.

I slide down the ledge slowly, holding the roots of the trees to make sure I don't fall and meet the same fate.

When I reach his body, I quickly kick away the gun. Then I go to my knees in front of him, inspecting his body, his breathing, his heartbeat.

Nothing.

A smile creeps onto my face.

"Cage?"

Her voice makes me glance over my shoulder. She's there, standing right on the edge of the ledge, clutching a tree as she watches us.

Her jaw drops, and her eyes widen.

"Is he …?"

"Dead," I reply.

"He … died … where my sister died," she mumbles, grimacing.

She sinks to the ground as she comes to the realization

we're finally safe now. "Finally… it's over. And he got what he deserved."

If she's right, and this is the place her sister died … then this is what he deserved.

I pick up his body and attempt to drag it away.

"What are you doing?" Her shout makes me stop.

"Burying him," I reply, still holding him as I stare at her.

"No, we can't do that," she says.

"Why not?" I ask, frowning.

I want to get rid of him. I don't want to be reminded of his body lying here, so close to her house. What if someone finds him?

"Because it's not the right thing to do. We can't hide a body. We have to report this."

"Why?" It's much easier if we just bury it and pretend nothing happened.

"Because that's how things work. How else are you going to explain the crashed car? We have to be honest. We don't want them to think you killed him. If you bury the body now, and they find out, they're going to say you did it." She sighs. "Please, Cage. Do it for me. Do the right thing."

I mull it over for a second, not liking the idea.

"What if they blame me?" I ask. "Will I get hurt?"

She shakes her head. "No. I won't let them. Please, trust me on this. We have to do it the right way. Just leave the body. The police will be here soon."

I nod.

I'm not agreeing, but I'll do it for her.

Because this is what she wants me to be.

Not a killer … but a protector.

So that's what I'll be.

457

FIFTY-SIX

Ella

When the police come, I'm the one who guides them to the body. I don't want Cage to talk too much because I worry he might incriminate himself. So I ask them to give me a notepad and a pen so I can write the story down.

I tell them exactly what happened, from his father coming to our home to take me to the gun, the chase, and the crash. How Cage saved me and then ran after his father, who then fell to his death. No detail is left out because I believe that honesty will get us the furthest. They've already called someone to come pick up the body too.

Meanwhile, Cage is getting his wounds taken care of by the paramedics who arrived too. And it doesn't take long for the reporters to arrive. Apparently, a neighbor saw what happened on the road and called the station. And now they're here, too, as if this situation wasn't hard enough already.

However, things take a turn for the worse the moment the police officer mentions he wants to take Cage in for questioning.

I write frantically.

What? Why? He's innocent.

The police officer holds up his hand. "We don't know that, ma'am. We still need to question him at the station. And he did try to attack the driver of the car, according to eye witnesses."

He was trying to save me! I write as fast as I can, but it's not fast enough for me.

"That may be the case, ma'am, but we've gotten multiple reports pertaining to this man."

I frown and pen down more. **What reports?**

"We can't discuss that, ma'am. All I can tell you is that he'll need to come with us. Thank you for sharing all the information. We'll probably need more later, though, so expect a phone call of some sorts."

He turns around and goes toward his fellow cop who's talking with Cage.

I watch them force him to get up and walk with them to their car.

Wait! I sign, but no one here can understand me.

"Ella?" Cage mutters, his voice breaking, despair in his eyes.

No, they can't lock him up.

Not again.

Please, not again.

He can't deal with that. He's been through enough.

You can't lock him up, I write, and I quickly run to the police officer and hold it up to his face.

"Ma'am, please get out of our way. Let the paramedics take care of you," he says, pointing at the man waiting behind us with the ambulance.

"What's happening?" Cage asks.

"Get in," the officer commands, opening the car door.

No, he's been stuck in a cage all his life. Don't do this to him, I frantically write.

But it's no use. They've already shoved him into the car.

"Ella ..." he mumbles, placing his hand on the window.

"Cage ..."

I place my hand on top, tears welling up in my eyes. But I don't want him to see my pain; I don't want him to worry too, so I swallow them down. "It'll be okay. It's just for routine questioning. Nothing more. I'll get you a lawyer."

The officers talk amongst themselves, but I know they're whispering about me and the fact I'm suddenly able to talk. They don't understand. They don't know us.

"You told me they wouldn't ..." Cage says, but I can barely hear him through the closed window.

"I know. I'm sorry, Cage. They just need to know what happened. Stay strong, okay? Do it for me?"

The engine is turned on, and I tremble as I realize what's going to happen.

"Cage, I'll be with you soon. Just wait for me. Do what they ask. Please," I plead.

He nods right before they take off, leaving me behind.

All I see is Cage's troubled face staring at me through

the rear window as they drive off.

I failed him again.

***

The press that was kept at a distance by the cops immediately swarms toward me, screaming questions at my face that I didn't want to answer. So I shut myself off and let the paramedic take care of me. He calls my family for me, and I wait anxiously for them to take me home.

Not long after, my mom and dad arrive, and she immediately rushes to my side. Because of all the press hanging around, they wait until we get back to my house before they question me.

However, the moment I step into my own house, I collapse on the floor and begin to cry.

I don't know why I feel so broken, but I do.

"Cage … I'm sorry …" I mumble even though he can't hear me.

I lie down and curl up into a ball, trying to console myself and work through everything that happened, wondering if I could've prevented them from taking him.

"Oh, honey … what happened?" Mom asks.

She helps me sit up, and I immediately bury my face in her shirt, crying my eyes out.

She caresses my back and wraps her arms around me, sitting down beside me on the floor. Dad, too, comes to hug me tight, and I tell them the entire story, just like I told the police.

"Oh, no … he came at you with a gun?" Mom says in shock.

461

I nod. "He's dead, but the police took Cage, Mom. He didn't do anything. He's innocent."

Mom sighs and asks, "Well, there must be something we can do?"

"I don't know ... they were so serious about wanting to question him; even though I told them everything, I don't think they believed me. They must think we're killers."

"But they know what that man did!" she shouts.

"Yes, but that doesn't mean we can just kill him," I reply.

"But you didn't."

"No, but they don't know that, and I have no proof. Just my story." I sniff. "I feel like it's hopeless."

"What are they gonna do? Charge him with murder?"

I nod. "They might."

We look at each other, and I bury my face in her chest again.

"Oh, I'm sorry, honey ... just when you thought everything was going well. I hope that man who did this to you rots in hell."

"Agreed," Dad chimes in. "And I think you should fight this."

"But what can I do?" I ask.

"You're stronger than ever. You've been through so much, and this doesn't even compare. You can face it and win. I'm sure of it," he says, kissing my forehead. "I believe in you."

"What if they charge him and take him to trial? What then?" I say. "I'm pregnant. They'll try to make it seem like he's the bad guy."

"Then you'll prove them wrong," Dad says, nodding.

He's so sure of himself. I wish I was that levelheaded.

But all I feel is heartache for Cage as he sits there in that tiny cell.

"Oh, Cage …" I mumble, hugging my parents tight.

Their presence is the only comfort I have right now, but I don't feel like I deserve it.

Cage deserves it … but he has none.

No one except me.

And I can't be there for him.

***

It doesn't take them long to charge him officially. But it still shocks me … because they aren't just bringing charging him with murder.

They want him in jail for making me pregnant too.

I can't believe they're actually trying to do this.

I'm going to talk to Cage right now. I know he has a lawyer, but he needs me too.

When I get to the police station, I slam my notebook on the counter and write some words.

I'm Ella Rosenberg. Let me see Cage. Now.

"I'm sorry, ma'am. I—"

I slam my hand down on the counter and write more.

How dare you keep him in there. He's innocent. Now let me see him.

"Okay, ma'am, let me speak to my supervisor, please," the woman says as she holds up her hand, then walks away.

Not soon after, another police officer comes up to the counter.

Sighing, he says, "All right. You can visit him for five

minutes." He walks to the front and commands, "Come with me."

I follow him down the corridor and into a room, where I sit down on a chair in front of a table. Shortly after, Cage comes in, his hands cuffed. He sits down on the chair in front of me.

"Cage," I mumble, tearing up.

My voice makes him lean forward as far as he can.

I reach for his hand. "I'm here."

"Ella ..." he mumbles, holding my hand so tight it hurts. He brings it to his face and kisses it multiple times, almost making me cry.

"I'm sorry. I'm so sorry they put you through this. You're innocent. I tried to tell them, but they wouldn't listen to me."

"You can talk?" the man behind me asks.

I frown at him, giving him the meanest look I can muster.

"Selective mutism," Cage fills in for me.

"Ah ..." the police officer mumbles. "Whatever. Do your thing. Five minutes, that's it."

I wait until the man is gone before talking to Cage again.

"Please tell me you're okay. Are they treating you well?" I ask.

"Well ... I have food and water. And a bed."

His description reminds me too much of the cells we were in, and it makes me shiver.

"Hold on, okay? I'm going to get you out of here," I say. "The lawyer you have is a good one. He'll help us."

"How?" His pleading voice cuts into my soul.

"I don't know yet, but we will. We have our story and

facts. We'll figure it out somehow," I say, smiling softly even though it's fake. I want him to know I'm okay, and he doesn't have to worry about me.

"What about the baby?" he asks.

"Still alive and well." I place a hand on my belly and bite my lip, seeing him stare at it, probably wishing he could touch me too. I wish I could do something *now*, but I don't know what to do except wait until they decide what to do to him.

"What's going to happen to me?" he asks.

"They … want to bring you to trial," I reply.

"Trial?"

"Yes. To convict you. A jury will decide whether you're guilty or not, but only after hearing all the facts."

"But I'm not guilty," he says.

"Exactly. But they'll probably try to pin it on you anyway because this case is going to get a lot of media attention."

"Media?"

"The reporters, remember?"

He nods, but I can tell from the look in his eyes he still doesn't understand anything about what's happening to him. I feel so sorry for him. He doesn't even know what's going on. How can they do this to him? To someone so scarred and broken? He doesn't deserve this.

I lick my lips and say, "I'll make sure they don't get you, okay? I won't let them convict you."

He nods, and we entwine fingers. It's all I can do right now. Just give him hope. Because I can't go on knowing he's in here, suffering without me. I need him to hope. For us. Because I've lost all mine, and it kills me.

But then the officer returns and says those two dreaded words that cut into my heart.

"Time's up."

FIFTY-SEVEN

Ella

The reporters have already gathered in front of the courthouse. Today's the day we've waited for. The day they want me to testify against Cage for what he's done …

Even though he's innocent, they actually think they can prove he killed his father.

And the fact he impregnated me only adds to their case.

It's despicable that they want to throw us under the bus like that, but I guess it was the only outcome, considering the amount of attention this whole story has garnered. They needed someone to punish for everything that happened at the compound … so they chose Cage.

Mom and Dad protect me from the barrage of questions

the reporters throw at me while we walk up the stairs. Still, their cameras and eyes make me feel vulnerable, naked almost, as if I've been stripped of everything that makes me human. I'm an object for them, and I'm so done with them.

Done with everything.

I wish it could be over, so we could live our life in peace and not be bothered by anyone ever again.

But I want to do it with Cage. Him, and only him.

I love him. I don't doubt it for a second. I know what I want; I'm not crazy, like they're trying to prove today. But I'll show them.

When we're finally inside the building, I breathe a sigh of relief.

"Those reporters will leave once they figure out we've got nothing to tell them," Dad says.

"Exactly," Mom chimes in.

Behind me, I hear my own name being called out. "Ella!"

I turn around and see Bo running inside.

"Oh …" Mom mumbles.

She's not the only one who's shocked to see him here.

"Ella, wait," he says, practically out of breath.

"Um … Should we go grab some coffee?" Dad suggests. "Yeah, we should." He quickly grabs my mom and pulls her with him, leaving me alone with Bo who's bent over, huffing.

He holds up a finger. "One sec."

I nod, licking my lips as I wait for him to come to his breath.

"Sorry about that," he says.

What did you do? I sign.

He shrugs, casually scratching the back of his head. "I biked."

I frown and sign, *All the way from home?*

"Yup."

I smile and sign, *But why?*

His skin flushes as he murmurs, "Well, I just wanted to …" He gazes down at the stones on the floor, unable to look me in the eyes as he mumbles. "You know, I just wanted to be here. To show my support for you." He clears his throat. "And Cage."

I can't help but feel the warmth of his heart, knowing he's doing his best even though he probably hates Cage because I love him and not Bo. But I can't blame him for that. No one chooses who they love. It just happens.

I place a hand on his shoulder and sign, *Thank you. I really appreciate it.*

He grabs my hand and says, "Listen. I'm really sorry about … everything. What I said was wrong, and I wanted to apologize. I've been a bad friend to you," he confides, biting his lip. "And I should've known better than to say those things. It was mean. It was inconsiderate. And I don't want to lose you over something like that."

I cock my head, unable to look away as he's stolen my heart in a different way. What we share is something more than love … It's a bond that can't be broken. He's like family to me, and what he's doing right now means a lot to me.

"I … I …" I mumble, struggling to convert the words in my head and make them come out of my mouth.

His lips part, and he stares at my mouth as I fight as hard as I can to give him what he needs.

My voice.

"I'm h-here." The letters come out slowly, but I'm doing my best.

I want to be able to talk to him the way I did with Syrena. With my parents. With Cage.

Because he is important to me.

"Y-you ..." I place my hand on his chest. "A-nd ... m-me." Then I place my hand on my own heart.

He smiles, his eyes tearing up, and he pulls me in for a hug.

"You and me," he repeats. "I'm sorry, Ella. Can you forgive me?"

I pat him on the back and say, "Y-yes."

Each word that comes from my mouth is a little less hard to speak than the one before.

"I promise I'll never be a jerk like that again," he says as we slowly unravel from each other's arms. "And if it does almost happen, I give you permission to slap me again."

I laugh and shake my head. "S-sorry."

"Don't be," he says, grabbing my shoulders. "I deserved it. I've been an asshole and a bad friend."

"Are w-e f-friends?" I ask, my voice still scratchy, but I'm managing.

It isn't an issue of trust with him. It's me getting used to him being here while I use my voice.

"Yes," he affirms, leaning over to stare into my eyes. "Nothing has changed. At least, I hope not." He grins. "And I'm here to support you."

I nod, thankful we could resolve our issues before I lost Cage too. I wouldn't have anyone left if that happened.

"Now, I heard what happened. Read about it in the

newspaper. It's quite the show."

I take a deep breath and nod again, staring at the tiles underneath my feet, wondering how it ever got so far.

"Sorry, that was insensitive. Are you okay?" he asks, clearing his throat.

I nod and fold my arms. "M-managing."

"I understand. So that man who took you … he really came to take you back? Everything they wrote was true? The car chase and the showdown in the forest?"

I nod and then shake my head. "C-Cage didn't d-do it."

"Wow," he says. "So are they really trying to convict him of killing his own father? And for … making you pregnant?"

I nod again.

"Shit …" he hisses. "That's bad. I'm sorry."

"Ella?" I hear my dad call out my name. "It's about to start. Are you coming?"

"Oh, right," Bo says. "Yes, I guess it's time to go then. I'll be sitting in the back, sending you mental cheers, okay?" He winks as he walks toward the room entrance meant for spectators.

I wave him off and go back to my parents who are waiting up ahead. Dad places a hand on my back while Mom kisses me on the cheeks.

"Good luck, honey. Do your best," she says. "I know you can do it."

"We believe in you," Dad adds, pressing a kiss to my forehead too.

"Thanks," I say as they release me.

"We'll see you in there," Mom says, as they both walk back toward the same entrance Bo went through too.

I nod, my heart feeling heavy and my stomach in knots.
There's no running away now.
This is it.
This is the moment of truth.
So I take a deep breath and enter the room.

FIFTY-EIGHT

CAGE

The moment I see her sitting on that wooden seat in the front, I want to run to her, but I know I can't. These two officers behind me keep me in line and force me to sit down across from her, unable to reach out to her. The shackles around my wrists force me to keep my hands together, and I hate that she has to see them.

That she has to see me like this ... chained up ... like a monster.

Everyone in the room looks at me with disdain, with fear in their eyes, shutting me out. They don't know me as she does. They think I'm a beast, an animal that'll only hurt and cause pain.

That's what that DA person describes when she begins

her case. How I'm a savage, born in a cage, and not useful for anything other than fighting and killing. That I was raised as a beast and should be kept away from society. I'm not fit for life out in the real world.

Her words hurt, but none of them are as bad as seeing the look on Ella's face while she endures it all. Her watery eyes stain my soul, corrupt me to the point of wanting to lash out.

I can't take it much longer. Can't take being unable to defend myself.

I know she told me not to do anything and to let the defense do their job for me, but I hate sitting around and doing nothing. I want to be in control over my own fate for once in my life.

Biting my lip, I hear every single word the woman on the stand says. About how my handprints are all over him and the knife that cut my father. That I made him drive into a tree by jumping onto the car. How I murdered my own father by pushing him down a cliff.

None of it's true, yet when she presents the facts the way she does, it all makes sense.

To the people around us, at least.

Not to me.

But that doesn't matter.

Not to anyone but Ella, her parents, and her friend.

Because all the other people in this room seem to stare at me with disgust, probably thinking I'm part of the problem. That I somehow helped my father set up his scheme and do all those things to those girls. That I impregnated her ... and that she never wanted that.

I did none of that.

All I did was love a girl. And now I might be locked up forever because of it.

Ella is called forward, and she sits down on the bench near the judge, right in front of me. Her eyes never leave mine as she holds her hand up in the air and speaks out the words the judge wants her to repeat.

I'm hung on her lips, wanting to hear every single word she has to say.

"Miss Rosenberg, were you captured by this man?" The woman holds up a picture.

Ella nods and signs. There's a signer present who can interpret everything she signs to speech.

"Yes, that's him," the interpreter says.

"Did he come to your house and threaten you?"

"Yes," she signs, and the interpreter speaks.

"And then he forced you into a car, and the defendant here chased after it, jumped onto it, and shoved a knife into the glass?"

She nods. "Yes," the interpreter says.

"Did the defendant intend to physically harm his father with that same knife?"

She nods again, and the interpreter speaks the word. "Yes."

"When the defendant managed to pull you out, according to your story, the car crashed into a tree. His father then ran into the forest, and the defendant chased him. Were you there to see that happen?"

"Yes, but I did not follow him into the woods until after his father was dead," Ella explains with the help of the interpreter.

"So it's safe to say you don't know how he died?"

The room erupts into whispers, and the judge has to call the room to order.

It takes a few seconds for everything to be quiet again and for Ella to answer. "Yes."

The woman nods. "So he could've killed his own dad by pushing him down the ledge."

"That's not what happened," Ella signs, with her interpreter speaking the words for her. "I trust Cage's story. He didn't kill him. His father fell."

"Right …" The woman narrows her eyes, knowing she's cornered us. "But you both had the means and reasons to kill him."

We have no proof of anything, but neither does she. It's our story against hers.

"But let's discuss what happened to you personally. A few months ago, you were taken by this same man, his father. And were you put into a cage? A cage that was right beside the defendant's?"

Ella signs. "Yes. We were kept separate," the interpreter says.

"Can you describe it please?"

"There were three cages in total, and one room connecting them all together."

"And yours was connected to the defendant's cage? Who is the son of the man who took you?"

She signs. "Yes," the interpreter interprets.

"And when this man"—she holds up the picture again—"Graham, opened the cages … you were allowed to enter the other room on your own volition?"

"Yes, but he would use gas if we didn't listen," the interpreter says for Ella, who signed it.

"But he would never use gas in the defendant's cage?"

She shakes her head. "No," the interpreter says.

"So when the defendant saw the opportunity to go into your cage to grab you, he did so of his own free will. Correct?"

Ella signs. "No," the interpreter says. "His father would hurt the prisoners if he didn't do as told."

"But he would never hurt his own son, would he?" the woman asks.

"Objection, calls for speculation," the laywer says.

Ella looks at him for a second, but the judge speaks first. "Overruled."

Ella signs. "He did harm Cage with a chip inside his body that fired electricity into his muscles," the interpreter says.

"But has his father used that on him to make him go into your cell?"

Ella shakes her head. "No," the interpreter says.

"So then we can safely say he went into your cage on his own volition and took you into the room to proceed to have sex with you."

The whole room erupts into a collective gasp, and I bite my lip to stop myself from roaring out of rage. They don't know our story. Her words are paper thin compared to what we experienced. But that woman is clever enough to know it'll work to her advantage. To leave out the crucial stuff and focus on the bad bits. The things I can't take back.

"And then he impregnated you," the woman continues, "while you were in captivity."

More sighs and gasps can be heard.

I hate the sound.

Hate that they don't approve of our relationship. That they're trying to spin it into something it's not.

"And he did this knowing it was wrong," she says.

"Objection, argumentative," the lawyer says. And the judge says she sustains it.

But Ella answers anyway. "No," Ella's interpreter says as she signs. "He never knew it was wrong."

But the woman asking the questions has already made up her mind. "Did he ever try to defy his father? Did he ever say no? Did he ever stop himself or his father from harming you?"

I don't understand why she keeps pushing it in this direction.

Why are we no longer focusing on my father's death, but on Ella. On what happened to her and me.

And then it hits me.

It's because she can never prove my father died because of me.

But she can prove what I did with Ella … because the proof is inside her, growing as we speak. And going there is her only option to get me convicted. Because that's what this woman ultimately wants.

Me. Behind bars.

I'm the only one she can punish now that my father is gone, so she'll do anything she can to get me there.

Ella shakes her head, almost on the verge of crying, but she persists as she signs. "He helped me escape. He fought his father, and I had to leave him there."

"After he'd already impregnated you," she adds. "We have video footage showing the fact that you got pregnant from him as shown here." The woman turns on a television and shows the images from my father's camera that has Ella sitting on the ground in my cage with the pregnancy stick. I still feel warm, thinking about the moment I found out she was pregnant with my child.

"And we have footage of the day you were tied up to a wooden contraption. Now, I won't show it to the audience because it's quite upsetting, but I have already shown it to the judge and jury. The rest of the files were unfortunately destroyed, but the two we do have are substantial evidence to claim you were not in the position to decide. Agreed?"

"Objection, calls for a conclusion," the lawyer says.

But Ella refuses to let it go. "No," Ella signs, her interpreter saying the word. "I chose to let him take me. Contraption or not, I said yes. I wanted him, and he wanted me. Contraptions aren't that uncommon."

The woman is momentarily taken aback. "I guess you could say that. But who tied you to that contraption? Him or his father? And who put you in the cage? What was the sole purpose of you being there?" she asks. "Was it sex?"

Ella grimaces and briefly glances at me. I wonder if that woman is right. The rest of the room seems to believe it. I'm even starting to doubt myself.

What if I *am* really the bad guy?

Because I did something to her without her wanting the same thing?

Is she better off without me?

If all those things are true, maybe I should be locked up. Maybe I should go away forever because I hurt her ... and I never wanted to hurt her.

I want her to be happy, and if that means being rid of me, then so be it.

She deserves the life my father took away from her.

I have no right to stake my claim on that.

Not if it's not right.

If it isn't what she wants.

But as I gaze at her with my unrelenting love, I can see a strength in her eyes that I haven't seen before. A fire burns inside them that seems inextinguishable.

***

"Did he use you for sex?" the woman asks as the entire room grows silent.

Ella gazes at the woman with her head held high and not an inch of regret on her face as she signs. "No."

Everyone is silent even though I can see the faces of the people around me fill with shock.

"I love him," the interpreter says for Ella.

The woman stands there flabbergasted as Ella keeps signing.

"I willingly let him take me, and I participated out of my own free will. Our baby is the product of love."

"But ... are you sure you're not just saying that out of fear?"

"My counselor checked me and said I was perfectly sane, and I have proof," the interpreter says after Ella signs. Ella holds up two pieces of paper and hands one to the woman and another one to the judge. "I am sane, and I choose to love Cage."

She focuses on me now, signing as she gives her heart to me. "There's nothing difficult about it ... I fell in love with this man, and I owe him my life."

Something inside me breaks, forcing me to witness the power of her love for me.

"He is a victim. Born without ever having the ability to make decisions on his own. But we made this decision together, and I wanted him as much as he wanted me," she explains, signing as the interpreter fills in her missing words. "And I want nothing more than to have him in my life ... and our baby that we made by our own choice."

She chose to lie even when it's forbidden.

Chose to say that she wanted everything for the sake of saving me.

Because rules don't matter when you want to save the person you love.

No one can prove her wrong. Her heart and mind are unshakable, impenetrable. No one can touch the truth she's forged for herself.

And as long as she upholds that truth ... no one can take me down.

No one can lock me up as long as she believes in my innocence.

"Cage is innocent. He protected me from his father, and now you're trying to prosecute him? Where is the humanity? The compassion? Since when did we start locking up victims? Since when did we forget how to forgive and forget? He did nothing wrong. Nothing." Ella's signing is furious, and I feel so proud of her that I can feel the fire burn inside me, wishing I could go to her right now.

"L-let. H-him. Go." It's her voice now, speaking through the microphone. Scratchy, but still clear nonetheless.

Her final words slam into me like a fist, but I'll willingly

481

go down for her.

My Ella ... she's the warrior, not me.

She went through the worst experience in her life, fought it all with tenderness and hope, and now she stands here to defend me after everything she's been through.

She's the woman I never deserved but got anyway.

And I intend to cherish that forever ... if I still get the chance.

The woman nods and swallows, saying, "No further questions, your honor."

The lawyers each talk one more time, and now we have to wait. How long, I don't know, but I'll wait.

The officers tell me to get up, so I do, and in these same chains I walk out of the room again ... but they don't quite feel as heavy as they did before.

***

Hours pass as I sit in this office, drinking water from a cup while being watched by two officers. When the call comes that the jury is back and has reached a verdict, my heart almost pounds out of my chest.

The men escort me outside and bring me back to the big room, setting me down on the same chair I sat on before.

Ella is right there too in the audience, staring at me as the jury people come into the room.

Everyone is quiet as the foreperson reads from a piece of paper. I only understand some of it, but it's enough to know what my fate is.

"Without substantial proof, and with Miss Rosenberg's statement, we came to the conclusion that we cannot willfully submit this man to any more incarceration. He has suffered enough. So we find the defendant … not guilty." The judge dismisses the case, and I'm free to go.

I sit back and breathe out a sigh of relief while half the room erupts into yelling and the other half into cheers.

My eyes feel watery as I watch Ella's fear and anxiety burst out into droplets rolling down her cheeks. She's nodding constantly, staring at me, and I'm unable to look away.

The officers undo the shackles around my hands, and I rub my red wrists as I step out of the seat. Ella pushes past the people surrounding her, rushing toward me.

I hold out my arms, and she falls into me with open arms, ready to receive my love.

I'm here.

I'm free.

And I'm hers.

FIFTY-NINE

Ella

He's free.

Finally, truly free.

Free of the judgment others laid on him.

Free of the burden of hurting me.

Even if it meant I had to lie about what went down in that compound, I have no regrets. Zero.

My love for him is not a lie.

Nor is his devotion to me.

There's nothing anyone can tell me that'll sway my feelings toward him or my need for him. I want him in my life, and nothing will ever change that.

Not even a courtroom full of people, seeking justice for

what went down in that compound.

Even if they couldn't put his father in jail, I wouldn't allow them to take Cage in his stead.

He did nothing wrong. He's innocent, just like I am.

And now he's finally mine again.

As we walk out of the courthouse, I can't stop holding him, desperately clinging to his hand with our fingers entwined. I refuse to let anyone's opinion change my own, despite the barrage of questions from the reporters, asking me why I did what I did.

I didn't say it on a whim. I'd made my decision a long time ago.

I would protect him at all cost … just as he protected me all these times.

He may be a beast, but he is my beast.

I won't judge him for it.

He's safe with me, in my arms, and he'll always be.

Together we can stand through it all.

My mom and dad push past the people in front of us, giving us room to walk down the steps. Bo follows behind, keeping them at bay by repeating the same words.

"No comment."

I'm thankful to have them here as I bring Cage back to the car, back to safety, back to where we belong.

Home.

I usher him into the back seat of the car, desperate to get away from it all. Mom and Dad quickly get into the front seat, and Dad starts the engine. Bo taps on the window, and I roll it down slightly.

"I'll go back home, okay?"

"S-sure … t-thank y-you," I say, smiling at him.

He nods. "Of course. That's what friends are for." The smile that follows warms my heart. He quickly gets on his bike and says, "See ya."

Then he bikes off, and Dad drives off too.

I hold Cage's hand all the way. I can't keep my eyes off him. Can't stop inching closer and resting my head against his shoulder. We're okay. We're finally okay.

He grabs my face with one hand, gently caressing my cheek as he kisses my forehead.

I don't even care that my parents can see him do it.

I want them to know this is it for me.

He's the one. I want nobody else.

But Mom can only smile at us as she gazes into the rearview mirror, and I know then that she'll accept whoever I pick because I chose him with my heart.

I chose him, and he chose me. That's all that matters.

***

When we get to my place, Mom and Dad drop us off without getting out of the car. Mom rolls down her window and says, "Well, I'm glad you got your happy ever after anyway."

"Thanks, Mom," I say, giving her a kiss, and then I look at Dad. "You too, Dad."

"My pleasure, honey. I'm just happy you're happy."

"You're not coming inside?" I ask.

"I figured you two would like some private time." Mom winks. "So we'll excuse ourselves now."

I blush as Mom waves, and the car drives off.

When I turn around, Cage has already walked to the

front door, so I traipse behind him and quickly pull out the key. Smiling at him, I open the door and let him go in first. He breathes in deeply, staring at the walls and the floor before stepping in.

With his hand, he touches the walls as he saunters through the room slowly as if he's savoring this moment. And I can't help but watch him with admiration as he goes straight for the glass door, sliding it open to stare outside.

He takes off his shoes ... and then his clothes. One by one, he tears everything off until he's naked. Then he steps outside, into the sunshine, right into my garden. We're lucky it's closed off from the rest of the world with all these trees in the back because he'd make a lot of heads turn.

He wriggles his toes in the grass as he stretches out. And I can't help but watch him from afar. Grinning, I wonder what he's up to as he stares up at the sky.

And I know just the thing to do.

***

CAGE

I stand in the open air, enjoying the wind brushing along my body. I love the smell of the forest, the taste of freedom.

However, when I hear a creak behind me, I turn around only to see Ella standing in the doorway ... completely naked.

Her clothes lie behind her on the wooden floor inside.

I swallow at the sight of her. She's beautiful. So pretty ... and all mine.

She slowly walks toward me through the grass, licking her lips as she approaches me. I smile and stand tall, waiting for her to come. I could take her at any time, but that's not what I want right now. What I want is for her to take control of her own needs. That she's certain she wants me.

But I see no hesitation in her eyes as she stands before me. They only flicker with joy and excitement ... with love.

Her fingers entangle with mine, curling up until we're holding hands. She tiptoes closer and softly pecks me on the cheek. My eyes can't help but follow hers as they go down to my cock and trail all the way back up again, lingering on my abs. She bites her lip as she gazes up at me, and then she whispers into my ear.

"Take me, Cage. I'm yours."

It's all I need to know.

All I need to let the beast out of its cage again.

I nudge a strand of loose pearl white hair behind her ear and grab her face, kissing her deeply. Hard. I take her mouth with mine, my tongue dipping out to lay claim to her. I want her, body and soul. Completely mine.

She wraps both arms around my neck and pulls me in, desperate for more, and I answer her plea by kissing her faster, more aggressively. My hands can't help but slide down her sweet curves, clutching her ass to pull her closer to my body.

"Mine," I growl against her lips, and she grins.

"Yours ..." she mumbles, and I smash my lips to hers again.

I can't help myself because that word sets me off like nothing else.

I let my hands loose on her body, caressing the small of

her back with one while squeezing her tit with the other. I plant kisses all over her neck and all the way down to her chest where I suck on her nipples until they're hard.

My mouth draws a line all the way down her body until I reach her belly, and I place kiss after kiss until she's giggling. I love the sound of her voice, but I love the feel of her belly even more.

"Mine …" I repeat as my tongue slides down between her slit while I sink to my knees in front of her. I want to lick her, taste her on my tongue, and have her come all over my mouth.

I suck and lick, alternating with kisses until she's shaking on her feet.

Moans leaving her mouth make me hard as a rock, but I persist, wanting to give my woman everything she needs.

She's more important to me than my own cock.

Her pleasure is my pleasure.

So I let my tongue do all the work, circling around her clit until she grasps my hair, pushing me into her pussy. I love it when she does that; when she's not afraid of what she wants.

I keep kissing and licking her until I feel her body quake, and I hold her steady. She clutches me, moaning loudly, and then I feel the orgasm roll through her. She shivers as I hold her tight, sucking up all her sweetness. Fuck, she tastes so good. I want to do this every single fucking day for the rest of my life.

As she pants, I pull her down toward me. Quickly, we sink to the ground, still kissing, still embracing. I can't stop touching her and neither can she. We're locked in place by our desire to be together, no matter the cost.

As I bury my face in the nook of her neck, I push my cock into her sweet, wet pussy, unable to control myself. I grab her wrists and pin them above her head, our hands clutching as I make sweet love to her.

I may be an animal ... but I'm her animal.

Only for her.

So I kiss her as hard as I can, fuck her as hard as I can, own her because she's mine and mine alone.

She greedily accepts every thrust I give her, wrapping her legs around me as I plow into her. Our mouths are almost unable to unlatch, even to take a breath. As I plunge in, my tongue dips out to lick her wherever I can, wanting to taste her very essence.

I fuck her hard and deep on the grass, letting the world know she's mine. I don't give a fuck that we're outside; it only adds to the rawness of it all and how much we want each other. How much I need her.

I roar out loud and come as I bury myself deep inside her, my cock pulsing with need. Again and again, I jet my seed, filling her up until I'm sated. Until we're both sated.

But I don't roll off her or pull out. I want her to know I'm here to stay. And I shower her with kisses, endless kisses everywhere; on her mouth, jaw, nose, cheeks. I don't stop until she giggles and practically begs me.

But I won't ever stop loving her.

My girl. My woman. My Ella.

She belongs to me.

EPILOGUE

Ella

A few weeks later

Cage places his hand over my big belly, feeling the baby kick. Only a few more months and then it's finally time. When he smiles at me, I feel happy, complete.

At this moment, I'm at peace.

Even though I know we have so many more things to do.

Explore the world. Let Cage see the beauty of it.

Find Syrena.

And maybe even his brother.

All those things are important to me, to us, but we'll

take it one step at a time.

Besides, we're going to need to buy a new car first before we can travel anywhere. And there's no use starting our search now when we've got a baby on the way.

The doctors told me to take it easy anyway, so I'm going to take their advice now—as I should have all along. But that feeling of unfinished business still nags deep down inside me.

"Cage?" I mumble.

He lifts his head from the book he was reading.

It still amazes me he's learned to read so quickly.

"Do you ... ever think about your brother?" I ask.

"Sometimes. Why?"

I shrug. "Just wondering ... Don't you wish you could meet him?"

"Maybe," he says, frowning.

"I do ... I mean, I want to ask him things about my sister, you know?"

"Oh, that ..." He clears his throat, scratching the back of his head. "I don't know."

"You don't know what? That you want to meet him? Or talk to him?"

"Do we? He's a ... killer."

"So are you," I say, raising my brows. He knows it too.

He nods, grimacing. "Right. But ..." He sighs.

"What?" I grab his hand. "Tell me."

He looks afraid. "What if he isn't ... like me?"

"You mean what if he still is a bad person?"

He nods.

I smile. "There's only one way to find out. We have to find him and talk to him." Who knows, maybe the police have already found something based on the evidence they found at the compound. Graham must've kept some information about him.

Cage narrows his eyes. "Are you sure?"

It's as if he's seeking approval even though I can see in his eyes he's desperate to know more. Now that Cage knows his brother's name is Lock, it's like a fire has been lit inside his heart that's impossible to extinguish.

I know the feeling all too well. That's why I mentioned him. I don't want Cage to feel locked up in his own mind. He doesn't have to go through that alone. I'm here for him. Even if the man who caused my sister's death is his brother, I still think we should give him a chance. For Cage.

"Yes," I reply. "So let's put that on our list of things to do."

"Right ... along with Syrena," he adds.

But the mere mention of her name makes my heart sink into my shoes again.

"What's wrong?" Cage asks as I shift on the couch.

"Well ..." I sigh, propping my elbow up. "I'm just worried about Syrena."

He nods, frowning. "I understand."

"What if she's in trouble?"

"She'll figure it out. She can handle herself," he says.

"I know," I say. "But what if that man who bought her is treating her badly?"

"You want to save her," Cage fills in for me, taking a strand of my hair and tucking it behind my ears. He always manages to read my mind.

"Yes," I say. "But ... we have to wait." I gaze down at my belly. "For this."

Cage places a hand on top of mine. "You will save her."

"You think? But what good am I going to be with a baby in my arms?"

"You have me," he says, raising his brow.

"Are you saying you're going to take care of our baby too?" I still can't believe he actually wants to nurture his own baby like a real dad instead of a savage fighter.

"Of course." The smug smile on his face is infectious. "I take care of what's mine."

I giggle as he places a kiss below my ear.

"Okay, I'll take you up on that offer," I muse.

"Good. I know you can do it," he replies, lowering his head as he gazes at me. "You *will* find her."

I bite my lip. "You think?"

He nods and then whispers into my ear. "You found me too, remember?"

***

Months later

"Push, push, push!" the nurse coaxes, but it makes me want to scream at her.

It's not helping, and my body fucking hurts. It feels like my crotch is exploding as I'm trying to push out an elephant or something. And I can barely breathe even though she tells me to every goddamn second she gets.

I don't swear much, but this pain ... God, it makes me want to curse like a motherfucker.

The only thing holding me back, keeping me from going

insane, is the man standing beside me, whispering to me.

"You can do it," Cage says, holding my hand.

I squeeze tight, wanting to channel every inch of my anger into him.

I know he won't mind. He already told me. But from the look on his face, I can definitely tell he didn't expect it to be this extreme. Still, he refuses to speak up. He takes it like the warrior he is.

"And breathe," the nurse says, but I'm barely able to catch up. "I can see the head!"

I whimper, wanting to look too, but I can't because my belly is in the way.

I feel like I'm falling apart.

"Just a little more," Cage says as I squeeze hard.

The nurse remarks, "One final push!"

And I give it all I have. Finally, I feel the pain bursting out of me as I release the breath I was holding. A loud crying ensues.

The baby.

It's really the baby.

The nurse holds him up for us to see and quickly wipes him off. "And … it's a boy!"

I can't believe it's actually a boy.

Just like Cage told me whenever he rubbed my belly these past few months.

I didn't want to know the gender … I wanted it to be a surprise. But it doesn't even matter. I'm just happy he's alive and well.

The moment she places him on me, I begin to cry, unable to hold it together any longer. He's beautiful. Perfect. Mine.

Cage's eyes tear up too, and he caresses the baby's tiny cheeks, whispering, "My little man …"

And he kisses him on the forehead.

I smile, exhausted but happy.

I did it. I brought this little life into the world with love.

In a place he deserves to be.

Safe.

***

Mom and Dad come to visit me in the afternoon after the baby has already been bathed and is sleeping in my arms. Mom almost immediately begins to cry when she sees him.

"Oh … he's so beautiful!" she murmurs, caressing his head. "Can I?" she asks me.

I nod. "Of course."

She gently takes him from my arms, cradling him. "He's so big …"

"A warrior," Cage muses, making my mom chuckle.

Dad grabs my camera and snaps a quick shot. "Look into the camera," he tells my mom.

He takes some more pictures of her, the baby, us together, everyone embracing with our little man between.

Then the baby gets hungry, so I put him on my breast again. Feeding him has been a very strange experience, and I never imagined it'd feel this way to have a baby suckle, but I can get used to it. It makes me feel very protective of him. Like a big bear momma who will chase away anyone trying to hurt him.

Not that I'll ever need to, with that hunk of a man standing beside my bed at all times. He's refused to go home since I came here—not to sleep, eat, or anything else. He just wants to stay by my side until he can take me home, and I can appreciate that.

We're all sitting together, the men with a cup of coffee and Mom with some tea. Then someone knocks on the door. Bo's head peeks through and then a whole array of flowers pops into the room.

"Hi!" he says. "Sorry, is this a bad time?"

"No, no, come in," Mom says, beckoning him.

"Okay. I brought you some flowers," he says to me, smiling as he comes inside. But when he sees the baby, I can see him melt. "He ... looks just like you," he says, leaning in to kiss me on the cheeks. "Well done."

"T-thank you," I mutter, rubbing away the happy tears.

"How are you feeling?" Bo asks.

"T-tired." Everyone laughs because it's so obvious, but it's the truth.

"I can imagine, with a boy the size of him popping out of you," Dad says.

Mom immediately shoves him. "Hank!"

"What? It's true," he quips, making me laugh.

"He'll be a champ," Cage says, making a fist with his hand. "Just like his father."

I grin. "Or a photographer. That'd be nice."

Cage winks. "A fighting photographer." And everyone chuckles again.

Bo clears his throat. "So ... have you decided on a name yet?"

I nod, and I lick my lips as I stare at Cage, wondering who will say the word.

But he intently gazes at me, giving me the honor of

naming our baby.

Our son.

Created in captivity.

Born in freedom.

But never without love.

"Everyone …" I gently tickle his face until he wakes up and shows his eyes to my family. "Meet Forest."

THANK YOU FOR READING!

Thank you so much for reading Caged & Uncaged. I hope you enjoyed the story!

For updates about upcoming books, please visit my website, www.clarissawild.blogspot.com or sign up for my newsletter here: www.bit.ly/clarissanewsletter.

I'd love to talk to you! You can find me on Facebook: www.facebook.com/ClarissaWildAuthor, make sure to click LIKE. You can also join the Fan Club: www.facebook.com/groups/FanClubClarissaWild/ and talk with other readers!

Enjoyed this book? You could really help out by leaving a review on Amazon and Goodreads. Thank you!

ALSO BY CLARISSA WILD

Dark Romance

Debts & Vengeance Series
House Of Sin Series
Dellucci Mafia Duet
The Debt Duet
Delirious Series
Company Series
Indecent Games Series
FATHER

New Adult Romance

Fierce Series
Blissful Series
Ruin
Cruel Boy
Rowdy Boy

Erotic Romance

The Billionaire's Bet Series
Enflamed Series
Unprofessional Bad Boys Series

Visit Clarissa Wild's website for current titles.
www.clarissawild.com

ABOUT THE AUTHOR

Clarissa Wild is a New York Times & USA Today Bestselling author with ASD (Asperger's Syndrome), who was born and raised in the Netherlands. She loves to write Dark Romance and Contemporary Romance novels featuring dangerous men and feisty women. Her other loves include her hilarious husband, her cutie pie son, and her two crazy but cute dogs. In her free time, she enjoys watching all sorts of movies, playing video games, and cooking up some delicious meals.

Want to be informed of new releases and special offers? Sign up for Clarissa Wild's newsletter on her website www.clarissawild.com.

Visit Clarissa Wild on Amazon for current titles.